AF606806

CAMP STARLIGHT SERIES
BOOK TWO

Camp Enemies

ELLIE BELMONT
& LACEY COLE

ISBN: 978-1-967383-03-0 (paperback)

Developmental editing by Kristen with Kristen's Red Pen

Editing by Sara with Telltail Editing

Proofreading by Chelly with Ink it Out Editing

Cover artist: Andra Murarasu with @andra.mdesigns

Map artist: Mary with Books and Moods

AX RANGE
THE BONFIRE
MEDITATION MEADOW
LAKE STARLIGHT
CAMP STARLIGHT
ZIPLINE
CRAFT CABIN
THE MESS HALL
FRONT OFFICE
CAMP STARLIGHT
FOXGLOVE STABLES
WILDWOOD

To all the stubborn hearts out there. We hope you meet your match.

ONE
Jack

My best friend had a slideshow.

And one of those little laser pointer clicker things.

I didn't even know we had a projector, let alone a movie screen, but this place was full of surprises.

Autumn sat off to the side as our boss, Hazel, went over our summer preparation meeting for the start of the season at Camp Starlight—a summer camp for adults.

The resort I worked at was a popular travel destination on Mount Hood, in Wildwood, Oregon. A hideaway that emphasized the nostalgia of childhood summers under the stars, while giving it an adult spin, of course.

Hazel pointed at the slideshow behind her. "The updated menu will be more farm-forward and feature..."

As a permanent staffer, I knew most of this already, but man, why was I zoning out?

Maybe it was because I knew this place like the back of my hand. After all, I'd been working here since its inception six years ago. And that wasn't even counting the months it'd taken to get it up and running.

I loved the beginning of the summer. It meant I got to see old friends returning from off-season excursions and jobs, meet people who were new to the team, and catch up with friends I'd missed for months. Our kickoff meeting was the best way to inform those staff members about any changes to the camp that Hazel, Leo, Autumn, and I had worked our asses off to bring to fruition.

Still, the only thing keeping me present was Autumn and that damn clicker.

"Jack, please take a bow."

I rolled my eyes at Hazel, who apparently wanted a literal bow in front of my coworkers. Okay, I might as well lean into it.

I stood, bent over dramatically, and shook my ass so that my coworkers had a full view of the goods. It wasn't all for naught because Lamar whistled, causing me to wince. That sound could probably be heard in space.

"The staff reviews are in, and we've heard nothing but good things about the new pod." Hazel was referring to the clusters of cabins spread throughout the camp that I'd built. Each pod consisted of a counselor cabin and five guest cabins that could host up to two campers. Each counselor served as a fun coordinator of sorts as well as someone campers could turn to if they had any issues, from first aid to room needs. "I'm sure you've stopped by to check out Lynx, but if not, take the time. It's beautiful. I'd be remiss not to mention the hours of labor, several near misses with a pneumatic air nailer"—she looked to Leo, whose help was instrumental everywhere around camp except for when it involved power tools. He'd been banned after nearly harming himself—"and how many two-by-fours did we use?"

Hazel was known for her sarcastic humor, her deadpan wit, and her ability to put people on the spot.

"Nine hundred sixty-seven," I answered without hesitation. I didn't have a clue how many had been used. Actually, that number felt a little off.

She tilted her head at me, obviously surprised that I had a

number at all. "Let's thank him for the painstaking labor and the fact that we have a new pod for our campers."

Cheers rose from my camp family, and I let them wash over me. I wore many hats at Camp Starlight, but my primary roles in the off-season were head of maintenance and construction foreman. It'd taken me a little under a year to build the six cabins, so I knew to take credit where credit was due. I did have a team, which I tried to explain for the umpteenth time, but they ignored me. Someone behind me patted me on the back.

"Speaking of Lynx, let's give a Starlight welcome to Chase, our new counselor who will be taking residence on the north side of camp."

The Montana transplant lifted the cowboy hat sitting in front of him on the table and waved it to us in hello. "I'm happy to be here. Thank you so much for hiring me, Hazel. I love what you've built here."

Hazel's cheeks reddened at the attention.

I had already met Chase when he arrived, and his approachability and down-to-earth smile, not to mention the short, curly blonde hair and that charming laugh, already had the majority of us swooning. Was there a halo over his head?

I might have been the only one who noticed the flash of annoyance that took over Leo's face before he interjected, all smiles once more, "Chase is a former rancher. Apparently, that's a real job, even outside of romance novels. And he will also be our liaison with Foxglove Horse Camp next door."

We had an agreement with the equestrian camp we shared a border with. We had the whole camp for one full day each camp session, so that our attendees could ride trails and spend time with nature's walking monstrosities. I had nothing to do with it. I had feelings about this.

Leo pushed back his messy brown hair, which we all knew was a pointless task, before giving up. "Another new addition to our amazing counselors is Emerson Delgado, who many of you may recognize as a guest from last year."

"I'm so excited to be back," Emerson said happily, her pink-tinted retro curls bouncing. "There's no place like Camp Starlight."

"Don't I know it," Lamar agreed. We hadn't thought he'd be returning after he signed up with a wilderness excursion company, but we'd been delightfully surprised when he asked to come back.

Hazel and Leo both looked proud, as they should be. We called them camp mom and camp dad, regardless of our ages. They were the creators of the camp and had every right to be praised.

Leo continued. "While we're discussing staff, it's important that we announce that this will be Bobby's final summer with us."

Everyone turned to the seventy-year-old sous-chef with sad glances and smiles.

His boss, Azalea, squeezed his shoulder. "Bobby has been with us from the start, and we plan to make this his best summer ever."

Several woos echoed off the dining hall walls, and Felicia patted Bobby's shoulder as he swiped at his eyes with the back of his hand.

Hazel quickly put us back on track, probably for Bobby's sake, but possibly for her own. She didn't like to show vulnerability, especially in public. She'd been like this since I'd known her, back in high school when we became friends. She'd been a freshman when I was a sophomore, and we'd bonded over punk music and our distaste for discussing our family drama, which I later learned was rather dire for her. I often regretted not pushing her to discuss it more back then.

"Now, I'll pass the baton to Autumn," Hazel said to eager applause. We all knew what was coming from our newly appointed assistant director: an update on the shipping board.

"Quiet down, people. Quiet down," Autumn declared to the crowd of camp counselors, owners, chefs, and bartenders. "I have an important announcement, and I don't want to repeat myself."

She took a deep breath, clutching her fingers as though she were about to deliver a death sentence to our staff, before starting her slide show. An image of a dry-erase board with staff names and rankings took over the screen. "This year, we aren't doing the shipping board."

A giant red X animated over the image.

Okay, apparently, it *was* a death sentence.

There were literal gasps and shouts of disagreement all around. People were shocked and dismayed. I may have seen tears.

"What's the shipping board?" Emerson asked.

That shut everyone up for a minute. We kept this game from our campers because it was our way of blowing off steam, making each of them contestants in a dating-style game and betting on the results.

"The shipping board has been around for four years," Leo said pointedly of the unofficial competition that Autumn ran in her free time. "It's a time-honored tradition. People use camper profiles to pair them together—"

"And then maybe try to push them in the right direction," Felicia, our resident horndog, added.

Sometimes it worked, and the person betting on the couple won a few bucks. Most of the time, nothing happened at all. Last year, the winner had been Leo by a landslide. It was the same every year. Leo also won an honorable mention by guessing that Autumn and her now-boyfriend Jamie would get together.

Camp Starlight was a place to get away from the monotony of real life, a respite from the mundanity of cubicles and familial obligations. The majority of campers were just there for a good time in the open air. But there were always hookups, which went hand in hand with rumors and conjecture. Our camp made it easy to spread the gossip since it was so small, and the staff was a huge part of that. That didn't mean our lives were spared from the grapevine, as Autumn had learned firsthand last session.

"Holy shit, y'all are diabolical." Emerson's gleeful smile put us at ease. "I want to play."

"When everyone decides to let me speak," my friend said with the tact of a middle school librarian, "I'll explain."

There were more groans and a cluster of angry words shouted. Someone even threw a rolled-up piece of paper at her, which she ducked from with catlike grace before it hit the projector screen. If she didn't get it together quickly, this was going to turn into an angry mob.

"We're going to be doing something else," she said, raising her voice over the din and hitting next on her slides. A list appeared, and she pointed the laser at the screen. "Because the shipping board caused more harm than good."

"Tell that to the people who got together!" shouted Sawyer, our resident yoga expert and the loudest person in this place.

"We have no idea if the people who *got together* ended up in lasting relationships," Autumn said. "But my guess is they were mostly hookups. And we are not running a bordello—"

A bordello? Really?

"The corkboard of wedding invites in our office would say otherwise," Hazel said carefully, adjusting her aviators on the top of her head. She had her hand on a bouncing Leo's shoulder, who looked like he wanted to fire Autumn on the spot. Our boss's indignation could have been cause for concern to a normal staffer, but we all knew that Autumn was unshakable, so it didn't matter. "And considering your relationship was one of Leo's success stories, you don't have room to talk."

Autumn ignored her. "And frankly, it was costing everyone too much money."

She had that right. I couldn't calculate how many twenties I'd lost during that competition, and I wasn't about to count.

"I'm still owed my fee from some people." She fake-coughed. "Lamar." She glared at the man who had tried to pair her now-boyfriend off with a woman we called Cherry Lips Cheryl. To be fair, he'd had no idea that Autumn and Jamie had a history or would end up together. "And I was sick of doling out fake sympathy after hearing you all were going broke."

"And we won't lose money on this stupid replacement?" Leo said, unconcerned with his confrontational attitude.

Autumn put her hands on her hips, a look of scorn on her face. Man, she was especially heartless today. I liked it. Leo was unwavering, not even breaking eye contact as he pushed his black-rimmed glasses up his nose.

"Does anyone want to hear about my alternative?" Autumn said to a crowd that was ignoring her. She raised her voice. "Yes? That's what I thought. So shut up," she chastised. "I wouldn't take this away without having a better alternative." She directed that at Leo, whose crossed arms said he wasn't interested. He looked like a four-year-old being told he had to eat his green beans if he ever wanted to see dessert. "This year, we're going to start a tournament-style competition I'm calling Camp Wars."

She clicked on to the next slide, and a banner with that same name crossed over a stock image of a group of adults playing tug-of-war.

That shut everyone up. The title alone had me interested. I pictured ducking in a battle zone with hand-made projectiles and beach balls zooming from every angle. Water balloon grenades thrown over sand hills with explosions of glitter cascading over our well-loved beach.

Autumn hit next on the slideshow, which displayed a blank list with dates for each competition. She hit next on her clicker, and the top bullet point appeared with the first competition—poker.

"Nice," Lamar said happily. He loved the game and was always playing it with his pod.

"Keep your board shorts on, Lamar. You haven't won yet," Sawyer said.

"We'll see about that," Lamar jested.

"So how is this going to work? We're going to spread out the competitions over the course of ten weeks. For campers, it'll just be fun and games, but for counselors, there'll be a running score. If it goes well, we'll do it again. The leaders of each pod will go against each other, should you choose to participate."

We had seven pods—Orion, Phoenix, Andromeda, Cygnus, Delphinus, Corvus, and Lynx—all of which were named after star systems. My pod was Corvus, and it was arguably the best because crows were badass, and so was I.

"What about the seventh pod?" Sawyer asked.

It hadn't gone without notice that the leader of Andromeda was missing. It'd been hard to fill that position last year as well, but we'd finished out the year with Nat, a social media influencer who also happened to be the woman my now ex-girlfriend cheated on me with. She would not be missed. If the other staffers knew what happened, they would be on my side, but there was no point in digging up the past.

Because Camp Starlight only ran from May to September, our counselors came and went each year. We were always fortunate to see some returning faces because it was such a fun place to work. We'd never had a returning staffer for Andromeda, and we'd had people leave earlier than they were contracted. I was beginning to think that pod was cursed, because the person who was slated to replace her had ghosted us a week ago.

"I'll be filling in since we're down a counselor—" Autumn started.

"Actually—" Hazel interrupted.

"What's the prize for the competition?"

"Can all the pods team up against Lamar at poker?"

"Are campers spectators, or...?"

Autumn picked from the barrage of questions and continued. "Sorry, I wasn't clear: for much of the tournament, the campers will be involved in a pod versus pod showdown, but there are some activities where it will just be counselor pitted against counselor."

"Wait, we don't even get to compete?" I could see the vein in Leo's forehead twitch from here.

"You've got enough going on with Camp Sunlight." The second camp was being launched next week, and Leo and Hazel were traveling to Northern California to make sure it went off without a hitch. If it were to be anything like the launch of Camp Starlight, it wouldn't be perfect right off the bat.

Leo looked mollified but definitely not happy. "Fine."

His acceptance prompted Autumn to continue. "As always, the true competition will be going on behind the scenes. We got lucky that no one discovered our meddling with the shipping board, but this is another sensitive issue. Campers won't suspect a thing, as long as we don't get too competitive." Yeah, right.

Autumn eyed me and several other people. She had to know what she was doing. After all, the competitiveness around the shipping board nearly came to physical blows. Maybe I was exaggerating, but it did get pretty cutthroat. That might have been another reason it was getting shut down.

She clicked several more times so the remaining bullets appeared with all of the competitions.

I scanned the categories, feeling all too pleased. This was going to be fun. We had poker, flag football, swimming, archery, and a—

"We're doing a bake-off?" Bobby asked, practically bouncing.

"That one will be hosted by you," Autumn said to our sous-chef, who was also our head baker. We all knew Bobby wanted to have his own cooking show. "Ready to tell people their cakes aren't up to snuff?"

"Everyone's cakes will be perfect." He beamed at us. Either Bobby would be the most impartial host ever, or he'd be terrible at dishing out criticism, pun intended. Only time would tell.

Autumn went on to explain some important particulars. Each event had assigned judges, from camp staffers to friends from the town of Wildwood. She'd organized this thing to go off without a hitch. Now it was just up to us to provide the entertainment. I already knew my pod was going to sweep most of these. I mean, an obstacle race? Come on.

Emerson narrowed her eyes. "Autumn, what if there's a tie? Will there be a tiebreaker?"

"Oooh, like fastest friendship bracelet making?" Sawyer suggested.

Lamar lifted his finger in the air. "Cleanest bunks?"

"We're still a destination resort," Hazel chimed in. "We will not be checking people's living areas."

"I vote we have a hot pepper challenge to see who can eat the spiciest one," Azalea offered.

"Um, no thanks," I blurted, and I was quickly backed up by other agreeing murmurs. That sounded painful.

Leo was barely containing his laughter, his shoulders shaking.

Autumn chuckled. "Fantastic. If there's a tie, we'll figure it out."

"Though it shouldn't need to be on your radar since I'll be the one winning," I interjected.

People turned on me, laughing like it was the funniest joke they'd ever heard, even though I'd definitely be a strong contender. They'd all lick their wounds when they lost.

Just then, the door burst open, demanding our attention with a large creak and the sun shining through everything but the silhouette of a woman.

"Oof, that door still does that, huh?" she said, stepping inside to reveal herself. Of course, she would make her entrance by pointing out one of the many things on my laundry list of tasks that I was behind on. What a surprise.

Nat Breckenridge's caramel-brown hair couldn't be confused with someone else's. Her sun-kissed cheeks and deep brown eyes had mesmerized more than a few campers. Her voice was rushed, which paired nicely with the sheen of sweat on her brow. She was late after all.

Her arrival elicited excitement and several gasps as people

waved at her. I wasn't the only one who hadn't known about her arrival. Visit? I didn't know what she was doing here.

"Go back to what you were doing." She waved us off with the grace of Marie Antoinette, and I wondered if the exasperation in her voice was directed at us or if it was because she'd just run here. Probably the former. The woman was entitled. That might sound judgmental, but still, who did she think she was? *And what was she doing here?*

Autumn chose that moment to explain what we were doing. "To catch you up, the shipping board's canceled, and we're doing Camp Wars." She pointed to the list behind her. "All the counselors are going head-to-head. I'll explain in detail later."

"I think I got it. So what do I get when I win?" Her lips quirked up on one side.

Oh god, she was staying.

"That's the spirit." Autumn's raised eyebrows made it seem as though she was just as surprised to see Nat as I was. She hurried the rest of her presentation along, nonetheless. "So, is everybody in?"

The room erupted in positive murmurs. I threw in my own, "Fuck yes," which came off a little more cutthroat than my fellow staffers. There was no way I was going to lose this competition. I had more than one reason to take this seriously, and the woman who just walked through the door was one of them.

I MAY HAVE BEEN DONE WITH THE EXPANSION, BUT THAT didn't mean there wasn't a ton of work to do.

Unfortunately, it was hard to focus on my task list when I ruminated on the fact that Nat was back. I couldn't believe I was stuck with the princess of the West Coast, who people had swarmed the second our kickoff meeting ended. I'd been gone half an hour, and people were probably still fawning over her instead of doing something important like, I don't know… their jobs.

Someone knocked at my door as I grabbed new drill batteries from the bedroom in my cabin that served as a garage of sorts.

"Hey, Jack? What do I do if my gutter looks like it's about to fall off?" an apologetic Sawyer asked.

"You wait for me to reattach it." People frequently tried to take stuff off my plate the closer we got to launch, but I was always happy to help. "How about you go take a break, and I'll meet you over there after?" I had a door to fix.

Sawyer nodded gratefully. "I can do that."

I walked over to the mess hall to take care of the issue. The offending door wasn't properly aligned because the hinges were worn, which caused it to swing open with too much force. I had already bought replacement hinges, but no, we were focusing on what I *hadn't* done.

I combed through my toolbox and realized I'd left the hinges in my truck. Why couldn't things just be easy today? I did a one-eighty and headed toward the parking lot.

"Psst," a conspicuous Leo whispered loudly from the side of the mess hall. "If you want to discuss the shipping board 2.0, we meet at dawn. Or tonight at nine thirty, whichever comes first."

He was probably going to get some takers, but I wouldn't be one of them. I used to have fun with the shipping board, but I wouldn't be participating anymore, and it had nothing to do with losing the money.

"I don't have time for that. I'm behind as is." My words came out harsher than I'd meant them to, but the sentiment was correct.

"You're telling me you aren't interested?" Leo raised his eyebrows in astonishment. "Does nobody care about me being able to afford the new addition on my house?" he quipped.

He and Hazel each had one half of a duplex-style cabin near the entry of the camp. And if he needed a new addition, which he didn't have the space for, he'd come to me for it. I remained unmoved.

"Whatever, Jack," he said petulantly, waving me off before rushing to speak with Azalea, who was carrying some newly cleaned chef's coats. She looked like she didn't have time to deal with his antics either.

I opened the door to my old pickup truck, and it creaked. Great. Another crappy hinge. Couldn't I catch a break when it came to doors? Was I being dramatic? I did my best to take care of the things that mattered when it came to my truck, even though she looked like she'd seen better days. I could blame her peeling paint and dented roof, but there was no point in fixing superficial issues. What I cared about was the fact that she was reliable and nostalgic. After all, she'd stuck with me since high school, so I wasn't about to trade her in.

"Oh, come on. For real?" The dulcet tones of a stranger came from two cars over.

I threw the hinges in my toolbox and looked for the source of the noise. I wished I'd just ignored it.

Nat stood on the tire of her green Subaru, jumping to reach something in the corner of her hard-shelled cargo box to no avail. The car was a surprising choice for someone like her. I'd figured she was more of a luxury car kind of girl. After all, the Breckenridges owned one of the most expensive car companies in the world.

I didn't know if she was hiding it, but most of us knew her last name. She was basically American royalty, and her family probably considered themselves the backbone of America. They'd been involved in numerous industries, from cars to tech. And that didn't even take into account her family's political legacy and the detrimental mark it'd left on the country. They were rich, entitled, selfish people, and hiding behind a social media alias didn't make her any better.

It might have sounded judgy, but after what happened last year, she'd proven the kind of person she was.

TWO
Nat

HAD JACK GOTTEN HOTTER?

That was the first thought that popped into my head as I saw the blond-haired, broad-chested, lumberjack of a man standing in the same parking lot as my trusty Subie and the pile of stuff beside it.

Maybe it was the whole smoldering thing he had going on or the fact that he looked like he wanted to fuck me against a door. Was I reading that correctly?

"Oh, Jack." Relief washed over me. "You have long arms. Can you...?"

Suddenly, that smolder came off as something more like indignation. Or maybe annoyance.

Why was I starting to feel like a rabbit in the sights of a bear?

"What is it, Nat?" He didn't sound like he cared to know.

My lack of an answer due to sheer confusion must have irritated him, because he walked with determination and reached above my head to grab the duffel bag I'd been trying to get while standing on a tire to give me the edge.

He placed my bag of hiking gear with the rest of my pile of crap and made to walk away before I called him back. His words were confusing, but maybe he was just in a bad mood. Or the sun was in his eyes? When he turned to me, he looked less angry and more apathetic.

Perhaps I'd misread the situation. Only one way to find out. "Any chance you could tell me the code to my cabin? Hazel told me, but I forgot." My sweaty face probably said as much.

"Call Hazel." He lifted the red metal toolbox I hadn't noticed and waved toward camp. "Gotta fix a door."

Okay, that was definitely contempt in his voice.

"My phone's dead, but that's fine..." I felt like a chastened child. "Sorry I asked." I tried smiling self-deprecatingly, but he didn't return it. Something was obviously wrong.

He looked at my passenger seat, which held a cute pink mini fridge that could store six soda cans at most. "You know you have your own fridge in your cabin, right?"

Oof, I didn't want to have to explain the need I had for a fridge to keep my skincare essentials at the proper temperature. Not when he was looking at me like that.

"I need two."

His eyebrow went up as if that was the most ridiculous thing he'd ever heard. If he learned what it was for, his handsome head would probably explode.

Jack sighed in frustration, scrolling through his phone for my door code. He lifted his eyes and took a breath as if he needed to get something off his chest. Instead, he asked, "Why are you back here, Natalie?"

"Oh," I said dumbly. *Why am I back here?* Words escaped me. And why was he saying it like *that*? "Hazel asked—"

"Hazel," he said, frustrated. "Hazel." He looked as if he was about to go tell our boss to suck an egg.

"Is there a problem, Jack?"

"Nope. Not at all. I mean, no one asks my opinion about these things. Your code is zero-eight-zero-five."

Maybe I was taking someone's place. Hazel had sounded

desperate when we talked, but maybe I'd misheard the desperation in her voice. Obviously, he had someone else in mind for the position.

I tried to come up with something to say. The man had caught me off guard twice in one conversation. But I chose to stand here like an open-mouthed fish instead.

"If that's all—" he started, but it felt like the end of a sentence.

The last thing I'd ask for at this juncture was more help.

"No, I'm good. Thank you." There they were. *Words.*

He turned on his heel and lugged his banged-up toolbox with him, while I stood frozen among the things I couldn't live without. I watched him walk past the Camp Starlight sign and down the trail until he disappeared, still trying to make sense of the abrasive encounter.

I didn't know Jack all that well, but we'd had much less hostile conversations during the month I'd worked here last summer, and he hadn't seemed to have a problem with me then. Clearly, I'd caught him on an off day. I wasn't going to let that get to me, so I shrugged it off and removed the last item from my car, ready to reenter the only place that had felt like home in a long time.

I'D TRAVELED FAR AND WIDE, BUT CAMP STARLIGHT WAS just special. As if it lived in a bubble in one of the prettiest places in the world. There was a feeling every time I walked into this place like it was... magic.

The air smelled woodsy-er, the birds sang a prettier song, and s'mores never turned out the same when I tried to make them on the road. Even the cabin that had been ignored for several months felt more welcoming than any hotel or homeshare I'd visited in the past two years.

I wiped the sweat from my brow as people walked past my pod

to get the place ready for the new guests that would be arriving. I would have helped, but I'd just driven something close to eight hours, and I had to get my house in order if I was going to function for my activities in less than a day.

By midday tomorrow, my cabin would be surrounded by campers. There would be liveliness and happy activity as people unloaded their things into one-room cabins.

The place I was staying in was somewhat larger than the cabins our guests stayed in. It had a small kitchenette and a bathroom. With campers coming and going each week, it was nice having our cabins close together so that we could facilitate bonding around the picnic table and firepit.

I liked my location because it was only fifty feet from the bathrooms and communal showers, which my pod members always loved. After all, it was nice to be closer to the facilities. People came here for the camp experience, though bougiefied, and that meant sharing some things. It was worth it for the camaraderie you got from spending time with fellow campers, and it added to the camp experience. And Camp Starlight went above and beyond to make this adults-only glamping experience unique and worth the cost.

For one thing, there was the food.

Hazel and Leo had recruited an amazing chef, Azalea, and she'd found a skilled team that made anything from caprese wraps to shakshuka. The standard fare alternated on a nightly basis, so if you wanted a sloppy joe or a hot dog, odds were you could find them, but most chose the delicacies offered.

There were full bars in the mess hall and the bonfire pit for those who chose to partake in alcoholic beverages, and the bartenders, Lola and Luis, a married couple who owned a bar in town, were happy to serve up immaculate creations.

"Hellooo?"

Sunlight shone around my friend, creating this pretty halo she'd probably hate if she knew about, but as enigmatic as Hazel could be, she was also a softy with a big heart.

"Well, if it isn't the most gorgeous fighter pilot I've ever seen." I cocked my head in admiration.

She frequently wore jumpsuits and overalls and was never without her aviator sunglasses. This was a big change from my former college roommate, who used to be a little more goth before she found her style. Even if she still liked to sport the chunky black boots and ripped tights once in a while.

I grew up in Maryland, just a hop and a skip away from DC. I'd gone to the West Coast for college to be closer to my mother's mother, my favorite grandmother, who happened to be in a retirement community in Oregon. The agreement between my controlling parents and me had been that I'd get my degree in business and come back to join the Breckenridge Group once I'd finished my master's. For the most part, I'd done what they wanted, but that had changed after I'd disappointed them in a big way.

She put her hand on her hip and posed. "I need you for a mission."

"Really? I thought the mission was for me to come here in your hour of need to fill the role of camp counselor. Speaking of which, was everyone on board with me coming back?"

Hazel quirked an eyebrow. "What do you mean?"

"Just curious."

Hazel didn't ask me to elaborate. "To answer your question, yes, we do need you. But your mission, should you choose to accept it, is to go pick up marshmallows for tomorrow's festivities. Because we'd look like fools if we didn't have enough for s'mores."

I laughed. "Well, we can't have that. Let me finish this up, and then I'd be happy to go."

"Thank goodness, because I don't want to." She tossed a pair of rolled-up socks back and forth as she stared into my nearly empty bag. "You've got this packing thing down."

"It's easy when you don't have a permanent address. Less stuff to hold on to." Did that sound depressing? Hopefully not.

"I wish I could live the way you do. You should see my place.

It's inundated with the randomest shit. Childhood craft projects, photos. Probably every paper airplane Leo has ever made for me. Lots of tangible memories. In fact, I bet I still have the paper fortune-teller games we made from that night we got drunk on White Claws and ate nachos until we threw up."

"I'm surprised they survived that horrendous night."

I may not have carried everything with me, but I wondered if my mom and stepfather had any sort of class photos or projects I'd worked hard on from my past. But I shrugged it off, knowing the truth. They'd probably thrown those things away the second they came across them. That sort of thing didn't fit their aesthetic, curated to an inch of its life. They definitely didn't have some box in the attic with my name on it.

But I wasn't about to say that out loud.

"I didn't get to talk to him yet, but how's Leo?"

"Leo is… Leo." The smile that took over her face had me wishing I'd had my own… whatever Leo was to Hazel.

I'd known her since our freshman year of college, where she'd talked about him constantly. They'd been friends since their own days at camp as adolescents, and they'd been practically inseparable, even when hundreds of miles away from each other. I always wondered if there was more to their relationship than they let on. Any observer would have questions. She never outwardly claimed to have feelings for him, but she was also excellent at deflecting whenever the topic was brought up.

"He's currently trying to bribe a deer to leave the garden with a basket of apples attached to a fishing rod," she said, beaming. "He's so funny."

I turned my back so she didn't see my knowing smile. "And the second camp?"

Hazel let out a deep sigh, one tinged with exhaustion. "It's going good. Leo and I just got back in time for campers to arrive here, but we'll go back down next week to help them launch. For some reason, I think I'm more nervous than the first time we opened this camp. I can't wait for things to be up and running so we can take a second to just... breathe."

In the short time since I arrived, I'd noticed my friend carried herself differently. Her shoulders were slumped as though she'd forgotten what posture was, her face carrying dark circles underneath her eyes. But she still looked happy. Running was what she was used to.

Last year, a backer had approached Hazel and her counterpart about opening a second Camp Starlight, now called Camp Sunlight, and they'd been working tirelessly at the former kids' summer camp to get things up and running. I hadn't been sure they'd be able to do it in the nine months they'd had, but they'd pulled out a miracle. It helped that the bones were there, and this place was like a well-oiled machine, so they knew what they were doing after six years. I couldn't wait to go to Northern California to see it.

I closed my dresser and found Hazel biting her lip as she scrolled on her phone.

"Oof, looks like Poppy liked your latest post." Her eyebrows jumped to her hairline as if she didn't mean to say the words, but there they were, hanging between us like a breath on a cold fall night.

"She can like all she likes." I tried not to sound bitter as I fought the urge to pull out my phone. Pulling up the post would lead to checking out her profile, which would lead to remembering that I was less bitter and more sad than anything. Her account hadn't seen the growth she'd expected it to have after dating me for six months, which meant her plan to date me for likes had blown up in her face. It had been two months since we'd broken up, which made this the second time I'd come to camp on the heels of a breakup. This was officially a pattern. Great.

I fell back onto the bed, causing Hazel to bounce slightly. She let out a small giggle, a sound she didn't normally make outside of being drunk.

"Is everything going well here? You haven't mentioned how the start of Starlight has been going."

"Well, we've been very focused on our other project, so Autumn has been picking up the slack and kicking ass as assistant director. She's not acting as a camp counselor this year, so she has more time. I think we can look forward to a chaos-free year." She knocked on my oak bed frame. "With the exception of these camp games. They're already turning into something." Hazel's eyebrows went up as I grinned maniacally. "You're going to be good, right? We both know how competitive you can get."

I rolled my eyes dramatically enough to hurt. "Hey, that resident advisor was able to walk straight a couple of weeks after our spring softball tournament. You and I both agreed that had he tied his shoes properly, he wouldn't have face-planted when I tagged him out at third base."

"And the black eye did go away, so no harm done."

"Exactly." I rolled to the side, and my keys fell out onto the ground. I got out of bed and picked them up, dangling them from my fingers.

"You don't still have that frog keychain. Why don't you just buy a new one?"

"You obviously can't buy luck, Hazel. This thing has gotten me through a lot of major events and milestones."

"The first car you bought yourself."

I raised a finger. "Every one of my finals in college."

"That time we got free tickets to that metal show senior year."

I nodded. "That was pretty sick. Even after they showed up two hours late and the kegs ran out. Now, if only it could help me find a person who isn't dating me for all the wrong reasons. What am I saying? Don't feel bad, Bernice." I squeezed my keychain. "No one said you have to be perfect." I placed my keys carefully on top of my dresser, instantly realizing that I'd made a mistake. I turned to Hazel, who stared at me gleefully. "Don't even think about it."

"I know someone who would be perfect for you—"

"Hazel. You're not good at this. You're not Leo."

Leo was the infamous matchmaker at Camp. Though he sure did fail when it came to his own relationships. He'd won the shipping board every year since its inception, always figuring out which pairs went best together. He even had a bulletin board in his office filled with wedding and birth announcements, which he prided himself on, even though he hadn't had a hand in every single one. To him, it was close enough.

Everything at camp screamed family and belonging, and while I knew Hazel's relationship with her own family was complex, I also had my fair share of family complications and was glad she didn't ask me about mine, just like I wasn't about to ask about hers. It was one of those unspoken things that I appreciated about her.

"Really, Nat, thank you so much for helping out again. I've never had a new hire no-show before."

This was the second consecutive year that I'd been a fill-in counselor at Camp Starlight. Last year, I'd jumped at the chance to finish out the summer when a counselor had to leave because his pregnant sister went on bed rest and needed him to come help out. I'd just come off a bad breakup and happened to have some downtime, so I'd spent six weeks helping out. To be honest, I'd been ecstatic when she called me. We had recently rekindled our friendship after a few years of separation due to distance. We'd kept up with each other, but last year was the first time I'd seen her in years, and that was one of the best summers of my life.

"It's okay. I was planning on going where the wind took me this summer, anyway."

My job was great, so I wasn't complaining. I'd been a travel blogger since I was twenty-three. Before I went full time several years ago, I'd worked at my mom's company, in a soul-killing job, doing influencing on the side. I decided to leave after my accounts blew up, and I started making enough money to sustain myself. My mom hadn't taken it well.

"It's no problem." I'd still be able to keep up with my other job. Camp Starlight was surrounded by great hikes and viewpoints, and I planned to take short jaunts around Oregon during my time off for content.

Taking a break wasn't the worst idea anyway. At least that was what the therapist I hadn't spoken to in months had told me, but what did she know? Sure, I hadn't stopped moving since the last time I was at Starlight, and before that, I hadn't had a place to land in years. But who needed a *home*, amiright?

"I know we left it open-ended for now, and longevity with counselors is never guaranteed, but we liked having you around last summer. Your advice on increasing engagement and the changes you made to our website helped enrollments go more smoothly. Not to mention, you're such a positive light, which is always right at home here."

My cheeks heated at her compliments. She didn't usually dole them out like candy, and it was a little overwhelming all at once. "I just don't want you to worry about staffing while everything else is going on. Like I told you, I'd be happy to stick around for a few months."

Hazel narrowed her eyes skeptically. "If you're sure."

"I'm sure." I didn't know exactly how long I'd be here because the season was long, and I didn't have a plan just yet, but I didn't want this to be a stressor on anyone. And not to mention, being here just felt... right.

I wanted to chase that feeling.

THREE
Nat

The water rippled around my calves as I sat on the Lake Starlight dock and finally felt restored. It was so pretty out here that I wished I'd brought my camera. But there would be plenty of time for photo opportunities later. The campers were arriving soon, and this lake water cooling me off was my only hope at normalcy, my only reprieve from the sweltering desert that was currently my studio cabin. I was sweating in places that I didn't know I could sweat.

My shorts were sticking to me, and even though I considered myself fairly acclimated to the Pacific Northwest's changing weather patterns, this heatwave caught me off guard. Of course, it would happen the first week of camp.

Having grown up in Maryland, I was familiar with heatwaves and snowstorms. But I felt lied to. Oregon was supposed to be different. Everyone warned me about the rain, nice summers, and more rain, so where was all of that? Instead, we were fighting an unprecedented heatwave, and the cabin AC unit I thought I could rely on had packed its bags, leaving me high and dry. The large evergreen trees provided a little shade at least, and I could get a light cross-breeze with all the windows open, but it still wasn't enough.

There was still a little time to gather myself before the campers for this week arrived. I'd already gone over my packets, magically deciphering Leo's god-awful handwriting. Maybe I was just getting better at reading it, or maybe after some mild harassment, he'd made them halfway legible.

I was getting used to the many changes between now and last summer. For one thing, there was the new pod, Lynx, built just off the meditation meadow. I hadn't had a moment to talk with Lynx's new counselor, Chase, but I would eventually. Then there was Emerson. She and I had met briefly last year when she was in Jamie's infamous pod.

I had been lucky to witness Jamie and Autumn's love take shape over their time together last summer. I hadn't known Emerson back then, but this time, I intended to learn more about her.

After I finally felt like a human again, I pulled my legs from the lake water and slid my flip-flops back on, ready to walk the grounds to see what people were up to. Maybe even bump into a tall, broody blond who could fix my AC. I found myself under the zipline platform—my old stomping grounds. I'd be splitting my time between the zipline and craft cabin just like last year, as well as taking on some of Autumn's activities. At least I wouldn't be bored. First stop, the mess hall for a snack and a refill of my water bottle. I had an hour before I was needed at the parking lot to help campers find their pods in the madness that was Friday, better known as campers' arrival day.

The doors to the mess hall echoed strangely when campers weren't occupying the large space, running back and forth and talking excitedly over one another.

I snagged some trail mix when I heard commotion coming from the kitchen. I poked my head in to see our new intern, Shayne, as well as Azalea and Bobby, in a clamor to finish trays of snack foods that traveling campers could enjoy before dinner. I went to the nearest ice and water station and filled up my water bottle.

"Can I help?" I called out.

Azalea gave me a look that said I was today's miracle. She immediately took me up on my offer, and moments later, I was bustling trays from the kitchen and laying them out on the buffet tables at their warming stations. That was when I realized I wasn't the only noncook in the kitchen.

Chase nodded at me as he rid himself of a pile of napkins and put his palms down on the counter. "Are these them?" he asked in a hopeful tone. His flushed cheeks gave away that he must have been searching for a while.

"Yup, at the front of the buffet, please," Bobby confirmed, and Chase turned and spun, nearly taking me out.

"Sorry." He abruptly took a step back, momentarily stunned, before letting out a little laugh. "You're Nat, right?"

"That's right. And you're the newbie."

We chatted for a few minutes, and he reminded me of a cowboy who, as far as I could tell, didn't have a mean bone in his body.

"Did you get your packets from Leo? Do you know who you'll be looking for?" I asked, making sure he hadn't been in here all morning.

"Yeah, I have an eclectic group. I got the former child actor, a baker, a tarot reader, a beautician, and a lovely introvert who I know nothing about yet."

"That sounds fun. I got the already bonded group of self-identified nerds celebrating a twenty-first birthday." I almost asked who his shipping board picks were, but we weren't doing it this year. Which was probably for the best. Leo always won anyway. Most likely because I hadn't had enough time last year to properly put him in his place. He'd be out of the competition this time around, but I'd still have my opportunity to compete, which was all I cared about. Camp Wars sounded much more my style anyway.

EMERSON, SAWYER, CHASE, LAMAR, FELICIA, JACK, AND I stood up on the stage in front of this week's cohort of campers, and we introduced ourselves. It was the same every week. We were called on the stage during dinner, and then we went into the get to know your counselor game: two truths and a lie. We all made it fun and interesting, garnering some laughs and playful gasps. New facts were presented by most of the counselors. Since I'd just arrived and was living in a sweatbox, I hadn't given my answers much thought and instead focused on delivery.

I kept my two truths and a lie the same as last year. I talked about my follower count, which was significantly higher now than last summer.

Then I told them I'd danced with Dolly Parton, which most people assumed I hadn't done, so it was an easy misdirect. When I was ten, my grandfather, who'd been running for office, had scheduled an interview with my family on a popular morning show. We were supposed to sit and answer a couple of questions on the same show that Dolly was later performing on. I had seen her backstage, and she'd danced with me when I admitted I was nervous to go on TV. Those three minutes had been spectacular.

I ended the game by saying my favorite movie was *The Goonies*, which wasn't true since I hadn't seen the Pacific Northwest staple. I'd always gotten gasps for that lie, as well as a few good-natured boos. I still needed to watch that one, or Hazel just might make good on her threats to kick me out of camp until I did.

Once the initial awkwardness of on-stage introductions was out of the way, the counselors and campers all headed out to play more icebreaker games around the bonfire and to just unwind.

Many campers had traveled a great distance to be here. Some would go to bed early, while others would soak up the nostalgia and fun vibes of stories around the campfire.

The groups of campers were usually fun, but my current group was exceptionally so. There were five of them, and the youngest in their friend group, Jessica, was turning twenty-one and chose to celebrate it at camp. Turned out, *self-described nerds* meant challenging each other in chess one minute and playing a long-running D&D campaign the next. Their dedication to strategy and story was incredible.

I'd felt like a cool aunt as I helped them get settled in their cabins earlier, and even more so now as I learned about the deep lore of the world they'd built and the time that Brandon had been backstabbed by the birthday girl, which had led to the implosion of that campaign.

My group was all ready to relax and enjoy crafting and campfires. Anything to get away from their regular lives, which I could relate to. Sometimes getting away meant partying with your friends and trying to get your counselor to agree to a one-shot campaign. Other times, it meant driving your ass back to camp when your friend needed you.

The stories they told around the bonfire got louder and sillier over time. Once they got into another nearly heated but ultimately for fun debate, I excused myself. I looked around the group of counselors hanging with their pods and caught those piercing eyes I'd been looking for through the fire's flame. I was predictably drawn in by Jack Hawthorne. I wanted to know more about him.

Jack's campers were having a blast getting to know one another, and the way he interacted with them had me hanging on every word as well. He stood up and headed away from his cohort with a grin, turning toward the bar, and I made my move.

His jaw was set in a firm line, and those eyes were intense when they met mine. It took everything to keep myself on track.

"Hey, so it's like one hundred and ten degrees in my cabin

right now. Think you could help a girl out after this?" I pushed my hair behind my ear, and he tracked my movement, scowling at me.

"Why is it that you're always asking me for something?" His tone was a rattlesnake warning that any further interaction meant venom. It stung, but mostly because it didn't make sense.

"Excuse me?" This was definitely not about the frizz. "All I'm asking is for an air conditioner that works."

He crossed his arms over his broad chest and gave me a look that felt like a door slamming in my face. "You're just going to have to deal. I don't have time for this," he clipped and began to walk around me.

Stunned, I let him pass, wondering what had crawled up his ass. Guess I needed to try to figure out how to survive by myself. There was no way I was spending the rest of the summer like this.

I couldn't imagine going back to my sweatbox of a cabin right now. Instead, I let out an annoyed sigh and made my way toward the closest communal bathroom.

I swung the door open aggressively, and a startled Autumn gasped and put her hand to her chest as I stormed in. I could feel my face taking on that familiar, frustrating shade of beet red, and I knew my eyes were wild with the need to take a frigid shower and scream into the void. I'd have to settle on splashing myself with cold water instead. But now my boss was looking at me, and I had to be at least somewhat professional. Screaming into the void would have to wait.

"Oh, sorry," I said in a huff.

"You about sent me into next week." Autumn's hands gripped the sink behind her, and that was when I saw it. Half of her blonde, wavy hair was wet and stringy.

She turned back to lean over the sink. "Jamie's bad at feeding me s'mores." She smiled wryly at me through the bathroom mirror as she scrubbed marshmallow remnants out of her hair.

I held back my laughter. "Do you need any help?"

"I'll wash it again when I get back to my cabin tonight." It was so cute how she and Jamie lived here at camp.

I grabbed a washcloth and offered it to her, but she waved me off.

"Thanks, but it's under control now." She eyed me up and down. "I hate to say it, but you're looking a bit frizzier than usual. Don't you use a plethora of fancy hair care products?"

I rolled my eyes at her. "You'd look like a bog witch, too, if you had my cabin. I've been sweating my ass off since my AC whispered its last breath. And since Jack's not able to get another one, I'll probably be frizzy and stuck taking cold showers."

"What do you mean? Of course, we can get another AC." Autumn cocked her head in my direction and finished wringing out her hair.

"Seriously? That would be amazing," I practically screeched.

Autumn had her ways, so she must have known something that Jack didn't. I swiped away some sweat and used the washcloth she had rejected, letting out a sigh of sheer relief as I wiped cold water all over my face.

FOUR
Nat

My inbox mocked me as I did my best to open unread messages in bed. With the chaos of arriving late and settling in, I was still playing catch-up on emails and direct messages. I usually stayed meticulously on top of it, something I'd learned from my CEO mom, but offers for brand partnerships kept coming in, and I hadn't had the capacity lately to connect with them all yet. The more I looked at each email draft I'd started with half-thought-out replies, the more I felt overwhelmed, which made me feel like a failure, and my little ADHD brain couldn't handle it.

If I could just break through this mental block, then I could delegate to my amazing assistant, Kim. She lived in Chicago, was an excellent communicator, and handled a lot of the behind-the-scenes minutiae. But ultimately, it was up to me to decide what brands I wanted to take on and how much I was willing to put on the line. Too many offers was a good problem to have, but my decision fatigue was running higher these days.

All I knew was that a higher follower count meant more obligations, which was demanding when I was feeling creatively blocked. I did my best to reinvigorate my spark any chance I could to prevent things from going stale. This was one of the reasons I was happy to help Hazel out. Last time I'd been at camp, I'd left with more energy and inspiration than I'd had in years.

People loved to think that influencing was easy, but that was the furthest thing from the truth. I'd done trends, interviews, and collaborations with other travel bloggers. I took photos and made content months in advance. And I had to be on twenty-four seven. There was a level of authenticity to my brand, which was just as important as showing off the beautiful parts of the world. Not everyone could travel and experience things as I did, but it could be exhausting waiting for the perfect atmospheric shot or dealing with strangers who asked invasive questions. Not to mention blocking gross commenters. Researching and exploring were fun, but sometimes it was challenging. Getting lost in unfamiliar places and the constant moving and living out of a suitcase sometimes meant I needed to just stay in one place for a moment.

It was time for some fresh air. If I was going to get a hike in before camp was awake, I had to disconnect.

That would be easier done if I'd gotten any sleep last night. The heat in my cabin was appalling. That was one of the reasons I was looking forward to getting outside in the fresh air.

Recharge. Reconnect.

I slipped on my hiking boots, nurturing the flame of my inner creative, as though she'd run away if I weren't careful. Hiking in the wilderness was where I always belonged. Send me into the trees with a rain jacket and hiking boots and I would be home. Give me a camera and sunscreen and I'd be gone all day. However, that wasn't feasible today, since I had a full day scheduled. The only time I'd have to myself for the first couple of weeks would be the mornings before activities began.

I was also looking forward to the first competition in Camp Wars later this afternoon. I knew how to play Texas Hold'em, even if it had been a while. I had a surprisingly good game face. Most competitors underestimated me, and I loved proving them wrong.

I loved upping the bets and pulling through with something unexpected.

After I finished lacing my boots, I took off. The air was crisp and fresh at five in the morning. Though I hadn't slept well, the cool tree canopy and the branches under my feet were rejuvenating in the way only the wilderness could be. I took the walking trail that went around Lake Starlight and caught the sunrise from the east. Oranges and pinks melded into a sherbet sky as the breeze blew wisps of hair out of my eyes.

I'd brought my camera this time and made sure to utilize it, already feeling more motivated to post than I had all last month. It was my first solo hike in forever. Maybe that was why? I was already coming up with a collaboration I could do with Starlight. I'd have to show it to Hazel.

I sat on a large moss-covered rock and stretched my legs out. A dragonfly drifted on the wind around me, and I followed it until it disappeared from view. My younger sister had once told me they symbolized adapting to change and embracing transformation, while enjoying the present. So I was on a mission to be myself, reconnect with acquaintances and my inner child. Deciding to come to camp, no matter how temporary the respite, felt like the right choice.

I'd felt this way last summer, too. I remembered taking this exact walk, sitting on this same rock, looking over the lake, and contemplating what I'd done wrong when another relationship had ended. I'd promised myself I wouldn't let those past mistakes ruin my chance at a good summer, and for the most part, it'd worked.

Was I about to make the same promise? In the same spot? If the Nat-sized shoe fit.

Suddenly, something moved beside me. No—not moved, slithered. I let out a suppressed shriek instead of unleashing a terrified wail, like my inner self wanted to do. I didn't want to be responsible for waking up the whole camp. I scrambled off the once-serene rock, taking a few clumsy steps backward to see if I could get eyes on the snake. Usually, I got along well in nature, but I had a line, and my line was snakes. They didn't have legs. They were fast and unpredictable. The only thing snakes were good for was looking badass in Medusa's hair or on my college ex's hot bicep tattoo. Nowhere else.

I hightailed it back to camp in double time, ready to shower.

I HEADED INTO THE CRAFT CABIN STORAGE TO GET ready for my afternoon activity. Autumn definitely had a system. Was it color-coded or up to my level of organization? No. But at least it made sense for the most part. It didn't matter, though. Autumn might host a few craft nights here and there, but she was busier than ever, so this was my territory now.

I easily found the supplies for pottery. I loved her carefree brain. Sometimes I wished mine was—

No, I wasn't going there. I could appreciate my neuro-spicy brain for what it was. I was organized. Too organized, according to my last girlfriend. But she didn't realize how one domino out of place meant everything could topple over, and once the chaos set in, it was hard to get myself grounded again. I was scheduled, I paid for help from my assistant, and I had multiple alarms to keep me on task. Thankfully, my system worked.

I selected the clay and began working it while campers piled in. I squished the slippery substance between my fingers and reveled in how it molded so easily, which made me think of my reintegration into camp. How I'd just slid right back in as if nothing had happened. With the exception of Jack noticing. I mashed the clay between my fingers and destroyed what I was doing, ready to start again, until the sound of campers pulled me out of my reverie.

The room filled up without my noticing, and I overheard snippets of conversations. They told stories of only being able to make a bowl in their high school pottery classes. Or on the opposite end of the spectrum, someone who fell in love with ceramics and now owns an online store selling cute mugs.

My demonstration on how to make a leaf-like soap dish went well. The class had fun, and we all had different creations to show for the hour well spent. I'd fire these, and they'd get picked up later.

I tucked my hair behind my ears and began cleaning up the space. A gasp left me when I took in the broad-shouldered, blond man sitting at the back table.

"Shit, I didn't see you there." My hackles went up at his unaffected shrug. "What do you want, Jack?"

"Why did you go behind my back? I told you I couldn't get you an AC this week."

I folded my arms across my chest and stood my ground. "I didn't go behind your back."

His eyes narrowed as if he'd caught me in a lie. "Yeah, you did. I've got enough going on without Autumn breathing down my neck."

Jack stood up as I rounded the table to get to him, standing toe to toe. I was not backing down. "It still feels like Death Valley in my cabin."

"I have to build a photo booth setup for our last-minute poker night and reinforce the garden fencing after a deer got in, all while tending to my pod. I didn't have time to go around the mountain to pick up your precious AC at the drop of a dime when it could have waited a couple of days. But yeah. I did it anyway. I'll install it tomorrow morning since it's clear you can't live without luxury."

There had been many moments in my life where I lost my voice because I was in total shock. Luckily, this wasn't one of them. I blamed the rage.

"Are you done? First off, you didn't say you'd get it in a couple of days. You left me to deal with it on my own. I've got an idea:

how about we switch cabins so you can experience living in a sauna and hoping you don't die of heat exhaustion? No? I didn't think so."

There was a spark of something in his eyes as they widened at my snark. As though he relished this interaction. Was he enjoying this?

He leaned down to my level, and I was happy to see him have to hunch. Maybe it'd give him some neck pain. "You want to know what I think?"

"Not unless it's a list of why you're wrong. Or how you plan to make it up to me," I quipped.

He seemed all too eager to deliver the final blow. "I think princesses like you don't belong in the wilderness."

I let out a small gasp, and my fists balled up. "How fucking dare—"

But he was already pushing out the door. I may have been livid, but at least there was one beacon of light. I'd have blessed AC. Even if it was being installed by the most condescending, infantilizing asshole in the world.

He'd won this round, but this was just one battle in what was shaping up to be a war.

THE NEXT MORNING, MY DOOR CREAKED AS JACK MADE his way inside my cabin with a massive box and a drill in his hands. He cringed at the sound but didn't say anything. In fact, neither of us said anything. I'd call it awkward, but the tension was more angry than anything.

Part of that was on me. I'd spent yet another night in my sweatbox, tossing and turning as I thought of ways to get away with sabotage. Maybe we'd see how he'd deal without an air conditioner.

He pushed my couch out of the way and used a drill to remove the screws from the board the AC was mounted to. Then he unceremoniously pushed the piece of crap out the window, and it crunched onto the bush behind the cabin. I would say the man had a problem with aggression, but he was smiling, so I figured he was just being lazy instead of doing it in a normal way.

He wiped a bead of sweat from his brow, and I basked in his wrongness. I was so close to saying something about how right I was regarding the debilitating heat, but another drip rolled down the side of his face, and I found myself practically salivating. Damn, why did someone who looked like that have to be such a douche canoe?

It was ridiculous to question whether we'd gotten off on the wrong foot just because he was hot, right?

Right.

I was beginning to wonder if I should break the silence. It was starting to drive me up the wall. Then I talked myself out of it, because no, I would not cave first. He could live in his discomfort. He was the one who needed to apologize, and I was the one who'd done nothing wrong. But chances were, if I waited for an apology, I'd be waiting forever.

Jack ignored me as he efficiently got to work using a pocketknife to slice open the box, drawing attention to his rippling muscles in his too-tight T-shirt. I knew I shouldn't be looking, and I knew I was right about that when he scowled at me as he started to lift it without assistance.

I figured now was the time to prove I wasn't the precious princess I'd been dubbed by the king asshole. I took one side of the unit and lifted with him, seeing the relief in his face when he realized I was helping. We walked to the window and placed it gently. The unit started to shift, and we both reached on top to stabilize it, my hand landing on his. That was when I realized it was just the two of us in my too-small, too-hot cabin. And he had those forearms.

I needed a slap across the cheek or an air horn to get my head together. He stared at me, and I could see the twilight blue spark of his eyes. Were they beckoning me closer? Or were mine playing tricks on me? My breaths became short, light puffs, and I almost said something embarrassing, but Jack broke first, taking back his hand. I held onto the air conditioner, wondering if he'd felt it, too. That all too hazy buzz of... something.

"Thanks." There was a rough edge to his low tone, but it wasn't in the same way I'd heard before. I reminded myself that I was grateful, not disappointed, and that we hadn't both pulled away and broken yet another AC. Not that the first one was my fault.

Jack drilled the AC into place on the inside, then made his way around the back of the cabin, and I heard the screws going into place.

I let go of the unit, and it didn't move, which was enough for me to hightail it to my small kitchen, open my freezer door, and stick my head inside. I didn't have a plan, but I needed to cool off if that man was coming back in here. Anything to get my mind off Jack. Then I saw the ice cubes. I grabbed them and dropped them the second I turned around and found him in a freaking backward cap, hair curled behind his ears.

"You okay?" he asked, the divot between his eyebrows deepening. A coherent version of me would have realized that was the nicest thing he'd said to me this year.

"Yeah." I quickly picked up the tray and set it on the counter, reaching for two glasses as he started cleaning up. I cracked the tray and dropped ice cubes into each glass, pouring the sweet tea I'd made yesterday over top. Then came the sound of heaven. The AC unit burst to life, and I was probably dreaming it, but I swear the air instantly reached me across the room. I turned, glasses in hand, squealing in delight as I saw the air blowing his long hair off his shoulders. He sighed in relief, and yet again, I wanted to point out just how hypocritical he was. But I didn't. Because the circulating oxygen went straight to my brain, and I kept my foot out of my mouth.

Nothing could take away this high. Even Jack let out a satisfied grin, and it made him seem almost bearable. What was more bearable was the hum of the machine and the cool, refreshing air as we both leaned into it. The contrast of the cold air on my way-too-hot skin caused me to tremble.

He stepped closer to me, and I froze as he nodded to my hand. I looked down at the drink, realizing what he was asking, and shoved it at him a little too eagerly. He didn't appear to notice.

"It's finally manageable in here."

"Don't mention it," he deadpanned. He took the tea carefully, as if to avoid my fingers this time, and gulped it down in two quick swallows. Even the way the man's throat worked was irritating. Were my eyes wandering again? Was I being obvious? I had to get it together. But his shirt, covered in sweat, annoyingly clung to him, and of course, he had the gall to smell good, even in tight quarters like this. It wasn't as if I was seeking this out, but it was just so... pornographic.

Shit, there was no denying this after all.

Jack let out a little puff of air, the relief loosening up his form. "Thanks." He set the glass in the sink and looked like he wanted to say something else, but instead, he grabbed the cardboard box and went through the door. "Don't break this one," he called over his shoulder.

I slammed the door shut behind him.

FIVE
Nat

CHASE HANDED ME THE FINAL BALLOON FOR THE ARCH we were building as we transformed the mess hall into a Vegas-themed casino for tonight's poker night. The décor could only be described as *camp glam*, and we were doing the best we could with the short window of time we had to do it.

Sawyer and Autumn handled the lighting while Chase and I moved to the next task on Autumn's list and began setting up the tables, placing chips, cards, and markers in their proper places. There were eight tables in all: one for each pod, and one for the counselors to kick off our Camp Wars competition.

The occasional trash talk could be heard between counselors as we set up. This was shaping up to be a cutthroat event. Tonight, we'd all battle for dominance so we could put ourselves on the scoreboard. I'd say people were taking this too seriously, but I was no better. I'd gone as far as watching *World Poker Championship* videos in preparation.

I jumped at Jack's voice from behind me.

"Where's the photo booth going to be?"

I pointed toward the corner where Emerson and Sawyer were hanging up lights. Jack set the long boards down next to the prop table where I'd indicated to build the photo booth frame we'd reuse for future events.

As the tournament time drew closer, Autumn hopped up on the stage and announced the rules, and we helped campers get situated. Some campers, like my current pod, had already bonded to each other at the hip. Others hadn't quite clicked yet, but I hoped this poker night would bring them together.

Jack hovered as everyone got to their tables. "I feel like I should warn you. I'm damn good at poker."

I rolled my eyes. "So am I."

A devious look crossed over his face. "Why don't we make it interesting then?"

My mind went to a highly inappropriate place where he'd suggest strip poker, and my face heated. "How so?"

"If you win, which I'll add is highly unlikely, I'll clean those zipline harnesses you were always complaining about last summer. For a month."

That stopped me in my tracks. Somehow, he remembered my least favorite task at this camp. The idea of giving that responsibility to Jack was beyond tempting.

"Don't look so cocky. Those harnesses are hand-wash only, Jack," I lied. I would have quit if I had to squeeze out the butt sweat from those things. I waited for some indication that he'd made a mistake, but he didn't seem fazed. "And I'd be doing what? Giving you notes on how to have a better attitude?"

The look he gave me was ominous. "You'll be cleaning the drains in the communal showers."

Okay, not ominous. More like a curse.

"I can agree to those terms." Either way, I'd be winning, so I figured I'd toss him a bone. I couldn't wait to see his face when he scrubbed those harnesses by hand.

The counselors all took seats at the table. Chase sat on my left, and Emerson was on my right. Jack sat directly across from me as if he were personally challenging me. I still didn't know why he seemed to have a vendetta against me in particular, but no matter the reason, he was going to regret making an enemy of me. If he was dead set on a rival, I'd give him the pettiest, fiercest, most stubborn rival he'd ever seen.

Once all the tables were full, campers began shuffling their decks and explaining the rules to each other. I overheard one table making their own camp rules, where if they raised the bet, they had to quote a line from a movie before doing so. I shook my head, laughing. I turned to Jack and found him glowering from behind sunglasses, as if he actually thought he could deceive us. It was so intense I caught a chill.

"You can try to hide your tells all you like, but just so you know, those are reflective lenses," I remarked, proud of myself.

Jack scoffed as if I were wrong, looked at them, and casually slid the offending sunglasses up on top of his head with a pout. It would have been cute, had he not been annoying the shit out of me.

I laughed to spite him.

"You're so immature," he groused.

"And you're so prickly," I shot back.

Everyone turned to Autumn as she got up on the stage, projecting a graphic of the rankings of poker hands for Texas Hold'em. She went over the rules and the value of each chip, of which we'd been given three hundred imaginary dollars.

Felicia's eyes went around the table. "Who's the first dealer?"

"How about the newest counselor deals?" Lamar offered as Felicia handed Chase the deck.

"Technically, Nat is the newest," Jack pointed out.

"Am not," I argued. "I was here last year."

He narrowed his eyes at me. "Actually, you are. You showed up for this session halfway through the kickoff, the last arrival among all of us. Therefore, you deal first."

I didn't feel like arguing further, so I took the deck. We made it through our first two rounds, with most of us folding, because the cards showing were garbage.

Chase leaned into me after I took my turn. "Hazel mentioned that you love Fritos and chocolate. I haven't tried it yet, but I love sweet pickles on pepperoni pizza, so which of us do you think is stranger?"

I laughed at his conspiratorial whisper and admitted, "I'd be willing to try yours."

Chase beamed, while Jack's face scrunched up as if he'd just eaten a lemon.

"Don't knock it 'til you try it," I defended. "Sweet and salty always go well together."

He let out an exasperated sigh and folded his cards when the bet was called.

That's right, Jack. I've got you beat.

I collected the next two pots, explaining the rules to Emerson as we went, because this was her first time. I'd offered her a few tips since I'd played more than enough poker in my college years, and not because of my dormmates or friends. No, it was my Grandma Carol.

Some grandmothers played bunco or pinochle. Mine, however, was a hustler who'd take you for everything you had, and she'd taught me to play. I smiled at the memory.

Feeling cocky, I upped my game and my trash talk. "Put your money where your mouth is."

Knowing my pile of chips was bigger than my enemies' had me excited, but the fact that mine was bigger than Jack's? Well, that was just the cherry on the cake.

Soon, Jack and Lamar were in a one-on-one showdown.

"Get him, Lamar," I cheered, guessing Jack was up against the ropes.

"What did you have?" Jack asked a gloating Lamar as the final card was laid.

Lamar looked into his eyes with all seriousness. "You beat."

He showed my rival the straight he'd managed to pull on the flop, and I beamed. Sawyer cackled at the playful trash talk, which got snickers from the rest of us. Even grumpy Jack seemed to be having fun.

In the next round, both Sawyer and Emerson lost after going all in. I promised Emerson we could play again soon, to her delight.

"Kenny Rogers was supposed to be on my side," Sawyer complained, and I felt that in my bones. That seventies silver fox wasn't on either of our sides. My pile of chips had dwindled slightly. I guessed I also needed a refresher on when to fold them, when to walk away, and when to run. My dignity was at stake, and I needed to get it together.

Sawyer left the table, vowing to destroy us next time. We all took a quick break after refilling drinks and stretching.

Chase, Lamar, and I all went head-to-head when we came back for the next round, and I managed to squeak out a victory by sheer bluffing as they folded. I shoved my two-seven off-suit hand into the pile of discards, making sure no one saw.

Jack's eyes searched my face before he smirked, as if he could see right through me. But he was about to see just how wrong he was.

Felicia went out next, and things were getting serious. By the time Chase went out, Jack was looking all too smug.

Chase stood up next to me and leaned down while Jack dealt out our cards. "Maybe I'll see you around for those chocolate-dipped Fritos later."

I gave him a quick, "Sure," practically waving him off. I needed to focus on taking down Jack. Lamar, too, but mostly Jack.

The game went on, and soon I was certain of my impending victory.

"You're on. I'll call," I said, dropping my cards down with gusto. My large pile had been shrinking, but I was still on a mission to put Jack in his place.

Lamar folded, setting his cards down in front of him. "Too rich for my blood."

Two losses later, however, Jack was looking a little too pleased with himself.

"Looking a little sparse over there, Lamar. But I suppose it's time to get you off this board," a high-handed Jack gloated.

"Keep talking, Jack. It won't matter when I knock you out of the game," I replied as if Jack had taunted me.

I pushed my bet into the community pot, and Lamar went all in after me. If I were going to lose, I'd much rather it be to Lamar.

Jack and Lamar were all in, and it was down to me. I had nothing left to give, but I believed in my pocket queens. And while I couldn't help but pout at my significantly weakened standing, I wasn't about to give up.

I nearly gave away my hand when a third queen was revealed on the flop, which meant a full house, or four of a kind, was on my radar. Either way, it was a solid bet. Jack raised, trying to get me to fold before the turn, and it wasn't happening.

The infuriating man was trying to bait me into a bad decision, but I didn't fold pocket queens, ever, and especially not when it was just between Jack and me. He might have thought he could bluff me out with this new bet, but he was dead wrong.

The answering smile on Jack's face told me he thought he'd backed me into a corner. He had a gleam in his eye, and it screamed trouble.

"Since Nat can't call—" Lamar started.

"I have this," I blurted, then dangled Bernice in front of them. I'd brought her to give me an edge. The frog talisman had been sitting in my pocket all night. This wasn't what I'd had planned for her, but I had to do what I had to do.

Jack's gaze went from me to Bernice. "A keychain?"

I ran my fingers over her metal form. "She's not just a keychain. She's my lucky charm."

Lamar looked at Bernice skeptically. "It looks like it's on its last legs."

I shook my head. "As I said, she's lucky. And priceless."

Jack's eyes lit up, and it almost seemed as if he wanted her more after that. "I'm fine with it if you are, Lamar." Then he shrugged noncommittally, as if he hadn't just played his hand. How this man had been at the top of this game, I had no clue. He couldn't bluff his way out of a paper bag.

"You must really need some luck." Lamar ran his hand over his brow and grinned. "Yeah, okay, let the frog in."

I wasn't going to lose, so I kissed Bernice and set her on top of the pile of chips. "Just for a moment, baby," I murmured.

Jack's eyebrows went high, as if he were trying to decipher this interaction. I wasn't about to explain.

"You're gonna wish you'd folded," Jack said as if my prized possession wasn't on the line. His tone was all too playful in front of the audience I hadn't noticed had gathered. The mess hall was so quiet you could hear a pin drop. Apparently, we were now the entertainment.

With that added pressure, I decided the only folding I'd be doing was my arms across my chest. "You'd love that, wouldn't you?"

We all flipped our cards, and I tried not to give away anything I was feeling. Jack had two low clubs. He was obviously going for the flush I hadn't considered. Lamar had two pairs. And I desperately needed that full house. Three of a kind was no longer an option.

My gut clenched as I questioned my impulsive actions that had gotten my cute little keychain into this mess. No, it would be okay. I was going to get the full house. And the next card revealed was going to grant my wish.

The final card was turned. A four of clubs.

Lamar gracefully pushed in his cards. I looked over to Jack, his face split into an infuriating smile.

No, no, no. This wasn't happening. Jack showed off his pocket clubs, completing his flush with low cards. I could have screamed at myself.

Jack was already gloating, seeing my expression. Lamar gave me a conciliatory glance that said he understood.

The cheers in the room didn't overshadow Jack's villainous laugh as he scooped up his pile of winnings, taking both of us out in one fell swoop.

"Looks like you have a new home, little frog," he gloated, dangling my keychain, and I was *this* close to flipping the table. But Grandma Carol had taught me better than that.

"You don't actually want that garbage," Lamar joked.

I held out my hand. "He's right, I'll take it back."

"No way. You lost, princess. But I think you're right, this little frog *is* lucky. For me, at least."

I looked at my frog, then back to his obnoxious face. I was done letting his rugged good looks distract me. This man was poisonous, and now, as he swung my frog around his finger, laughing, I was more determined than ever.

Taking Jack Hawthorne down was personal.

SIX
Jack

The past week had been confusing at best. My attempts to get Nat out of my head had only backfired. I'd ended up fixating on her more. I'd won at poker, but that wasn't what I kept thinking about. No, I kept picturing her working with me to install her AC in that too-hot cabin. The way we'd looked into each other's eyes for longer than was appropriate. And that hand touch.

Images of her kept flooding my mind. Her too-tight yoga pants. That relieved sigh when the AC kicked on after our efforts. At the mess hall, happy and playful as she set up the event. Then riled up as she stormed off after I took her precious frog, Bernice. Who names a keychain, anyway? The little thing was worn down and kinda cute in a been-through-the-wringer kind of way.

I'd set it on my coffee table over a stack of mail I hadn't gotten to yet and looked at it like the trophy it was.

At the office, Autumn was running around with an air of deadlines about her. I tapped her shoulder, and she jumped. "So, how are things going?"

"Normally, amazing. But this week? Exhausting, if I'm being honest. Everything runs smoothly until the owners are gone, and

I'm basically doing three jobs. I'm also the counselor supervisor, so if you could do me a favor and not need any supervision, that would be great."

"They're back later today, aren't they?" And not a minute too soon, apparently.

"Yes, thank goodness." Relief flooded her face as she blew her bangs out of her eyes and melted into her chair. "It's been a long week, Jack. I mean, I've loved stepping up. I'm totally capable. But last night, Jamie asked if I was auditioning for a new role as camp ghost since I'm never home."

I cracked a grin. My friendship with Autumn was the best thing to come out of my time in Palo Alto. At the bright, bushy-tailed age of twenty-two, I'd decided to move down to California to work for my dad's construction company. He'd moved from Oregon after my parents' messy divorce when I was in high school. When a bad breakup had me feeling untethered, I'd figured there was no better time to move to California and reconnect with my dad. He took me under his wing and taught me the ins and outs of his construction company. Quickly, I fell in love with the work and learned everything I could.

I'd been in my mid-twenties when I met Autumn. She'd been a barista at the coffee shop I frequented. Come to think of it, she'd had an air of deadlines even back then, slinging orders like she was being chased. Only now, there was more of a love and purpose surrounding everything she did.

When Hazel called me with the job offer to come help her and Leo restore a former resort into their vision of Camp Starlight, I'd known she would need more help, and I'd recommended Autumn. They video called that night, and two weeks later, Autumn and I were both packing and moving to the Oregon wilderness, thrilled for the opportunity.

I took in the room. Autumn's space was a whole other level of destruction than usual. When she hit a fugue state, my best friend buried her desk space and any other available surface in sticky notes. There was an abundance of the color-coded squares, and I considered swapping the colors around just to mess with her, before thinking better of it.

Instead, I picked up a photo of her and Jamie. They looked amazing, all heart eyes and hugs. "Aw, the couple in love."

Autumn snatched the photo frame out of my hands. "Don't knock it 'til you try it," she said lovingly as she looked at the picture. It was of them holding each other all cute-like at the dock.

"Been there, done that, bought the T-shirt. Burned the T-shirt, spread the ashes at sea," I said sardonically.

Autumn let out a little laugh, despite the tense conversation. "You mean the lake?"

I let out an exasperated sigh. "It's a metaphor."

She clasped her hands, her eyes filled with sadness. "So you're never going to... ever?"

It was as if she didn't know my shitty backstory. Parents put the kids through a terrible divorce, dad moved to another state, both parents put pressure on me to choose who I'd live with, and they still can't talk to one another, blah blah blah. And that was just their relationship. My past was rife with cheating exes.

"Not everything ends up like how it did for you and Jamie."

She set the picture back down with a sigh. "Listen, just in case it wasn't clear before, I didn't know that Nat was coming back. I swear I would have warned you."

Just then, my phone started vibrating. I took it out to see my ex's name pop up on the screen, telling me she was thinking about me and wanted to talk. As if she had any right to such a thing.

My hawkeyed bestie had no qualms about being nosy AF and saw the message. I hastily shoved my phone into my pocket, as if hiding it would make the text go away.

"What does Gia want?" Autumn arched a brow defensively, as if she were ready to jump to my aid.

I let out a sigh. "Don't know, don't care."

Autumn must have felt my cold tone because she wisely didn't press, and my shoulders relaxed, only to be bunched right back up a moment later when she used her too casual tone. "So how are you doing with the Nat of it all? Having her back here?"

I shrugged. "I couldn't care less. It doesn't matter to me. Not even a little."

Autumn's eyes met mine, as if she could see right through me. This wouldn't be a problem if I could just ignore Nat, but instead, I was doing the opposite. For some annoying reason, I couldn't get her being almost kind to me out of my head.

Luckily, Autumn went on, so I didn't have to elaborate. "Look, I'm team Jack, always, but I'm also assistant director, so I can't be mean to Nat. And neither can you." She gave me a look that said I needed to suck it up. "We all have to work together."

"Like I said, I don't care. Having her around is no big deal." And before Autumn could question the validity of that statement, I waved and gave her an excuse about needing to snake the drains, even though that was now Nat's job.

Leo and Hazel arrived just before flag football, looking jet-lagged. I figured they'd both take a break from the festivities and get some rest, but Hazel said she was riding a second wind and was excited to be the referee. Apparently, she wasn't messing around when she came out wearing a vertical black-and-white striped shirt with a whistle around her neck. She looked like someone you didn't want to fuck with.

We started the second Camp Wars competition with all seven counselors, and the new week's campers who'd chosen to participate were lined up on the beach, ready to learn the rules and watch the first game between Chase's and Lamar's teams.

Sawyer had been a quarterback in high school, so they announced the rules as Hazel gave each of us bandanas. I tied my blue bandana on my bicep, and Nat tied her red one into her hair. I watched as she moved the long locks out of her face as if this meant showtime. I wanted to remind her that it wasn't even her round, but that'd sound petty, and Autumn had just mentioned I should get my shit together.

We'd chosen the beach over the meditation meadow as our field because, as Leo had pointed out, the meditation meadow was all about serenity and didn't need to be tainted with our aggression. The field would have five team members from each side, with subs on the sidelines.

"The main difference is that this is a no-contact game. No fumbles, it'll be a dead ball. No tackling. That's what the flags are for, people. No blocking," Sawyer explained before putting their yellow bandana over their forehead like they were the Karate Kid or something. The majority of us moved to the seating area to watch the games begin.

Autumn had created a bracket, which she displayed on an easel. The plan was for each team to play a game until they lost, and the winners would move on to play each other.

Things didn't turn out so well for Sawyer's team. They lost in their only round when they went up against Nat's team, who'd won their first match against Emerson's team. Felicia was out after my team bested hers. Chase and Lamar had faced off, with Lamar coming out on top. When I won my match against Lamar's team, it only meant one thing: there would be a Nat and Jack showdown. What a surprise.

I'd just come off from the field after an arduous win and wiped the sweat from my brow. Nat, meanwhile, looked all too happy, soaking up the sun and laughing with Chase. Chase had just flashed himself in the face with the sun on her compact mirror, and they both couldn't stop laughing about it. She then held the mirror and touched up her eyeblack. And of course, it looked cute on her.

Just what I needed, more reason to think she was cute. I

couldn't let her get to me like this. Gia had thought Nat was cute, too. Ugh, I hated how my ex kept popping into my mind after that text. We were over. It had been months of no contact. Why was she messing with me now? Maybe it was good to remember, since it reinvigorated my hatred of Nat. I could use that.

Throughout the day, people had come and gone, choosing to sit in to cheer teams on or participate themselves. Most didn't choose a side, but Chase, the poor sucker, seemed all too happy to cheer Nat on during both her games. Was he trying to flirt with her? That man was a kind soul, too sweet for Nat, that was for sure. But based on her track record, she'd chew him up and spit him out. I shouldn't have cared who was into her.

We walked toward Hazel for the coin toss. "Okay, heads is Nat. Tails is Jack," Hazel said, flipping the coin in the air.

Of course, my nemesis won. But she wouldn't be winning this game. That was all that mattered.

Hazel blew her whistle and headed over to Leo.

Nat tightened the bandana in her hair so it didn't fall out. "Can't wait 'til I get your flags, Jack." Her voice made my blood boil. Her every expression had me bursting at the seams. Then I remembered my secret weapon.

I removed the trophy keychain from my shorts and spun it on my finger, purposely antagonizing her. "What were you saying?" I taunted, and Nat looked ready to blow a gasket. I probably looked like a cartoon villain.

The more she stared, the more her eyes filled with longing. "How about this, the winner gets Bernice? If you win, I'll make you a hundred bucks richer." Man, she was desperate.

"Get lost, Nat. This is my lucky keychain now." I tucked Bernice back into my pocket with a smirk, and Nat turned on her heel. "That's right, walk away." I grinned to myself. Needling her was so much fun.

Autumn sidled up to me, looking accusatory. "What did we just talk about, Jack?" Before I could respond, she chastised me. "I know you have your reasons, but grumpy being mean to sunshine is not a good look. You're coming off like an asshole in front of the campers. Be a professional."

My gaze immediately tracked for Nat, and I shook my head, angry that I did care about what she was doing, where she was, if I was pissing her off or not. But it was fun to piss her off. And the truth was, Nat was competitive, a worthy adversary. She was a lit fuse ready to blow if I said or did the wrong thing, which was infuriating and impossible to ignore.

"I can do that," I groused.

Autumn nodded at me and seemed appeased as she turned away.

When we finally started the game, I lost confidence that we'd have it in the bag. Nat's team was formidable. They stole flags left and right, had bursts of energy that led to scoring, and were all-around athletic. Our teams were evenly matched, which made it harder to get ahead on the scoreboard.

We each had more than five players on our team, so we'd cycle out for subs and cheer on our teammates remaining on the field.

I saw Nat sub out, and I followed her, tagging in one of my teammates who charged in with gusto.

She cupped her hands around her mouth and yelled to her camper. "You've got this. Go in for the kill. Destroy them!"

Hazel paused mid-run to warn her. "Violence."

"That's right, look for the opening," I directed, downright gleeful as we scored.

Nat regrouped and called out a play. "Time for the classic Flea Flicker."

Flea Flicker? Well, whatever that was, it was working because their team tossed the ball from player to player until everyone on their team had touched it before scoring. And just like that, we were tied yet again.

I took a page from her book and began using football terms on my team, much to their dismay. Annoyance? Yes, it was definitely annoyance.

"Go for the Hail Mary!" I shouted, letting my voice boom over her cheering. I didn't know what a Hail Mary was, but it didn't matter. I was annoying Nat, and that was more important. But I'd lost the plot apparently, because my shouting distracted my teammate, Ben, and one of Nat's players snatched one of his flags and scored.

Great.

Now their team was up.

Nat celebrated, obnoxiously dancing next to me in her red athletic shorts and dirty red tank top. I needed to look away from her diversionary tactics disguised as playful dance moves. I gave her an icy look as we retook the field.

"Careful, Jack. You keep making that face, it'll stay that way. People will ask about the stick up your ass."

I stepped closer, looking down into her unflinching eyes. "You've gotten so good at relying on me to fix things, but the one thing I can't fix for you is your game."

She didn't back down. "You're just jealous because your team does better when you're off the field."

"In order to be jealous, I'd have to care what you think," I shot back.

Nat gave me a look that burned into the side of my face, and I cheerfully jogged over to my team, proud of myself for getting under her skin.

I was more determined than ever to take her down. The whistle blew, and my team had possession, with me leading the charge. On the next play, we lined up, and I readied myself for the hike, already planning to target one of Nat's campers, when a blur of red in my periphery snagged my attention just before I was knocked off my feet.

Everything was in slow motion as Nat tackled me to the ground in an illegal quarterback blitz and sack.

"Oof." I fell hard on my back and heard people all clamoring around me. I took a moment to gather my senses and sat up, pissed. Nat brushed sand from her leg before reaching down to help me, but I ignored her offer and got up by myself.

Hazel interjected and blew her whistle loudly at a smug-looking Nat. "Fifteen-yard penalty." Nat had the nerve to hold up my flag as if she'd won it fair and square. "This isn't tackle football." Hazel made a wild *you're out of here* hand motion.

"Come on," Nat complained as if she had a leg to stand on.

Hazel pointed to the sidelines. She wasn't having any of it. "Take a two-minute penalty for unsportsmanlike behavior. And you can come back onto the field only if you pinky promise not to do it again."

"Eject her," I argued.

Hazel gave me a *my rules* look, settling the matter. "Not for a first offense."

"I'll show you unsportsmanlike behavior," Nat uttered under her breath as she exited the field. She immediately tried to justify her actions to a bemused Sawyer, who was shaking their head.

While Nat was out, I looked over at her and couldn't believe my eyes. She had her phone in her hand, and it pissed me off. She always had it on her. She couldn't even play a whole game without her precious hot-pink bejeweled phone, and unfortunately, I couldn't focus on anything else. She was insufferable. When she cheered and took photos of her teammates, she had the gall to look like the hottest villain I'd ever seen, and I hated it. I hated that she pulled my attention to her at every turn.

It was nearing the end of the second half. Nat's team scored another touchdown while she was in Hazel's imposed time-out. She ran back onto the sand while another teammate subbed out. Our team fought, and we managed to get back another point, but just as we were making our final drive to tie the game, the whistle blew. Time was up.

Nat celebrated with her team. They gathered around each

other, and she was hoisted up briefly, while they all clapped excitedly.

I had lost.

A few torturous minutes later, both teams lined up and high-fived each other, dispersing as they finished. Nat reached out to shake my hand, and I didn't do the same. She pulled away, a look of surprise on her face.

"This is ridiculous, and you know it. That wasn't fair play. That was an ambush."

"Come on, Jack. Take the loss and learn from it," she said smugly. We were just out of earshot of everyone, but I wished people could see her true colors.

"You just can't win the right way, now can you, Nat?"

"Are you implying that I'm a cheater?"

"I'm not *implying* anything." My voice caught in my throat, and I cleared it and looked away from her before spitting out, "But it's no surprise. You know all about cheating, don't you?"

Nat narrowed her eyes in confusion as I turned my back on her and left her alone on the field. I expected a retort, but the silence was deafening.

My harmful imagination latched on to a made-up image of Nat and my ex wrapped around each other. Thankfully, I'd only been told by Jamie about the cheating, not witnessed it firsthand, but the pang of hurt lashed through me all the same. She knew what she did back then. I'd had more than enough of Nat Breckenridge.

SEVEN
Nat

Justifiable homicide.

It was the defense I planned to use when I was tried for murdering Jack for making me snake drains.

And sure, he had to do this regularly, which sucked. And yeah, it was a fair bet. But still, I was pretty sure I had grounds for murder.

I had many facets. Girly girl, gets-dirt-under-her-nails girl, and hyperactive girl, but this girl I was not. And I couldn't believe this would be my life for the next six weeks.

The major takeaway from this unfortunate event was that, clearly, Jack was bad at his job.

I kicked the garbage can I'd been using back into its place like a petulant child and cleaned off the snake to the best of my ability. Snake. Even the cleaning tool was disgustingly named.

Staring at the surprisingly helpful object, I wondered if I could do something to get back at him for this. Because he would pay for what he'd done to me, fair or not. I'd make sure of it.

"I never would have thought to do that." Hazel watched me take a photo of sword ferns in the foreground, framing the blurred Camp Starlight sign in the background. It was obvious what we were advertising, but it was an artsier way of showing the Starlight entrance.

"You post a lot of photos with guests in them, and that definitely shows the heart of camp. But I'd take some more photos of Starlight itself. Build a story around the landmarks. I'd also do some profiles on our staff. Highlight their backgrounds and what attracted them to this place."

Hazel took the same shot and turned her head sideways as she viewed it. "You're really good at this."

I bobbed my shoulders self-deprecatingly. Just like Hazel, I was never good at taking compliments. "What about the camp's socials? There's a lot of good content on there."

"It's pretty easy to capture joy here. It translates really well for the most part. But man, am I getting tired."

The bags under her eyes were just as severe as when I'd seen her a couple of days ago. The lines on her forehead were more prominent than usual, and she wasn't making her usual jokes. Still, she was beautiful in a mysterious, haunting sort of way. She had sharp edges from the tender parts of her that had been put back together and often hid behind jokes, but she had the softest heart once she let you in. She was a head shorter than me but always felt so much bigger. Confident and strong, she was the coolest person I'd ever met.

For as long as I'd known her, Hazel had had high expectations for herself. And even though she had Leo and Autumn to help carry the load, I was sure she took on too much. I didn't want them to feel like they were lacking in any area, especially when I could help. They'd done well enough with their social profiles, but I could see glaring areas where they could be better curated.

So, I zeroed in on the crux of the issue. "Do you still not have a designated person in charge of social media?"

"It's still divided between me, Leo, and Autumn, depending on who's free at the time. We've been doing social media for both camps. They send us photos, and we take our own as well. Then we make a plan for the month, pulling from a folder on the... I know. We sound like hacks."

I chuckled. "No, you don't. Like I said, it doesn't reflect poorly on your accounts. You're doing a lot."

"It's what we've always done." It dawned on me how much of herself she gave to this place, as well as to Camp Sunlight. Between the three of them, there was still so much to do, and my friend looked like she could use a bit of a respite.

"Well, if you need some help, I'd be happy to do some posts for the Starlight account while I'm here."

Hazel lit up like that was the best thing she'd heard. "Really? We'd pay you."

"No need. I'll just throw a few things together and see if you like them. Your branding is on point. You probably just need a little more content so you have stories, right? A bit more of a consistent online presence?"

"That's exactly what we need. Man, Nat, you are a force to be reckoned with." She reached over my shoulder and swiped through several photos. "But we will pay you. That's not up for debate."

"Sure, sure."

Hazel rolled her eyes at my blowoff. I had a feeling this wasn't the end of it.

Once we were finished, I headed to the showers to wash off the day. Newly clean and ready for bed, I pulled on my pajamas and grabbed my skincare out of the mini fridge. It was the perfect size for all of my serums and lotions. Due to my travel, I usually lived spontaneously, which did not mean bringing appliances with me. But since my work at Camp Starlight was open-ended and I was actually standing still for a little bit, I'd bought the most self-indulgent skincare I could.

I got a call right as I sat down at my desk to apply everything.

My stepsister, Mandy, was seven years younger than me and lived on the East Coast near my mom and stepfather, Dean.

My world fell apart after we lost my dad to a brain aneurysm when I was ten years old. He wasn't perfect, but he loved me and always gave me affection. My mom remarried when I was twelve, and the best thing that came with Dean was Mandy, who I'd gotten to see grow up.

"Well, if it isn't my favorite genius." I'd been calling her that ever since she won a spelling bee in grade school. She excelled at everything she did, and I was so proud of her.

"And if it isn't the social media maven."

I laughed a little too hard at that. Things were always changing in my field, and sometimes I felt like I was flying by the seat of my pants. But maybe I wasn't giving myself enough credit.

"Last I checked, you're over a million followers, Natty." Her nickname for me stemmed from her inability to pronounce Natalie as a toddler, and it'd stuck. My mother hated it, which made me love it more.

"Yeah, well..." I shrugged, even though she couldn't see it. "How's Shoshanna?"

She'd been in a relationship with Sho for two years. If they didn't get married soon, I'd be surprised. My sister had it all figured out. The job at my mom's holding company, which set her up for big things, the girlfriend who doted on her, and more friends than I'd know what to do with.

"Don't think I didn't catch that deflection, but she's doing well. We just went to that cliffside resort you mentioned. It was amazing. They upgraded us just for mentioning you." It was a surprise that Mandy had gotten away from work, considering the hours she put in. I was glad I got to add to the experience. "You make friends everywhere you go, don't you?"

"It's not hard. There are a lot of interesting people out there." *Friends* was a loose term. The friends I'd had over the years usually didn't answer the phone much, let alone stick around. Most people I met weren't looking for lasting relationships with the woman who rolled in and out of their lives in the span of a few days, unfortunately.

But it was a hazard of the job. I met people, had amazing moments with them, and then moved on. I could reach out and see if they wanted to see me again, sure, but I was always off to the next place and didn't often revisit places.

That was why I loved my relationship with Hazel. We'd stayed friends after college. We may have drifted apart for a while, but we'd grown up a lot, and I knew we'd stick it out, no matter how far apart we were.

"Pretty sure that's a you thing. Even my friends wanted to be your bestie."

I chuckled. "That's because I was the cool high schooler when y'all were just tweens."

"No, Nat. It's definitely a you thing," my sister said firmly. She didn't usually get like this. It was jarring. "Take the compliment."

I twiddled with my eye repair serum. "Okay, I'm awesome, I guess."

"That's right. Now on to the reason I'm calling you."

"You aren't just calling to tell me how amazing I am?"

"No, I'm calling to ask you to visit us this summer. *All* of us."

Wow. She was really ripping the bandage off.

"I already have plans this summer." It sounded final, but maybe because it was. "Why don't you visit me in Oregon? I'm sure we can find a place nearby that isn't sold out."

"Nat, it's been years. You're going to have to see them eventually."

"Why don't you tell them that? Because I'm pretty sure I was the one who was cut out."

It had been four long years since I was unceremoniously kicked out of my family. Mandy was incredibly naïve when it came to our parents and what they were capable of. I'd tried to explain it before, but she'd shut down. Someday she'd learn how much the truth hurt.

"I'm so sick of being in the middle of this."

"I don't even bring them up with you, Mandy." I sighed. Damn, she was getting more and more persistent. She wasn't getting it. "I can only be in charge of my own feelings. I can't change theirs." Thousands of dollars in therapy had taught me that. "And I agreed to work at Camp Starlight."

"Okay," she acquiesced. "Maybe we'll be able to come by."

Something told me that wouldn't be happening, but I didn't say it. I may have been lonely, but there was no chance in hell I was going back to my supposed home. Not if I had to see them.

THE WARMTH FROM SUNLIGHT BLARING THROUGH MY window was my natural alarm clock. I listened as the breeze from the mountain trees carried songs of birds and rustling leaves through my window, and took a breath of fresh air.

Today was a great day to decimate my foe.

The entire camp met on the beach near the dock, prepared to swim in a relay race that was bound to be interesting. We divided into pod teams, intending to have five members in total. Fortunately, I had one pod member opting out, leaving a space on the team for me. Just like any of the competitions, there were always some people who wouldn't want to participate, and we weren't about to force anyone to do so. If we had too many people, a counselor would stand to the side and root for their team to pull out a win. If more competitors were needed, we'd just have someone go twice.

Jack and I stood on the edge of the dock, bumping elbows as we stared at the buoy, which was approximately sixty yards away.

He was probably thinking the same thing as me: one small push and he'd be in the water. The sadistic side of me imagined him floundering before disappearing beneath the surface, small bubbles rising to the top of the water. Was this my new happy place?

Man, he turned me into a monster.

"Two enter the ring," Emerson said beside us in a dramatic tone. "The grumpy handyman versus the sunshine social media queen. Only one will walk away with their dignity. The other will leave Camp Starlight in shame, never to return again."

Emerson must have been proud of herself because we both turned to find her smirking in her blue polka dot bikini.

"Hilarious," Jack deadpanned.

"You two look like you're trying to blast that buoy out of the water using just your eyes. You might be taking this too seriously," she went on, unfazed by our annoyance.

I wanted to say she'd be taking it seriously, too, if she were even on the scoreboard, but I didn't.

Jack spoke out of the corner of his mouth as Emerson retreated to her team. "I'd rather just blast you out of the water."

"You are *so* mature, Jack. Really. A genuine adult." I sounded like a seven-year-old.

He waved me off and headed down the dock. "Okay, team Corvus, huddle up."

Huddle up? What was he, a high school football coach? Was he compensating after his poor performance at flag football?

I couldn't hold back my grin. I loved this week's group of campers. I had a newly married couple from Rhode Island, Hannah and Amy, and a best friend duo named Jen and Lexa, both of whose abilities to spin pottery made me question my decision to teach the class myself. Then there was Emily, the Pilates instructor with an eight-pack. I only knew this because she was rightfully proud to show anyone who questioned it. And Jen kept questioning it.

I walked to my group and gave them a speech worth remembering. "Let me just start this off by saying, there are no winners or losers here."

Jen arched her brow. "For real? How seriously are we taking this?"

"Doesn't matter. What does matter is that we give this our all. We can and we will prove that we are competitors in this race. So let's focus up." Shit, was I going too far this time? I had to tone it down. "We jump off the dock at the whistle, then swim to the buoy and back. The second someone touches that dock, the next person needs to be in the water. Do we have anyone with respiratory issues? Delayed recognition of touch, if that's a thing? No one? Good, then we can go hard."

My teammates had mixed looks of excitement and confusion. It didn't exactly bode well.

"Who's going first?" Lexa asked, her excitement palpable.

"You can if you like. Then Jen, Emily, and Amy will go. And I'll end the relay. Hannah will be cheering us on from the sidelines."

"Go, sports." Hannah threw her arms in the air cheerleader-style, ending in jazz hands. It wasn't exactly sarcastic, but it wasn't not sarcastic either.

"Hell yes," Amy said.

Lexa tied her hair back and stood at the edge of the dock, waiting diligently for the whistle to blow.

"Okay, I know we're on the outskirts of this dock, so it might seem daunting to get to the buoy." We couldn't have gotten a center space. No, not like Jack. Mr. I'm Above Cheating.

"I'm not worried, Coach." She stretched her arms above her head.

I turned to find Jack glaring beside our group. "That's what I like to hear."

"Everybody ready?" Autumn shouted over the seven teams. A few *woos* sounded as people took their places. "On your mark, get set—"

She whistled, and seven people jumped into the water. Lexa took off like an Olympian and made it first to the marker, smacking it quickly before turning back around. She touched the dock, and Jen dove in after. This was feeling good. Maybe we had a shot at this.

Cheers resounded as each team swam their hearts out. Even Hannah was screaming. We were two lengths ahead of everyone, and I was practically giddy. Until I saw Jack whooping beside me, reminding me that this was going to be close.

I knew Emily had dived in due to the splash to the face I received. It was a helpful reminder to stop getting distracted. After all, I had just one more person ahead of me, and then I could take Jack down.

Ready for my chance, I bounced on my toes as my final teammate touched the buoy, moving to the edge of the dock. And when it came, I dove in and swam my heart out, not knowing how close behind Jack was. I couldn't worry about him right now. Instead, I focused on my stroke, the glide of the water over my fingers. Each breath fueled me. It was just me and the water. Soon to be me and the buoy. Then me and... Jack's hand? Because we touched the marker at the same time. We both looked at our hands for a millisecond before realizing what we were doing and separated as though we'd had an electric shock.

I rushed back to the dock, heart pounding as I swam the fastest I'd ever swum. And by the time I made it, my team was shouting affirmations at me, just as Jack's were. I wiped away the excess water from my brow, feeling the goose bumps prickling on my skin. I didn't know who had won, who'd been closer. But I was feeling good.

I swam to the ladder, right behind Jack, who kicked in the water extra hard before climbing the ladder, so that he splashed me in the face. I knew he'd done it on purpose. I cupped some water and splashed right back as I waited, but it just dripped down his muscled calves. It was mesmerizing. I wanted to see them up close.

Was I secretly a calf girl and didn't know it?

By the time I made it back to my excited team, I learned the devastating news. Not only had we gotten second place, but we'd tied. With Jack's team.

"You can't be sure," Jack whisper-argued with Autumn. "You're one person. How can you see two people touching the dock at the same time? Why didn't you have a second set of eyes? What kind of competition is this?"

Autumn tilted her head in exasperation. "It was very obvious, Jack. And if you're going to call into question the validity of this competition, I did have a second set of eyes. Azalea was watching, too. But if I had the option, I would have chosen Nat because of your bad attitude."

"Some best friend you are."

"Are you really arguing about getting second place right now? You get that you lost, right?"

Jack threw up his arms and turned on his heel. He looked like a four-year-old throwing a tantrum, but unfortunately, no one appeared to notice. Why was no one paying attention?

I learned later that Sawyer had been the winner. Not that it mattered. I was still tied with Jackass.

"This will not stand," Jack said from beside me. We were the only two people left on the dock. Everyone else was happily walking away, as if this were just a game. "Let's make one thing clear: I don't care who wins Camp Wars as long as I beat you."

If there were a living personification of a cartoon character turning bright red before blowing her top, I was that. The man infuriated me. He was so cocky. So combative. So... So...

"I need a tie with you like I need a snake in my sheets," I seethed.

"Then we fix this. Swim-off. Tonight. After campfire," he said through gritted teeth. "Don't be late."

I stepped toe to toe with him. "Oh, I know. The last thing I need is you calling it on a technicality."

Apparently, we were doing this. I didn't ask if this was a part of the main competition, but I was guessing it wasn't. Maybe it was just a side, side bet? But who was going to bring logic into this mess? One of us had to break the tie. That was all that mattered.

EIGHT

Jack

NAT AND I COULD AGREE ON ONE THING AT LEAST, AND that was there would be no ties between us. I watched as she walked away, wrapping a towel around her waist and wringing out her long braid. An unbidden image of said braid wrapping around my hand invaded my mind, and my horny brain fixated on it.

This, unfortunately, wasn't the first time Nat had destroyed my peace. Was it because she was such a challenge? Or was it that I liked her competitive spirit? Her persistence. The fact that she made me want to win that much more.

And then there was her laugh, which always grabbed my attention, no matter how far apart we were.

"We can agree, if I'd done this competition, I would've won, right?" Autumn's higher voice snapped me out of the ridiculous thoughts I shouldn't be having about my enemy. Her hands were firmly planted on her hips as she talked emphatically with Jamie. He must have just gotten off work since he was still in his suit and tie. He looked down at my best friend, grinning and shaking his head at her.

I walked off the dock and met them at the boathouse. "What's going on over here?"

Autumn's eyes snapped to mine. "Oh, nothing. Just talking about how I would have destroyed all of you at this relay if I'd been participating."

Jamie reached out and put his hands over hers as he tugged her closer to him. "I know, sunflower."

I cleared my throat, reminding the lovebirds I was still here. Autumn narrowed her eyes at me, and I regretted drawing her attention.

"Why were you giving me so much grief earlier? You were acting like a child." The disdain in her voice could be felt down to my toes.

I had hoped she would instantly get over my outburst, but of course, my behavior had caught up to me. I had to remember that not everyone appreciated arguing just for the sake of arguing, even though it felt natural when it came to Nat. I hated that she brought out my pettiness, my need to be right, and the little bit of a mean streak I had.

"You have to admit Nat's the worst," I tried, clinging to the fantastical idea that Autumn would take my side.

She tilted her head at me, clearly at her limit. "What happened to being a professional? You need to stop letting her get under your skin."

Jamie gave me a look as if to say he was sorry. He was the one who'd caught Gia and Nat making out last year. The one who told me about seeing the two of them kissing by his cabin. Who knew if Gia even would have divulged her betrayal. I knew Jamie was on my side, but I also knew that Autumn was right, even if I didn't want her to be.

"This will be the last time." I was probably lying, but it didn't matter. Whatever was between us was driving me mad, and I needed to squash it.

Autumn crossed her arms. "Will it now? And let me guess, you need a mediator to make sure you two don't squabble all night?"

The word mediator made me think of Nat and me sitting

together cross-legged as Autumn forced us to talk this out like adults. Yeah, no. "We need a ref, not a marriage counselor."

"That was an interesting jump." Her tone was full of judgment, which I didn't appreciate, but maybe I had it coming. "Fine, I'll do it, but I need something from you."

"You're going to extort your best friend in his time of need," I bellyached, and Autumn looked pleased with herself.

"I prefer the term negotiate," she corrected pointedly. "I'll help you with this, but it'll be the last time you bring me into something with Nat. And"—she lifted a finger as if to stop me from interjecting—"we need fifty tires for the obstacle race. Which means... you'll be liaising with the junkmaster."

The junkmaster in question was Herman Peters, the local curmudgeon and a constant pain in Wildwood's side. He had the best yard in Wildwood and had once won a feature in the *Wildwoodian*, the town's local newspaper. But his house and backyard were a mystery. If you were looking for an old boat without a motor or a Toyota Tercel bumper, he'd find it for you—for a price—usually in the form of your dignity. But the true price was interacting with him.

"If by *liaise*, you mean getting my head bitten off for talking to him about anything other than tennis or raccoons?" I said, but Autumn remained unshakable. I resorted to begging. "Please don't make me do this."

Autumn shook her head. "If it's not you, it'll be me, and that's not happening. The last time I needed something, he made me recite the town song, Jack. It's three minutes long."

"We have a town song?" Jamie jumped in, eager to learn more.

She nodded. "Each grade at Wildwood Elementary came up with a verse. It's set to Miley Cyrus's 'Party in the USA.' He had the lyrics printed out for me and everything."

I tried to imagine what horrendous thing he might do to me, but that could be anything. He enjoyed others' humiliation. "You think the man has fifty tires lying around somewhere?"

"Have you seen his backyard?"

"No. Have you?" The town curmudgeon was notoriously secretive, and I didn't have a spy kit.

Autumn shuddered. "It's rumored he has an entire pile of garden gnomes back there. Like, hundreds."

"So if I don't come back alive?" I raised my eyebrows expectantly.

"We'll be blaming the gnomes."

I'd bet she'd plan me a nice funeral. "This is going to suck."

"Well, if you go into it with that mindset..." She shrugged before she and Jamie walked off.

I changed back at my cabin and rushed my way through dinner, which was perfect because I was radioed to help a camper with an electronic lock that wasn't working. Then I took out some lingering frustration on unpacking a massive net for the upcoming obstacle race. This was turning out to be my least favorite competition. I'd better win.

By the time I made my way over to the campfire, the party was already in full swing. New lively faces sat on wooden bleachers, conversing with drinks in hand. I sat next to one of my pod members, Erin, as she told us her worst first date story while crocheting a sweater.

"So, he took me to a timeshare meeting just to get a free dinner. We were trapped for hours." She shook her head gravely as several campers gasped at the injustice. "It's okay, though, because he got sidled into a ski chalet, and I got out of there before they conned me into anything."

The conversation quickly evolved into bad first date stories, but all I could think about was how relationships always ended poorly for me. The cheating ex who had broken my heart in the most obliterating clichés of all time popped into my head. She'd left me for my former best friend. That one was probably the worst breakup, but it had prompted my move to California, which was how I'd met my actual best friend, Autumn.

The night should have been lovely, but of course, my gaze immediately found Nat. The fire backlit her, and the image showed all these endearing little flyaway hairs that only made her look more beautiful. She gestured as she told a story, enrapturing her audience.

Her gaze met mine for a moment, and the sounds around me vanished. I imagined her wrapped in a blanket under my arm, close enough that I could see the fire reflected in her eyes before she nuzzled into my neck.

What was wrong with me?

Our gazes remained fixed on each other until Chase came up and handed her a drink. I no longer felt her penetrating stare, and strangely, I wanted it back. I wanted to be the one she was too friendly with. I wanted to feel that point of contact where our arms brushed, where her breath danced along my skin.

I was beginning to think I had a problem on my hands.

Then, for no good reason, Chase gave her a lingering hug, and I nearly lost my head.

The crowd around the campfire dissipated as the fire burned lower, and I made my way toward the dock. Nat had left a couple of minutes before I did, and I didn't want to seem too eager. But when I got to the dock, it was empty. The moon lit the lake in a serene picture, but it didn't do anything to calm my nerves.

After about fifteen minutes, I started pacing. Campfire was definitely over, and Nat was late for our showdown.

Was she blowing me off? Just the thought of it infuriated me. I'd thought she wanted to see this tie ended as much as I did. It was irrational, I knew it was, but the more I thought of the possibilities, the more frustrated I got. Maybe she'd forgotten and was with Chase. She was prone to late-night make-outs, after all.

Then, as if summoned, she gracefully came toward me, disarming as she confidently walked down the dock.

"You're late." It was the only thing I could think of, even though it made me sound like an asshole.

She shrugged. "I was getting changed. *After campfire* is an arbitrary time, anyway."

"Sure you were." I reached behind my neck, pulled my shirt off, and wrapped it around my shoulders, wondering where Autumn was so we could get this over with.

"What's up your ass this time, Jack?" Her eyes went up and down my body, and I felt her gaze before she diverted her attention. If she was going to check me out, well, I'd give her something to drool over. I flexed my chest slightly.

"See something you like?" I smirked. This was good. She'd caught me staring at her more than a couple of times, so this leveled the playing field.

"You are so... so—" Her eyes flared as she tried to find words. She was strong-willed and challenging, to say the least. Full of a defiance I wanted to break. I hated that I was egged on by every word out of her pretty mouth. And I hated thinking it, but that was exactly what she was. Pretty. No, not pretty. Nat was the most gorgeous woman I'd ever laid eyes on.

She stepped closer to me and stared into my eyes. I wanted her to touch me. Anywhere. Just the idea of feeling her skin on mine covered me in goose bumps. I didn't need this. I didn't need to be jealous of golden boy Chase. And I didn't need to have feelings at all.

Wait, feelings? No. This was just an attraction, plain and simple.

I shook my head, trying not to look at her. Why was I so infatuated with her?

She continued, oblivious to the ridiculous realization plaguing me. "Look, I'm just trying to have a good time at camp. I'm not looking for a fight."

Not looking to fight? Of course, she'd want me to just forget what she'd done. "Well, you should have thought about that before—"

"Before what? Are you still hurt over being tackled? How tiny is your male ego?" she shot back, her voice going up an octave.

My heart pounded, ready to jump out of my chest. All my misplaced attraction turned to anger over something so trivial, but she brought it out in me. "You one hundred percent did not deserve to win at flag football."

"I was always going to win, Jack. Football is in my blood," she teased, but it only disgusted me. Everyone knew that the Breckenridges owned Baltimore's football team, among other things, and apparently, she was proud of it.

"Careful, Nat. Your spoiled rich girl is showing."

Her pupils dilated, exposing the tender spot, and I prepared to push on it like a bruise.

Nat gave me a look of pure contempt. "Stop talking."

"I didn't realize that's what got you off. Rubbing power and privilege in the faces of the common folk? Should I bow?"

"You don't know a thing about me," she seethed.

Maybe I should have listened, but I wasn't inclined to do what she wanted me to do, and if I were being honest, I liked getting under her skin. Just being around her brought out something in me that I wasn't proud of. "You're a Breckenridge through and through. With the integrity to match."

Her jaw looked like it was going to come unhinged as she gaped at me before narrowing her eyes. And just like when she'd tackled me on the field last week, I was caught off guard.

Nat shoved my shoulder hard, sending me off-balance, my arms flailing out wide to no avail. I toppled into the cold lake water with an awkward splash. I came up quickly and sputtered out water, wiping a hand down my face.

It took me a second to catch up to just what I'd done. "Nat. Wait—" I tried as I grabbed my floating T-shirt and swam to the ladder. I looked up to see her receding form, already halfway down the dock, muttering obscenities as she stormed away from me. Shit, she booked it fast.

I pulled myself up using the ladder. My T-shirt clung to my neck, like my bad choices. I wrung it out aggressively. I may have gone too far this time. The thought sat uneasily as guilt began to eat at me.

On top of me coming off like a jerk, there were professional ramifications to my behavior I hadn't fully considered yet. Like how stupid I was. Nat was close to Hazel, and if she told her what I did, how I was behaving, I could lose Starlight, the best thing that had ever happened to me. What would I do then? Go back to construction without whimsy? No, thank you. I needed to get my hotheaded nature under control before I completely lost sight of what was important.

My phone started ringing, interrupting my thoughts as I saw my brother's face appear. I bent down and grabbed it from on top of my towel, answering in my mostly normal, cheery voice. "Hey, what's going on?"

"Sorry, I know it's late, but I wanted to let you know that Jordy's been asking about you lately. He misses you."

I pictured my nephew, now ten and growing up fast. It was always fun to see him running around camp as a carefree little boy. I loved it when he visited. It gave me such pride that my nephew wanted to spend time with me, and it was a stark reminder that I needed to get my act together and set a good example for him. Possibly even get my head out of my ass when it came to this whole rivalry.

"I'm free Thursdays," I said, needing something positive to focus on. "He can come over and chastise me about my cabin being too messy."

"Can he chastise you about that on a Saturday? There's a winery in Emerald Falls I've been wanting to take Molly to. I know she's going to love it."

I chuckled. "Yeah, I can make that happen."

"Awesome." I could hear the joy in his voice at the prospect of surprising her. It was proof that Foster was a better husband than our dad was for our mom.

A sour feeling flopped in my stomach, and I wanted off the phone. My family would be so disappointed if they knew how I was behaving. Letting anger and negativity infect me and others around me.

I felt Autumn's presence behind me on the dock and turned to see her kind wave when she realized I was on the phone. "Listen, I gotta run. Autumn's here."

Autumn stopped walking and waited for me to finish the call.

My brother's cheery tone did nothing but dampen my mood. "Don't give Autumn too much trouble. See you next week." Little did he know, Autumn wasn't in my sights. Nat was.

"You're late," I muttered for the second time, annoyed but not with her.

"*After campfire* is an arbitrary time, Jack." Did she and Nat talk or something? "And I had to find calamine lotion for a camper with poison ivy. Where's Nat?" She looked around the dock as if she would just appear. Pop up out of the lake like a mermaid, all magical and shit.

My chest tightened as I pictured Nat storming off because of me. "She left."

"Well, you clearly took part in your epic showdown without me. So what happened?" She watched as I continued aggressively wringing out my T-shirt, squeezing every last droplet of water out of it as though it would rid me of my shame. "You're pouty. So I'm guessing Nat won?"

I looked back over the night water, seeing the buoy floating in the distance, and let out a long sigh. "I got what I deserved."

NINE
Nat

Shock wasn't a strong enough word for what I felt after what Jack had said last night. The man had no right to be so harsh. I'd wondered for a while what he had against me, but maybe my family was reason enough. Maybe it was valid.

My grandfather was politically divisive and frequently antagonistic to those who opposed his views. He'd been known for his smear campaigns back when he was attempting to win the presidency and hadn't been well-liked as a vice president.

As his granddaughter, I was a face of his *family first* campaign, and the vitriol toward my family and me was well-known. I'd only fallen away from the spotlight after my father's tragic passing. I still resented my parents for putting me in that position.

But that wasn't where the animosity toward my family ended. My mother was a billionaire who ran an empire that had its own host of problems, and I'd contributed to it by working for them. It was one of the reasons I'd left. I couldn't be proud of the company I worked for.

I'd hoped getting out of the public eye would have been enough for the country to forget about me, but obviously, Jack hadn't. Maybe he was in the same camp as the objectors and assumed I shared my family's values.

I swiped left and right on my lock screen over and over. And because I was a glutton for punishment, I made a choice.

Was today the best time to call my mom? Definitely not. But my sister's words had been ringing in my head, and I knew she was right. Someone needed to extend the olive branch, and if past experiences had taught me anything, it wasn't going to be them.

I quickly unlocked my phone, pulling up my contacts and hitting send on *Mom* before I could back out. God, what was I doing?

It rang.

And went to voicemail.

"You've reached the voicemail of Catherine Breckenridge..."

I pulled it away from my ear and stared. Had my mom just bitch-buttoned me? I hung up. What the fuck?

I called back, and it rang once before immediately going to voicemail again. Okay, definitely bitch-buttoning me.

My blood started to boil. Excuses piled up, and none of them were comforting. Maybe she was in a meeting. Maybe she was driving. Maybe she'd meant it when she'd told me I was no longer a part of the family. I thought about sending a text to my sister telling her I was right, but this was one thing I didn't want to be right about. There was no winning in this situation.

I wiped away the moisture collecting in the corner of my eye and put my phone down. Maybe it was time to throw on some hiking boots. The outdoors never did me dirty, though I was afraid of it being too quiet and allowing me too much time to think. Dammit, why were my cheeks wet?

Two knocks sounded. Then another. I opened my door and found Jack standing on my front porch, hand clenched in a fist to knock again.

So it was going to be one of *those* days.

"What do you want?" I sniffed. He probably thought it was something a stuck-up *Breckenridge* would do.

His throat constricted as he swallowed down his shittiness. Probably.

"I'm sorry to bother you," he spoke, softer than I'd ever heard him. This wasn't going how I thought it would. "I came to apologize."

Okay, really not going how I thought it would.

"Apologize?" It came out sounding more truculent than I'd meant.

"I was out of line last night. You were pushing me, and I..." He took a half-step back as I glared, hopefully searing a hole through his undersized heart. "No. I never should have said what I said."

I nodded, and he waited for a response, leaving dead air between us. Breaking the silence was a small mercy he didn't deserve, but I did it anyway. "You're right, you shouldn't have. I'm glad you recognize you did something wrong."

He gave me a small nod. An acceptance of his wrongness. It caught me off guard, but not enough for me to want this interaction to go any longer than it had to.

"Is that all?"

"Yeah, Nat. That's all."

"Cool." I shut the door in his face and walked to the bed again, already overthinking my interaction, as any anxiety-ridden person would do.

It may have been salty, a little impulsive, and maybe immature, but I wasn't ready to accept his apology. This was a major sore spot, and he didn't have a goddamn clue what he was talking about.

The urge to explain myself to him started to pick at me, but I fought it. I didn't need to reveal that I'd worked my ass off not to be like my family. That choosing myself for once meant losing my home. That made me feel like I was all alone.

I wanted to go see Hazel, but she'd notified me just hours ago that she and Leo were going back to California to deal with a problem at Camp Sunlight. She was vague about it, but if she had to leave the state, there must have been a major issue.

It wouldn't have mattered anyway. I'd been keeping the animosity between Jack and me under wraps with my friend, mostly because it felt tattletale-y to go to her. Maybe even petty. I didn't want our issues to reflect poorly on him, because I wasn't a monster. This had been his job for years. If I were pushed out for being unprofessional, at least I would still have my primary source of income.

But money was the only thing I had. And I would have traded all of it for one person to hug me right now.

It had been days, and everything he'd said that night on the dock still stung. I needed a distraction, which was perfect because today was our day off and we were about to take part in another competition: the bake-off. We'd moved it up to Thursday, after campers had left, with the express purpose of keeping them out of this contest. I couldn't say I wasn't nervous, because I barely cooked these days. I was too busy traveling, and when I did have a kitchen, I tried. But there was no baking, per se. I could read directions. That was all I'd need, right?

It took all of five minutes for me to be reminded that Jack Hawthorne was a douche. Especially since he made everyone like him, making me look vindictive for no reason.

Mouth gaping, I watched him goof off with Emerson. And Autumn. And Lamar. Even Kristy from Wildwood's bakery, the Cozy Crumb, had a rapport with him.

What the hell had I done to make him hate me so much?

I realized I was glaring at him as he told the stupid punchline to his stupid joke.

"So I said, 'Why do you have three flip-flops when I only have one?'"

Cue raucous applause. Cue my hackles rising.

If I kept responding like this, my shoulders were going to stay that way.

Everyone except for Mr. Hilarious dispersed and took their spots at their stations, leaving the space right next to me open.

For fuck's sake.

Jack stopped in his tracks when he realized what he was left with. He looked left, then right, probably calculating the level of effort it would take to have someone switch places with him. But everyone around us was engaged with their seatmates, completely unaware of the drama that had the capacity to unfold.

I, however, could feel the tension weighing me down like a five-hundred-pound boulder on my chest.

He made his way to his spot, sitting down in front of his convection toaster oven. We were seated in the mess hall at the long tables, in front of cooking stations set up for each counselor. Our supplies and ingredients were beside each other. That seemed like an oversight. Who knew what kind of sabotage could take place if your seatmate was a conniving jerk?

He tapped on the table, took a breath, and turned an inch toward me before looking back at his oven. Then he did it again. He was starting to earn the moniker of weirdo on top of asshole. "Natalie, I—"

"Jack attack, can you hand me that whisk right by you? I didn't get one." Sawyer pointed at his station.

Jack nodded and grabbed his second whisk, tossing it at Sawyer before stabbing his own whisk at them. Sawyer parried as though they were fencing. Jack then flipped his whisk between his fingers and placed it back on the table.

I mock coughed once Sawyer walked away. "Two-faced." I coughed again. Maturity was overrated when you were in your thirties.

"What'd you just say?"

"You may have everyone here convinced that you're some wonderful guy, but I know better."

"*Okay.*" Jack's voice dripped with condescension. I imagined him taking a long hike off a short cliff and smiled to myself, which garnered a confused expression from the man who haunted my dreams. And my reality.

"It's all right. You've already made your mind up about me. But I figured something out." I leaned in, making sure that no one else could hear me. "You're just the hater in the comments. And I deal with those on the daily, so..."

His jaw clenched. "I am not. And it's not like you're an innocent party here."

"Right. Go ahead and deflect. But you should ask yourself, if you're such a nice person, how can you justify your treatment of me?"

Then I saw it. A wince. Dipped eyebrows. A break in his resolve. "Princess." His fingers flexed, almost as if he wanted to reach out and touch me, but that made no sense. Right?

"Chop chop, now." Bobby broke through the noise and addressed the room.

I turned to face him, leaving Jack right where I wanted him: behind me and out of my line of sight.

"Hello, everyone, and welcome to the first-ever Starlight bake-off. For today's competition, we're making toaster oven cake." Bobby stood in front of two tables with gingham cloths spread over them and gestured grandly. "As you've noticed, each station has a recipe book and some basic baking supplies.

"In a moment, you'll randomly come up one at a time and choose a Wildwood wild ingredient from the first table here, then two ingredients that will complement it from the second table. Remember to use your wild ingredient to make the best cake we've ever tasted."

Azalea held up a fishbowl with papers inside it and made a

show of putting her hand in and spinning the papers around. She drew names, and Sawyer was drawn first. I tried to see what was on the wild table, but our view was obstructed, probably so we couldn't plan ahead. Sawyer brought back a bottle of Coca-Cola, along with a fancy chocolate bar and marshmallows. I had no idea what their plan was or if you could even bake with Coke, but my best guess was that I'd be stuck with something weird.

Felicia was up next, coming back with her arms filled with raisins, cream cheese, and... applesauce? Chase came back with matcha, cherries, and edible violet flowers. Then it was my turn.

I walked up to the table and cringed. The only remaining items were bacon, ginger, vodka, chili pepper, sage, and... mayonnaise. That seemed less controversial than bacon and ginger, and I had no idea what to do with the vodka. But mayo was made with eggs and oil, if I remembered correctly, so it had to bake well, right? I grabbed the jar and moved to the other table, lifting the gingham tablecloth, and grabbed raspberries and gelatin. I could make this work.

I smirked at Jack as I walked my goodies back to my station. Lamar was called, and he ended up with the ginger, then took his time selecting almond milk and lemon. Jack came back with the bacon, as well as maple syrup and espresso to go with it. And lastly was Emerson, who was gifted with the vodka. She also chose lavender and vanilla bean flavorings, which sounded yummy together.

Bobby gestured to Azalea, who took over. "Random ingredient cake baking is a camper favorite during cooking class. You may think that's beyond the scope of what these toaster ovens can achieve, but those little things can get up to four hundred and fifty degrees."

Bobby jumped in. "We'll be judging you on three criteria: taste, texture, and décor. Be sure to focus on all three areas. If you fail in one of these categories, that will be the yeast of your problems. Get it? Yeast?"

"It's always funnier when you have to explain the joke, Bobby," Azalea deadpanned.

Jack snorted, and I realized how close he was behind me. Was I actually able to feel his breath? The goose bumps breaking out over my skin were either caused by a figment of my imagination or he'd moved closer. And why did that excite me so much? It couldn't. Just because he was hot did not mean he turned me on. Personality mattered.

Did I even like his personality?

The man had many facets, especially when it came to everyone but me. As much as I didn't want to admit to my *awareness* of his interactions, it was glaringly obvious. His campers loved him, and he was playful and amiable with his friends, of whom he had many. I questioned why I'd even noticed this. This was starting to become a problem.

I reminded myself that I had a competition to win, and I was going to rub it in his face when I—

"For our panel of judges today, we have three Wildwood business owners. Felix, the owner of Beans and Beans. Our favorite Wildwood baker, Kristy. And Cherie, the owner of our antique and secondhand store, the Treasure Trove."

Everyone cheered, probably for points. Man, I needed to get this competitive streak under control. I was turning into an asshole, just like my nemesis. I had to be better than this. Better than him.

"All right, counselors, you know what to do. One, two, tree!"

Some light chuckling resounded at Bobby's flair, and I grabbed the recipe book from my station and started flipping through the pages. We didn't know what we'd be making ahead of time, so this was helpful. Baking was a science, so you needed to know the exact measurements to make sure the batter would turn into a cake, let alone one that tasted good. I scanned each of the pages and found what I hoped to be a crowd-pleaser: a raspberry layered cake. Of course, I'd call it something more Starlight-focused.

"Reminder to preheat your ovens," Azalea offered.

Bobby jumped on this. "Yeah, batter to be safe than sorry."

Jack watched me carefully measure my ingredients, and I wondered if he was going to mimic my every movement because he didn't know what he was doing or if it was for some nefarious purpose. It went without saying that I wouldn't sabotage anything, but I wasn't about to broach the "no cheating" discussion. And who knew if he was trying to get me back for wrongs he'd thought I'd committed. The man was ridiculous.

Azalea and Bobby had started their walk-throughs with all the contestants, and I doubled down on my focus. I mixed the batter until it was ready to pour. I bit my lip as I carefully did so, only to find Jack staring. I let go of my lip, and his gaze bounced up, as if he'd been caught. I could never guess what was going on in this man's brain.

"How are we doing over here?" Azalea asked.

"You can taste the tension," Bobby said in a voice that sounded like it belonged on a TV show. "I'll tell you what, Azalea, if their rivalry ruins good cake, it'll just *bake* my heart."

"Does he always use baking puns in your kitchen?" Jack asked Azalea.

She shrugged. "You get used to it."

"Aw, you know you're going to miss me." Bobby booped her on the nose, and Azalea batted his hand away before smiling lovingly at her friend.

"Always." She cleared her throat. "Now, what are you making here, Nat?"

"It's a classic raspberry cake with fruit filling and frosting. It'll have a Starlight touch, though, I promise."

Azalea waved her hand, as if wafting the smell toward her. "Can't wait to try it. Shayne actually picked out these recipes."

This year's cooking intern wasn't here today, but what twenty-two-year-old would be enthralled by this shit show when they could be doing... whatever twenty-two-year-olds did on their days off?

"And you, Jack?"

Charming as ever, Jack walked the judges through his bacon, coffee, and maple syrup concoction. He dropped some of his batter into his pan, but it was looking a little more... soupy than I expected. Maybe this would be his downfall.

"Did you remember to—" Bobby started before Azalea cut him off.

"No helping," she reminded him.

"Right." His right hand clenched, as if he were fighting the urge to be his sweet self and come to Jack's aid.

Jack tilted his head as he stared at the mixture, going back to his recipe and running his finger down the instructions with a puzzled look on his face. I fought back the urge to smile like the Cheshire Cat and turned back to my own batter. I'd added different colors of food coloring to three bowls to simulate different planets. All I had to do was use a rounded scoop to drop them in the plain batter, and I'd be good. But as I did the first one, it kind of... spread. Was this even going to work?

I glanced around at my competitors, who were already putting their pans in the oven. I was running behind. I plopped the other two planets and poured the remaining plain-colored batter over them before placing them in the oven a little too roughly. I winced. Jack was already standing with his arms crossed. He wasn't gloating, but I couldn't quite get a read on him. His furrowed brow did look more pensive than frustrated with me, which was an upgrade.

"Psst," Emerson whispered.

I subtly glanced at her beside me.

Unwrapping her butter, she spoke out of the corner of her mouth. "What say you to an alliance?"

An alliance? "And how would that work?"

"I don't know. You put your cake on top of mine or vice versa. The end result: *super cake.* We'd have this competition in the bag."

I burst into laughter, and she dramatically shushed me. "And who gets the point for winning?" I whispered back.

"Well, obviously that would be me. You already have a point for stomping on Jack at flag football. Great job, by the way." She raised and lowered her eyebrows several times, I assumed as a way to show she was impressed. What it ended up looking like was a woman trying to regain the feeling in her face.

"Don't think complimenting me will be enough for me to forget that you're the only one coming out on top in this scenario."

Emerson waved me off. "That's not what matters. What matters is that we're a team. And teamwork makes the dreamwork."

"You're ridiculous."

"You love me," she said with a smile that made her mischievous dimple I'd never noticed before pop adorably. These people were such weirdos.

I turned to find Jack shaking his head with a smile at Emerson's antics. At least he wasn't jumping down my throat over this fake alliance offering.

He looked so good when he smiled. But I ignored the warmth in my cheeks as I thought of him and got back to work, measuring powdered sugar for my frosting.

Time was called just as I pulled my cake from the oven, and I wasn't surprised to see that most people were at a similar place. I was surprised that Jack's cake looked perfectly cooked. But that didn't mean it tasted good.

I turned away from Bobby and bumped right into Jack. He let out an *umph* before dusting himself off. Even stunned Jack was hot.

"You've got something right there." I pointed at his cheekbone, which had a bit of batter on it. He wiped flour off his hands onto the same spot, almost purposely, which made me smile. Not because it was cute. Definitely not that. He then proceeded to brush it into a dangling lock of hair, which had me laughing. Was this the feeling people got when he was being playful with them? I wanted to eat it up with a spoon.

"To allow time for our cakes to cool, we're going to break for lunch." Bobby's interruption was both welcome and unappreciated, because I wanted this moment to go on, even if I shouldn't.

I cleaned my area up before going to the other side of the mess hall to a sandwich-making station. The staff didn't cook for us on our days off, but they were nice enough to do this for us today, which was much appreciated. I was starving.

I made my way to the table everyone was sharing and found my spot between Autumn and Jack. Really, universe? Jack was kind enough to scoot over for me to sit down, an uncharacteristic move, but maybe he was just trying to keep space between us.

The whole group was ravenous.

Felicia broke the silence. "Where are Hazel and Leo?"

Eyes met as we questioned the same thing. Leo would be excited about eating whatever we ended up making, but he was a garbage disposal. Last year, he told me he was a judge for the town's tuna melt competition, which sounded disgusting.

Autumn gave a long sigh. "The director for Sunlight was fired."

Murmurs came from the group. Hazel hadn't been specific as to why she bailed in our text message, but obviously, it was a big deal.

"They looked for that person for months," a resigned Jack said. "What the hell happened?"

"Apparently, they were arrested for embezzling money from their child's PTA. Luckily, they weren't in charge of the finances for Sunlight yet."

"You've got to be kidding me." Lamar's shocked expression matched everyone else's. "Who steals money from kids?"

There were murmurs of agreement and outrage.

"So what are they going to do?" I asked. Autumn was always in the know, but this new development likely had no solution yet.

"They don't know. Leo mentioned that the assistant director was incredibly qualified for their position, so it's possible they'll move them up and then look for their replacement. Until then, it looks like it'll be just me running things here."

"I can help with whatever you need," I offered. "Especially when it comes to communications." It didn't go without my noticing that Jack's gaze was on me. I turned, prepared to defend myself from I didn't know what, but his stare was something more like awe. There was no way. I could only do wrong in his eyes.

Felicia offered to separate and distribute the mail to campers, and Lamar said he would coordinate with the cleaning crew on his day off. Sawyer, Emerson, and Azalea offered up similar projects they could help out on.

"You're not doing this alone," Jack said seriously.

Autumn teared up at the support from her friends. "I'll be sure to ask for help this time around," she promised. "This is a well-oiled machine, and we had a system set up for when they were gone the first time, but this time..."

I'd planned on calling Hazel after this competition because of how down I felt this morning, but I decided to put my feelings on the back burner. She had enough on her plate already.

We returned to our places and found our cakes had cooled. I jumped back into action, prepared to decorate better than I'd ever decorated before. Though that experience was very limited. One year, for a friend's birthday, I made a mirror glaze that went over some buttercream icing. Complete with my edible glitter, the idea formed itself. Galaxy glaze. I tried not to bolster my ego too much, but the words *genius* and *brilliant* both came to mind.

Then I noticed that my cake had cracked a little. Had I baked it for too long? I touched the worst side, and a piece fell. Dammit. I grabbed some buttercream and added it before placing it back together. It would be fine. What I needed to worry about was my glaze. Despite my careful reading of the recipe, the consistency wasn't quite right.

I glanced at my competition and found mixed reactions to everyone's creations, but the confident, smiling faces concerned me the most. I should have been happy for them, but I found myself more jealous than anything. My ambition was starting to get the best of me. I took a breath and told myself to take it down a notch.

It was out of my control. I could lose this one, but as long as Jack didn't win, I'd be okay with the result.

It was now or never. I poured the glaze over the frosted cake, but it spread too quickly and almost melted the frosting below. Oh god, I must have put it on when it was too hot. I tried scooping it off the wax paper so I could respread, but the entire thing was dripping, and it was too thin to pick up.

I looked at the clock. I had fewer than ten minutes to make this into a masterpiece. I took a breath and assessed. So the glaze didn't work. That was okay. But it had melted the frosting below, and that was also sliding off the cake. I took a spreading knife to try to blend it, but the gelatin mixture plus the frosting was turning into this chunky monstrosity.

We had less than a minute to go. I continued to fix the frosting, which was still melting off. Then, with ten seconds left, I threw some glitter onto the thing, and voilà.

It looked horrendous.

I didn't want to present to the judges. Maybe I could just throw the cake at Jack and run out of the mess hall. Could there really be consequences for that? People would probably get a kick out of it. I would.

A pathetic whimper came from behind me, and I did a one-eighty. Jack's cake was looking sad and kind of collapsing on itself.

"I don't want to hear it," he warned the second he saw my face. I was trying to hold back from laughing and the tears caused by the full-body shaking I was doing.

"Is yours supposed to look like a collapsing soufflé?" I barely got it out. And despite trying my very best, I burst into laughter.

He did not look pleased.

Then he leaned around me to see my creation, which was looking more and more like the Frankenstein of cakes, now that the broken piece was separating from the mainland.

"It's a galaxy cake," I tried.

"Galaxy? That thing needs to be taken out by a meteor."

"Hey!"

We were gaining the attention of other counselors, some of whom had placating faces, while the rest were chuckling.

"Ooh, Nat, are you gonna put that on your socials?" my ex-friend Sawyer snarked.

"No, don't do it," Emerson said seriously. "That will lose you followers."

Jack cackled.

Bobby clapped. "Okay, everyone, please leave your creations on your workstations and stand in a line. We'll call each of you up. Starting with Sawyer."

Sawyer's Coke cake was lauded because of their decorative ingenuity. They'd made a swirly design with the marshmallows and even made little chocolate trees that wrapped around the side. How had they found the time for that? The judges loved Lamar's cake for its layered lemon design placed over his drizzled almond icing.

Chase's matcha cherry cake was the perfect bright green and had edible violets on top that made it look like a garden.

By the time it was Emerson's turn, I wondered what my train-wreck of a cake looked like.

"Tell us about your cake, Emerson." Bobby's eyes lit up even though Emerson's cake looked a little wonkier than the others.

"It's a lavender, vanilla bean, vodka cake."

"And how do you think you did?"

"It certainly smelled good. But the thing that's going to give me an edge is that it was baked with love."

I turned my head to find Jack rolling his eyes. I pressed my lips together, trying not to scoff. He shook his head and tilted it toward the judges, so I returned my attention to them.

"Thank you, Emerson. Up next is Jack."

Jack went to our table and visibly exhaled. "Do I have to?"

"What was that?" Azalea shouted from her spot.

I was beginning to think my sides were going to collapse just like his cake from held-back laughter.

"Nothing." He brought his *cake* to the front and placed it before the judges.

Felix's eyebrows shot off his forehead. Cherie looked like she was chewing on the inside of her cheeks. And Kristy, well, she was touching her fingers to her temples as if she were doing complex math.

"This is my coffee and maple bacon lover's dream. It's my attempt at a soufflé," he lied.

"Soufflés were not in the book. Did you do this by memory?"

"Yes." Another lie.

Cherie chewed slowly before swallowing. "Well, Jack, I appreciate your effort." Oh, this was going to be good. "But despite its collapse, this is still not a soufflé. Also, traditional soufflés don't have frosting."

I should remove myself from this room because I was going to lose it.

"Fair enough." Jack rejoined us, looking a little disheveled.

Then my name was called. His was so bad, I'd forgotten mine was about to be a trainwreck.

"This is called Stargazer's Delight. It's a raspberry sponge cake with planets on the inside." Maybe I shouldn't have mentioned that part. "It has a planetary glaze, which I made with gelatin."

"And your mystery ingredient?" Kristy asked.

"It was mayonnaise."

Two of the judges cringed at hearing my mystery ingredient, which didn't bode well. But I heard several hums, so I knew the flavor was on point. But were they bypassing the frosting?

"Is the cake supposed to, um, ooze?" Felix asked as sweetly as he could.

I knew exactly who the snort behind me came from.

"Not really." Might as well be honest.

Kristy pushed a piece around her plate. "The gelatin is probably the reason it's congealing."

Ew. What a word.

"Thank you, Nat," Bobby said.

Dismissed. Thank god. I went back to stand in line with my fellow counselors, all of whom had shit-eating grins.

The judges deliberated, and after an ungodly amount of time, they came back with a winner: Chase. Thankfully, they didn't have a loser category, because I was pretty sure I'd be in it alongside Jack.

"Thank you so much, bakers. You did a wonderful job." Bobby congratulated us on the hard work we'd put in, and everyone went back to their stations to clean.

Jack pointed at my cake. "You know, if it'd be helpful, I can get a shovel and dig you a crater out back so you can bury that thing."

"Yours was shit, too, Hawthorne."

"What did they call it again? Oozy? You should let me try it."

I batted his greedy hands away. "Not a chance in hell."

Jack burst into laughter, and that was the moment I decided once and for all.

It was on.

TEN

Jack

MATING SEASON WAS FINALLY HERE. SO I WAS UP AND dressed at the crack of dawn, which meant a crisp four thirty. That might scare some people off, but I only slept a few hours a night anyway, and bird-watching was one of my favorite hobbies. Fellow birders always looked forward to reporting the birds throughout all of the Mount Hood National Forest region, and Camp Starlight's acreage had some of the best viewing spots to catch some rare little songbirds.

I'd be taking a small group of campers out here later this week as well, and maybe they'd see the same rare birds I hoped to catch in action today. I planned to share my findings from this week with the Bird Alliance of Oregon. I had some friends in the coalition, and we were always excited to hear what each other had spotted.

I filled my thermos with my favorite Beans and Beans whole bean blend that I'd ground at home before brewing into the steaming, rich, bold perfection that it was now. This coffee, paired with my favorite bird-watching shirt, always put me in a good mood. The shirt was faded, the cotton loose and well-worn, with *Hawksome* written in bold lettering above a picture of a hawk. My nephew surprised me with a bird-themed T-shirt every birthday, and I loved all of them, but this one was my favorite.

I walked quietly and found my perch, slowing my breathing as I lifted my binoculars to scan the area. A few long moments of tranquility and peace surrounded me.

There.

I focused my gaze on a small bird, a yellow-rumped warbler, and minutes later spotted a hermit warbler deep in the conifers. I documented their locations, and even though these weren't rare per se, it was fun to keep track of their behaviors and patterns.

I moved locations, walking deeper into the forest to see what else I could find.

There, in all its glory, was a northern goshawk in hunting formation. I imagined there was a nest nearby that the hawk was looking to provide food for in an undisturbed part of the forest. I crept and waited in the nooks and crannies of the forest, careful not to spook or frighten it as I lifted my binoculars and focused in on the dive movement of the majestic creature. Something in me settled.

I enjoyed the moment with my coffee and snapped an amateur series of photos on my phone. Not even a certain brunette could ruin this.

☆☆☆

I HURRIED TOWARD THE BOATHOUSE. USUALLY, I'D HEAD back to my cabin to change, but I'd foregone those moments to stay longer in the forest, and I had spare Crocs there.

Camp was bustling as I made my way through its winding paths. Laughter greeted me as I passed each pod. That wasn't too concerning, because most people laughed while at camp, but the stares were... new.

I kept moving in a hurry to the lake. Were those more stares?

Another camper, someone from Sawyer's pod, seemed to do a double take when our paths crossed. She giggled. "Whoa."

I turned my head, wondering what that was all about, when another group of campers broke into laughter. But they upped the ante by pointing directly at me. Did I have something on my shirt? I looked down at myself, and my shirt looked amazing as usual. Maybe they just loved puns? No. No one liked puns that much.

I shook off that strange interaction and redirected my thoughts to getting the boat ready for the campers who were already showing up. They had their towels slung over their shoulders, big sunglasses, and a few beers in hand. I grinned at them.

But my grin quickly fell. Even they laughed when they saw me.

They climbed into the boat, and I started it up after my safety check, feeling self-conscious. I tried to push the feeling aside, assuming it would go once we got out on the water and I made the introductions. Unfortunately, the snickers continued, much to my chagrin.

"What is it?" I finally asked, exasperation in my tone.

Best friends Liza and Celeste were librarians in my pod this week. They both mimed a large ring around my eye area.

"You just have a little something here," Liza clarified.

"What do you mean, *something*?"

"It's like black makeup in a heavy ring. Did you lose a bet?" Celeste asked.

"Or take a dare?" Liza added with a wince.

Oh. No.

I pictured my binoculars sitting peacefully with my thermos at the boathouse before I procured them yesterday.

I rubbed at the marks and looked at my fingers, seeing the residue spread all over them. Apparently, that had only made it worse. I went to use my T-shirt to wipe when Liza stopped me.

"That'll probably stain," she warned with a pitying look. "You'll need makeup remover or probably an oil to take it off. I have some back in my cabin."

Celeste pulled out her phone camera to show me the damage that had been done. Yep, I'd walked around camp with literal black circles rimming my eyes, transforming me into a raccoon that watched birds. And I instantly knew who the culprit was.

I put my sunglasses on and hoped that time wouldn't make things worse. Luckily, I had this boat trip around the lake to plot my revenge.

"We could put their staplers in Jell-O?" Celeste suggested.

Camille gently shut that down. "Nat doesn't seem like she has a pressing need for a stapler. And I don't think campers bring staplers to camp."

Darek looked pensive. "We don't want to go after one person. We have to take out all of Andromeda." The fervent way he said this made me realize that maybe I wasn't the only one with a camp vendetta. Maybe this went beyond pod loyalty.

"Okay, how about we cover their picnic table in sticky notes?" Liza mused. "I did it at work to a colleague once."

"Oh my gosh. That was you?" Celeste looked betrayed and then burst into a loud belly laugh. We all joined in as we drifted along the lake.

Autumn would have a conniption if I stole her sticky notes to prank Nat back.

"How about something that's not as stationary-focused?" I suggested.

Darek scratched his beard. "Well, if not office supplies, how about food?"

Turned out, there were a lot of different food-related pranks we could choose from. As a group, we considered and debated the best options. We settled on an easy one that we could pull off flawlessly, each with our own parts to play.

The following morning, I stood in front of a beautifully decorated wicker basket of revenge eclairs. Delicious looking, perfect ovals of light pastry, iced with chocolate. If they expected them to be filled with Boston cream, they were in for a surprise.

Instead, they were getting what they deserved… Well, what Nat deserved.

Did I feel bad for Nat's other campers caught in the crosshairs? No. Being at camp sometimes meant you got pranked, and that was that. They were unlucky enough to be in a venomous snake's pod.

It hadn't taken long for the five of us to plot our revenge mission. Darek found a random basket in the craft room. Camille snagged the relish and filled the eclair shells, courtesy of Azalea, with Celeste and Liza. When it was all together, I put the final touch on a perfect ganache topping, after taking my critiques from the bake-off to heart.

I was so proud of us. They were diabolical.

I carried the Trojan Horse over in the early hours of the next morning with utter delight and placed them on Nat's pod's picnic table. The basket looked innocent and welcoming, with a note that said,

Happy eating!

Love, Azalea.

She'd forgive me for that later.

My boat conspirators all tucked behind trees in the forest, far from the view of Nat's pod, with clean binoculars at the ready.

Nat started every morning with a cheery greeting, checking in to see how people in Andromeda slept. I knew this because I'd witnessed her playing music from her speaker, not so loud it'd wake the couple that might sleep in but loud enough to energize the newly woken campers. She played the randomest songs, from Hamilton to Huntrix to some indie music I'd never heard of before, and her campers seemed to love it.

From our position in the trees, I saw three of Nat's newest batch of campers, Russell, Curtis, and Drew, sluggishly emerge from their cabins. It took a minute for the tired-looking campers to see the trick eclairs, perking up as they each reached for one.

They took their bites in tandem until the moment things went awry.

Russell was the most boisterous in his vehemence, upset after a significant bite. He spat it out and kept spitting while a couple of my podmates snickered at his reaction.

Did I feel a little bad? Yes. Did it make it that much funnier when he started using his fingers to wipe the relish flavor from his tongue? Absolutely.

Curtis spat his out with little flair and mouthed, "What the hell?"

Drew threw his donut on the ground and stomped on it like it might jump back up without some interference.

As if they were of one mind, Curtis and Russell looked at each other and played right into our hands, going for the cooler at the side of the table. The cooler, which we refilled daily, usually had a variety of beverages, but they'd only find tampered-with Gatorades inside.

Nat was right there in the thick of it with her pod. She was clearly not expecting the relish either, and her face scrunched up adorably upon first taste. Only, she didn't spit it out or complain. The chaos continued around her, but she didn't pay attention. Instead, the feisty counselor lifted her head and looked into the trees, chewing slowly, her eyes narrowed, as if she were searching for us. She knew we were out here, and she stood her ground. I nearly revealed myself, just to show I wasn't backing down either.

Nat broke her stare as Russell turned to her in disbelief. "Why would someone do this?"

She gave him a double take, then looked at Curtis, who was also chugging a sports drink. Curtis saw Russell, then looked to his tampered Gatorade. Drew started laughing at how Curtis's lips were a bright blue thanks to the food coloring we'd added.

We ducked behind our trees. My campers' laughs could no longer be contained. Celeste had dropped her binoculars around her neck, instead clutching her side. Camille wiped away tears.

From an outsider's view, it would appear that we had lost our minds, unable to take our eyes off the show before us.

I kept an eye on Nat from my hiding spot. She scanned her surroundings, locking onto our area with a look that said *this means war.*

Soon, the mayhem died down, with Nat's pod members regaining their composure and leaving, presumably to clean their mouths out. Nat remained fixed in her position, pouring out the tainted Gatorade and throwing the bottles back into the cooler. My campers had left, bored once the activity died down, but I couldn't look away.

She lifted her head in my direction, mouthing, "Game on, Hawthorne," a promise that I'd regret my actions. Maybe I would eventually, but right now, it was worth it to see that sinister smile on Nat's face.

Bring it on, princess.

☆ ☆ ☆

IT DIDN'T TAKE LONG FOR NEWS OF OUR EXPLOITS TO spread throughout camp, but I couldn't have predicted what it would unleash. Apparently, others wanted in on the fun. I'd heard reports of hot sauce being added to the maraschino cherries, Felicia's pod adding vinegar to water bottles. That didn't surprise me. Food was the easiest go-to prank. No one had done that to me, thankfully. That would have been gross.

When Autumn cornered me later to ask if I knew how this started, I went with the tried-and-true method of lying through my teeth. Come to find out, Nat must have lied, too. By the end of the second day, Autumn still didn't have her culprit, and the pranks were still going on.

On the second day, I woke up feeling groggy as ever, but with a new motivation as I recalled the look on Nat's face yesterday. I opened my bedroom door, planning to make coffee, but as I stepped into the hallway, a loud burst and a pop startled me. I jumped back at the noise, only to jerk at another pop.

My heart raced before my sleep-deprived mind realized what it was. Slowly, my eyes adjusted to the light, and I found the entire floor of my cabin was covered in colorful balloons. This must have taken them forever. I stumbled out of the rainbow mess with a huge smile on my face. I kinda loved these pranks. What was wrong with me?

I got ready, dragging my feet along the floor, careful not to pop any other balloons, and tried my best not to allow them to leave my cabin. I stopped by to see if any of my campers had something similar done to them, but they were gathered around the table, oblivious.

When I made my way to the office, I sighed. Our Camp Starlight flag had been replaced with none other than my Hawk-some T-shirt. Rude. Because of its age and status as my most beloved T-shirt, I often air-dried it and spread it out on my porch banister in the sun. I must have forgotten to bring it back inside. Even when it was clean, my pit stains were showing. Ugh, gross. Nat was playing with fire, and it looked like camp prank wars were officially on.

As I vegged on the couch that night, three stomps sounded on the steps of my front porch, and I knew exactly who was about to grace me with her presence. It gave me the high I was hoping for. The one you experience after getting revenge.

If I'd have known she was going to come by so soon, I would have at least worn a shirt.

A burst of knocks ricocheted off the wood, loud enough

that her knuckles were probably hurting. Oh, the sweet sounds of my upset nemesis. I grinned and opened the door, right as she leaned in to pound again, catching her in my arms as she fell forward.

In a moment suspended in time, I held her and couldn't help but notice how perfectly we fit together.

Something about her made me notice things about myself I usually paid no attention to. The tautness of my skin. The rise and fall of my chest. The way her hot breath against my throat caused goose bumps to climb up my neck.

I twitched at the feeling, which apparently reminded her that she was here on a mission, and cuddling with me was not it.

She pulled away quickly, and her sightline glazed a path from my abs to my eyes.

"What's up?"

"How about you put a shirt on for this conversation?" If I wasn't mistaken, her words were part hostile and part... aroused?

I casually leaned against the doorframe. "If I'd known you were going to come by, princess, I would have dressed up."

The stormy clouds overhead matched her mood as she leveled me with a glare that told me she was not backing down. But I wasn't either, and leaving her to follow me inside wasn't on the agenda. So I opted out of putting on a shirt and waited for the barrage of frustration to spill from her pretty mouth.

"Where is it, Jack?" she practically growled at me, and her intensity was intoxicating. She peered around my body, but I filled out the frame, blocking her vision.

I feigned innocence. "Where's what?"

"Don't give me that bullshit. I want my mini fridge back. It's important—" A gasp left her as she spotted what I'd purposely displayed on the counter behind me.

My smile curled up as she pushed me to the side so she could get a better view. I straightened my arm so she couldn't bypass me and grab the Barbie-pink mini fridge.

"That doesn't belong to you." She clenched her jaw and gave me exactly what I wanted.

There was something so satisfying about getting a rise out of her. The way she looked at me when she was pissed off made me feel electric. I was becoming addicted to the feelings she evoked in me.

"Oh, that? That's my new beer fridge. What do you think?" I lied, loving how her face went from disbelief to panic to rage. Her hands fisted as she prepared to rip me a new one. Of course, I hadn't actually touched her stuff. The little fridge was organized within an inch of its life with different lotions and shit, and I didn't want to touch anything and have to puzzle it back together.

"If you took out my products, so help me, I'll—"

I egged her on, aware I was walking a fine line. "Take something else of mine? That's a pity, because it makes a perfect beer fridge."

She held her ground, something else I was becoming more and more responsive to. "You'd better be joking. That's my skin care routine. Those antioxidant face masks are temperature dependent."

"Joking? Like how you filled my cabin with balloons?"

She doubled down, feigning innocence. "What makes you think I had anything to do with that little prank anyway?"

"Because it has you written all over it. So answer me this, Nat: did you or did you not take my favorite T-shirt and hang it on our flagpole today?" That shirt and I had been through some things. "I got it down earlier, but I demand recompense. For my pain and suffering."

She scoffed and went up on her tiptoes to look me in my eyes. I leaned down. Fuck, she was cute.

"The only thing you're getting is a swift kick in the—"

"Oh, now we're negotiating?"

This was going better than I could have imagined. She squared up to me. She was direct and unapologetic as she stared me down, just like she'd done in the craft cabin when she'd requested a new AC unit. My blood felt ready to boil, but not from anger.

Surprisingly, I couldn't fight the grin on my face as I glanced down at her pursed lips. They were pretty lips. Pretty lips that her tongue just swiped across. And was she biting her bottom one? My brain went offline as I pushed a lock of hair behind her ear, my fingers remaining on the curve of her jaw as her eyes fluttered closed.

"What are you doing?" There was something like curiosity in her breathy tone. Not hatred, not reprehension, but maybe interest.

The images that flooded me took hold and wouldn't let me breathe. Her hands around my neck, my lips on that sweet skin, my tongue licking her lower lip, asking for entry. All of it was a rapid-fire bombardment I didn't need.

Nat's cheeks were pink. Was she thinking what I was thinking, too? I dropped my hand and rushed inside. The need to put some distance between us, and quickly, was staggering. I unplugged her little fridge and brought it outside, placing it in her outstretched hands, careful not to touch her this time. If I touched her, I'd want to keep touching her, and that was beginning to be a problem.

I met her eyes, not sure what I wanted, not sure what I needed. "Here. It's exactly as you left it."

She held the pink fridge close to her chest like a shield. "We'll see about that."

Then she turned and set it down on the banister to look inside. Relief flooded her face as her shoulders went down, and she let out a soft sigh when she faced me. Her venom was diluted as she noticed her lotions and serums, or whatever, were all perfectly intact.

She huffed, looking at me as if she were going to lay into me again. Only she didn't. She stood there, eyes boring into mine. Why was she still here? What was she waiting for?

I let the silence between us hang a moment before I opened my door wider. It looked like an invitation. Now that would be stupid. I grabbed the doorknob and hastily pulled it closed, opting to step out onto my porch instead.

Nat didn't give me room to step out. Instead, she stayed put and made me close the distance. She ran her manicured nails through her hair, and the pink sparkles showed through her loose brown strands as she moved them off one shoulder, revealing the expanse of her sun-kissed neck. I could almost feel her warmth under my lips as I imagined playfully nipping and sucking on her neck. Running my hands through all her beautiful hair as I teased and kissed her. Shit. She was becoming an addiction.

"What are you staring at, Jack?"

"Nothing good," I admitted. But like her, I didn't move away. I liked that she was within arm's reach. I liked seeing her faint freckles this close and the distinct striations in her warm brown eyes.

Again, I debated leaning forward, letting her sweet honeysuckle scent entrance me, wondering what it would be like to press my lips to hers. But I knew better.

We didn't say anything for a long moment. Or maybe it just felt long. She shook her head and finally took a step back, turning to leave. Then she froze and turned back around.

My heart galloped. I was in trouble. Real trouble. "What are you doing?"

I swallowed hard and reached for the doorknob behind me, prepared to let her in. Her eyes softened. Her whole demeanor changed. But instead of closing the distance between us, she scooped up the cute little fridge off my banister. I'd completely forgotten about it. But once it was in her arms, she turned and left without another word.

ELEVEN
Jack

I'd like to say I woke to the thunder and rain pelting my cabin window at two thirty this morning, but unfortunately, that was not the case.

No, I was too busy lying awake thinking about her, feeling frustrated and annoyed.

I hated that this seemed like my new normal, but even before she showed up demanding her property back, I hadn't been able to get her out of my head.

I opened my ears to the sounds around me, hoping for a distraction. I usually liked the sounds of a storm. It was beautiful, the way the sky opened up and unleashed the smell of petrichor and damp trees. I lived in the right place to experience the joys of nature, as cheesy as that sounded.

But that wasn't enough of a distraction. No, I was too confused about the way I'd lost myself this past month, and I could only blame her. What was the word for when you couldn't stop thinking of your enemy's smile and the way her hair curved around her ear? Discombobulation?

All I knew was that I wanted her here in my bed with me.

I rolled over, lifting my hair off the pillow so it didn't stick to my neck if I passed out. Then I heard it. A huge crack, a crash, and ten seconds of silence.

I jumped out of bed, hoping it was my imagination and the worst hadn't just happened. I yanked my hiking boots on, grabbed my raincoat, and burst through the door.

I took in my surroundings, noting that my cabin looked normal, and my pod was dead asleep. I didn't know what I was looking for or what direction to go in, but on instinct, I headed toward her pod.

The trail was empty, which was a good sign. Maybe there wasn't some disaster awaiting me. Maybe I'd been in that strange place between sleep and consciousness. I batted at the hair that stuck to my soaked face and realized I hadn't even pulled my hood up. Well, it was too late now.

The second I made it to the Andromeda pod, I lifted my head and caught sight of the cabin, slipping in a puddle and nearly losing my footing before righting myself.

I didn't have time to stop and think because I was running toward her, mud be damned.

Every cabin in Andromeda was fine. Every one but hers.

The collapsed fir tree had destroyed the roof. But the rain was coming down so hard, I could barely see the rest of the damage. I expected a sound to come from her side of the forest. A scream. A yell. Anything to tell me she was alive. The silence took the wind right out of me.

Two doors opened in my periphery, but I was too busy to ask for help, rushing to the front door. I tried to open the thing, but it didn't budge. And the two people who attempted to help weren't achieving anything either.

I didn't say anything as more people joined, their voices blurred. My throat was filled with cotton balls, my eyes stinging.

Please be okay. Please be okay. Please be okay.

Then I remembered that Nat's bed was on the other side of the cabin. I made my way, slipping down the tiny embankment, and reached the back side.

"Natalie!" I shouted, but it could have been a whisper in the cacophony of this wind and rain. I climbed over branches, losing my footing on needles and not caring. Why wasn't she making a sound? "Nat?"

A branch from the downed tree cracked and shifted under my weight, but the lack of noise coming from her window had my stomach churning. Then it came: the best sound I'd ever heard.

"Over here!"

But those words weren't enough. I needed to see her, feel her, and know that she was okay.

I took a tentative step on a large branch, grateful that it held as I made it to her window. It had shattered, but at least it wasn't blocked.

"Jack," she cried, and my heart broke.

"Natalie!" I yelled louder. "I'm here. Don't move, princess. I'm going to get you."

"The window won't open. There's shattered glass everywhere."

She was right, the tree had bent the frame so it dipped. There was no opening it. I took off my jacket and used one side to knock the remaining shards out of the way before placing it on the frame.

"Can you get out?" I tried, hoping I didn't need to go get a ladder. Or a chainsaw, for god's sake.

"I—I think so," she said, but the damn rain had it sounding like a murmur. God, was she hurt? Not knowing killed me. I was about to jump through the window when I saw one knee on the sill, then her head poking through. I reached up to help her out and pulled her into a cradle in my arms.

"I'm right here. I've got you." My voice sounded broken, even to my own ears.

Nat clung to me as I held her, resting her face in my neck for a moment before pulling away. "I'm okay. I'm okay."

Why was she trying to make me feel better?

She pushed my hair out of my eyes, and I blinked away the blur. Was I crying?

"I thought I'd lost you."

Nat trembled in my arms but didn't break eye contact, her gaze soft and vulnerable.

"Is she okay?" someone shouted, and the world around us became Technicolor once more. The rain hadn't let up. Goose bumps crawled up my skin to the point that they hurt. The people holding my elbows to help lower me and Nat down from the tree were drenched. One offered to carry her, but I wasn't letting go of her, and I wasn't questioning why.

She was breathing. She was alive. And she was safe in my arms.

TWELVE

Nat

I PANTED AND CLUNG TO JACK AS HE CRADLED ME IN HIS arms, away from my destroyed cabin and into the clearing past my pod's campfire. The commotion of voices and movement around us blended into the wind's howling as the rain soaked us. I didn't speak as Jack held me to his chest and kept walking.

He fielded questions and concerns from the counselors and campers who'd heard the tree fall onto my cabin and were trying to be helpful in the aftermath. My fear-riddled state had me hearing bits and pieces, but I didn't miss it when he asked someone to call Dr. Alyse.

"I don't need a doctor." It was the middle of the night. I would be fine.

Jack squeezed me tighter, his face etched with worry and something else as he stopped and looked at me. "Yeah, you do, princess."

I didn't argue again. Jack was certain, and that meant the discussion was over.

Someone from my pod offered to carry me, but Jack gently refused. He had me, and I wasn't going to question him. There was something different about this version of Jack, who'd come to my window with a panicked look and was now prioritizing helping me over anything else.

I'd never imagined myself being rescued before or being attracted to the man doing said rescuing. But as Jack held me as if I were precious and delegated tasks to campers and counselors alike, I felt that stupid, familiar fizziness swirl around in my stomach. It wasn't only the intensity of the night. No, it was the realization that Jack was carrying me as if he'd carried me hundreds of times. It was the look in his eyes and the reassurance in his hold with every step we took.

I never would have expected this kind of reaction from my enemy or from myself, but I was done questioning the events of tonight as I rested my head in the nook between his shoulder and neck and breathed in deeply.

I couldn't help myself. He was comforting, so I instinctively held him closer. His grip tightened around me as if he'd never let me go, and he kept walking us in the rain toward the parking lot. I shivered against him. Cold. Wet. Then a wool blanket was thrown over me, its scratchy material barely noticeable. I could hear the tenor of Autumn's voice as she and Jack talked in clipped sentences while I shamelessly clutched onto him. Grateful for the warmth. Grateful for him.

Slowly, my senses settled down. Adrenaline released its vise grip on me, and it hit me again that Jack was carrying me. That he'd rescued me. But also, now my feet were throbbing in pain. I had to admit he was right. I was hurt.

I remembered the harrowing steps I'd taken over shattered glass to get to the window. Which only reminded me of Jack's desperate face as he'd reached for me. I'd never seen him so serious. So focused. I hadn't thought then; I'd just moved into his arms.

Jack had murmured soft words into the air around us. "I've got you." He'd puffed the promise into the air. More reassurances had quickly joined. "You're safe."

And in that moment, I'd known it was true. It was that simple. Jack was principled and wouldn't say things he didn't mean.

Autumn's worried gaze met Jack's, and her hand landed on his shoulder, which gave him pause. "I can drive her," she offered.

I felt more than I saw Jack's firm shake of his head. "I've got her. I'll get her there. Can you make sure Dr. Alyse is coming? Please?"

I gazed up at him through wet lashes. I'd never heard Jack ask something of someone like that, as if he were desperate for it. His jaw was set in a line, fierce determination in his eyes. He was on a singular mission as he held me.

He flung his truck door open, but I was gently lowered onto the bench seat. Jack tucked the blanket in around me, and he reached across to buckle me in.

I was annoyed at the sweet gesture. I could buckle myself. Jack and I both looked down at my shaking hands and it spurred him into action. Suddenly, he ran around the hood of the truck and hopped in, and we were off. Jack's knuckles were pressed white as he gripped the wheel. We drove to the clinic in silence, processing everything that had happened.

The lights to the clinic flickered as we arrived and, combined with the fallen branches and violent rain, it resembled a zombie apocalypse movie—eerie as hell.

Jack didn't seem to notice as he slammed the truck into park and charged around the hood to open my door for me. Jack scooped me up and out of the truck, back into his arms, where I'd be warm and safe. He didn't avoid the large puddles in the front row of the parking lot by going around. No, Jack took the quickest route to get me inside the Wildwood clinic.

Each step jostled me, and I clung to him tighter. Short breaths were pushed out from my lungs as he flexed below me. Of course, he just had to rescue me in a T-shirt that obscenely clung to him, soaked within an inch of its life. The nerve.

Not only did he look good and his body heat radiated warmth

into my soaking wet skin, but he also had the audacity to smell good, too. It was impossible to be annoyed with someone who rescued you and smelled this delectable.

He opened the door just as the lights stabilized, and its bright art-covered walls made it look a lot less ominous.

"Dr. Alyse," Jack greeted her as she met us at the door. I assumed she didn't normally go to work in banana pajamas, but who was I to judge? This was Wildwood. That, combined with her bedhead, reminded me she'd flown out of bed to help me.

Jack kept hold of me as he followed the doctor into the first examination room.

"It's her feet." His voice was uncharacteristically tight as he continued. "I didn't apply pressure. But I got here as quickly as I could."

"You can set her down over there. Let's have a look." Alyse washed her hands and put on some gloves before gathering some supplies.

Jack lifted me onto the medical bed, then stepped back. When he set me down, though, the blanket I'd been wearing fell off my shoulders, and Jack made a noise I'd never heard come out of him before. My gaze went to him, but he was already turning away. He rubbed his hand over the back of his neck as he stared off at the wall, his back facing me.

Was he blushing? I looked down at my soaked blue tank as it clung obscenely. The material outlined the shape of my chest, the tips of my breasts on full display. Now it was my turn to blush, and of course, Alyse saw the whole awkward interaction. Her gaze shot between us. She gave me an interested, pointed look, and I shook my head. Luckily, she had a modicum of tact as she busied herself by applying a saline solution to my cut feet.

My left foot was obviously worse than the right, but both of them throbbed as Alyse applied the saline solution and extracted the small shards embedded in the pads. Luckily, I'd just walked on my toes, and my whole foot hadn't been damaged.

"Ouch, girl. What happened?"

I winced as she worked on them, and Jack left to get me water, which was nice since he'd been hovering just over my shoulder ever since he brought me here.

"Mother Nature decided my cabin needed a renovation." I winced as Alyse removed a piece of glass from my toe. I took the water from Jack after he returned. "I cut them on glass while getting out of my cabin. How very John McClane of me."

Alyse laughed at the joke. Jack even cracked a smile, so my mission was accomplished.

"Yeah, sure, if John McClane wore short shorts," she added, finished washing off both my feet, and applied an ointment. She handed Jack the rest of the tube when he reached for it and started talking again before I could protest. "Good news, they don't look deep enough to warrant stitches. Stay off them for a few days, change the bandages every few hours, and call me right away if there's any sign of infection."

Jack nodded and hung on Alyse's every word as if he were mentally taking notes about my care regimen.

"And, Jack, let me have a look at that for you, too."

Jack's face twisted in confusion. "Look at what?"

Alyse's eyes softened, and she gestured toward his left forearm, which sported dried blood.

His gaze followed hers.

"Oh, that?" he said sheepishly. "It's nothing."

Alyse rolled her eyes while she washed her hands again and applied fresh gloves before turning back toward him. "Give me that," she said with an unamused tone. She held his wrist gently, analyzing the wound on his forearm. She washed it out and checked for any glass pieces, just like she had with me.

"It's shallow," she said, and it was my turn to let out a little puff of relief. Dr. Alyse looked between us, then faced Jack. "So are you going to be taking care of her?"

Her eyebrows raised as her voice lingered, and I knew what she was getting at. She also ran Wildwood's local romance book club. I'd been invited to attend, but I hadn't found the time yet. I could only imagine what hurt/comfort scenarios were playing through her head.

Jack interrupted when he answered her in a serious tone. "Yes, ma'am, I'll make sure she's taken care of."

Alyse gave us a knowing look, and I couldn't help but think that she was already shipping us. I didn't argue with her. After this strange night, maybe I was shipping us now, too.

"No, it'll be too much trouble." I somehow mustered the energy to argue with Jack after finding myself once again in his strong arms. He transported me as if I were some hurt bride, backing up into each door until we reached his truck. The rain hadn't let up, but that didn't hinder Jack, who confidently drove the short distance down the winding road from downtown Wildwood back to Camp Starlight.

"No, you're right. Sleeping on the floor isn't insane at all." His sarcastic tone softened into something kind. "The easiest solution is for you to sleep at my place. I have a shirt and sweats you can borrow."

Everyone else at camp had gone back to bed, no doubt. We'd have a long day dealing with the aftermath tomorrow. Right now, I had Jack to deal with.

When we arrived at camp, he picked me up again and carried me toward his cabin as if the decision had already been made.

"Look, it's already three in the morning, and it's only for a few hours. I think we can manage, just this once. I'll sleep on the couch," he insisted.

Jack lived in the former bunkhouse, so his cabin was much

larger than mine and had communal spaces. It made sense since he lived here year-round. Didn't mean I wasn't jealous, though.

"You're right," I whispered, mindful of the late hour.

Jack looked almost surprised. He let out a hushed laugh. "Finally, you admit it," he whispered back, mirroring my tone, before opening the door.

I narrowed my eyes at him, which was much easier at this angle. "You know, a girl could get used to this."

Jack's laugh vibrated through me as he held me close. "What a surprise coming from you, princess."

"None of my other subjects complain like you do," I tacked on in a haughty, playful tone once we made it inside his cabin.

The cabin was dark, but a part of me knew he was grinning. I felt a strange bit of relief knowing he could still smile after everything that had happened tonight. That man had been too close to permanent scowl territory.

Jack walked through the dark living room to the bedroom and leaned down slowly. I didn't want to let go of him, a silly notion. Eventually, he made a soft noise, and I untwined my arms from around him and found myself gently placed onto his bed. My heart thudded, and I needed to express my gratitude.

"Jack—"

He set a folded T-shirt and the promised pair of sweats down on the bed. "Be right back."

He walked away with purpose. Cool air whooshed between us, which was okay because when I stopped to think about it, I didn't know what I was even trying to say.

Jack returned with two throw pillows. He didn't look at me as he carefully lifted my calves and placed the pillows under each of my legs, propping up my feet. "There you go." His voice was softer than I was used to.

"Jack, wait." It was hard to remember that just hours ago, we'd been enemies. The juxtaposition was off-putting, and it didn't make sense. The one person I never thought I could trust was now the person I felt the safest with. I wanted to say something that conveyed the gravity of the swirling emotions I felt, but when he turned toward me from the doorway, his face lightly lined by the moonlight, all I could manage was a simple, "Thank you."

"Goodnight, princess."

I could hear the warmth in his voice as he softly closed the door, but I only let out a small, "Night," that he probably didn't even hear.

What else was there to say to the man who had literally swept you off your feet?

THIRTEEN
Jack

THE SOUND OF NAT TOSSING AND TURNING IN THE other room was getting to me. But when the scared gasp and the whimpering kicked in, I burst into action. I rushed inside the partially open door and got on my knees beside the queen-size bed, touching her shoulder gently, but she didn't stop thrashing. Her hair stuck to her face, and her pallor was all wrong.

"Nat," I said firmly, pushing her shoulder a little harder.

Her eyes burst open, and she scanned her surroundings, taking in the bed she was lying on and the bunk beds I hadn't removed across the room, before she blinked and focused on my face once more. "Jack?"

I pushed away the hair sticking to her face. "You're in my cabin, Nat. You're okay."

"Okay," she breathed. "Yeah. I'm okay." She closed her eyes and leaned into my touch as she let out a longer breath. Even disheveled, she was beautiful. "Did a tree fall on my cabin?"

"It did." I reluctantly removed my hand.

She absentmindedly touched her temple where my fingers had just been, breaking eye contact as she sat up. Her eyebrows pulled together as she looked around. "Did a tree hit this place, too?"

Was she concussed?

I moved my head into her line of sight, looking for blown pupils or something. I didn't actually know what I was doing. I wasn't a medical professional, but she was acting strangely.

"No."

"Then why is it so messy?"

And just like that, my pity was gone.

I sighed and shook my head, standing up and turning to walk away. She followed, apparently, because she was touching my elbow within seconds.

"Ow. Ow. Ow," she said with every step. I almost swept her off her feet to take away the pain, but thought better of it. She was wincing, but that wasn't what caught my attention. No, it was the fact that she was in my bedroom, wearing my T-shirt and a pair of my sweatpants. Why was that so hot? Why did I want to pick up an injured woman and pin her against the wall with my hips and mouth?

"Are you okay?"

"Yeah," she squeaked out. This time, I couldn't help myself. I reached out for her so I could take her into my arms and soothe her pain, but she touched my shoulder and shook her head. "I'm okay, Jack." Now she was the one reassuring me?

Flashes of last night popped into my head. Her voice had been barely intelligible from her room as the rain poured overhead. The way she'd clung to me as I carried her. I'd barely noticed my surroundings or who came to help last night. I got her to the doctor, but the rest of it? Everything was so blurry.

The sound of rain broke me out of my stupor.

"It's still storming outside? Seriously?" She walked on her heels over to the window. Her bandages seemed intact, so I didn't give her shit about it.

"It's not supposed to let up for a couple of days or so."

"Too bad your weather app can't predict falling trees. Then we wouldn't be in this mess. Or—" She scanned my living room. "I guess you still would have been in a mess of your own."

I surveyed my surroundings. Okay, so it was a little cluttered. I'd sort of swept the clean laundry that had been on the couch onto the floor last night, and mail and manuals were lying on all surfaces around the room. Not to mention the water glasses on my end table only added to the aesthetic. But the toolboxes and drywall supplies I hadn't moved into my second room were job-related since I treated it like a garage. She certainly couldn't judge me for that, right?

As she scrutinized the room, I eyed her and shook my head. It was time to get out of here. "Bathroom's down the hall. Towels are in the closet, and first aid is under the sink. And there's orange juice in the fridge." Why was I babbling?

"Where are you going?" she asked as I reached for the door.

"Out. Help yourself to anything. I'll be back in a bit."

I could have stayed to help her, but I chose not to. I needed to put as much distance between the woman wearing my clothes and me as possible.

"Wait a minute. What happened?" A distressed Leo stared at me and Autumn through our video chat, and I sort of wished I hadn't involved him in this mess.

"A storm took out Nat's cabin," I repeated patiently. He had to feel out of control being in California.

Autumn jumped in. "Nothing else appears to be damaged. We checked on all the campers last night while Jack took Nat to the hospital."

"*Hospital?* What the hell?" Leo looked two seconds away from pulling out his hair or maybe jumping on an airplane to see that Nat was okay.

"It wasn't the hospital," I interjected. "I took her to see Dr. Alyse."

That didn't give him the relief I was hoping for. "I need more, Jack."

"Nat stepped on some glass last night. Alyse removed it and bandaged her up. She's a little shaken, but she's fine."

He breathed a sigh of relief. "I'd like to talk to her today and hear that from her."

"Of course," I promised.

"So, what kind of damage are we looking at?" Leo asked.

Ever the fixer, Autumn tried to assuage his fears. "I'll start by saying that none of the campers were affected, beyond having a big scare. Damage-wise, there's a whole-ass tree going down the middle of Nat's cabin. Then, there are the downed tree branches all over. We're in damage control in more ways than one, but as far as the camper experience goes, we've got some indoor activities planned for the time being. We might bring back poker just to distract people from the rain."

"And the repairs?"

I shook my head. "I need to assess, but based on what I saw last night, we're looking at weeks of repairs, at minimum. She's going to need a place to go."

I tracked Leo's eyes to my best friend, who had already considered this.

"We're completely booked up," Autumn said apprehensively. "I have one spot in a month, but that would only be for the week. What about your cabin, Leo? Or Hazel's."

Leo sighed, defeated. "We both have our keys here."

And I didn't have keys to their places because technically, they were their homes. "And no one here has a spare key?"

"We do have spares, it's just... I have Hazel's—"

"And Hazel has yours." Shit. There was no way we didn't have an alternative.

"I'll talk with Hazel, and we'll pop the key in the mail, but for now, don't you have bunk beds in your cabin, Jack?" Leo asked.

Autumn side-eyed me, and I knew what was coming next.

"They can't live together. They'll kill each other," she said without preamble. "And my second bedroom was turned into an office after Jamie moved in. But someone can sleep on my couch? The only problem is, Jamie wakes up at five and is loud as hell in the morning, so I wouldn't recommend it."

"Leo, how long are you going to be gone?"

He cringed. "At least a week. Look, Hazel is at her limit. Now, we're going to have to deal with insurance and repairs, and I don't even want to bring this up to her. I need you two to figure something out."

"We can do that," we said in unison.

"Okay, thank you. Call if you need anything else."

The screen went blank, leaving Autumn and me to stare at each other until she broke the silence with an undeniable truth: "This is a terrible idea."

"Yeah, well..."

"Don't you remember when it was just you and Leo?"

Leo had stayed with me during a squirrel infestation in his cabin. He'd discovered it when he'd fallen asleep with a piece of pizza crust in his hand and woken up with a squirrel on his chest holding said piece of crust. Then it bit him, which led to him bitching and moaning for a week.

But as horrifying as that was, it'd been worse when we lived together. We'd thought it'd be fine since we'd all lived together in one room at the very beginning, but we'd been wrong. Apparently, the girls had balanced us out.

It was time for me to rip the bandage off. "Did you see this morning?"

She closed her eyes. "It's not great."

"I'll take all these options back to Nat and see what she wants to do." I stood from my chair and grabbed my baseball cap, putting it back on. "And I'll let you know how bad it is, damage-wise."

It wasn't good. I sat Nat down gently. She'd begrudgingly let me give her a piggyback ride over to her cabin. She'd slid on a pair of my shoes that were definitely too big for her.

We assessed the damage. The fallen tree had smashed her door to the point that it couldn't be opened until I broke it out of its casing. I'd need to take a chainsaw to unblock the entrance. The roof was caved in, and I could only assume there would be water damage.

"Ow. Ow."

I turned to find her walking gingerly on her heels just like this morning. Only now, it looked like she was wearing clown shoes. She looked ridiculous. And yet again, I rushed to pick her up.

She touched my forearm to stop me, kindness in her eyes. "You don't have to carry me."

"But you shouldn't be walking." I couldn't stand the idea of her in pain. It made me physically ill. "And the doctor said to get some rest."

She stared at me quizzically. "I hurt my feet, Jack. I didn't get a concussion."

Okay, that made sense. Despite everything, I offered my arm. When she took it, I breathed in relief. We walked the perimeter at a snail's pace together.

Nat lifted a broken pot to a nasturtium plant. "What do we do?"

I winced as the pot fell to pieces when she tried to cover the exposed roots with dirt. "We need to retarp the roof since it wasn't secured properly. I need to take photos for insurance and get the go-ahead to chop this up and get through the door."

She nodded, swallowing loud enough that I heard it.

"Are you okay?"

"Yeah, fine." She didn't look fine. She stood in front of the ruins, and even in her distressed state, she looked beautiful. The juxtaposition of her light with the harsh destruction caused a lump in my throat.

"It's okay to be upset that your home just got destroyed."

A flash of something crossed her face, but she quickly wiped it away with a smile. "It's okay. I'm used to living without a home anyway. I haven't had one of those in a long time."

I wanted to pry, because this was clearly affecting her, but she seemed determined to put on a brave face.

"So, I'm guessing I can't live here..." There was a melancholy quality to her voice as she toed a fallen branch and kicked it off her front porch before setting her foot back down and wincing.

"No, you can't. And it's going to be a minute before you can get inside. I'm sorry, Nat."

"Not your fault," she offered, but the dejected look on her face had me wishing I could fix it.

"This brings me to my next point," I started, but she cut me off.

"You mean where I'm going to live?"

"Yeah. Hazel and Leo are gone for a week. Leo offered to mail a key, but they seem a little stressed right now—"

Nat shook her head. "We don't need to involve them."

"That's what I was thinking. I'll tell them they don't have to go to the trouble." He pulled out his phone and sent a quick text. "So, the way I see it, you have a couple of options. Option one is that you stay with me. You take one of the bunks, and I sleep in the bed you used last night."

She looked up and carefully considered my words. "And option two?" she said hopefully.

"Option two is one of us sleeps on Autumn's couch."

"I don't want to put them out. Not to mention, those two are like newlyweds, and it would be awkward as hell." She was right about that. "What's wrong with your couch?"

"The permanent indent in my side from the broken spring says we should not sleep there. That thing is like a modern-day torture device."

"Jesus, Jack, how old is it?" She looked skeptical.

"A few decades?" I shrugged. "I haven't gotten around to changing it."

Just like I hadn't gotten around to getting rid of the bunk bed in my bedroom, which had previously been a bunkhouse. I remembered the early days. Nights when Hazel, Leo, Autumn, and I slept in that room, laughing into the early hours of the morning. Maybe I hadn't moved them because I was nostalgic.

"Look, I spoke with Leo, and they're going to be gone at least a week, and even then, neither Hazel nor Leo has an available spare bed. We've converted our second bedrooms into offices or storage. Which, as much as it pains me to say this, my place sounds like the best option, for now." Man, I needed to build some storage sheds.

"Maybe I could tough it out once the tree is gone," she offered. That was the moment the west-side gutter fell, right on top of the bush. I lifted an eyebrow, and she rolled her eyes. "Okay, maybe not."

"I don't love the idea of you or me sleeping on a couch for however long this takes." I took her hands in mine and rubbed the back of her palms with my thumbs in reassurance. "I promise I'll get into this place as soon as I can, so you can at least get some of your things."

She glanced down at where we were joined and back into my eyes. "I know you will." We dropped hands, and the disappearing heat from her fingers felt like a loss I wasn't willing to analyze. "I probably have some clothes in my car. Don't stress, okay?"

That was the nicest thing she'd said to me this year. I thought about the reasons for her vitriol and quickly pushed them away on the walk back to my cabin.

Nice went out the door the minute we went inside. She let out a puff of air, almost as if in disbelief.

"I'd say there's good news and bad news to this living arrangement." She lifted a pile of mail with her pointer finger, her chipped blue nail tapping on it before she dropped it. "The good news is you have a roof." Here we go. "And the bad news is: this is almost as bad as my cabin."

If it had been any other person, I would have snorted at her sarcasm, but this was Nat. Even if she had a point. It wasn't just drywall supplies and tools. There were also buckets of paint. A few shovels. Tiling supplies and bags of thin-set adhesive. When I took my cabin in through her eyes, a wave of embarrassment hit me. None of this should have been in a place that was supposed to be habitable. I needed to move it into the second bedroom. Or better yet, outside somewhere.

Nat folded her arms over her chest. "If I'm to live here"—we both physically cringed at that—"we need to have some rules."

"Just what every person wants to hear."

"Fine, some guidelines. Regulations? Boundaries?"

I shrugged. "Number one, you stay out of my way, and I'll stay out of yours."

"Easy. Done. Number two, this"—she gestured to my living room—"needs to be cleaner." She ran a finger on a bookshelf as if she were Mary fucking Poppins in gloves and raised it so I could see how the dust and wood shavings had accumulated.

"I used a table saw in here once."

"Well, since it was just once." Her tone wasn't appreciated.

"It was a rainy day, and it wasn't until afterward that I realized it was a mistake."

She pointed to the fireplace and the paper around it. "That's a fire hazard." The vehemence in her tone had me questioning if either of us would be safe with her under the same roof. Nat turned, then she saw her beloved keychain sticking out from under a pizza box on the coffee table. "And Bernice is sitting under garbage!"

I squeezed my hands into fists to hold back from saying something I'd regret.

"Jesus, is that paint thinner, Jack?" Shit. What was that doing here?

"I'll get rid of that," I said dumbly. "Anything else?"

Nat took in her surroundings, leaving me hanging for a long moment. "TBD."

FOURTEEN
Nat

"So how are you doing?" Hazel's voice was doing that worried thing it did sometimes.

Leo must have told her everything after our quick phone call, where he'd checked on me before jokingly asking if he had to rename the place Camp Natalie to prevent me from suing.

While her question was of concern and care, there was also a weariness in her tone that advised me against venting about the prospect of living with Jack. Part of me wanted to let the dam break and tell her that Jack was becoming a little too distracting. That I might be in trouble. But her voice was smaller than I'd ever heard it, and it was clear she was going through something much bigger than I was. So I gave her the sanitized answer.

"It's a mess, but we're handling it. Everyone banded together after it happened, and I got out, so it's nothing to worry about." I hoped she didn't use her superpower to read between the lines. While everything I'd said was true, it was also… lacking.

Hazel hummed, letting the moment stretch out. It was one of her tactics that always worked on me, leaving me no choice but to fill the silence.

"It was a little bit scary."

"I bet it was." She let out a sigh, and I wondered how much she wished she were here. "You went to Alyse, right? What did she say?"

"She said I'm good. No stitches, just a little sore."

It was obvious she wanted to focus this conversation on me, not her, and while it was a signature Hazel move, I needed to redirect the conversation. Take a page out of her book.

"Enough about me. What's going on with you?" I asked.

Hazel sniffed hollowly. "There's just a lot going on, and I'm not handling it as well as I would like." There was a plea in her brittle tone confirming she was just barely keeping it together. So I didn't press.

I expected an *I've got to go.* What I didn't expect were the next words out of her mouth.

"Jack isn't being mean, right? If he is, you'll let me know?"

Mean definitely wasn't the word I'd use. Challenging? Exhausting? Getting under my skin? Those all seemed much more fitting.

"No more than before." And while I had my doubts about living with the man, I was also very resourceful. I already knew how I'd be dealing with him.

"Well, good. In that case, let's call this penance for that double date."

I barked out a laugh at her audacity. "For the last time, it wasn't a double date." I'd made my case before and lost this argument every time.

In her words, I'd tricked her into going on a double date with a guy whose hot roommate I wanted to hook up with. It was more like a hangout where we were scoping out if he was decent or not. It wasn't my fault that his roommate talked Hazel's ear off about Greek mythology for two hours while I flirted with the hot one.

Still, I played along for a moment before gently offering, "You know I'm here if you wanna talk some more. Whenever."

"Thanks, babe. We will. But Leo's here, and he brought soup."

We all had our comfort foods. Hazel's was any type of soup. No matter how hot it was outside.

It made me think of the comfort meal I'd had the morning after the storm. My campers had brought me goodies from the mess hall and checked how I was doing with my injuries. They'd left with quite the story to tell from their week at camp after being woken up and helping tarp my caved-in cabin while I was at the clinic.

By the time I made it back to the cabin to rest my aching feet, Jack had cleared the tools and random stuff off the bunk beds as promised. Even though he was making an effort, his messier space was still throwing me off, but I didn't complain because he was at least diligently working on my cabin repairs. He'd gotten my busted laptop, my dead phone, and my meds from my nightstand. What I didn't expect him to bring back was my mini fridge, which was a little dinged up but completely functional. I appreciated how considerate he was of my needs when I didn't even ask him. But I was still out of my comfort zone, which stressed me out.

My gaze shot between the bunk beds and Jack's bed. I hadn't slept in a twin bed in ages, much less a bunk bed. I would have preferred the top bunk—all the better to look down upon Jack. However, it was only used as storage. I sure as hell couldn't sleep in the bed directly across from that man again. While the bed itself was comfortable enough, the problem was Jack. The man's e-reader brightened up the entire room. And for some annoying reason, I wanted to know what he was reading. I shouldn't care, but I had seen the bluish glow highlighting his stupid grin, and it was enough to make anyone curious. Not to mention it made me miss my own e-reader, probably buried in that pile of rubble.

I longed for the perfect distraction that only books could provide. Plus, the book I had been reading before the storm was just starting to get good. The mystery was unfolding perfectly, and the protagonist had finally learned they liked their quirky neighbor. They were going to kiss any page now.

Jack reacted to his book again, and I couldn't help myself. "What are you reading?"

"It's a sweet little story about a man who lives by himself in the forest and the woman who knocks on his door in the middle of the night."

For some reason, I knew the plot wasn't going to have a hot one-bed situation like one of my books would have.

"Jack, we're literally at a cabin. In the woods. What are you thinking?"

"It soothes me. Plus, I'm getting some good ideas in case someone crosses me," he deadpanned.

That pulled a laugh out of me that I didn't expect. Actually, it sounded closer to a snort. "Aren't you hilarious tonight?"

He looked pleased with my reaction and went on. "Did you know that more than four hundred people have gone missing on Mt. Rainier since it became a national park?"

"Isn't that only a few hours away?"

"That number is pretty high. They say conditions make it nearly impossible to find people. Something about fog rolling in out of nowhere and hidden crevasses people just... fall into."

I didn't have many options, so I threw the closest thing I could find at him. His T-shirt hit him square in the face, and I reveled at my prowess. "I don't want to know that! Now I'm not going to be able to sleep," I screeched.

"I'm the one who's reading it, princess. I think you'll be just fine." He chuckled to himself, then stopped abruptly, holding the material in front of his face and staring at it a little too long. I knew I was going to regret whatever he said next. "Wait a second. Were you sleeping with my T-shirt?"

"No," I lied.

"Then why was it in your bed?" The humor in his voice had my cheeks going so hot, I wondered if they were illuminating the room.

"You worry about things on your half of the room."

I expected something cocky and annoying to follow that statement. Instead, he surprised me. "Speaking of worrying, did you change your bandage tonight?"

I wasn't about to give in to some sweet response, so I went with the first thing I could. "Yes, Mom," I joked.

"I only ask because Alyse scares me."

I laughed at that one. Alyse was as scary as Leo. "So do horses, right?" I teased.

Jack's face scrunched up adorably at the mention of the amazing animals. He set his e-reader down on his chest and let the darkness engulf us. "You remember that?"

My voice came out softer in the dark. "It's easy to remember someone hating something you love."

Jack's voice had a smile in it. "You would love horses."

"And you would love being a dick," I bit back but regretted the harsh words. "What do you have against horses, anyway?" There had to be a reason behind his clear hatred toward the majestic animals.

"I didn't grow up going to camps, like most everyone else here." His voice was quiet, and I waited with bated breath for him to continue. "But I was a Boy Scout. Our troop went to a horse ranch, and it was stupid." He emitted a soft sigh. "A kid spooked the horse I was learning to ride, and it took off running. I clutched the reins, but I was thrown off anyway. I got a broken arm and a forced apology out of the ordeal when his mother found out what had happened. I swore I wouldn't get back on one of those deathtraps if I could help it."

"That sounds awful." My heart squeezed for him. I almost hadn't expected him to answer, and now that he had, I oddly felt the need to keep this conversation alive. "Maybe the reason you can't sleep is that you read scary books before bed," I observed.

He lifted his screen back up, his face taking on that soft blue aura again as he turned back to his book. "It's not. And sleep is overrated."

I laughed, surprised. "Um, no, it's one of the best things a human can do."

"I wouldn't know." There was a wistfulness to his tone that I wasn't used to from him.

"So this is normal for you? Up at all hours?"

"Insomnia is a bitch. But it means I'm up early for bird-watching. Or whatever I'm doing that day."

I also remembered last year's admission, when Jack commented about never sleeping more than four hours a night during a game of two truths and a lie. Back then, I'd thought it was an exaggeration, but now I figured that might actually be the case for him. "I've never been bird-watching."

"It's one of my favorite things to do. That, and yoga, help clear my head. You could probably use something like that," he suggested.

It surprised me to hear that Jack did yoga when I saw him as more of a lumberjack, but the man clearly contained multitudes.

"I've tried meditation, but I couldn't turn my brain off." I thought about all the noise in my life and the things I was behind on. I'd never felt settled. There was always something I should be doing.

He paused, as if considering my words. "I hate to offer this, because it always annoys me when someone says it to me, but maybe you could use a break?"

I let him in on a little-known secret. "Let's just say my running to-do list is a mile long."

"Tell me about it. I've been go, go, go for years. My time out there is the only quiet I usually allow myself."

"So, what I'm hearing is we're two completely healthy individuals."

A puff of a laugh escaped him. "You're not wrong. But I've recently decided to live by a new mantra: that list will always be there tomorrow. And I'm going to adopt it the moment I'm done with your cabin."

"When you figure out how to do it, you can teach me your ways."

He nodded softly. "Time for bed, princess. We'll work on ourselves tomorrow," he said, turning back to his e-reader.

I smiled to the ceiling and tried to go back to sleep. Tomorrow meant new campers. Even though I worried that sleeping this close to Jack would be impossible, I was out within minutes.

The hauling of debris should not have been this sexy. But unfortunately, not being able to sleep for the couple of days since the storm meant my sleep-deprived brain didn't get that memo, as the man who'd kept me up the past couple of nights with his constant movement wasted no time getting to work on my mangled cabin.

It had been a few days since the storm. The bad weather had made cleanup difficult, but Jack had done what he could. Things had been tense in the cabin because we were tiptoeing around each other. Every day, I worried about doing or saying something I'd regret. Because, of course, I was getting too familiar and far too close to someone who didn't like me. That was always going to be a stupid risk that I didn't need to explore.

Jack worked behind my campers as I sat with my podmates at the Andromeda campfire, just as I did every morning before breakfast. This morning time was usually my chance to talk with campers, to build some camaraderie. It would have been helpful, considering this new cohort of campers was a motley crew of a family that wasn't getting along, but I kept getting distracted by the sultry view of Jack hauling the large branches out of my cabin.

He'd been friendly as he greeted my podmates and asked them to excuse the noise as he got to work. But when said noises were mostly grunts from swinging an ax to chop branches, combined with the way his T-shirt clung to him, I found myself questioning if this whole display was ethical.

When I heard him hauling what sounded like glass, emotions clogged my throat as I continued to process that night. The fear, pain, and adrenaline. All of it came back in an instant, and then I calmed myself down by remembering how I'd felt oddly safe in his hold.

I've got you.

And he hadn't been lying. I'd felt it in my bones that he wouldn't let anything happen to me. It was as if the imprint of his strong arms had been left on my body. But this fascination with listening to that broad-shouldered, muscled man was so much better than listening to my current pod members bicker, which was what they were dead set on doing.

I didn't know how much time had passed, but by the time Jack pulled the starter cord on a chainsaw, I knew I'd be done for if I watched him lumberjack anymore. It was time for a change of scenery.

I broke out of my stupor to encourage everyone to follow me, using the tactic of feeding them good food to get them to relax. "Let's go to the mess hall."

And if going to the mess hall happened to get me away from a far too attractive and unsolicited roommate... well, that was icing on the cake.

Food always brought people together. But somehow, even while drinking mimosas and snacking on Bobby's heavenly pastries, they still found a way to bicker. They were a close-knit family whose motto seemed to be picking on each other and driving one another mad. Most people took a vacation to try to reconnect and relax together, but not the Millers. I'd already heard all about the reason for their squabble from the youngest sister. She'd filled me in that there were issues around a trust and that their recently deceased long-lost aunt thought family bonding at a camp for adults would do the trick. So far, it hadn't.

I rubbed my temples and tried to meditate for a moment, but I remembered these were grown-ass adults, and they should theoretically be able to sort their own issues out.

Usually, I had more patience, and I'd suggest fun things to get them out of their funk, but to be fair, this week had been challenging, and there wasn't enough tea in the world for this. Missing a couple of days of my medication and not having my phone back until last night meant that my carefully crafted morning rituals were gone. Everything felt unorganized and chaotic, as if a rug had been pulled out from under me. Most mornings, I was an early bird. I'd put on music and go about the inconvenient task of changing my bandages before doing my skincare routine, but today, I was dragging.

Part of that was getting back on my Adderall routine, but the other part was Jack.

I had some time off, so I went back to my cabin, planning to take a catnap before lunch, when a knock at the door startled me. It was still early, and no one knocked much at camp. Unless maybe a camper was lost? I walked to the door, still wrapped in my blanket. What I didn't expect to find on the doorstep was a middle-school-aged boy standing there with his eyes somehow both lit up and bugged out.

"You're Naturegirlnat."

This was a first. Being spotted was rare here at camp, especially not by a kid while I was wearing my fuzzy bunny slippers. I was so grateful that Jack had let me into my cabin to get some *necessities* early this morning.

"That's right. And you are?" I took in his brown crew cut and dimples.

The boy's wits seemed to return when Jack sidled up beside me. He was newly showered with his hair in a half-up, half-down man bun. Why was that so hot?

"Uncle Jack, you really know Naturegirlnat?" The boy's big eyes flew from me to Jack and back to me.

Jack smiled and ushered the kid inside. Jack clearly didn't understand why the boy would be so enamored with me. That made two of us.

"I live here. Isn't that right, Jack? Now, who do I have the pleasure of meeting?" I nudged Jack when he didn't introduce us right away.

Jack pushed a hand through his messy hair and grinned at the kid, who set his backpack down. "Sorry. Nat, this is Jordan, my nephew. We're hanging out today."

He poured himself coffee before he began making something on the kitchen stovetop. I still wasn't used to the fact that Jack had his own full kitchen, a fireplace, much more space, and now, apparently, a sweet nephew who was making himself right at home.

"You can call me Jordy," he said before turning to his uncle. "Is she your girlfriend?" He seemed so excited, we both turned to shatter his dreams at the same time.

"No," and, "No way," were spoken in unison with enough fervor to light the room on fire.

Jack clarified quickly. "Nat is a friend of mine. She's a counselor here."

"Oh my gosh. So this is what you do on your off time?" Jordy asked as Jack handed him a mug of cocoa, and he took a sip before he continued talking excitedly. "What are you working on now?"

I adored his sweet energy. I was recognized for my social media presence from time to time, but it never ceased to amaze me. I started to answer when a steaming mug of cocoa was placed into my hands. I looked up and smiled at the considerate gesture, resisting the urge to pat him on his cheek. Jack smiled at me and turned back to the stovetop.

"Well, what are you doing today?" I asked.

Jack answered for him. "We're just hanging around camp. Might go into Wildwood."

"Well, if you and your uncle don't have too many plans, why don't you help me with my latest post?" I looked to Jack to make sure I wasn't overstepping, but he smiled at me warmly. I turned back to Jordy. "If you'd like. I could use an assistant today. I'm free until this afternoon."

"Really? You'd let me help you?" Jordy asked eagerly.

I couldn't help but be warmed by that. Some kids would balk at the idea, but Jordy was filled with such enthusiasm over helping me with my work that I almost wanted him to lower his expectations. But I'd find a way to make it fun.

Jack shrugged with a smile, and Jordan looked like he was going to combust from excitement. I grabbed my phone, since I had no way of uploading from my camera. My phone had miraculously made it through the storm, but my laptop was not so lucky.

"I have a video channel, too." As we laced up our boots, Jordan stopped me with a serious look on his adorable face. "I actually started it because of you."

I smiled so wide my cheeks hurt. That was the best compliment I'd ever received. I loved that I was inspiring him. "You did?"

Jack popped back into our field of vision with his own stunned look, before his eyes crinkled at the corners. "That's so cool, bud. Sounds like you two have lots in common."

So he thought what I did was cool. Well, at least when his nephew did.

"Why don't you tell us about your channel?" I encouraged Jordy, who, as it turned out, didn't need much encouragement as he became the cutest professional. He explained his channel's goal, which was to explore the world like me.

"I'm just getting started, but I have all these ideas, and where I live, there are these trails. Don't you think people would love to see them?" He looked to Jack, hoping his uncle would back him up. Jack nodded, and I pictured them hiking together, one pointing out birds while the other took video.

Jack ruffled his hair. "Yeah, Jordy, they'll love it."

I could tell he was a really good uncle with how he cared about everything Jordy said. Apparently, they talked weekly, and Jack seemed to know all about his nephew's life and what was going on with him at school. Seeing this side of Jack had me warming even more to him. Who knew?

We walked down the main path through the camp, and it was clear Jordy had been here many times before. He looked so comfortable chatting with Jack. And Jack was smiling with a child. It was so surprising and at complete odds with how I thought of him. I was still wrapping my mind around it when I realized I'd missed part of the conversation.

"What's that, Jordy?" I asked as I tried to catch up.

"Have you had a Sasquatch sighting yet?"

I shook my head, and the ten-year-old gave me an incredulous look. "Not yet, no," I hedged.

Jordy shook his head but gave me a reassuring look. "Don't worry, Nat, if I can see him with my family on the drive up here, I'm sure you will too, one day."

I looked to Jack. A lock of hair obscured his face, but it didn't hide the corner of his lips tilting up.

"Is that so? Guess we'll have to keep a lookout."

Jack and I exchanged an amused glance. We skipped through camp, dodging puddles and enjoying the drizzly day. We spent the morning filming and writing copy for a camp post.

Even after a storm, Camp Starlight shone beautifully.

On the way back, we passed through the meditation meadow, and a fuzzy caterpillar had crawled up the sign. I took the opportunity to show Jordy how to find light sources and angle the shots. When we captured the little bug perfectly as it crawled next to droplets of condensation, his excitement was palpable.

Jordy didn't let up on his barrage of insightful questions until we got back to Jack's cabin, where we worked on the copy and posted it.

"How about we give the lil' critter a name?" I offered, thinking of cute post title ideas.

Jordy turned out to be a natural. He put his finger on his chin, like I'd seen Jack do while considering something. "Or maybe we title it *Camp Starlight: fuzzy caterpillar approved.*"

Jack went to make us all sandwiches while we continued sharing ideas, and by the time he came back, Jordy and I had the post up and were responding to our first comment.

"You're really good at this, Jordy. Thanks so much for your help," I said, meaning it. I'd been less inspired the past few days, and his spirit reinvigorated me more than he knew. He was also really good at making me laugh.

Jack sat next to Jordy, who played my compliment off as though it were no big deal. But it was a big deal. Jordy had no idea that because of him, I hadn't thought about maiming his uncle even once today.

Jordy didn't argue when I closed the app on my phone a few minutes later. He gently touched my hand and looked into my eyes the way only a kid could. "Thanks, Nat. That was so much fun."

"Yeah." Jack smiled at me, and there was no sarcasm detected when he offered his own "Thanks, Nat."

Jordy told me about his new account, and I tagged him in the post. The request would have to be approved by his parents, but either way, it warmed my heart seeing his eyes light up. Witnessing Jordy's love of photography as an artistic expression reminded me of one of the reasons why I chose to do what I did.

I did my activities and met back up with them to eat dinner in the mess hall, before going back to our cabin, where Jack insisted I sit down and rest because my feet were still healing. Foster came by and picked up Jordy after dinner. Jack and I sat on the lumpy couch, exhausted and... happy? Yeah. Happy together.

I WAS STILL FEELING WARM WHEN MY SISTER CALLED later that night.

"Hey, Mandy, it's good to hear from you." I looked at her beautiful face in our video chat. I could picture her feet kicked up, books stacked up in the space under her coffee table because there weren't enough bookshelves anymore in her and Sho's apartment.

My sister lived for learning. She'd always had an academic drive that I'd never had. I'd agreed to get my master's in marketing and work for my mom's company, but that was before my passion showed up when I started exploring different places and sharing them with the world.

My sister, however, had had a love of school since kindergarten. She'd known she wanted to thrive in business, so she did. Mandy worked hard, and if she made up her mind about something, it happened. I was just as determined, but all throughout school, I'd had to fight my way through assignments until I'd realized later in life that I had an undiagnosed learning disability.

Mandy was usually unstoppable, but now she also looked a little worn around the edges. That drive and excitement she'd once exuded had been pulled out of her.

I noticed the floral-painted picture on the wall in the background and realized she was calling me from her office and not her home. "Working late again?"

"Yeah, my current project has been kicking my ass a little," she said, cheeks tinged with embarrassment.

"Mom and Dean should not be pushing you like that," I inserted, feeling protective.

Mandy shook her head. "It's not them. My team needs me." My sister always held herself to ridiculous standards. "Sho's probably expecting me home by now."

"Don't let your soul get crushed by the corporate world." I tried for a joke, but Mandy's eyebrows pinched together.

"I'm not like you." She sounded uncharacteristically defensive. "Mom and Dad work hard. They run a tight ship here, and sometimes they demand a little more than most people can give, but that's okay. I'm not most people."

I was surprised by Mandy's reaction. I hadn't meant to rile her up. "I didn't mean it like that."

But she doubled down, something that surprised me again. "How did you mean it? That I'm somehow just a cog in a machine? Not everyone wants to live your life, Nat."

My own defenses rose. "Mandy, listen to yourself. I just don't want to see what happened to me happen to you." I worried our parents would turn on her the instant she wasn't their perfect protégé, but she didn't have to be treated like that. She could still get out of their clutches.

"You left us, remember? And I'm not unhappy with my life."

Her words felt like a slap, and I wasn't prepared for the sting. I knew what our parents were capable of, and if they manipulated her, then cut her off abruptly as they did to me, I worried it would destroy her.

"I'm sorry. I just don't want them taking advantage of you."

"You don't get it, Natty. I want them to be able to rely on me, and they should be able to. I'm a project manager, and yeah, it's been an undertaking, but I can handle it."

What would a good sister say to that? "Of course, you can, but also, you don't have to follow in their footsteps."

My mother was difficult to get along with, unless you fit the exact mold she laid you into, which I'd tried over and over to do. But over time, I'd learned that there was nothing I could do to make her proud, and when it became apparent that I wasn't that daughter anymore, I'd been cut off, and Mandy became my mom's shining star.

"You know what they did to me," I reasoned.

The prolonged silence had me questioning if Mandy was pulling away. She never really listened to my side of the story, and I always worried about what they'd told her. I could just hear Dean's voice saying, "Nat chose her passion project over her family."

Mandy cleared her throat and answered in a neutral tone. "There are two sides to every story." Ever the diplomat. Maybe she was trying to do peacekeeping, but after I'd tried to reach out last week twice with no reciprocation from my mom, it just felt like a low blow.

"Have you talked to them lately? Did they ask about me?" I asked tentatively.

"No, they haven't said anything about you lately." Her voice was a little sad at the admission, and I wished I hadn't asked. Eventually, I'd have to face my mother, but hopefully, when I did, she wouldn't bitch-button me again. I realized I hadn't responded as tears pricked my eyes. "Nat, wait—"

"No, it's okay, I'll talk with you soon, all right?" Before she could respond, I hung up the phone and pulled the throw blanket up to my chin.

All my emotions were swirling around. It was like she didn't believe me. Her experience with our family was night and day from mine. And I hadn't ever questioned if I'd made the right choice for myself by pursuing my dream, but the truth was, I didn't have the option to be in their lives. They cut me out and started treating me like the black sheep they were ashamed of, all while teaching my younger sister to follow in their footsteps.

Mandy had their shared ambition, yes, but she was also a kind soul. She was someone who saw the good in people. I didn't want that to be the thing they crushed.

Thankfully, Jack gave me privacy. I wasn't ready to go into our room. I pictured his sweet nephew and the fun day we'd had. The way Jack smiled at me as if he had reason to. I'd seen even more of their family. His brother's jovial demeanor as he joked with his lovely wife, Molly. Everyone laughing and chatting.

What would my family become if Mandy decided to have a child with Shoshanna?

I'd want to be that cool aunt for the kid, even if they were on the East Coast, and with that dream also came the knowledge that I'd have to see my family more. My mom's disapproving judgment of my life choices. Their disappointed faces and attitudes whenever I tried to be myself.

I let out a longing sigh. Maybe things would be different by the time children came into the picture, but maybe not. Either way, Jack didn't seem to realize what he had. He was obviously close with his family, and no matter what they'd gone through, he had people who loved him.

FIFTEEN
Nat

THE WORST THING HAPPENED THIS MORNING. I HAD A sex dream about Jack.

His rugged face hadn't annoyed me as much. Especially when it was between my legs. And why was he good at literally everything? Dream Nat didn't have a hard time coming on his tongue. Not one bit.

Which should have been fine. I'd had dreams about people I knew before, and I took them with a grain of salt. But not with people I hated. And definitely not with people I was also stuck living with.

I stared out the window as I washed dishes, zoning out because I could not rid myself of this persistent state of horniness.

Jack grabbed a glass from the drying rack and filled it from the tap, pointing at my hands, which were vigorously scrubbing a cup in the soapy water. "You okay?"

"What? Yeah."

He tilted his head, his eyebrow lifted in disbelief. "Okay."

Then he adjusted his tool belt and went out the front door. The moment the screen slapped against the frame, I turned to make sure he was gone and made my decision. I dropped the plastic cup I'd been cleaning, and bubbles sprayed up my forearms, but I didn't care. I needed to get this out of my system.

I rushed into our room and dug into my suitcase, throwing clothes onto my bed as I searched. How long had it been since I'd last had an orgasm? Just the fact that I was having a hard time remembering meant it had been too long. Then I found it, purple and perfect, my trusty friend that never let me down.

I dropped my yoga pants on the floor and jumped into bed, pulling the sheet up as fast as I could, and closed my eyes.

I let out a breath and turned it on, slipping it inside my underwear. The buzz was a welcome relief as the first vibrations hit their mark. I rolled my neck into the pillow in an attempt to loosen my muscles, but it wasn't that easy to get in the right mood. It could have been because his smell lingered even though he was gone.

I tried to clear my mind.

Relax. I am relaxed. Sooo relaxed.

I didn't expect that to work, but it started feeling good. Adding pressure only improved the experience. I opened my eyes and stared at the bunk above me. At night, I frequently counted all the slats to try to go to sleep, and now I had the urge to do it again. Why couldn't I just turn my brain off and focus on the task at hand? Literally.

But I had no mental stimuli to keep me in it. I turned my head quickly, looking at my empty nightstand. I didn't know what I was thinking, leaving my phone in the kitchen. There were a couple of romance novels on my dresser across the room, but that would mean getting them, finding a scene on the fly, and then holding the book like an eighteenth-century masturbator. No.

Flashes of this morning's dream invaded my brain, but I shoved them down as best I could.

"Lift your shirt, princess."

Dammit.

The words entered my brain without my consent, but I listened to them anyway. I slid the fabric up my stomach, over my bra. I did the same for the bra itself, lifting it over my breasts until they were bare above the sheet.

Dream Jack had been bossy, which wasn't really a surprise, but I'd be lying if I said I didn't enjoy it. His persona was replaced by Fantasy Jack, who placed his hands over my nipples, looking deep into my eyes as he pinched them just hard enough to hurt so good. I let out a whine as I did the same with one hand, the other pulling the vibrator up, then down lightly—a little tease.

Fantasy Jack was wearing too many clothes. Then he wasn't. His bare chest, which I'd seen multiple times, touched my skin, and I imagined what that might feel like. I'd probably never be able to see him without thinking that again, but here we were. He kissed my neck, up the curve of my jaw, to the corner of my mouth. A slight tremor went through my legs as I imagined his other hand working its way down my torso. God, I bet the man would be good with his hands. They were large and calloused, with long fingers. He'd...

I turned up the vibrator and whimpered, looking over to his side of the room. His pillow was right there. Would it be wrong if I just put it under my head and sniffed it while I—

Nope. Not going there. No way.

Fantasy Jack had gotten my pants off and was fingering me oh so good. Then he was entering me, his grip on my hips impossibly tight.

"That's it, Nat. Take all my dick."

Fuck.

"Do you quiver like this for everyone, or am I just special?"

Even Fantasy Jack was a tool. So why did I like it?

How were thoughts of him working so well to scratch this itch? It wasn't like I hadn't caught myself looking at his lips. The way he walked with purpose. That cocky grin that came out at all the wrong times and infuriated me to no end.

I upped the vibrations again, on the precipice. His hand crept up my collarbone, right to my neck, his thumb pressing on my...

The vibrator slipped down, and I couldn't feel it in the right spot. I tried to get it back to where it belonged.

Right as the door slammed in the other room.

My eyes burst open. Was I making that up?

Then I heard boots walking in the living room. "You here, Nat?"

Oh. God. I rushed to turn the vibrator off, but it only upped the setting, which felt fucking amazing. I pressed it again. Then again. And finally, it turned off. As the steps got closer, I let it drop, realizing my tits were just out, and yanked the blanket over them just as Jack entered.

"Oh."

"Hey." The word came out breathy. I cleared my throat. "Hey."

Jack tilted his head in confusion. "You okay? The sink is still filled with water and dishes."

"What?" I croaked. "Yeah, I'll get to them. I was just..." The words hovered in the air as my mind went blank. *Say. Something.* "I got a headache."

Jack turned to leave. He must have known something was up. But he came back thirty seconds later with an ice pack wrapped in a dish towel. He approached me, and I reached under the sheet, stopping myself before he saw that I was semi-topless. I must have looked like the big bad wolf with this thing pulled up to my chin.

He pushed my hair away from my forehead and placed the pack in its place.

"Thank you."

Jack nodded. "You sure you're okay? I thought I heard you groan, and you look flushed. Do you want me to grab you some—"

"No. No. I already took something. I'm just lying in the dark, trying to chill."

He narrowed his eyes. "The light's on."

"Not when my eyes are closed." Again, the urge to pull my

hand out of this blanket and point at my eyes came, and I clutched my thigh to stop myself.

"Those meds must be kicking in. You sure you don't need anything else?" Man, of all the times for him to be nice to me.

"Nope. Thank you." I tried to sound sincere, but I was more stressed than anything. He had no reason to peel the blanket down, thank god.

By the time he left, mentioning something about missing his favorite hammer or whatever, I was amped up and desperate. Details of him flooded in. He'd had sweat on his brow, probably from walking in the heat, and a hole in his shirt just below his collarbone. I wondered what it'd feel like to stick my finger between the broken fibers, touching solid muscle, feeling the warmth of his skin.

I lifted my head off the pillow and listened as best I could. He was gone. I was safe. I turned it back on, doing my best to get back into the moment. I'd seen the outline of him under his sweats a dozen times, and that wasn't even with him being hard. He had to be big. It would fit so well between my thighs...

The vibrations ended. I pressed the button again. And again. And again and again.

The whine that came out of me was unseemly. I turned my head, and the ice pack I'd forgotten about slipped along with its towel, the cold side landing on my neck. The sound that followed that was no more dignified than the first. I pulled the vibrator from beneath the sheets and had the world's worst staring contest.

I was wrong. Apparently, it could fail me.

"If you're stumped, you should try the lobster gyoza. It's my favorite."

A smiling Chase peeked at me from behind his menu. He

seemed so naturally friendly, and it had me contemplating why Jack had looked so weird when my date picked me up. He'd been confused when Chase arrived and more confused when Chase told him he was taking me out to dinner. The look had been a flash of something I'd never seen from him before, but I wasn't going to read into it.

"I love lobster gyoza," I said, though I'd never had it in my life. At least I knew I liked lobster.

We went to the Pinecrest Lodge's Asian fusion restaurant, Sakura, whose dress code was semi-casual. My feet were nearly healed, so I was able to wear flats and a sundress, which I appreciated.

Sakura was one of three restaurants at the resort. There was also Hidden Hearth, their Michelin-star restaurant, and Après-Ski, a quirky hole-in-the-wall on top of the mountain that primarily dealt in warm cocktails. This one was more mid-tier and was one of my favorites in town.

Chase had offered to take me out of Wildwood, but I'd told him there was no need. Something about the familiarity made me happy. And this restaurant was unique in that it had a life-size fake cherry tree in the middle, with pink-petaled flowers dangling overhead.

Chase was the quintessential gentleman. He wore a button-up plaid shirt, with sleeves and everything, even in eighty-five-degree heat. It must have been stifling. It also may have explained why they were accidentally misbuttoned, but I didn't want to say anything. His jeans were dark blue and snug. His shoes weren't covered in dirt. It might have been a low bar, but we did live in the wilderness. Despite his overeager look, he seemed perfectly comfortable and was easy to talk to.

We ordered our food, along with their nicest thirty-dollar bottle of sake, which Chase had asked for with a grin.

Once the small talk was out of the way and our server had left, we were all alone. I twiddled with the napkin in my lap and stared at the paper tablecloth, which was temporarily blocked from view when Chase handed me a crayon to draw.

"I've always wanted to know, what's it like to be a travel influencer?"

I sketched some evergreen trees. Chase was drawing what looked like a dog. "It's great. I get to go all over the place, obviously. Um... I try food from all over. I meet a lot of cool people." Why did this sound like a middle school report on what I did last summer?

I lifted my head and found him smiling at me. Again.

I continued, this time a little more eloquently. "I like being able to see how different cultures are, even across the continental US. The helpful locals, their favorite hole-in-the-wall restaurants, and the waterfalls off the beaten path. I create my itineraries in advance, but I always leave some wiggle room for when someone local recommends somewhere specific I need to try. It's a lot of work maintaining both the business and social sides, but it's worth it." I took a sip of my wine, swishing it in my mouth. "I like being a nomad because it allows me to fly under the radar a little."

"Under the radar? You don't run into people who know who you are?"

"I mean, occasionally, but interactions are usually harmless these days. It's nothing compared to how they used to be when I was little." Shit. I tried to let it go, but he waited patiently for an explanation. "I was in the public eye, even before this, I guess. My last name is Breckenridge." I kicked myself for my slipup. I didn't need people to know who I was.

Chase's eyes went wide. "Like, the famous Breckenridges?" His face shifted from confusion to understanding. "Wasn't your grandfather a vice president?"

"Yep." My grandfather's platform when he ran for president was family first. I'd been to more political events than I could count. My father's unexpected death had been fodder for months.

And now my mother ran one of the biggest holding companies in the country, spanning generations.

"That must have been really hard as a kid."

I had a lot of privilege, but my childhood wasn't a cakewalk. "It got a lot better once they stopped forcing me to go to events. But there is a reason my real name isn't tied to my account. I still get randos messaging me when they figure it out." I shrugged, ready for a subject change. "What about you? What state are you from again?"

He talked about his hometown in Montana, which was even smaller than Wildwood. I watched him light up, talking about the differences, and found myself thinking about how handsome he was when he smiled, which was pretty much always. He'd never fit into my family, who were more known for their drive, not their kindness.

Chase had this boy-next-door look. He exuded friendliness in a way Jack never could. His face couldn't hide anything if he tried, and his dimple made me want to pat his cheek like an auntie. He had cared about his outfit today. There wasn't a wrinkle in sight, unlike the well-worn T-shirt Jack had on before I left. His ruggedness and off-putting attitude that he always showed around me definitely didn't belong in a nice restaurant like this.

And now Jack was back in my head, the last place I wanted him to be.

Had I really just attempted to get myself off to him on the same day as this date? Guilt washed over me. Was it wrong to use your enemy as masturbation material when you had a date with another person? If the orgasm didn't happen, did it even count? My answer was no, and this was a first date anyway, so I should stop being hard on myself. The event was a fluke, triggered by feelings stirred by a dream. They weren't real. And it was never going to happen. But it still aggravated me.

"Nat?"

"Sorry, what?"

Chase seemed unfazed by my inability to pay attention. "I asked about your time at Starlight last year. Were you a counselor the entire summer?"

"No, I was only here for six weeks. Someone had to leave, and Hazel asked if I could make myself free. It's nice having a regular bed for a little while. It can get rough living out of a car."

He nodded. "I bet. And now you're dealing with it again. How has that living arrangement been?"

"Oh. Well, that's been tricky."

Chase smiled, waiting for me to elaborate. I reached for my nearly empty glass of wine and realized it was starting to go to my head, so I held back.

"If it had been anyone other than Jack, I'd be fine. But he's exhausting. And messy. And he does this thing where he thinks the temperature should be kept at sixty. I'm going to freeze, Chase. Death by AC. Not to mention he's more moody than he'll admit to and even more stubborn."

"Oh, boy."

"He also wears shoes in the house and purposely uses the hot water while I'm showering." I was on a roll. "And he doesn't know when to just admit he's wrong. And he has zero taste in music. But it's fine. Just fine."

Right as I realized I'd been bitching, I noticed a couple walking our way. Kai, the craft store owner, greeted us, accompanied by his boyfriend, Simon, the general store owner.

I waved. "Hi, you two. How was dinner?"

"Good," they said in unison. "Great," they both tried, as if to sound original but failing. The four of us laughed, garnering the attention of a few patrons.

"The lobster gyoza is really good if you haven't ordered yet," Simon pointed out.

Chase nodded in agreement. "That's what I said."

The men lingered as if waiting for something, and I realized how rude I'd been. "I don't know if you've met, but this is Chase. He's a counselor, too."

I made their introductions, and Chase stood to shake hands, garnering supportive looks from the couple.

Kai smiled at me as if we were in cahoots. He seemed to approve. So why was my head not here with Chase?

"Well, we'll leave you to it." Kai grinned. "Nat."

"Kai," I said with the tone of a disgruntled teenager. "Simon."

The two walked away, whispering as if they had a juicy secret.

I lightly drew a sideways oval on the paper. Without thinking, I sketched a bird. A fucking bird.

"So, who do you think is going to win the competition? First person to say themself pays for dinner." He beamed.

"I don't know. If it's not me—and no, that didn't count—I'd say Lamar. What about you?"

Before he could answer that question, our server arrived with our food. It smelled like perfection, and for a moment, I almost forgot about the competition.

"My money's on Sawyer. Or Jack."

Blood rushed in my ears. "Jack." I stabbed a gyoza with a little too much force.

"Well, I figured it'd come off as pandering if I said you. But if it isn't one of us, I'd put money on him. He's pretty ruthless."

"Ruthless, petty, asinine. Take your pick." I took another sip of wine, finishing the glass, and Chase bit his lip, probably regretting his choice instantly. "He's a perpetual annoyance. Oh, and he snores."

The server dropped our bill on our table, and Chase pulled out his card at the same time as I did. I planned to place it on the bill, but instead of gracefully landing where it belonged, it flung across the table and landed in Chase's water glass.

I had a feeling I'd completely fucked up this date.

CHASE WALKED ME TO MY DOOR EVEN THOUGH I TOLD him I'd be fine. My previous interactions with him had proven that arguing with him was pointless when it came to chivalry.

The flickering light on Jack's porch went out suddenly, catching both of our attention and creating a romantic ambience I didn't think either of us wanted. Chase smiled at what was probably a wince on my part.

"Well, I had a great time," I said, like you were supposed to. I didn't want him to read into it.

"Yeah, me too." The strain in his voice further cemented my failure.

"I'm sorry, I was a bad date," I blurted.

"You're not a bad date. You're just... Look, I've been on enough first dates to tell when it's not going to happen."

"You have?"

"Let's just say I'm a hopeful romantic who hasn't been at the right place at the right time. Yet. But it's all good. Have a nice night, Nat."

"You too." My eyes hadn't quite adjusted as I reached out a hand to shake his, but he pulled me into a hug with my arm trapped between us, putting the cherry on top of this awkward date sundae.

I opened the screen door, surprised to find Jack pacing back and forth in the kitchen. Had he seen that interaction? God, I hoped not.

"The porch light went out." I pointed behind me as the screen door creaked shut.

Jack looked up, stunned. "Oh. I'll get to that."

Might as well make "I'll get to that" his middle name. His schedule was challenging, but did he really not see that he was putting off his own needs for those of every other person in this camp?

"You know I can help, right?"

He stared at me, but didn't respond.

I shrugged, toeing off my shoes, and made my way to the couch, pulling my feet up and massaging my tired instep. I let out a groan and lifted my eyes to find him staring. "Did you want to sit down? I can move over." I didn't expect him to take me up on the offer, but he was there in five seconds, and I pulled my feet under me.

He popped the top off a beer and handed it to me before doing the same with his own.

I took the drink gratefully. "How was your night?"

"My night? Great. It was great. What about yours?" His delivery was stern, almost as if he didn't actually want to know. Why was he acting weird?

"It was... great." Apparently, awkward was all that was in the cards for my night. "It was a good date," I lied, the same way I did most times people asked me how I was doing. It wasn't like things were terrible, but they definitely weren't wonderful.

"I'm glad."

Confusion marred my thoughts as I admitted, "That was my first date in a while. I think I forgot how to do it." Was it just me, or did Jack's eyes brighten at that? "I should have known better. These things don't often go well for me. What about you?"

"I don't date." He peeled the label off his bottle and left it on the coffee table, but I didn't have it in me to fight right now. Then his words sank in.

"Really?" It was a bit of a surprise. The man was objectively handsome and usually not the bane of people's existence.

"Yeah." He didn't elaborate, just gave me very direct eye contact, as if he knew all my secrets. It was unnerving.

"Well, that's a shame."

What was I saying? The way he was acting was definitely

strange and had me running through every scenario where he could be annoyed or frustrated with me. I landed on the worst of all worst-case scenarios: wondering whether I'd put my vibrator away after cleaning it this morning. Oh. God. I scanned through my memories of this morning, stopping on the one where he squeezed my throat during my fantasy—I cringed at that thought—and remembered washing it in the bathroom sink, shaking it dry, putting it back in my suitcase. I let out a puff of air. Okay, that couldn't be it. But maybe he had seen my awkward goodbye?

"What were you up to?"

Jack took a sip of the beer he'd placed on the table. "I stayed in. Finished the dishes. Talked with my mom for a while."

"Must be nice." Apparently, the wine had gotten to me. I hadn't meant to say that out loud.

Jack didn't miss it, unfortunately. "What do you mean?"

"It's nothing. I just haven't spoken with my mom in a few years. The last time I called, she sent me to voicemail." I twisted the hair tie from my wrist, and it snapped against me. Ow. "I talk to my sister, though."

Jack did me a kindness by not asking why that was. "I didn't know you had a sister."

Really? Because you sure do know everything about me. The tone in my head was laced with resentment. I didn't care if it was spiteful.

"She's actually my stepsister. We're seven years apart. My mom and stepfather, Dean, married when I was twelve. But Mandy's my favorite thing about them getting together."

"What's she like?"

I leaned my head back on the couch and smiled. "She's sweet. Loves baking and reality TV. And she's funny. She was always putting on these plays when she was little. I occasionally contributed, but I don't have an acting bone in my body. She can do anything. She's working her way through the company at an alarming speed. I just hope she chooses to forge her own path, you know?"

"Are you concerned she won't?"

"I'm worried she'll become a little clone of our parents." I didn't usually reveal this information, but this was one of the only times Jack and I had ever had a heart-to-heart, and I figured I could give him something. Plus, it felt nice to say out loud instead of internalizing everything. "I worked for their company for years, until I quit to travel blog full time. Then I was no longer welcome at home."

Jack stared, his lips slightly open. "They disowned you?"

"Disowned me, shunned me, whatever you want to call it." I took a sip of my beer, my cheeks warming at my admission. "The Breckenridge reputation always comes first, the business a close second, and like a lot of families in our social circle, anything else was unacceptable. Mandy might not share our last name, but she's an honorary one, just the same. In this circumstance, I just want to be able to see my sister for the holidays. Even if she thinks I need to extend an olive branch first, also known as coming home with my tail between my legs. Who knows? Maybe someday they'll get over it and welcome me back, but I don't see that happening any time soon."

"And you'd want that?"

His question caught me off guard. I was surprised an answer rolled off the tip of my tongue. "I mean, they are my family."

"Yeah, but not everybody deserves a second chance."

I blinked a few times and considered this. I'd taken the first step in calling them, but I didn't have a real plan after they'd answered. I was almost desperate enough to apologize, but I didn't know what strings would come with that apology.

"Maybe. But enough about my family. What about yours?"

He took a long sip of his beer, and I considered getting up. It was hard enough to reveal my darkest secrets without any reciprocation. But then he offered something in return.

"My family isn't perfect either. My parents had a pretty awful divorce when I was a kid, so I ended up having to pick a side. I actually moved to Palo Alto in my twenties to spend some time with my dad and work for his construction company, but it didn't strengthen our relationship any. He still blames me for picking my mom when I was fourteen. It was like he took it as a personal betrayal that my brother and I stayed. I just didn't want to leave my mom and friends to start over at a new school, but he never seemed to get over that. He is known to blame everyone but himself anyway, so we never really recovered. But my mom is wonderful, and so is my brother. Sometimes I wish I saw my dad, but also, with how we left things, he doesn't deserve a second chance until he reaches out, and it's been years. So I guess in that way, we're in the same boat." He took a deep breath, and we let a long moment sit between us before he continued. "So yeah, I have a shitty dad, but at least he's still around. I can only imagine what you went through when you lost yours."

I hadn't expected that. When I met his steely blue eyes, he seemed unsure if he should have broached this topic with me or not. I put my hand over his for a second before returning to run my glittery nails along the empty beer bottle's label.

I was glad to talk about my dad. It had been a while since someone had asked me about him. "I miss him like crazy. He had this way of making you feel like you were the most important person in the universe. He didn't have the easiest life as a politician's son, and he gave me the attention he never had himself. He never lost his cool or made me feel like I didn't matter." I turned to face him. "You'd be a great dad, you know."

Jack raised an eyebrow. "What makes you think that?"

"The way you are with Jordy. The way you are with your friends. I get the feeling they could come to you with any problem, and you'd solve it."

"Wow, Nat. That's one of the best compliments I've ever received."

"I just thought it was obvious." It was hard not to think about how I didn't have anyone I could go to like that, and it didn't look like that was going to change anytime soon. I cleared my throat. "Do you want kids?"

"I love kids. But I don't know if that's in the cards for me," he said with a twinge of resignation. I wanted him to elaborate, but he turned the tables on me before I could ask for clarification. "What about you?"

"I'd like the same, but I'm hopeful. I'd love to be someone's person. And I'd love to raise my kids to know they can do whatever they want to do, and I'll still love them no matter what."

Jack smiled softly as if he understood exactly what I meant by that admission. "I'm sure you will."

I felt cut open, and yet, Jack didn't take advantage of my vulnerability. Instead, he offered me understanding and a tenderness that felt foreign and necessary. My heart pounded with the realization.

I needed to put some distance between us. "Well, I think I'm going to go take a shower." Maybe I could wash away the awkwardness that coated me after that date. "Night, Jack."

"Goodnight, princess."

SIXTEEN
Jack

After our unexpectedly personal conversation, Nat went to sleep, but I was wired. The moment Chase had picked her up, an emotion I couldn't define had filled my senses. Made me... jittery.

How did she have time to date someone out here?

I was not upset. I wasn't.

She could do what she wanted. After all, relationships were for fools. A huge percentage of them didn't work out, and then most marriages ended in divorce. I didn't care that it was cynical. I wasn't playing those odds.

She sure had looked beautiful when she left, though. Her hair was curly instead of wavy, and she wore this little sundress that had lacy shoulders that gave you the barest peek of skin, which was somehow more alluring than the places her body was visible. She just glowed.

And the talk we had when she'd gotten back, where I learned more about her? I'd enjoyed it, up until we got to the part about me not dating. I hadn't wanted to hash out the Gia stuff I'd been avoiding. Hoping to shove it under the rug, more like. I didn't want to deal with it myself and especially not with Nat.

I hated her. So why did images of her standing close to Chase under the moonlight keep flooding my mind?

I needed to remind myself that I didn't care about who people dated, least of all her. And even if I did have some kind of feelings for her, however small they were, I wouldn't act on them. I wasn't going to date anyone, not any time soon. Maybe ever again.

But I did have to admit she was the first person who had piqued my interest that way since Gia. I hated Nat even more for it.

Only, that wasn't true. When it came down to it, I enjoyed getting to know her more. I liked how she was slowly opening up to me, in the quiet space of our bedroom, more than I'd thought I would. I found myself hanging on to her every word when she did. Slowly, I realized I hated how much more I wanted to know about her.

A message popped up on my phone, and I swiped quickly upon seeing Jordy's name. What was he texting me so late about?

Nat. Of course, it was Nat. Apparently, she'd followed him on his socials. Before that, there had been just nine of us, most of whom were family. And Jordy was ecstatic, given the ten or so exclamation points after "*Naturegirlnat followed me.*"

I shot back my nicest "*That's awesome,*" with an exclamation point of my own, even though that wasn't really my thing. It was nice of her to follow Jordy. She had been so sweet with him, giving him tips and helping him learn about what she did. There was no condescension, only kindness. And from the way she explained her process, I realized there were a lot of things I'd made stupid assumptions about. With every bit of new information, she was more and more intriguing.

Maybe I should just let this whole thing go with her. If I were being honest with myself, I wanted to stop holding this anger. It wasn't sitting well, and it hadn't in a long time.

I decided to go for a walk to clear my head. My creaky door swung behind me, slamming into the frame. "Come on."

I waited in the dark of my porch for Nat to come out of our room and complain, but she didn't. The last thing I needed was to see her in those cute short shorts she slept in. I wondered if they would be the pink pair with red polka dots. Or the gray ones with llamas on them. And just like that, I was back to my internal debate of which was better: Nat in sleep shorts or in my T-shirt and sweats. Would I be forever cursed with these images?

Fuck. Now I really needed to clear my head.

The moon shone brightly over camp, so much so that I didn't need a flashlight, even under the cover of tall trees.

"Jack, wait."

I turned to find Jamie in athletic attire, sweaty and out of breath. I didn't realize the man even stayed up this late, but clearly, he had something on his mind.

"What's up?"

Jamie wiped the sweat from his brow and stopped jogging in place. "I need to talk to you about something. I'm planning on asking Autumn to marry me."

I couldn't stop my jaw from dropping at that admission. But it quickly morphed into a smile. It had been nearly a year since they'd gotten back together. He made my best friend happy, so he was good in my book.

"And you need my blessing? Well, James, I must say, I've been waiting for this moment for what feels like forever."

Jamie lifted a thumb over his shoulder. "I knew I should have gone to Leo about this."

"Wrong. Leo's a terrible secret keeper." The man couldn't even keep his secret Santa pick to himself. "Even with him being gone, all of camp would already know everything by now if you had."

Jamie shrugged. "I guess all of you suck."

"I'm willing to ignore that comment." After all, some days he was right. "That's great, though, Jamie. Really."

"I'd be excited if I wasn't so nervous. It's also her birthday. But it was the only way I could get both of our families here without her suspecting anything."

I could tell he needed a confidence boost. "She's going to say yes. You know she will." I gave him a pat on the back. "I usually get her a Super Soaker or LEGOs or something. Look at you getting her a ring."

Jamie shrugged, as if he wasn't convinced. "Yeah, maybe. I know it's fast, but I want to get started on our life, you know? And it just feels right. But I'm here because I need you to do me a huge favor. I found this ring that screamed Autumn, but it had to be shipped here. It's supposed to arrive on Wednesday, but I'm going to a mediation in Emerald Falls, so I can't sign for it."

"What's the window?"

"Sometime between one and three." He winced. "I can get coverage after that, but I need someone to hang out at my office. I couldn't get the thing delivered here, you know?"

Wednesday was two days away. I thought over my plans. I could make it happen. This was obviously important. "I can do that."

"You're a lifesaver. I'm going to propose on Thursday. Our families will be here for her birthday, and it's her day off, so..."

"That sounds great, Jamie. Looks like you have it all planned out."

"I need it to work. I can't keep holding on to this secret. She's the best thing that's ever happened to me."

I smiled at that. "Of course. It'll all work out."

"You have got to be kidding me, Jack." Nat swept in like a whirlwind, partially deflated multicolored balloons parting at her feet. Her face was two shades redder than usual, and I could already tell this was going to go poorly.

She burst onto my side of the room, which had been designated as such by a blue line of painter's tape right down the middle. The night she'd taped it, I'd had half a mind to tell her that it only allowed for her to use half the doorway, but I'd figured I should pick my battles.

"What is it, Nat?"

"How can you be lying there when this place is such a pigsty?" She gestured to the empty stack of bins at the base of my bed and the pile of stuff I'd placed there after making space for her in front of it. I'd had every intention of shoving things inside after I'd bought them, but I hadn't gotten around to it. "And how have you still not cleaned up these balloons?"

She shoved a creeping pile of winter clothes over the line with her foot, and my blood started to boil.

Nat acted as if she had been living in a warzone. Sure, this room was the worst, but at least I knew where everything was. She had yet to see the second bedroom, which was a blessing considering her reaction to this.

I'd tidied the living room, removed all the work supplies, and piled up the mail. But before all this, the kitchen and bathroom had always been clean. I wasn't an animal. And she could walk from point A to point B easily. Wasn't that enough?

"Maybe I'm waiting for the perpetrator to clean them."

"Good luck with that." A smug look spread across her face, further instilling my belief that she had been the one to prank me. How she'd gotten into my cabin, though, I was still trying to figure out. Maybe she'd popped out a screen to an open window?

"And to answer your question, the reason I'm lying down is that I'm tired." And man, was that an understatement. Between doing my daily camp duties, attending to my pod, and working on her cabin, I'd barely had time to breathe. Which was why her griping like I was lazy the second I had a moment to sit down was getting on my last nerve.

"You're tired? I'm tired of functioning in this mess. This is where I sleep. This is where I work."

"Then maybe you should work elsewhere. Maybe you should get out of the cabin more."

Her face twisted with shock and indignation. Apparently, that was the wrong thing to say.

"My job," she said through clenched teeth, "requires my attention sixteen hours a day. I can't just sit at a desk and stop at five o'clock. And I don't have time to just rest."

"Not all of us work the way you do, Nat. And it sounds like even you're doing too much." Coming from me, that was a hypocritical statement. We had a surprising number of things in common because I'd often been told the same thing, and just like her, I ignored it.

"I'm not about to justify..." She took a breath. "You know what? No."

She threw her purple hard-shelled suitcase on her bunk bed and started shoving things from her nightstand into it.

I jumped to my feet. "What are you doing?"

"You just told me to get out of the house more, and this isn't working. I'm just going to sleep outside." That was the moment the rain started to clatter against the window. What was with this summer? Her eyes raised, and she sighed in frustration. "I've done it before."

"It's pouring."

"Fine. Then I'll sleep in my car."

This time, I was the one with clenched teeth. "You're sleeping in your car over my dead body."

I shut the case, and she turned around to find me right in her face. How were we always finding ourselves in this position?

"That's what's going to happen if I don't get out of here."

I sighed, resigned. I wasn't mad at her. This was a product of circumstance. I had to remember that. "Look, I'm doing my best. I haven't been able to get any of my crew to work on the cabin with me, and I keep running into supply issues. But someone just reached out, so I'll follow up and see what we can do. It would make things go a lot faster, and I'll have more energy to do… all of this."

"Okay." Her hackles lowered. "But why can't I help?"

"At this juncture, the shit I have to do over there would take more time to explain than it would just to do it myself. Plus, there's electrical work that even I can't do." I contemplated all the jobs I could give her, but it wasn't the right time. "I'm sorry, Nat. I get that it's frustrating."

She let out a long breath. "It's okay. I know that you're doing a lot." For once, it felt like she was getting it. "But you'll let me know if I can help, right?"

Her optimistic gaze had me nearly crumbling. And she wanted us to spend more time together? That was a recipe for disaster, much like my cake during the baking competition.

"Yeah, I'll let you know."

THE NEXT DAY HAD ME RUSHING. IT WAS THE FINAL DAY for this session of campers, so I went through my typical last-day routine, followed by getting some time in at Nat's cabin. I'd even given Autumn an excuse for why I needed to go to the hardware store later, so she didn't ask questions about why I was gone while I accepted Jamie's ring delivery. The only thing I needed were my keys, and I'd be good to go.

My phone vibrated, and I pulled it from my pocket as I power walked on the trail to my cabin. As soon as I saw Gia's name, asking if we could please talk, I stopped dead in my tracks.

Talk? What did she need to talk about?

The week she cheated on me, Gia had been a visiting camper for the final camp session. After I'd confronted her about making out with someone else, she'd made her teary exit. I'd told her to ship the stuff I'd left at her apartment back to me, and I'd done the same for her. We'd had no contact in almost a year. Maybe she was trying to explain herself beyond *I was drunk*. But why now?

Maybe she'd learned Nat was here and wanted to see her? Then they could fuck each other in my cabin and really put the nail in the coffin.

Okay, that was a stretch. Sometimes I hated my brain.

I stared at the text for too long before I noticed the time. I had to get my ass in gear. I started into a light jog, grateful to see my cabin in the clearing, but nothing could have prepared me for what I was about to walk in on.

It was like Cinderella's rodent friends had visited. Everything was different. The balloons were gone. There was not a single project material or tool in view. The mail was separated into neat piles on my coffee table.

I walked into the kitchen, where the counters literally sparkled. The last place I remembered throwing my car keys was on the counter, but they weren't there. I went into my room and found an equally clean place, except for a basket of laundry I'd been meaning to get to sitting at the end of my bed. The winter clothes I'd been ignoring were placed in the bins at the end of my bed, all of them labeled. Where did she get a label maker?

I searched my nightstand, and they weren't there either.

I rushed out to find Nat with a new pile of mail she'd obviously picked up at the office.

She was playing "Home," by Edward Sharpe and the Magnetic Zeros, an indie song she'd been obsessed with, on her phone's speaker. The song made my hackles rise. It was okay the first dozen times I'd heard it, but now, it contaminated this place. That and the smell of lemon cleaner.

"*Nat,*" I said through gritted teeth.

"*Jack.*" Her voice was equally gritty, directly mocking my tone. "What did you do?"

She walked into the living room and put the mail into the sorted piles, holding three envelopes as the song repeated itself. She whistled the opening to the song as she opened one letter and focused on it instead of looking me in the eye. "I can't live in chaos, Jack."

"That doesn't answer my question." Maybe I was blowing this out of proportion, but all I could think about was that nothing was where it should be, and it would be a pain in the ass to find anything.

"If you can't get there with context clues, I guess I'll spell it out. This place was a mess, and you told me you don't have time to do anything about it. I was going out of my mind, so I fixed it."

"You fixed it." My cheeks heated. Why was this bothering me so much? Oh yeah, because she was overbearing.

"I couldn't live like that. My ADHD won't allow it."

That had me shrinking just a bit, but only enough to prevent me from blowing my top.

"Where is everything?" I sifted through a basket of miscellany that was sitting in my entryway, sifting for my keys. How did I have so many loose batteries and pushpins? I definitely hadn't bought those. It put things into perspective when they were gathered together like this.

She scoffed, leaning over the little entry table to place everything back in the basket. "In the place it belongs."

I lifted my chin, glaring at her with the fire of a thousand suns. "I don't have time for this. Where are my keys?"

"Where they should be." Why was she making this so difficult? "On the hook. Near the door." She pointed at the hooks I'd clearly forgotten about.

I reached for them, right beside that damn frog keychain, muttered, "Thanks a lot," and burst through the door, which slammed into the siding. I really needed to fix that.

She rushed around me, blocking my exit down the porch. "If

you think you're going to be pissed at me for helping, you're out of your mind."

"You'd deserve it," I barked. "Get out of my way."

This angered her even further. She was about to blow a fuse, I could see the signs as clear as day. Her breaths came in short, rapid-fire bursts, and she was practically vibrating. "No," she spat back.

I picked her up by her biceps and lifted her to the side of me, while she looked on in shock. That didn't stop her, though. She kept pace as she followed alongside me.

"I can't believe you just did that."

"You'll get over it. Or you can yell at me on the way. Your choice."

And man, did she yell.

I drove down the highway and learned that I was a slob. A bad roommate. A general drain on society. She was obviously tired from doing all that work, because her insults were not as impressive as usual. Honestly, I expected more from her.

She was annoyed at me for not being grateful and for, in her words, throwing a fit. She worked up a sweat and squared her shoulders as if prepared to go into battle. But I seemed to surprise her, because I didn't fight back. I let her get it all out.

Nat tilted her head at me as I parallel parked next to Jamie's office. "What are we even doing?"

I didn't answer. It was none of her business.

I glanced at Jamie's empty office and opted not to get out until this was over. Then I turned to her and gave her the fight she was looking for. "If you're so dead set on attacking me for all my flaws, how about we go over yours?" She looked shocked for a moment, and I pushed on, ticking each offense off my fingers in front of her face. "You're invasive. Exhausting. Petty. You knew I had too much on my plate—we'd just talked about that—"

"That's why I was helping—" She pulled my hand down, trying to meet my eyes, but this wasn't done.

I cut her off. "You did that for you. You did that to get a one-up on me. And you did it because you're self-satisfied, impatient, and annoying."

Nat was stunned silent for a moment, but that didn't last long. Her eyes flared with irritation. We stared each other down. She was so stubborn.

"You know what, Jack? If that's how you really feel, then you can go ahead and shove it up your—"

I placed my hand over her mouth. "Wait."

She blew a raspberry into my palm. I fought everything in me not to look at her, but I was focused on something much more jarring.

A little yellow paper on the office door fluttered in the breeze. I jumped out of the car, and surprise, surprise, so did she. We'd just missed the delivery.

How had we missed it? I took in my surroundings and saw a brown delivery truck right down the street. I chased after it, but it went past the stop sign, a little too fast for this small town's liking, and pulled onto the road. I made it halfway down the street before realizing that was pointless and rushed back to my car. She stood by the passenger side door, staring at me, dumbfounded.

I ripped the door open and jumped in. She clearly got her shit together because she did the same.

We chased the vehicle for thirty minutes, but we never got the opportunity to talk with the driver. Once I explained the situation to Nat, she immediately jumped into action, calling around, but was left on hold. It didn't matter. You couldn't drive a delivery vehicle off the road, especially when they were going sixty miles per hour, and you were low on gas.

I pulled over at a gas station and banged my head against the wheel. Nat had the decency not to fight with me anymore when she realized this was bigger than both of us.

Jamie was never going to trust me again. I'd failed, and I was fucked.

SEVENTEEN
Nat

I'D BEEN KEEPING MY EYES OPEN FOR JAMIE ALL NIGHT. The tall lawyer shouldn't have been this elusive. He had to be off work by now, which meant he should be at the campfire with his goofy, soon-to-be fiancée, but I'd checked the campfire three times already, and nothing.

The guilt I was lugging around felt heavier with each passing moment. Jack and I both agreed to find Jamie and apologize for the insane way we'd behaved earlier today. I had been right about the cabin needing to be cleaned and about how frustrating he was as a person, but even I could recognize when I was being childish and letting my nemesis get under my skin.

And speaking of my nemesis... Jack seemed equally antsy to get our apology over with. I'd heard regret in his voice as we both recognized that we'd messed up royally this afternoon. Tonight, we'd make it right.

I lapped the main parts of camp again. I found Autumn near the campfire, so I avoided her seeing me. Perhaps I'd catch him coming back from the mess hall with snacks. Or from the restrooms? Okay, maybe I was being a little obsessive, but I needed to get to Jamie before Jack threw me under the bus.

I'd already called Jamie twice, but his phone had gone straight to voicemail. For some reason, it felt like even apologizing to Jamie was a competition now. Jack seemed to have the same mindset, since we'd passed each other twice tonight, and both times, we'd eyed each other and kept walking.

On the third inconvenient run-in, however, Jack turned on his heel and walked in my direction outside the main office. "Nat," he acknowledged, slowing his stride.

I pushed my headphones off my ears. I'd been driving Jack up the wall with an old indie band I'd rediscovered recently. It was probably about time to change it up.

I matched his pace and, expertly, his glare. "Jack."

He quirked a grin, no doubt about to say something that I'd make him regret, when voices caught us off guard. Our heads whipped in unison toward the front office door.

Leo's voice was easy to pick out, but hearing Jamie's voice had Jack and me both start for the door. Annoyingly, the competition between us to apologize first would have to end in another tie. Great. Maybe I'd just make sure mine was better. Yeah.

We both stepped inside, hoping we weren't interrupting. Jamie greeted us kindly, which neither of us deserved.

Jack took another step inside and looked Jamie in the eyes. "I'm really sorry, man."

I nodded along, equally dejected. "Me too," I chimed in. So much for an award-winning apology.

"You didn't get it?" Jamie's eyes filled with worry as he stared at our guilty faces, and it made me feel ten times worse.

"I just missed it. I chased the driver for five miles. Right, Nat?"

"Right."

"Okay. I'll get this figured out." He started pacing. "Her birthday is tomorrow, and our parents are coming, but it's going to be fine." He repeated the phrase while wringing his hands.

We both cringed at his nervous words. We'd only succeeded in giving him more stress.

"Jack and I called the delivery company close to thirty times by now, but we keep getting told it's in transit." I was tired of doing it, but I would all night if that was what it took. I wanted Jamie to know we were doing everything we could to make this right.

When he didn't say anything, I kept talking. "Maybe you could propose on a different day?" I pondered, even though I hated the suggestion.

Jamie shook his head, firm this time. "No, it has to happen tomorrow." He didn't elaborate. Guess it needed to happen tomorrow. Then something like determination crossed Jamie's face, and he walked past us. "I have an idea," he muttered to himself, lost in thought.

"Let us know if you need anything," I offered, and Jack echoed the same behind me. Jamie smiled and took off with a little more confidence.

"I wish I could say I'm surprised." Leo's voice was calm and took on a serious tone I'd never heard him use. Jack and I both turned to face him. He rose from his desk, arms crossed, with an air of *you know what you did.* Camp dad didn't usually get mad, but here he was, looking at us with narrowed eyes and a disappointment that felt so much worse than being yelled at ever could. "After the trip Hazel and I just had, I really didn't want to deal with something like this, but I guess here we are."

I wanted to ask him how things went in the couple of weeks since they'd been gone. They'd promoted the former assistant director since she'd been their second choice during the initial hiring for the camp. They must have found a new replacement assistant director, but I could only imagine the lengths they'd had to go to when it came to hiring in the short window of time they had.

"It won't happen again," I started.

Jack joined me. "We just got a little carried away."

Leo stepped out from his desk and ran a hand through his hair. "Carried away? Like you did with the camp prank wars?" He looked between us. His raised eyebrow looked surprisingly intimidating. "I know it was you two who started it."

"That's not even going on anymore," I insisted, at the same time Jack said, "There's no proof of that."

Leo let out an exasperated sigh. "You've been going at each other for weeks. You're constantly fighting during the competitions. And now, whatever is going on between you two is affecting other people."

Jack and I held our heads low and nodded. Our arguing had affected Jamie, and that was too far. I thought of Chase and our horrendous date. Instead of trying to get to know the new counselor, even as a friend, I'd complained about someone I shouldn't have been thinking about.

Leo turned to me, his bright green eyes looking concerned. "Why don't you stay with Hazel?"

I thought about the offer for a second, but she only had a loveseat that my legs didn't fit comfortably on, and our habits contradicted each other. Sure, I'd considered it early on, but now I shook my head.

I recalled my recent conversation with Hazel, how she was barely keeping it together, and while she did well processing emotional things on her own or with Leo, I didn't want to strain her further. My turmoil with Jack would only be a burden, and I didn't want to bring that into her already tense life. She didn't handle changes to her routine well, so I'd already made up my mind that I was better off handling this on my own. Despite our drama, I'd gotten comfortable in Jack's cabin, even if he was there.

"My stuff is already at Jack's, and I know Hazel's been under a lot of stress. I don't want to add to it."

Leo looked forlorn at the mention of Hazel's stress.

I felt the need to reassure him. "And we're doing great. I mean, good. Better?" Wow, I was not convincing.

Jack smiled at my tailspin, and he almost seemed curious that I hadn't taken the offer to sleep elsewhere. He met my eyes again, searching them, then he backed my decision up without arguing.

"It's not as bad as it seems. We're doing okay now," I promised.

Leo considered my words.

"Yeah, she's even getting me to clean up a bit more," Jack added, and he said it like it was a good thing. Was he actually grateful?

This admission caused Leo to break his serious face as he laughed. "You got Jack to clean?"

"Yeah..." Jack looked chagrined. Hearing it out of Leo's mouth must have made him realize I wasn't wrong. "Once I remove all the work stuff, I won't have as hard a time keeping up with it."

"I've stayed in worse places in my travels, but it's nice to be able to breathe in there finally."

Jack took in my words. "I'll try to be more considerate."

I smiled softly. Maybe he was beginning to understand how I felt about being displaced. The truth was, I needed a little bit of control, even if that came in the form of cleaning up his cabin in a desperate attempt at normalcy again. I'd been upset yesterday, but all that anger had dissipated.

"We won't cause any more trouble," Jack promised. "And Andromeda's cabin will be remodeled and repaired soon anyway."

Leo seemed appeased when he looked between us. "Okay then, no more petty arguments?"

"It wasn't petty." I couldn't help myself, but Jack elbowed me in the side. I reflexively smiled at Leo and backtracked. "That's right, no more arguments," I promised, even if it was a lie.

Maybe Jack and I finally had a better understanding of each other, but that didn't mean we'd be able to change overnight. Our strained relationship was built on this feud, and I enjoyed our rivalry, even if no one else understood it. Jack was sort of growing on me.

I resolved to do better. We could make sure we only argued in private and save our best trash talk for the competitions, where it belonged.

TIMES LIKE THESE, I WAS GRATEFUL FOR OUR STAFF'S ability to band together to bring something to fruition under the guise of a lie. Yes, it was Autumn's birthday, but if she saw the congratulations sign we'd hung in the mess hall and the champagne chilling in the fridge, she'd have questions. So we waited until she ran errands to set everything up.

Bobby and Chase made the prettiest engagement cake, while Azalea crafted a birthday dinner with Leo's help. Hazel, Lamar, and I hung streamers and balloons. The other counselors entertained Autumn's and Jamie's parents, who'd told her they wanted to visit to celebrate the birthday girl. Jamie had secretly filled us in on his plans this morning, and we all got to work doing our part to make sure Autumn was none the wiser. Unfortunately, he wasn't able to get the ring's precise location after our mishap, but he'd come up with a backup plan. He didn't elaborate, and it had my stomach roiling in worry. I guess I had that coming.

We met at the ax range for a friendly competition, which Autumn was excited about, since she'd finally be able to participate. She helped Jamie's mom learn to throw, and it didn't go unnoticed that Jamie was unimpressed with her hit, which nearly touched the bull's-eye. When he threw his own practice throw, it was apparent that he was only jealous. At least he got it on the board that time.

"You really expect me to believe you haven't improved your swing after nearly a year of doing this? Jamie Davis, have I taught you nothing?" Autumn laughed and playfully razzed Jamie as he threw his ax and shamelessly missed the target.

"You might need to teach me a little more," Jamie teased.

"Hey, glad you all made it." His face was bright, even if he was also nervous.

Lola and Luis came rushing over, and Autumn's parents were chatting together with Chase and Emerson off to the side, looking like the perfect spectators.

"We didn't miss it, right?" Luis exclaimed, out of breath.

Autumn's eyes went up.

I stepped in. "No, the competition is just about to start. You're both right on time."

Jamie looked relieved, and I laughed, knowing that if Autumn wasn't distracted checking all the axes, she'd see right through this whole song and dance.

"This is a pretty great turnout," Autumn commented as the stragglers from our staff finally arrived. She was already so impressed and full of love. It was beautiful to see.

Jamie grinned and handed her an ax, but not just any ax. The handle of this one was painted bright yellow, and a sunflower had been painstakingly etched into the wood handle by Jamie as a gift for their six-month anniversary.

"Of course, they made the time, honey," Autumn's stepmom said as she picked up an ax. "You're a very special person."

She propped the ax over her shoulder. "You know buttering me up won't matter, right? I'm going to destroy all of you. It's not even fair."

Laughter erupted from everyone, except her father, whose crossed arms didn't pair well with the smile he was fighting.

Jamie was grinning and obviously enamored. "I don't know about that. I think you're going to have to prove it." His nerves seemed to melt away when she teased him, and witnessing the interaction made my heart squeeze. I felt grateful to be a part of their special moment.

Autumn was giddy as she tried to get more information. "So, should we do this as individuals or as teams?"

"Teams," Jamie declared with a boyish grin. "And you'll be on mine, won't you?"

"You're a terrible pick. But a good boyfriend. Sure. Why not?"

Jamie shook his head and nudged her shoulder. "Thanks for carrying me," he joked as their *team* stepped up and threw their axes.

To no one's surprise, Autumn nailed a bull's-eye. I had to hand it to her, she had excellent hand-eye coordination when it didn't involve feeding herself s'mores. Then again, maybe those messes were Jamie's fault, too.

I smiled as Jamie stepped up next and made a big show of telling everyone he was swinging and that he was ready to win. He wound up, released the ax, and just like he had the first time he'd met Autumn, according to the camp legend, it went through the woods in the direction of the lake. Jamie threw his hands in the air, feigning exasperation, as his gaze followed his ax.

"You did not just do that." Autumn took his hand and spouted mostly playful insults at her boyfriend as they trudged off together to get the wayward ax.

The group of us nonchalantly veered away from the range to a hidden piece of the beach, fifty feet from where Jamie was taking her. I'd recently learned about their second meet-cute last year and loved the way he was calling back to it.

When Autumn neared the beach a step ahead of him, she stopped abruptly and turned to Jamie, then back to the beach. We couldn't see it, but I'd watched him spell out the message *Will you marry me?* meticulously in stones on the sand.

"What do you think he's saying?" Hazel asked as Leo held her shoulders so she didn't fall off the precarious rocks she was teetering on. There were more than ten of us and barely enough space to see through the trees.

"Probably something like, 'All I do is dream of you,' followed by, 'This is all thanks to Leo,'" Leo boasted. He probably believed that.

The group chuckled until Jamie got down on one knee. I was pretty sure everyone held their breath until Autumn launched herself into his arms, nearly knocking him over. Once he got back on his feet, he lifted her and spun her around, which was enough for us to head in their direction.

We found Jamie with tears in his eyes as he slipped something onto her finger. They walked toward us with big smiles, and then I heard Jamie's voice.

"A real ring is coming, I promise."

Autumn smiled softly and cupped his face. "I don't care. I love this one."

They turned to see all of us cheering and jumping up and down, sharing in their excitement.

Jamie beamed at us with the biggest smile. "Thank you all so much!"

Autumn was pink-cheeked as she showed off the intricate ring Jamie had woven out of friendship bracelet string. The untarnished happiness in her eyes was only broken when she came to a realization. "Wait, so the competition?"

"Was all a setup for this. But we can finish it if you want, sunflower. I won't throw it out here again," he teased, and she lit up laughing.

She grabbed his hands in hers. "I love being on your team."

The group of us let out a collective *Aww* at the sweet moment, and the parents congratulated the couple.

After dinner and cake, we discussed options for how we could celebrate the new engagement. In the end, most of us decided to celebrate by going to the local bar.

The parents chose to stay back and let us *young folk* go out. The group ahead of me was exchanging their favorite Jamie and Autumn stories on our way to the cars when I caught Leo's strained voice behind me.

"But you used to be such a romantic. Now you're so cynical." He said it like a sad fact.

Jack's reply was barely above a whisper. "I'm happy for them. I'm happy for all the couples who find love, really. It's just not for me."

My heart squeezed at the raw quality in his low tone.

Leo seemed to feel it, too, as he tried to assuage him. "Not everything will blow up in your face like it did last year."

I thought back to last summer and considered the way Jack was now. It was like he'd had a personality transplant, at least around me. I hadn't known him well back then, but Leo definitely had. What had changed?

Jack didn't answer. Instead, he power walked past me. Over my shoulder, I saw Leo's pinched brows, right before he caught me looking. I turned back. Jack had made it up the trail to congratulate his best friend, but I would bet he wanted out of his conversation with Leo. Jack smiled and threw an arm around Autumn and then Jamie.

What the hell had happened to him last year?

EIGHTEEN

Jack

Fireside Bar was hopping for a Thursday night. The first of our group walked in, and I questioned if we should find somewhere else, but it was tradition to celebrate big events here.

Lola pushed past me and headed to the bar, jumping in to sling drinks with her daughter, Maya, who ran the place during the summer.

I couldn't get my conversation with Leo out of my head. He may have been annoyed with me over my newfound feelings about love, but he was a relentless romantic. He just didn't get it.

It wasn't like I wasn't happy for my friends. I wanted to believe things would work out, but I also knew that love didn't last. I just hoped they'd be the exception to the rule.

I'd watched countless relationships, including all of mine, end with disastrous results. It didn't inspire confidence. And after my most recent relationship blowup, I wasn't willing to try it again. I was fine with living a peaceful, busy life in the mountains, surrounded by my found family.

Autumn and Jamie were the last to walk in, and the bar erupted in cheers. It was no surprise that their engagement had already spread through town. You couldn't tie your shoelaces without someone talking about big news.

I walked to the bar, which was full of patrons eagerly awaiting drinks, and found my spot in line.

"Looking hot tonight, nature girl." Maya held a shaker in one hand as she spoke to Nat, who wore a summer dress with a heart-shaped neckline. I'd definitely noticed.

"Not as hot as you shaking that thing." Nat's smile lit up the room, and I found myself getting a little jealous, which was stupid. Maya was completely straight. And I wasn't into Nat. I repeated that in my head like a mantra.

"No way, twice in one week?" Kai sidled up to her. "How are those nails holding up?"

Nat extended her hand and chuckled. "We got our nails done at Wild Beauty the other day," she explained to Maya. "And they made it two days. I know better than to get pretty when I'm down and dirty all the time, but I can't help myself."

That phrasing had me thinking of her down and dirty in another way, and I mentally slapped myself.

He laughed. "But they're still glittery at least."

She took her hand back and looked. "The benefits of working with crafts."

Kai nodded. "Don't I know it. Speaking of which, your restock order came in today. Want me to drop it off?"

Nat's partially polished hand went to her chest. "You don't have to do that."

"I love stopping by Camp Starlight. Simon was just telling me about..."

I zoned out of the conversation and focused on ordering my beer from Lola. She poured a pint, and I took a long swig. Nat really was getting along in Wildwood. It was nice to see our town accept the new counselors each summer. Welcoming Nat had been no different. Except that they didn't just welcome her, everyone loved her, and when she wasn't driving me up the wall, I could almost see why.

A voice behind me got my attention. "Ladies and gentlemen, please welcome to the stage Hazel Matthews and Leo Lovejoy."

We all whooped and clapped as Maya introduced them on the tiny stage in the back of the bar. Someone handed Leo a guitar.

This was a special treat for the people of Wildwood. It wasn't often that we got a moment like this outside of the campfire. People loved our camp mom and dad and put pressure on them to perform, but that rarely worked.

"This one goes out to Autumn and Jamie, our favorite lovebirds," Hazel said as she stood at the mic. Someone lowered the lighting as Leo strummed the first chords of Maren Morris and Hozier's "The Bones."

I'd seen it dozens of times around the campfire, but it never failed to take my breath away. The two of them were like magic, their sounds melding together perfectly. Hazel wasn't a big fan of attention, so this was Leo bringing her out of her shell, just like he'd done when they'd performed for their first camp talent show together as kids. Or so I'd been told.

Autumn and Jamie came out to the center of the dance floor and looked at each other with heart eyes, and several others followed suit. It was hard not to feel the romance in the air, no matter how much I wanted to avoid it.

I glanced at Nat, who had her arms wrapped around herself as she swayed to our friends' song. She had a look about her, a wistfulness that said *I want to be them*.

Or maybe I was drawing conclusions I didn't know anything about.

Hazel smiled at Leo, who looked at his fingers for a moment before meeting her gaze.

I'd seen them deny it out of their teeth, and I'd known not to say anything, but it did look like there was something there. I carefully reminded myself that they were just friends. Best friends. And that didn't have to mean a romantic relationship. Not everything ended that way.

The bar erupted into cheers and applause as they finished their song. I noticed Nat looking at her drink, as if she were searching for her answer at the bottom of her glass. She threw it back and finished it, right as Lola came back with a tray of cocktails.

"Hey, there," a sweet voice said behind me.

I turned to find a pretty redhead with her hand in a little wave, standing beside a blonde with wavy hair.

I wasn't in the mood for this kind of interaction, but I was polite, nonetheless. "How's it going?"

"Pretty good. I'm Stephanie. And this is Lily."

"It's nice to meet you. I'm Jack. Are y'all from around here?"

Stephanie pushed her hair behind one ear and shook her head. "We're visiting from Arizona."

"And what brought you to our small town?" I took a gulp of my beer and found the bottom of my glass. I wondered how soon I could extricate myself from this situation and get another.

Lily jumped in. "Just trying to find ourselves some mountain men. You sure fit that bill." She was clearly tipsy. And loud.

I chuckled as Stephanie turned three shades of pink. She was pretty, with beachy waves and an embarrassed smile. She laughed it off and elbowed her friend, which would normally have done it for me, but for some reason, I wasn't one bit interested.

"If Jack's a mountain man, does that make me one, too?" Leo came up beside us and winked at me.

He seemed to be trying to be funny, because he considered himself a nerd, which didn't typically go hand in hand with a tough, ax-swinging man of the wilderness.

"That depends," I mock-pondered. "Do you live on a mountain?"

Leo's smile was pure sunshine. "I do."

"And do you do mountain man things? Ruggedly cutting wood? Throwing tree trunks? Looking into sunsets as you traverse rocky outcroppings?" I asked, watching the girls next to us as they waited for Leo's response.

He shrugged. "I'm really good with a GPS."

I patted him on the shoulder. "Might not count, buddy."

"Damn." Leo grinned before he took a drink of his beer. But the women I'd been talking to looked at him with stars in their eyes. That guitar playing had an undeniable effect on people. So did his voice.

"Artists are hot, too," Stephanie soothed, moving on from flirting with me. Her friend also angled her body toward him.

Leo had a certain kind of appeal that drew women to him. He was a much better catch than the guy who didn't want a relationship. At least he believed in that sort of thing.

Leo's eyes widened. "Oh, well, I mean. I'm not going to argue with that."

Hazel snorted beside him, joining the group and gathering herself as everyone stared at her. "Leo's great at a lot of things."

"He's great at board games." Autumn sidled up beside her as Jamie hugged her from behind. "Ooh, and he's in a one-man band." Was she trying to kill his game?

Lily had a puzzled expression. "A one-man..."

"He's got a full set of instruments he plays all at once. Like Bert. From *Mary Poppins*." Autumn lifted her beer in cheers.

Hazel burst into giggles.

Leo looked proud. "Don't even lie, Ms. Matthews. We all know you had a thing for Bert."

"I would never lie about that." She and Autumn started giggling again.

It was then that I went around the room to count how many of us were sloshed. I was feeling tipsy after our dinner celebration. Then there was Chase and Jamie, who were listening to Lamar tell a story; he waved his arms wildly and nearly knocked Luis over as he carried a tray of drinks. No one would ever accuse Starlighters of not knowing how to have a good time.

I tried to find Sawyer, Emerson, and Felicia to make sure they were doing all right, when my eyeline landed on Nat, whose cheeks were flushed as she spoke to a guy in a band tee and cargo shorts. Her eyes darted across the room as if she were looking for someone to step in before she caught my gaze.

Without telling my feet to move, I found myself in her vicinity.

The man leaned in to talk to her over the din of chatter. "I just love your account. I've been following for years. Are you here to do more footage? Do you need a guide?"

Nat smiled politely. "Oh, I'm actually—"

"Taking a break from working." I popped in. "She's on a vacation."

Nat gave me a look but nodded. "That's right."

"A vacation from your vacations?" He chuckled. "What's that like?"

A flash of annoyance passed over her features, probably because he made it sound like she didn't have a job. "I keep it low key. I mostly spend time with friends and my boyfriend."

Ah, so she wanted to get rid of him. I put my arm around her shoulder, and she tilted her head against my chest. I hated how much I liked that, but I could probably thank the booze.

"Are you visiting too?" I asked him.

"Yeah, just for the week. My friends and I are hiking the crest tomorrow."

I petted Nat's hair. "Very cool. Well, baby, I think we should say goodbye to our friends and head back to my place." Hey, it was true. "What do you think?"

"That sounds amazing. It was so nice to meet you, Todd."

The guy smiled, and it still came off a little too flirty for my taste, but I was in the fake boyfriend mindset. That explained it.

"Thank you," Nat whispered as I put my hand on her lower back and guided her to our group.

Leo handed back the redhead's phone. If I were to guess, he'd been putting his number in her contacts. The man had game even when I thought he didn't.

Hazel peeled at her beer bottle's label, looking anywhere but at her friend.

"What did I miss?" Nat questioned, looking at our camp mom.

"Leo's a mountain man," Hazel said, but her resigned tone didn't match her smile.

☆☆☆

Luis honked his horn goodbye after dropping us off at Camp Starlight. He and Leo had driven everyone home, which was good because none of us were fit to drive. We'd almost called the local rideshare guy, Herb, but Luis had been kind enough to step up.

Leo and Hazel were the first to peel off, heading to their duplex. Then went Sawyer and Lamar, who had been holding each other up until they reached Sawyer's cabin. Felicia gave us a peace sign as she headed to her place. And that left Nat and me.

We walked together in peaceful silence from the parking lot to my cabin.

Nat seemed contemplative as she drew my attention on the porch. "I think it's time for a truce, mountain man Jack."

I typed in my code and opened the door for her. "You heard that?"

She rolled her eyes. "The whole bar heard that."

I locked the door. It took a second for her words to register, but when they did, I jumped on the opportunity. "You jealous, princess?"

"Pfft. In your dreams. Which are probably of me, if we're being honest." Nat headed to the bedroom, kicked off her shoes, collapsed on her bunk, and let out a groan of comfort that went straight to my dick.

I leaned in the doorway, purposely avoiding a view of her sundress and the way the hem rode up along her thighs. "Oh yeah?"

She rolled over onto her back. "I see the way you wake up smiling." She pointed to her lips.

I barked out a laugh. She was cute drunk. I'd noticed the emphatic way she spoke with people all night and remembered the look she'd had when she was with that guy. I was glad I'd been there to rescue her. "Do you often get recognized out in the wild?"

Nat tapped her chin. "Sometimes."

"Doesn't it make you nervous?"

She shrugged. "Only when I'm alone, and it's a man. But that doesn't happen often. I do my best to stay safe."

I tried not to seethe at the idea of her feeling unsafe. "How do you do that?"

"I've taken self-defense classes, and I always travel with pepper spray. A lot of times, I'm with a guide or a friend. And I never post about where I am until after I've been gone a few days."

The idea of an obsessed fan cornering her didn't sit well with me. Sure, she was self-sufficient, but people could be horrible, and the idea of someone crossing any of her lines had me seeing red.

She must have read it on my face, because she spoke firmly, not lacking in confidence. "I pay attention to my surroundings. I was totally fine. You just helped move things along."

I didn't know what to say to that. I knew she was famous, in more ways than one, but she was down-to-earth. Her audience, however, was probably the same kind of people she'd run into on her travels, so it didn't assuage my fear.

"You're worried about me?"

I hated that she could even question that.

"Yeah, Nat." I cleared my throat because my words were barely decipherable. "Of course, I am." I crouched beside her, squeezing her hand in an attempt to prove my point.

Nat looked into my eyes with a serious gaze. "I was surrounded by people, and the guy was harmless. I don't always have that luxury, but I'm not that famous. I think you're blowing my status up in your head."

I'd seen it a dozen times, Nat downplaying her reach, but even my nephew knew who she was. I hadn't used social media up until now, but her account sounded like something I'd be interested in.

"You have over a million followers," I admitted. She probably didn't have a clue that I'd seen her posts. I'd done a deep dive on her account after Jordy told me she followed him back.

"A million friends that aren't actually friends," she said wistfully, rolling onto her side with a pillow in her arms. "Just like in real life."

Ah, so I was getting downcast drunk Nat. I didn't like it. "People love you."

She rolled onto her back and stared at the bunk above her. "Until they get to know me. That's the kind of friendships I make. Short, sweet, and superficial. I know I'm a good time. But I don't have an inner circle, let alone a group of friends. It's rare to find people who like me for me."

I thought back to the way I'd treated her, and it stung.

After too long a pause, I got my shit together. "Nat, I—"

"Don't worry about it. No more depressing Nat tonight." She closed her eyes as if that were the end of it, and it had me wondering, did she often mask her feelings to make herself more likable? "Maybe I liked that you showed up at my side." She spoke softly, as if it were a secret. "But that's probably just the residual crush talking. I know better now."

The sound of a record scratching went through my head.

"Wait, what?" Did I hear that right? Nat had a crush on me? Was that what she'd meant? "Nat, hey."

I waited a long moment, but her answering snore told me what

I already knew: that was the end of our conversation for the night. She also didn't respond when I poked her shoulder three times. Dammit.

I turned out the light and went to the kitchen to fill up two glasses of water and get some medicine we'd both need if being in our thirties had anything to say about it.

Nat looked beautiful, bathed in the light from the hallway, but that didn't stop me from poking her shoulder one last time, hoping to resume our conversation. I knew she'd be back to being closed off with me in the morning.

I set down medicine and water on her nightstand and turned my back on her, pausing as she spoke, her words garbled. I made out something about *too many marshmallows* and grinned at her.

"What was that?"

A warm smile spread across her lips. "Okay, if you really wanna cuddle, I'll be your teddy bear."

I choked on my laughter, my body shaking from holding it back.

By the time I got undressed and climbed into bed, my brain was wired. I couldn't get her unfiltered words out of my head. Nat Breckenridge used to have a crush on me? It had to have been last year, back when I'd been someone else's boyfriend—which she knew. We hadn't interacted all that much, but she might have been interested in me. How was I supposed to sleep on that?

NINETEEN
Jack

"OUCH." I LIFTED THE HAMMER OFF MY THUMB AND cringed. I hadn't hit the nail too hard. Actually, I hadn't hit the nail at all, and it hurt. Luckily, I had my work gloves on, so it was just a sharp pain that would be gone in a minute. My distracted brain, however, was another problem altogether.

Two days had passed since Nat's drunken confession, and I was having a hard time concentrating. What would happen if I brought it up? Would she deny it? Would she fill me in on what I'd clearly missed?

Whether or not she remembered it, she acted as if nothing had happened.

She'd told me she'd had a crush. And she might still have a little one, if I was understanding correctly. That blew my mind. I knew she had hatred for me, but it didn't seem that strong lately. Living together was still a struggle, but was that because we liked getting under each other's skin? And fuck it, I had to acknowledge I was very attracted to her.

It was finally time for me to admit I wasn't indifferent to her, and I was having a hard time with that.

Two knocks sounded on the frame of Nat's door, and I

happily put the hammer in my tool bag, tilting my head in confusion when Nat and Leo entered. What could this be about?

Nat's eyes darted to me, then to the side, where a buoyant Leo filled me with worry. Earlier this week, he'd been incredibly frustrated with us. So why was he so happy?

Leo cut to the chase. "I wanted to talk to you two. Together."

As they entered the cabin, Nat shrugged, looking around at my progress, running a finger down the wood framing, admiring my craftsmanship. It wouldn't be too long before she could move back in.

"What's up, Leo?" Nat asked. The anticipation was also killing me.

"As you know, tomorrow's Camp Wars competition is the obstacle relay, and it ends in a mud crawl." He said this like we didn't already know. The whole camp was excited. "So I decided that you two are going to go set up the mud pit. Call it your penance."

I figured I'd be the one to do this, but I wasn't expecting to do it with Nat.

I sighed. "Come on, Leo."

He gave me an unamused look. "I'm sorry, did you not ruin someone's engagement? Or am I misremembering?"

"You could argue that two people did end up engaged, so was it really ruined?" she tried.

I nearly laughed until Leo's eyes narrowed. He was still disappointed. Of course, he was. And he was not having it. He waited for an answer from us.

I let out a disgruntled, "Fine," at the same time as Nat.

Leo clapped his hands. "Great. And I know you're going to do a great job because you promised me you two would get along, so what could go wrong?"

☆
☆ ☆

Turned out, a lot could go wrong.

An hour later, Nat was frustrated with this as much as I was. "I don't know why he thinks we have to do this together. We can be around each other fine."

Was she delusional or just a liar?

"You're right," I lied. "And I'd be much more effective working on this alone."

That got under her skin. She stiffened and turned her head slowly at me as we walked to the location of the pit. "Adding me into the equation does not make you less effective. I can get my hands dirty. You know I can."

"That's not the point."

"Then what is the point?" she said, aggravated to the point that I regretted saying what I'd said. She grabbed one of the buckets we'd brought and angrily dunked it into the lake and poured it onto the dirt. I did the same once, then twice. It wasn't enough time to get my thoughts in order, however.

"The point is, this is a one-man job. One-person job," I corrected. "You'll just get in the way."

And if I hadn't shoved my foot in my mouth before, she made it abundantly clear that I had now.

She dumped another bucket of water, this time way too close to my feet. I picked up my heavy-duty rake and tried mixing the water into the dirt. We were lucky that it had rained overnight, because there was already some mud. We were just making it a little bit better.

"You think everything is a one-person job, and that's why it takes you forever."

I glared. "If you're talking about the cabin, that's entirely out of my control."

She threw her hands up, dropping her bucket in exasperation. "I'm talking about everything. You won't even delegate something as small as changing a lightbulb. Your place is falling apart, but you don't care because you'd rather help everyone else. And no, you don't want my help with *my* cabin. Did you ever think I'd be interested in learning a new skill?"

"And when would you have the time, exactly? When you're working here or working on content?" This argument was going off the rails. "You don't stop to take a breath."

"And neither do you," she practically screeched, stepping toward me. "You are a textbook hypocrite."

Steam had to be coming out of my ears. "Don't call me that."

"Don't tell me what to do." She grabbed the bucket, gathered more water, and poured it near me again.

Why was her defiance so hot?

She turned away, slipping slightly before regaining her footing. Then she gathered more water and poured it near me. Again. I ignored her display and kept raking, which was a lesson in patience if I'd ever seen one. I should have been studied.

"You know what your problem is?" she accused ten minutes later, as if she'd been ruminating on it this entire time. "You think you're the only competent person. You think you're better than people."

"I do not."

Her eyes flared hot as she dumped another bucket of water. "Fine, then you think you're better than me."

Was she right? No. I didn't think that. But had I acted this way? Maybe. It wasn't like I gave her the chance to help me with anything. But that was purely because I didn't want to be around her, and my reasons for not wanting to be around her were that I hated her. Not because I wanted her. It was absolutely not that. Just thinking about Nat's combativeness had my defensiveness rising.

The truth was, I'd been wrong about today. This job was going so much faster with her help, bringing the water while I mixed the mud. If we weren't at each other's throats, maybe we'd make a good team, but I couldn't control myself with her, and it was maddening.

Nat grabbed more water and walked it over to me, causing my hackles to rise. I was watching her more than raking mud now, and her raised eyebrows told me she took notice.

I needed to get some control back. "You don't know what you're talking about. And if you pour that thing near me one more time, you're going to regret it."

She squared her shoulders, her smugness shining through. "Ooh, threats. Just what I'd expect from you."

I reached for the bucket, yanking on the handle. Some water sloshed out, right on her shoes. She stared at her feet, then into my eyes, sending a death glare right at me.

Nat's next words were full of malice. "You did not just do that."

"Like you haven't been doing it the entire time."

She shook her head and yanked on the pail, which she didn't get back because I wasn't giving up. "Give that to me."

I gritted my teeth. "Take it."

She yanked harder, pulling it away from me, and sloshed even more on her shoes. I laughed, which must have been the final straw, because she pulled it and me, causing me to lose my footing, and I went down.

I slipped, landed, and wondered how young was too young to throw your back out. If it were going to happen, it'd be now. But one flex and I felt fine, more or less. Thankfully.

I lifted my hand to block the light from the sun, and a clump of mud fell on my cheek. That was when I heard the sound of pure, unadulterated laughter.

Nat bent in half, clutching her side, giggling at my misfortune. She was downright gleeful, and that little spark, the one I told myself to ignore, was creeping through me in full force.

In this moment, I could have remembered why we were here, why Leo was so upset with us, and what our mission was. Hell, I could have just had one brain cell devoted to thoughts an adult should have. But I didn't.

No, I wanted her to get down and dirty just like me. See if she laughed then.

I swept my leg and took her out at the knees. She flailed in slow motion, as if she were trying to grip the air, but it obviously didn't work. What I hadn't accounted for, however, was her falling right on top of me.

"*Jack!*" she yelled as I tried to catch my breath again after getting the wind knocked out of me. I wouldn't be surprised if wildlife scattered at the shrill sound.

Now I was the one who was laughing. No, it was more like wheezing.

"You." She took a huge breath, and I realized the gravity of what being chest to chest meant. How close all our parts were to each other. The way her face was inches from mine. "You—"

"What?" I cleared my throat, hoping she didn't notice the effect she had on me. If I wasn't careful, I was going to have a major problem on my hands. Or in my pants, if I were being honest. What I needed was a distraction.

Nat still hadn't moved from my hold. "I can't believe you—"

I pulled my hands from the muck. A loud slurping sound followed before I ran my hands to the small of her back. The squeak she let out as I found skin would have been precious had it not been coming from her. Her eyes widened as she took in what I assumed was a smirk on my face. And the rare moment of silence from her lips was broken as she purposely moved her hand in the mud and rubbed it on my biceps. Joke was on her. I was already covered in it anyway. But when she'd done the deed and should have been stopping, she kept rubbing them, looking down before realizing what she was doing and letting my arm go. Her gaze raised to mine, almost apologetically, but I didn't wait for her to take it back.

I lost all sense of reason, cupped her face, and pressed my lips to hers.

I would have expected some hesitancy, maybe even resistance, and a push away from either of us as we realized what had been done, but I was met with instant surrender. Nat leaned down, and my head met the ground again as she moved her mouth against mine, melting into me, begging for more. Her pillowy lips were soft as silk, just like I'd imagined. Because I'd dreamed about crushing my lips to her more times than I'd like to admit.

Nat leaned into my touch, and when we pulled apart, staring at each other, she closed the distance once more, extending this euphoric sensation of what I'd imagined kissing her might be like. And there was definitely nothing better.

And when I rolled us over so her back was in the mud, she didn't complain. No, she raised her thigh around me and allowed me to grind into her. There was no hiding the effect she had on me, and I didn't care anymore. She smelled of flowers, expensive and luxurious. She didn't belong in the mud, making out with a man like me, but she'd softly whimpered when we kissed again, so maybe she was fine with it. Her back arched slightly, and she kept hold of me.

My hand went up her other thigh until I reached the hem of her shorts, longing to be beneath them, but I squeezed her thigh instead, having the sense not to try anything further. Her fingers tightened around my arm ever so slightly, and I wondered if she'd try to break the mood or extend it. I gave her a moment to end this, to pull back. Only she didn't move away. Nat pulled me closer.

The place didn't matter. The mud clinging to our skin didn't matter. What mattered was that we were lost in each other.

And when I pulled away from her, she didn't glare or shy away. She stared into my eyes, breathing heavily, just like me.

TWENTY

Nat

What just happened? Was it real life or some strange dream about my addictive roommate?

All this need and want had only one place to go. He seemed frozen on top of me, his perfect lips still only millimeters from mine.

Jack's breath, a sweet puff of air, tingled over my face as he stared at me. One minute we'd been working, arguing, our normal. Next, we were this. Wrapped up and completely lost to the world, clinging and dirty without a care. He touched my cheek tenderly, and I let out the smallest gasp as he moved to hold my chin. Mud from his hand smeared across my face, and I smiled.

Was mud an aphrodisiac? Because I wanted those lips to meet mine, to linger and play and lavish me again. But Jack moved his hand, and he got to his knees, pensively staring down at me.

Why was this hotter than it should have been? I lay there, ready and waiting for him to move me into whatever position he wanted, but then he looked away.

The bubble we had been in just moments ago burst, and I wasn't ready for that. I wasn't ready for the quiet look on his face as he stood up and reached a hand down to me.

Apparently, the time to come out of the mud was now. It was all for the best anyway. I needed this spell to break. Needed to get myself together.

I took his hand and grinned at him while my arms shot out to each side of my body, and I caught my balance. "You look like you had a mud mask."

He chuffed out a strangled laugh at my joke and shook his head. His hand moved to my lower back, where he helped me regain my balance. I took a wobbly step, unsteady.

He kept a supportive hand on me. "And you look like a baby fawn."

I smiled and took another step, my stuck boot making a funny squelching noise. Jack's laugh escaped, and his grip on me tightened. Only the touch, grounding as it was, had me leaning into it rather than stabilizing myself. I tried for another step and promptly slipped and fell.

Correction. We fell.

I grabbed for Jack and took him down with me. We both sat on our asses, laughing with each other. His eyes were so beautiful like this. Crinkled at the sides. Blue and playful and, best of all, focused solely on me. There was no hatred, just heat.

Oh my god. I kissed my nemesis. Not just kissed. I made out with Jack. I wanted more from him, and I couldn't deny how right his hands felt on me. How perfect our lips were. His guiding touch, insistent and warm. Damn, I really wanted more.

As if it were written across my face, Jack seemed to realize what I was thinking. His expression went from dreamy to moon-eyed to surprised, until a gruffness settled over his face. If I were being honest, it was exactly what I'd expected from him. And just like that, the once-scorching moment morphed into an unbelievably awkward one.

Something about that made my heart sink in my chest like a battered ship.

"Jack, I—"

His eyes darted away from mine, and it was clear we weren't going to talk about this right now. "Let's go get cleaned up." He pulled me up again, sturdier this time. Not laughing at the state of our clothing or the sounds we made as we pulled ourselves out of the mud and into reality.

Finally, on solid ground, I resolved not to overthink my reaction to him. It was basic animalistic lust, that was all. It meant nothing.

As I walked a step behind Jack in the quiet, I was only comforted by the fact that I wasn't the only one shaken up by our actions. The surprise and heat of our kiss. Jack was probably just as confused about the whole thing as I was. I didn't know if that was comforting or not.

One thing was certain about this whole scenario. It couldn't happen again.

Heat gathered around my cheeks and neck, and I worried even the mud wouldn't be able to hide my blush as I recalled the embarrassing confession I'd made while drunk two nights ago. Traitorous words that had just flown out of my mouth. No thoughts or filters. No self-preservation. Just a late-night, tipsy confession no one had asked for. But in my defense, he had looked really good that night, even disheveled. He'd been friendly, not just to everyone but to me as well.

Was this impromptu mud make-out because of that inconvenient confession? Or had he been obsessing over how our lips might align, what I might taste like, just like I wondered about him?

Either way, we'd promised Leo we'd be professional. Which we would be if you considered bickering hyenas professional.

Professionalism had died the moment Jack's hands came around me, the second our tongues collided perfectly. Too perfectly.

But that was the problem with me.

I'd always been unlucky in love, and it seemed like that streak was far from over. Because falling for my enemy-turned-inconvenient roommate would seal my fate as really, really unlucky.

THIS WAS IT.

This was the epitome of *what the fuck am I doing?*

Jack mechanically stripped out of his clothes as we stood at the dock on the far end of camp. There wasn't anything particularly sexy about it, except for his stupid body.

It's just a body, I tried to tell myself. So why couldn't I take my eyes off him? *Get it together, lust-riddled brain*. Whatever this attraction was, it couldn't happen again. No matter how amazing he felt on top of me.

I jumped into the lazy lake water, and the mud came off in chunks. The memory of the kiss and all the fire? Well, that wasn't going to go away so easily.

The water was still cold in June. Tree cover and no days over eighty degrees meant chattering teeth, goose bumps, and way too much shivering, but not in the sexy way.

We ran our asses over to the communal showers. After several minutes of silence, I wondered how we were going to break this tension between us. The warm water washed the remaining mud away, thank goodness. I was just starting to relax when Jack's voice ruined all chances of that happening.

"You know, getting dirty looks good on you, princess," Jack commented from the stall next to mine. So he was going to lean into teasing me about this situation? Great.

I gave him a hearty, "Go fuck yourself, Jack." I could just picture his smile from the other side of the wall.

"Mmm, tempting. But I bet it's you who needs some relief. That imagination of yours is probably running rampant, isn't it?"

Ugh. This man.

"Are you projecting your need to relieve yourself or something?" I lathered my hair with the provided haircare products and tried not to sound as curious as I was for his answer.

"Stop deflecting. I couldn't help but notice the way you undressed me at the lake over there."

"First of all, you undressed yourself. Secondly, for your information, no, I am not imagining anything else. That kiss was more than enough, thank you very much."

He huffed a laugh. "Enough? Really? Because from where I stand, it seemed like you wanted more."

Was I that transparent? I needed the upper hand back and fast. His cockiness was stifling. His ego needed a reality check.

"In your dreams. I've got you clocked, Hawthorne. You're probably one of those dudes who's selfish in bed." I wrapped a towel around myself tightly and stepped out of the shower to grab another towel off the shelf for my hair.

Jack exited the shower, also in nothing but a towel, and his face met mine in the mirror. "You need me to prove how incorrect you are, princess? If you'd like, I can spell it out with my tongue."

I couldn't speak. My mouth was dry. And if I wasn't thinking about it before... well, now I couldn't stop thinking about it.

He seemed to realize he'd stolen my sanity as he lightly tapped his chin, a reminder to close my gaping lips. Then the asshole winked at me. That snapped me out of my stupor.

"In an alternate universe where I was somehow interested in all of... that"—I gestured up and down his body through the mirror —"you'd be the one moaning my name. Not the other way around."

Jack's face tilted down at me, and he looked intense, the way he did when just before kissing me, not even an hour ago. "Is that a challenge?" he asked, those burning eyes alive with a spark of rivalry in them.

This was one competition I wanted to have.

He stepped in front of me and cupped my jaw. Our eyes locked together. Was he going to kiss me again? I didn't step away. I just listened, my pulse beating a mile a minute. Jack was right, as infuriating as that was to admit. That kiss wasn't enough. That was a dangerous thought. Still, I leaned into him and tilted my neck ever so slightly.

But just like with everything, Jack ruined it.

He took a massive step back. "Whoa, what are we doing?" He sounded startled, as if he hadn't expected this turn of events between us. "This can't happen again."

It was as if I'd been doused in a bucket of cold water. "What?"

"We shouldn't do this." His face was panicked.

I may have been unlucky in love, but I'd never had this reaction from someone before. "You kissed me just as much as I kissed you. This isn't all my fault."

He opened his mouth, but whatever he was about to say was interrupted by a camper wearing flip-flops and a vengeful sunburn. Yikes.

We jumped apart as if we'd been caught doing something wrong. Was this wrong? Yes, it was.

I walked out the door, back to Jack's cabin, clutching the towel around me for dear life. How stupid. Of course, it couldn't happen.

Always on my heels, Jack walked with me and tried to talk to me all the way back to his cabin. "Nat, wait up."

I punched in the door code with ferocity. I didn't need to hear him reiterate what I already knew. Nearly kissing him again was stupid enough. That kiss was a one-and-done thing. It couldn't be more. Why had I almost let it happen again?

More mad at myself than at him, I stormed off to his room and shut the door behind me, our universal sign to stay out while the other dressed. I threw on comfy clothes as fast as humanly possible, opened the door, and changed places with him.

He didn't shut the door completely, still trying to talk to me from the other side. "I'm sorry that you're upset."

"Upset?" This man was infuriating. "You're so hot and cold. One minute, your tongue is down my throat. The next, you can't imagine the idea of us kissing?"

He opened the door in joggers, yanking a tee over his wet hair. "None of that matters. What matters is that this"—his hands flew wildly between us—"isn't happening."

"Can't happen anymore," I corrected haplessly as I pushed my way into the room and sat on my bed. He sat across from me and gave me a terse nod. The urge to regain control slammed into me. "You act like I'm begging for it. Believe me when I say this: I'm not."

"The point is, we will never be a thing." He said it unflinchingly, and I died a little bit inside. But not enough to stop pressing him.

"Because we're enemies?" I asked, still not entirely certain what had started the issue between us that had been boiling since day one.

"It's never going to happen for more reasons than that," he said, redirecting his gaze to the ceiling.

But it did bring up an interesting question. "What if I don't want to be enemies with you, Jack?" I asked his back, feeling less angry and more vulnerable.

Nothing made sense. Not his face as we almost kissed again. Not the tension he exuded. His eyes pleaded with me to listen. So I waited for him to start talking.

"I don't want to be enemies either, princess. But sometimes when I look at you, it's hard not to remember."

My heart raced. What was he getting at, and why did he look heartbroken?

"Remember what?" I asked softly.

His face changed from resigned to disappointed. "You're really going to act like you don't know?" he asked in disbelief. "You hooked up with my girlfriend last year, Nat."

Girlfriend? I flipped through my memories of last year like a photo album in my head. Jack had had a girlfriend? And I'd hooked up with her? The only one I'd done anything with was a blip on my radar, a deep kiss that had ended as soon as it had begun. And then she'd ghosted me.

"You were with Gia?" I recalled Gia, pixie-like and fun, then regretful when I'd moved to go further. My heart crumpled as the pieces I should have seen toppled into place.

"Yes, Gia. My girlfriend of two years. Who was *visiting me.*"

I hung my head. "I didn't know. I wouldn't have done that to you, to anyone—"

His face went from anger to understanding, ending with an, "Oh."

I let the word sink in. Jack thought I'd broken up his relationship last year, and he'd been angry with me ever since. It was sad. It was heartbreaking. It was... making me clench my fists.

My heart sped up, and I swallowed back tears I didn't want him to see, before I took a solid breath and spoke as calmly as I could. "So, what you're saying is, you were wrong about me? And all this time you've been putting me through hoops because your ex cheated when I didn't even know you were together?"

So many things made sense. The way he'd acted since my arrival. The pained look in his eyes after that romantic kiss, a moment neither of us could control. Then there was the distance between his best friend and me.

"Is this why Autumn has only been professional with me?" Autumn hadn't been rude or even cold, but she'd been closed off. In hindsight, it all made sense and felt night and day from how she'd treated me last year. We'd opened up to each other then. I'd talked with her after Jamie left camp. Now, the idea of her thinking I could be that type of person hurt. Almost as much as it hurt that Jack would think this of me. "Did she know about this?"

"Yeah, but—"

"Does everyone know?" I sounded so small. It felt like everything was crumbling around me.

"That's not the point—"

"Oh, my god. Everyone thinks I did this. I need to get out of here." All my insecurities came rushing back as anxiety pounded through me, circling and taunting.

I'd been used to people making assumptions about me my whole life. Thinking I had to fit into this box or another. *Breckenridges don't do this. You can't be like that.* No one considered how those boxes could be both suffocating and confusing. I hadn't felt that way at camp, but now it made sense.

Something crossed Jack's face, and he looked regretful.

"Everyone thinks Gia hooked up with a random camper, Nat. Only Jamie and Autumn know who she was with. And I don't think they hold that against you."

"How kind of them." My voice didn't sound like my own.

All this time, I'd been feeling something different about my place at Starlight, about Wildwood. Maybe this wasn't home after all.

Wasn't that the understatement of the year? I was living out of a suitcase. I was sleeping in Jack's bedroom, not my own. Of course, this place wasn't mine. This was Jack's home. Every cruel thing made sense now, and I hated it.

There was one thing I had to know. "Why didn't you confront me?"

He touched his fingers to his temple, resigned. "What would have been the point? I was told one thing, and it turned out to be true. Most of it."

"Not the important part." I fought back tears as emotions swarmed me.

"Look, I didn't realize—"

Tears turned to anger, and I didn't want to hear another word. "You *wanted* me to be your villain. Gia left you, and you needed someone to blame. Everything makes perfect sense now. You think I seduced her? That I enticed her back to my cabin? You couldn't be more wrong."

Jack looked desperate. He tugged at his hair. "That's not what I—"

"Tell that to me six weeks ago. Better yet, don't say anything. You have nothing to say that I want to hear." I pulled the blanket up over my head. My heart was pounding so loud that there was nothing that could calm me. I could hear Jack moving around our room. I could feel the tension of him wanting to say something, but he didn't. The silence was painful, and I knew just one touch from anyone would feel like the slice of a knife. I closed my eyes, willing the hurt away. Tears slowly dripped from my eyelids.

It was in that moment that I realized he never knew me, just like everyone else.

Maybe that was for the best.

TWENTY-ONE

Jack

BEFORE THE DESPERATE NEED TO GET NAT OUT OF MY house consumed me, I used to think of construction and building and repairs as their own kind of peace. Being able to put things together, making something new and sound out of something nonexistent or broken. All of it was rewarding.

But right now, none of the peace I usually carried through a project was with me. Instead, a vicious countdown ticked down in my head. It was a maddening need to finish this cabin and get Nat out of my space. Today. I needed to be done.

I attacked the problem of renovating Nat's cabin with a ferocity that almost surprised me. Ripping out the floors and taking down walls last week had been fun. Now, I was in the decidedly less-fun stage of putting it all back together again. No matter how much I pushed myself, the sweat, the back-breaking work, it didn't feel like enough. Ideally, there would be a team helping me restore the cabin this week, but unfortunately, work commitments and life obligations had come up with my go-to crew, leaving me on my own.

I rested with my hands on my knees, taking in the space, wishing more could be done. It had been a painstakingly long project already, but due to supplier issues, there would be at least another couple of weeks before the cabin could be finished. All the time I put in today felt as unnecessary as the anger I'd been hauling around for my roommate.

I pictured her upset face when she'd realized what I'd thought about her. How wrong I'd been.

Trying to apologize had been impossible. The words hadn't come out right last night, and before I could get it together, she'd cut me off. I had thought the worst of her. I'd thought she'd known who I was dating at the time and that she'd just tried to act like it hadn't happened. Like she was proud that she'd gotten away with it. And I'd been dead wrong.

So many things were coming back to me from that summer. Someone had dropped out of the last session, and when I'd told Gia, she'd jumped at the chance to visit. She'd wanted to see me, sure, but she'd also wanted to be in someone else's pod so she could have the authentic camp experience. She'd become fast friends with Jamie, Emerson, and everyone else she'd met, and she'd told me at the first campfire how much it meant to her.

Then she'd been spotted making out with another counselor.

My blood had boiled the moment I learned about her infidelity, but now, looking back, I just felt sad. Gia and I hadn't talked afterward, other than confirming it was over. Of course, she'd been trying to reach me sporadically over the past few weeks, but I didn't owe her anything.

Confrontation was overrated. Gia and I hadn't fought afterward. It just had its ending. A door that had quietly closed.

My parents had always jumped from fight to fight, and it was usually a tug-of-war between them and us kids. We'd often been encouraged to pick sides when we were younger, and as we got older, we'd found ourselves trying to keep the peace between our parents. For too many years, one would apologize to the other, they'd get back together and be happy for a few weeks, before the fighting inevitably started up again. Apologies never meant much, and even if they meant it at the time, placating words never stuck. When they finally gave up and got a divorce, I'd had plenty of time to see how bad relationships could be.

"Whoa, still at it, Hawthorne?" Lamar adjusted his sunglasses and gave me a lackadaisical smile as I picked up some nails I'd just spilled while thinking of my family. "You know you're about to compete, right?"

I grinned back at him. "Needed to get out of the house."

Lamar came closer. "And this has nothing to do with the brunette living at your place, then?"

"Nope," I said, letting the P pop. "Definitely not."

"Well, whether you're avoiding your roommate or not, the obstacle relay starts in twenty minutes."

"Right. Obstacle relay." The last place I wanted to be. Actually, that was the infamous finish line mud pit I'd practically tackled Nat into. I shook my head, but I couldn't shake the memory of how she'd arched so perfectly into me. How she'd kissed me back as if she needed my lips to breathe.

Shut up, brain.

"We have odd numbers, don't we? I'll sit this one out—" A part of me cringed at the suggestion. This was a perfect summary of how out of sorts I was. Giving up on the competition? The Jack of yesterday would have smacked himself upside the head.

Lamar grabbed my water bottle off the floor and handed it to me. "Not this time. We're meeting at the mess hall to assign obstacles to our teams. Just remember, your preference doesn't matter. What matters is that campers make their choice and we get what's left. Five bucks says you get the mud pit."

That would be just my luck.

I took a large swig of my water and cracked my back. An obstacle course sounded like hell. I'd already pushed my body to its limit. "Let's do this."

Lamar clapped. "Good. I don't want to have to change my bet."

"Bet?"

He looked a little sheepish, like maybe he wasn't supposed to tell. "Yeah, you know the counselors have been taking bets on which of you comes out ahead during this thing. You're just so competitive. I never thought we'd find someone who matched you in... spirit."

I rubbed my neck, which was killing me.

"Though looking at you now, I might need to change my choice." He winced as if he'd expected me to be treating this like an Olympic event instead of the casual obstacle relay that it was.

"Why do I feel like a horse right now?"

"You're manifesting your greatest fear?" Lamar guessed.

But horses had nothing on the unease I felt over being close to Nat. We were being bet on and pitted against each other before I even got there. My heart tightened in my chest. It would be even harder to get her alone to apologize. No matter what, I'd fix this before we faced another awkward night at our cabin.

I nodded and ran my hand through my hair, then put my hat back on. "Twenty minutes?"

"Maybe fifteen now." Lamar laughed as I took off in a quick jog back to my place for a quick change of clothes before meeting my pod at the mess hall.

I showed up to a flurry of campers running back and forth, finding their pods.

Nat waved a sparkly baton, indicating where Andromeda was gathering. I grinned, but I didn't catch her eye. I needed to gather my own pod. This week, my group consisted of half a team of roller derby players, the rest of whom were in Chase's pod. They were excited to compete, and a small rivalry had formed between their teams, which promised to be entertaining.

I was glad they seemed to have their shit together. None of the obstacles were particularly hard, but they'd still present a challenge to the other campers. My gaze instinctively went to Nat. She stood by Hazel and Lamar, discussing something. All the counselors were gathering, probably to go over the logistics.

"Be right back," I told my pod, and I jogged over and stood across from Nat, taking her in and barely listening to Hazel as she went over something having to do with out-of-bounds shortcuts. For all I knew, they were talking about NASCAR, because when I glanced at Nat, she had me questioning everything.

She looked beautiful, as she always did. She wore black workout shorts and a loose camp counselor tee, her hair tied up with a bandana as a headband. But there was also a weary quality to her. She had bags under her eyes and a sluggishness to her smile that was so unlike her. When I looked a little closer and saw her bloodshot eyes, I wondered if she'd slept at all last night. Knowing I was the reason for her sadness was a stab to the ribs.

Nat never looked at me. She turned away from the impromptu meeting as quickly as she could. I did the same and felt oddly hollowed out. I shook off the feeling and tried to concentrate on the relay.

Each of the pods was given a map of the five obstacles and their locations throughout camp.

My group huddled together to decide who was going to do which obstacle. Sue held out her hand for the map Hazel had given us and was clearly their roller derby team captain, ready to assign positions.

"Nat's gonna do the mud pit," I overheard as one of my teammates said my name and the word "mud" together.

"Jack?"

"Sorry. I'm really good at an egg carry," I tried.

They looked at me as if I were speaking gibberish, probably because I'd missed their entire conversation. The egg carry would be the first obstacle, and it was set up at the volleyball nets in the sand. There were four other perfectly good activities that I wouldn't mind doing, and yet the one I wanted to avoid was casually tossed my way. But I was prepared to plead for anything other than the mud pit crawl.

"I'd also crush that balance beam." It was a walkover, criss-crossed two-by-fours. "I'm really good with wood."

My pod member Bethany burst out in a surprised laugh, and the others gave each other *what the hell did he just say?* looks.

"Okay, that came out wrong. But look at these big feet. Perfect for balancing."

They didn't appear convinced.

Bethany gave me a curious look. "I'll be doing the two-by-four walk for our team, weirdo. We need you to do the crawl." Her finger was on the front office of the map, where the two-by-fours I'd screwed together last week were set up.

Said crawl meant I'd be trudging through the mud on my stomach under the woven net rope that Nat and I had set the posts for. Any other day, I'd love this obstacle, but now that Nat was doing it, I'd be experiencing déjà vu. Seriously, just my luck.

"I think there's a missed opportunity here. You're from the beach, Sue. Dirt is basically sand. It'll be just like you're home. You know you want to switch with me."

She shook her head, not budging. "I spend enough time cleaning dirt off my four kids, Jack. I like to be clean on my vacation." She was going to be doing the tire shuffle, which was the fourth obstacle set up at the meditation meadow, so it wasn't like she wouldn't be eating grass herself. Hypocrite much?

I pointed to the next activity, which was here at the mess hall just outside this building. "I can Hula-Hoop," I continued, even though I had never Hula-Hooped in my life. But we only had to hula ten times. How hard could it be?

Unfortunately, predictably, my pod wasn't persuaded, which made me the designated chump going into that ill-fated pit. Stupid frog.

A smile pulled at my lips as I turned the keychain over in my pocket. I'd taken Bernice from the hook that Nat had installed in her cleaning frenzy. For some reason, I liked having the cursed little critter, even if it had yet to be lucky for me.

"You're missing out," I said as everyone split up to go to the starting position for the obstacle they would be competing in.

I caught a glimpse of Nat still huddled up with her pod, no doubt doling out their own assignments. Maybe she'd walk over to the mud pit with me. I rubbed the little frog and realized that part of me didn't hate that idea as much as I should when my brain decided to bombard me with images of Nat in the mud. Her flushed cheeks and pouty lips lived rent-free in my brain.

My subconscious didn't stop there, though. I pictured our muddy make-out on repeat. I wanted to kiss her again. I pictured moving into her space, reaching out and threading my hands through her hair as I pulled her against me. Cherishing every moment of her soft, surprised moan as I pressed my lips to hers. Would it be an apology? Perhaps a declaration. No matter what it would mean, I pressed on the little frog and willed it to happen.

I wanted to do the mud pit now, as insane as that sounded. I watched like a falcon, but too soon, I found Nat laughing with one of her campers. For some stupid reason, my heart only sank further. I chided myself. My dumbass fantasy of Nat and me kissing after this relay wouldn't happen, especially not in front of campers. Focus on the competition.

Now that my initial reluctance to do the mud pit was assuaged, I was able to direct that feeling of want into winning. Then she was walking next to me. Fantasy back on. Shit. We didn't make eye contact. We didn't say anything. Luckily, there was so much commotion around us that no one noticed.

I checked on my campers to make sure they'd fanned out to go to their places, and I homed in on Sue, who was walking in the direction of the tire obstacle. Those tires had been painstakingly retrieved, just as I expected them to be. Herman had forced me to sell candy bars door to door for his grandniece's dance team fundraiser. He'd made me take a twirling ribbon with me, and the people of Wildwood had been happy to make me use it. I'd thought about buying the candy myself, but he'd stood on the sidewalk watching like a parent making sure their kid was safe.

Once the counselors and campers dissipated, Nat and Felicia joined me and the four other campers on the walk to the mud crawl.

Lola was monitoring the finish line and listened as Leo told us that the race had started over the radio. The quietest person in our pod, Tavis, would be kicking us off, but I couldn't see how that went, and it was killing me. I wished I could be there to cheer my campers on before they ran to the next obstacle, but I could only hear secondhand what was happening.

The events went quickly, and I found myself secretly glad my team hadn't taken me up on my doing the Hula-Hooping skills challenge, after Autumn had radioed that it was taking forever. On second thought, that shit sounded much more difficult, and I could only imagine how bad I'd do with these uncoordinated hips.

Someone finally emerged from the woods, and good sports that we were, our group cheered on the camper, who was on Lamar's team. When I moved closer to Nat during the hubbub, she subtly moved away and put Felicia in between us, pointedly ignoring me. Which was fine. I didn't want to hash anything out while we were competing anyway. Even if her silence felt like an open wound that needed cauterizing.

Tyler from Lamar's pod was the first of us mud-pitters tagged. Tyler army-crawled as if he were training for *American Ninja Warrior* or something. I was next after Sue came over the hill. She practically threw the baton at me, and I left Felicia, Nat, and the three other campers behind. I dove to my stomach and began the arduous crawl, the mud squishing and clinging to me as I made my way to the finish line on a mission. Tyler was still ahead by a fair bit, and I gave it everything I had, trying to pass Tyler, crawling my heart out. There was no more time for fantasies or looking back for beautiful counselors. I focused and held on to the competitive spirit, certain that Nat was right behind me. Tyler made it to the finish line first, and I was just behind him.

The rest of camp had arrived. My teammates jumped and cheered before taking two large steps back from me, despite my open arms snarkily searching for a muddy group hug. I cracked up at their looks of disgust. Their loss.

Then Nat was there, covered in mud and gorgeous. I couldn't help it. I was just drawn to her, and I hated how we'd left things last night. Hatred and competition were familiar defining characteristics in our dynamic, but now, there was another layer to it, a new distance between us that I didn't like.

Last night, I'd witnessed Nat's moment of clarity that, more than ever before, I wasn't someone she wanted to be around. The tender openness she'd tentatively shared with me before had closed down. When she had turned away from me, I hadn't pressed it because I was giving her space. But it still hurt more than I expected. I wanted to hear her voice, even if it was just to curse me out for the assumptions I'd made and the way I'd made her pay for them every day since.

I was captivated as she sliced through that mud pit. It was hard to ignore the determination in her gaze as she exhibited the same grit that I had. I couldn't help but cheer for her anyway.

Just yesterday, I'd been convinced she'd deserved everything I was putting her through. But today, everything shone in a new light. Nat hadn't known, and now I had to account for the very real fact that my actions had hurt her. I felt awful.

Nat celebrated her third-place win with her pod, and I hurried my ass to the dock. I didn't need to be on it again, covered in mud with her. So, after an obligatory jump to rinse mud off my body, I tried not to linger on the last time I'd jumped into this lake. Or the fact that Nat would be jumping in right behind me. I had the urge to pull her off to the side and apologize, but there were too many people around, and I'd see her tonight in our cabin.

I went back to my cabin to truly clean myself. My mind was

blissfully blank as the warm water cascaded down my limbs in a much-welcome reprieve. My arms were tired from working on the siding for Nat's cabin all day, then doing the arduous mud crawl. I let the heat soothe me as I efficiently scrubbed myself. I smiled as I reached into the linen closet and found it organized, the towels rolled as if we were in a hotel.

It was then that I took a look at the bathroom and how much it had changed. A Hawaiian pink shower caddy hung off a hook behind the door. Her toothbrush and toothpaste, the hair clip she'd worn yesterday, and some makeup brushes were all neatly arranged on the counter.

She was everywhere in this cabin, even though she had yet to step inside it tonight. I wondered if she'd come back here to clean up after the mud crawl, but she must have showered and changed at one of the communal bathrooms.

Dinner was an exhausting game of half listening to Felicia's animated story about a lock-picking adventure with a friend after they'd semi-stalked the quarterback of their high school football team and dropped her keys in his gym bag. Did I know why they'd ended up in his gym bag? No. Really, I was just looking for Nat. After an hour of this, it became obvious that Nat must have grabbed a prepared adult Lunchable and decided to eat somewhere else.

After leaving the mess hall, I played a fun game I liked to call *how many minutes have passed since I last looked at the clock?* while waiting for her to come back home. I was antsy to clear the air between us and caught myself opening her social media account to kill more time. I wished I could have said this was my first perusal, but the truth was, ever since she'd lit my nephew up like a happy little hellion by following him, I'd been pulling up her account more and more. Naturegirlnat had been easy to find, and she'd even posted the photos that she and my nephew had taken together during his visit last weekend.

By the time I'd caught myself smiling like a dumbass at my

phone, again, I decided it'd be best to get out of this cabin. What was taking her so long? Dinner was over. Her activity was over. Where was she?

Standing on my porch, I breathed deeply and took in the warm evening before I meandered around camp. I walked toward the craft cabin and saw a light on. Bingo. She may not have expected an apology, but I wasn't going to let this night pass us by without having said my piece. I would go back to giving her space if she preferred it that way, *after* apologizing.

TWENTY-TWO
Nat

TODAY WAS THE SECOND TIME I'D CLEANED MUD OUT OF crevices it didn't belong.

The second time I'd seen Jack covered in the stuff and had been somehow turned on by the image.

It wasn't my fault. That kiss the other day still had me squirming. It had been good. Mind-alteringly good.

But that didn't matter because I was the villain in Jack's story, and he'd treated me that way since I'd arrived. It'd been because of this that he'd brought things out in me I never expected to see. Things I still judged myself over.

I thought back to that night with Gia. I'd been on the rebound from a breakup. She'd obviously been with someone else. We'd hit it off over another camper's bad version of a cosmo, which neither of us had enjoyed but had drunk anyway. They'd made far too much, and I'd procured the pitcher and my silicone wine glass—because classy—and Gia and I had shared the drink back and forth, getting drunk as we sat on a dock on Lake Starlight.

I remembered our fingers brushing and the way I'd looked down to see the little stars painted on her blue nails.

But there was no romanticizing it beyond that. I'd barely known her.

I'd walked her back to her cabin and kissed her. No, she'd kissed me. That I remembered vividly because I'd been questioning what was about to happen and whether I was ready after the breakup I'd gone through earlier that month.

It was hard not to overanalyze everything now. The way she'd opened up to me over mixed drinks. She'd mentioned wanting the *true camp experience,* which must have been why she'd slept in her own cabin that week. The make-out was good. She'd giggled even. But out of nowhere, Gia had pulled away from me as though she'd made a huge mistake. Her reaction had left me wondering if I'd done something wrong. Now, I knew what that look was. She must have realized she'd cheated on Jack with a coworker of his.

The next day, she'd been gone.

She became the reason I'd decided against casual hookups. I'd leaned into making out with her because I'd been down on myself, but being ghosted by the hot girl at camp hadn't made me feel any better.

Before, I hadn't been opposed to one-night stands or intense make-outs with people I didn't know. It was hard to find a release when you were traveling constantly, so I'd occasionally ended up in the arms of someone new, knowing it wouldn't go anywhere. There was nothing wrong with that. But something had felt off with her. Now I knew why.

And other than Jack, at least two other people knew what had happened that night. It felt awful imagining what Jamie and Autumn must think of me.

They'd never outwardly treated me like shit, but were they just keeping it to themselves and secretly judging me? And which was worse? They'd obviously been above the former, but I had no idea about the latter.

I'd endured a lot the past six weeks, but the worst part was this cocktail of confusing emotions. First, I liked him, then I hated him, then I hate-liked him. Now I definitely hated him.

"Knock, knock."

Speak of the devil. And on another note, I really hated when people said knock, knock.

I sighed angrily, and that feeling didn't change just because he looked contrite.

The look quickly went away as Jack entered the craft cabin. "You have a minute?"

"I'm busy." I turned off the sink and shoved the paintbrushes I'd been cleaning into a mason jar to be used for the next class. I probably should have manhandled them a little less. They'd done nothing to deserve that.

"I can wait." The way he said it was patient and surprisingly not annoyed with my angry blowoff... It had me questioning things. Like maybe I should hear him out.

But I didn't want to. So there.

I took my time putting the paintbrushes away and cleaning paint stations, but he was still there. Sitting on the couch at the back, knotting and unknotting a macrame string he must have found on the floor or something. It had me wondering what else he could do with rope.

No. None of that.

I finished throwing away the last station's dirty paper towels when he must have gotten tired of waiting.

"So, we're just not gonna talk about it then?"

I threw a towel in the trash, but it took its time on the way down. When I gazed at him, he had an expression I couldn't read. Was he annoyed or was he determined? Confused?

"What is there to say, Jack?"

"I'd start with, I'm sorry."

I lifted my chin and glared at him, ripping the mason jar of paintbrushes off the desk at the front and making a beeline for the storage closet. He followed me. Of course.

"If you think I'm going to grovel when I had no idea she was your—"

Jack crowded me, and the already small closet shrank down to nothing. My eyes went wide, and he took a step toward the side, presumably so he wasn't blocking me in.

"This is a sacred space. You're not a crafter. You can't be in here." My voice sounded small as I whispered for no reason.

"The storage closet?" His cocky grin came out. I both hated and loved that grin. "We're going to get nowhere if you overreact to everything I say without letting me finish."

The absolute gall of this man. Was steam coming out of my ears? I wouldn't be surprised. "You might as well tell me to calm down."

He shook his head. "I may be an idiot, but I'm not stupid."

Was he being self-deprecating now? I wasn't falling for it. "Those both mean the same thing."

He took a step toward me. "No. They don't."

And just like in most of our interactions, I didn't back down. No, I stepped closer. "You're right about being an idiot."

Jack's eyes flared. "Do you ever let other people say what they need to say?"

"Do you ever stop pissing me off?" I struggled to think with his breath hot on my face. Had this room gone up twenty degrees? Was this a sauna now? That would surely destroy the crafting supplies.

He was amping up. "That sounds like a you problem."

"You're the only problem I have." I poked him in the chest. "And you're—"

Jack grabbed my hand and pulled me to him so we were chest to chest. He wrapped his hand loosely around my throat, using his thumb to tip my chin up, and before I could analyze how dangerous it was for the two of us to be this close, his mouth crashed onto mine.

Jack did a lot of things to clear my brain of thoughts. He

angered me. He frustrated me. But when he kissed me, every logical move I could make went out of my head.

This kiss was different from our mud-slicked make-out. That was indulgent and satisfying. This was frantic. It was fireworks going off where they didn't belong. Zipping and blowing up, incendiary and alarming.

He backed me against a wall of shelves, and the sound of a clay pot breaking as it hit the ground should have pulled me away from him, but I didn't care. I was too busy wrapping my arms around his neck as he ran his hands up my sides.

When we came apart, we were both panting messes. Strands of my hair had fallen out of my braid, dangling in my eyes, and Jack's lips looked swollen and redder than normal. I fanned my face and instantly regretted it.

"You hot and bothered for me, princess?"

My gaze followed the back of his hand down my shoulder to the tips of my fingers. Before that, I didn't know goose bumps could hurt.

"You are infuriating," I breathed, barely holding it together as he placed his hands on my hips, gripping them tightly and turning me around so I was facing the shelves. He pressed his thumbs into the space between my jean shorts and my tank top, and I nearly melted. When he ran a hand just below my belly button, my legs threatened to shake.

"Are you done?" he asked, his voice deep as he waited for my confirming nod. "That's right. Now unzip your pants like a good girl."

Oh god, did I like that or hate it? And why were my hands moving of their own volition?

"See? You can listen." His pleased tone almost had me crawling up the wall. The man had tormented me for weeks, and I was giving him everything he wanted.

"I can't stand you."

His lips dropped to just below my ear. "Tell me that in a minute when you can no longer stand."

God, the man was cocky. And that word brought our proximity to the forefront of my mind. With the way we were flush together, I could feel everything. He was affected by me, too.

I gripped the shelves and thanked whoever I needed to thank for their sturdiness before realizing he had probably built them. I'd always liked how handy he was. Jack knew how to build things. He used his hands and strength for all kinds of purposes, and now he was going to use them on me.

Jack's hands went below my beltline. His fingertips played with the top of my underwear, and I held my breath as he waited for my approval. Would I allow him to push this further? Because this would mean something. We'd had our mud make-out, and I'd barely reconstituted myself. Now, there was this undoing kiss and his exploring hands. This was more intimate. Something I wouldn't be able to call just a kiss afterward. I wouldn't be able to blow it off or forget it. I'd bet neither would he.

Lust overpowered me, and I gave his hand the subtlest push, enough to tell him that I was in this if he was. Just like with the competition, our goals were aligned.

Jack kissed the curve of my neck, and his fingers made a teasing pass over my clit to my center. My knees nearly gave way, but he clutched me tightly with his other arm, holding me steady against him as his fingers toyed with me. An embarrassing whimper left my lips as he delved deeper between my thighs.

"You get this wet for the man you hate?"

"Shut up, Jack." It was barely a demand. He had all the control, and I just... let him have his way because this felt too good. This man I'd been actively fighting had broken down my walls.

He pressed his lips to my ear and lowered his voice. "Do you know what you've been doing to me? Walking around in those tiny sleep shorts that are barely more than a slip of fabric? I've spent more nights tortured than tired. And I work hard, beautiful. I should be sleepy as hell."

Thank goodness it wasn't just me. I'd seen him shirtless more times than I could count. Showers in our shared space were the most frustrating. He didn't always plan ahead and bring clothes into the bathroom. Sometimes, he had the audacity to come out dripping wet in a towel, to the point that my tongue practically hung out every time he took a shower. I'd hear the water turn on, and my Pavlovian response was for my mouth to go dry.

I understood how he affected me, but I still couldn't believe I affected him. "You're an insomniac."

He let out a little chuckle. "You make it worse."

Jack dragged some of my wetness up to my clit and rubbed soft circles there. I leaned my head back against his shoulder and moaned. I should have been thinking about the possibility of someone coming in here, but I was too busy hoping I'd be the one who'd come. And thanks to Jack's skillful fingers, I was well on my way.

How was I going to go back to sleeping in the same room as him after he'd done dirty things to me? How long would I be able to resist taking his cock between my lips and testing just how hard I made him? If the thing pressed against me was any indication of size, I'd be in for it.

"Do you like being dirty at your place of work? Where anyone could see you leaving flushed and properly fucked?" Jack nipped at my earlobe and ran his free hand up my stomach and under my bra, coaxing another moan from me as he cupped my breast. "You're so beautiful when you moan, princess. It must kill you that I'm the one making you come undone."

Dirty talking Jack? Sign me up. I didn't care about our previous feelings toward each other, even if he was rubbing them in my face. I just cared that I was dangling on the edge, and this hot lumberjack was the one taking me there. My eyes blurred. I'd felt this nearly overwhelming sensation the closer I got to letting go.

My legs trembled slightly, and another soft noise left my lips. But I wasn't ready to give in just yet.

My breath came in short bursts. "Don't think so highly of yourself."

Jack kissed my neck and blew on the skin, causing me to shiver. "I can stop."

"Don't—don't do that either," I begged.

The small puff of a laugh leaving his lips confirmed he knew he'd won, but he kept it to himself. Instead, he increased his pace and the pressure he put on my clit, using his other hand to pinch my nipple until my mind went blank. I knocked containers of acrylic paint over, grinding my ass against him. A slew of words I wasn't proud of flew out of my mouth, many of them incoherent.

When my legs buckled, he held me firmly with his other arm while he continued to tease me.

"That's it, princess, give in. Give me what I want."

If he actually hated me, he would have stopped before I dissolved in his arms, but he didn't. A whine fell from my lips as I broke apart. His kisses softened against my neck, and as I tried to catch my breath, I thought that maybe he didn't hate me at all.

I caught my breath, then turned around, but I could barely make eye contact, the shame of what I'd done washing over me. "I can't believe I just did that. After you told me to apologize."

Jack lowered his head into my eyeline, a spark of recognition crossing his eyes. He touched my arm, and I didn't pull away. "No, Nat. I meant that I'm the one who's sorry."

Oh. "You—"

"Fucked up. So bad I don't know how to fix it. I should be the one apologizing. And I am sorry. So sorry for the way I treated you. I should have talked to you. Or acted like an adult and dealt with my feelings."

I swallowed slowly, the shame leaving just as quickly as it'd come. The sincerity on his face was foreign. I'd grown up in a household where I was always wrong. I'd had confrontations before, ones where I gave in and apologized for things I shouldn't have budged on. I'd never had someone take accountability for what they'd done, and never had they apologized to *me*. The one time I'd held my ground with my family had gone awfully. But this deserved a response. He deserved something for taking ownership of his treatment of me.

"I accept your apology." The words left my lips, and it sounded like someone else was saying them, but I meant it. He'd caused stress and aggravation, but he hadn't been harmful, not really. The time he'd gone too far, he'd apologized then, too.

"You... do?"

I smiled softly. "Yeah, Jack." I hugged him gently, and he responded with his whole body, as if he were desperate for this interaction.

"But I've been awful. The entire time you've been here. This whole contest—"

"Has been contentious, in part because of what you've done, yes. But the competitiveness between us would have come out regardless. Mine's just been directed at you. Now I don't know what I'm going to do."

Jack let out a burst of laughter. "You can still be competitive with me. In fact, I hope you will be. Because I have no intention of stopping or going easy on you."

It was good to hear him laugh. The air felt lighter. Tinged with sexual tension, yes, but lighter.

"But is it going to hit right?"

Jack licked his lips and smiled. "I'm sure you'll hate losing just as much, princess."

TWENTY-THREE

Nat

After Jack left, I pushed hair off my sweat-slicked skin and double-checked that my shorts were buttoned before I finished cleaning the craft cabin.

I debated going back home and taking a shower, but Jack would be there, along with those fingers I couldn't resist. I'd want to kiss him, and then I'd want more. Did I want more? Yes, but that was beside the point.

I hadn't even gotten to see him or touch him intimately during our tryst. I recalled the feeling of his hard length, and just the memory had me salivating. It was going to be so weird between us now. Would he expect this to turn into an enemies-with-benefits situation, or was it just a one-time thing?

Nothing about this situation was clear, except that it was awkward.

So once I was done, I bee-lined it to Hazel's duplex. She would know what I should do about Jack.

I planned to leave scandalous details unsaid, but I finally made up my mind to tell her something. She would be able to help me.

I took in the cute shared yard of Hazel and Leo's duplex, with their matching lawn chairs and a cooler nestled between them.

The screen door was the only thing blocking my view into Hazel's side, and I announced myself and opened it to find Hazel doing something I've never seen before: going through her trash can.

This was not just a dainty look at the top couple of items in case that was where the missing leftovers lid went. No, this was a spread-out, digging like a varmint in your garbage out back kind of search.

"What's going on here?" I used a tender voice as I peered at the raccoon version of my best friend. Luckily, she didn't startle. Instead, she glanced at her surroundings.

"This isn't what it looks like. I'm just looking for something." Hazel seemed embarrassed all of a sudden.

I sat down next to her and the spread-out pile of trash. "I see. And what do you think it looks like? Because I wouldn't exactly call this a healthy way to find materials for your next craft project, if that's what you're doing."

Hazel cracked a watery grin. "I wish."

"What happened?"

Hazel was rarely emotional, but she seemed overwhelmed. I immediately thought of the problems at Camp Sunlight, then worried it was something more serious.

"My friend Holli called. She saw my dad and gave me the heads up that he didn't look good. Apparently, she encouraged him to reach out. Then she gave me his new phone number. I wrote it down, but now I can't find it."

I understood the gravity of what she was saying and drew my own conclusion. "So you're worried it ended up in the garbage?" There was no judgment in my tone, only understanding.

Hazel nodded. So I got down on my knees next to her.

"I keep thinking that maybe he tried to reach out, but he couldn't get through to me because I... you know."

She'd mentioned how she'd commiserated with Leo the day

she blocked her dad's number. The man was a pit of greed and relentlessly hurt Hazel's kind spirit, but he was still her father. I wasn't one to judge. If anyone could relate to having a shitty family, it was me. So I helped her search. When we didn't find it in the garbage, I branched out, checking the table and counters. She finally found it hiding in plain sight on her coffee table.

My friend looked at the numbers scrawled onto the ripped part of the notebook paper. I met her beautiful hazel eyes. She'd always had pretty eyes, sometimes green, sometimes brown, and right now they were a little wild and a little hurt.

"Do you want some privacy? I can come back," I offered.

Hazel stared at the paper for a moment. "No, I'm okay."

She hastily took a picture of the scrap of paper to avoid this from happening again. When she turned around, I could see the overwhelm in her eyes and knew there was so much on her shoulders.

"How about you wash your hands and I take care of this?" I grabbed her broom and dustpan from the kitchen closet and shoveled the debris back into the bin. "Do you want to talk about it?" I asked when the mess was cleared and we'd cleaned up.

We sat in the middle of her purple velvet couch, each of us wrapped up in the softest blankets ever. Hazel shook her head at my question and picked up the remote. We began watching the Hallmark movie she'd muted to have her breakdown.

After a while, Hazel put her hand on my knee and squeezed softly. "I'm sorry. I know you didn't sign up for this today, but I'm glad you're here."

While I appreciated the sentiment, it also made me feel protective of her. This must be how Leo felt about her all the time.

That was the second apology I'd received tonight, although this one was completely uncalled for.

"You don't need to apologize. You should always be able to sift through garbage with friends."

This pried a smile and an eye roll from her. It was exactly what I was going for.

"Not many people would do that," she mused as we watched the couple on screen touch hands quickly, then pull away. Maybe I was feeling mushy, but I curled myself into her blanket and touched her shoulder. She turned to me, a puzzled look on her face.

"You have people here who love you. Leo loves you. I love you."

Hazel cocked her head as if she were telling me to take my own words to heart. "You know you have that, too, right? People who love you here?"

I smiled and shrugged. "Of course. How could they not love the girl who captures their best angles, makes strangers fall in love with camp, and who they love to ridicule for her eclectic taste in music?"

"Don't discount yourself. And there's nothing wrong with your taste in music. Anyone who says otherwise can fight me."

I believed Hazel to a degree when she said people loved me, but a scared part of me also believed I could lose her. The snide voice in the back of my head reminded me that my friendships didn't last. For many, I was too emotional, too loud. Just too much. I'd been rejected for this reason before, so now it was inherent to temper myself. To be mindful and not be a burden. Not to put too much strain on my relationships. So, I kept myself at bay around Hazel. It was necessary to ensure she'd keep wanting me around. Her just-right friend.

"I wasn't expecting to see you, but I'm glad you came," she said softly as if she'd just realized we didn't have plans together.

I thought about telling her about Jack again, but in the moment, my issues felt small and insignificant. She was already dealing with a lot.

I watched a little mobile of paper airplanes spin in the corner of the room as the air from a vent below blew upward. "Me too.

It's been a minute with the storm and the traveling. I've missed you." All true, even if I conveniently left out the selfish bits.

Hazel's whole body softened, and she wrapped her arms around me in a tight hug. "Missed you too, Nat," she said into my hair. "You know what we need? More friendship." She pulled back to face me with an unexpected gleam in her eyes. "To the group chat!"

I watched her as she texted her group chat, called *Girls, Gays, and Theys*, effectively sending out the bat signal.

Our phones both vibrated, a Morse code of hell-yeses, excuses, and wish-I-coulds.

Those who decided to join were headed over now, and that was when I decided to embrace it, pulling up an app to order pizza delivery.

Fifteen minutes later, a knock sounded at the screen door. Emerson and Felicia stood arm in arm, bursting with energy.

"It's been too long," Felicia lamented as she handed me a bottle of gin.

Hazel's eyebrows were raised as if she were doing the mental gymnastics to figure out when she'd last had a girls' night. I'd just assumed that the regular camp girls hung out all the time together. They all seemed so close.

"Yeah, that sounds fun. It's been forever for me, too." It wasn't quite a lie. I'd hung out with Mandy and Shoshanna before, if being a third wheel counted. And then there were all those times in college. Most of my travels included women, but we didn't get together in large groups. I was kind of out of my element.

I didn't need to harp on it. I was here now, and I wanted some of that feminine energy. If it coincided with getting away from my roommate, well, that was just a bonus.

The four of us giggled with pizza grease fingers and pink cheeks as we passed around the gin and a bottle of Pamplemousse sparkling water.

"Remember that couple with the bark burn?" Felicia giggled

before she opened up for Emerson to pour some gin and sparkling water into her mouth. She shook her body as though that were the only way to mix the two, and we all burst into laughter.

"There's no such thing as bark burn," Hazel said once things died down. She turned to Emerson and me and explained, "A couple was caught at the naked tree in the first year of Starlight. They had some... interesting injuries."

Emerson touched her chin, as if she were pondering something. "I think if you can get rug burn, you can probably get bark burn."

Felicia pointed enthusiastically. "Exactly!" she shouted a little too loudly.

The giggles didn't stop for much longer than was acceptable. The drinks made everything a bit funnier and made me happily fuzzy. Or maybe that was just a side effect of hanging with these amazing women. We shared story after story, and I heard about other ways they'd caught campers in compromising positions over the years.

Emerson delighted in having her own story to share with the group. "You know, the session I was here, I went with a group of friends to the East Side dock, and a couple was skinny-dipping there. They must have been under the dock, because we didn't see them, but I saw their clothes. I think they were just hiding there while we hung out."

Hazel bounced on her hands. "Oh my god, you do know that was Jamie and Autumn, right?"

"*No way*," Emerson screeched.

I was beside myself with this news. "How long were you there for?"

"Like twenty minutes," Emerson said, wheezing.

Everyone lost it. Then a knock sounded at the door, and several of us screamed.

"Shh, shh," Hazel whispered loudly. "Leo—"

"Can hear you through the screen door." He chuckled, opening said screen door to four women spread on the floor, cheeks red from laughing.

"Leo," Hazel whispered loudly. "You look so pretty with bedhead."

Leo patted his hair down. "And you look so pretty tipsy," he countered playfully. "But it's past your bedtime."

"Are you here to tuck her in?" Emerson asked, holding back a smile, and we lost it yet again.

Hazel's cheeks turned bright red, but she was still laughing, so that was a good sign.

I took Leo in, with his squirrel pajamas and sleep mask, pushing his hair up in more directions than usual.

"I thought you hated squirrels," I questioned, hoping to deflect the attention from my embarrassed friend.

"Hazel got these for me. They're super comfy."

Nope. Her cheeks just got redder.

Leo picked up a slice of pizza before heading to the door. "If you could just take it down two notches, I'd very much appreciate it."

"Okay, Daddy Leo!" Felicia called after him.

He looked over his shoulder, rolled his eyes, and left. I swore I heard him laugh from the porch and mutter, "I'm not getting any sleep tonight."

He probably didn't appreciate the laughs that followed as the screen door closed behind him.

As I approached, Jack's face lit up for just a moment before he seemed to catch himself. He had on his binoculars, and I giggled to myself, remembering my first prank on him.

He took them off and set them on the table, no doubt seeing where my mind went. I picked them up and hung them on his designated hook.

"Here, remember, we talked about this," I scolded, half serious.

Jack took off his boots next, leaving them in the space by the door. "Right." He walked past me to the kitchen and started making coffee for himself and hot cocoa for me. "So, where were you last night?" he asked, almost sounding too casual.

I looked over at him and was met with that large, broad-shouldered back. Had he been looking for me? My phone had died during the second Hallmark movie as Hazel and I spent the rest of last night finishing off our pizza and bingeing wholesome sweetness. By the time Felicia and Emerson left, we'd crawled into Hazel's bed, where I was reminded of another reason why we didn't spend the night together: her cold feet and the fact that she constantly kicked me. I was certain I was wearing the bags under my eyes like badges of survival to go with the bruises on my shins.

That was when I noticed Jack also appeared sleep deprived. Well, more sleep deprived than usual. Had he been worried?

"I had plans with Hazel," I lied.

Jack nodded as if this made perfect sense, even though we both knew I'd been avoiding him. "It doesn't have to be weird, you know. I mean, what happened. We live together. Goddammit, I should have thought this through. I just don't want you to feel uncomfortable. If you need me to leave, I'll sleep on a couch. I'll—"

I pressed my finger over his lips, stopping his unnecessary apology, and grinned. "You already showed me how very, *very* sorry you were."

Jack's eyebrows drew together. "I mean it."

"I know." My tone softened. "But you don't need to worry. I'm not uncomfortable around you. I mean, you gave me a lot to think about yesterday." My cheeks gathered all the warmth in my body as Jack's eyes lit up.

"So you're obsessed now? And that's why you didn't come home?"

"You wish. If anyone's obsessed, it's you."

"It's not a competition."

We both let out a ridiculous laugh, and I went on. "But you're right. Things don't have to be awkward between us. I should have texted."

Jack's eyes brightened. He must have been relieved. "Good."

"So you missed me, huh?" I teased.

Jack ran a hand through his hair and met my eyes. He paused as if he were thinking through his next words. "Yeah, I missed you. This place was so quiet."

Well, that was unexpected. I grinned, delighted. "You missed my soundtracks and random playlist, didn't you? Admit it. You love it when Broadway showtunes follow K-pop."

He mockingly winced at my words. "No, but I thought maybe you ditched this place for greener pastures."

When there was no antagonizing, I felt inclined to consider the comment for what it was. "I like being here."

Jack let out a long breath, as if he were relieved. My body relaxed at the realization of how true those words were. I liked being here. I liked being in Jack's apartment, in his bedroom, dealing with his e-reader and his failed tiptoeing around to make sure I slept. Setting up hot cocoa for me when he knew I didn't like coffee.

Did I like Jack? Like really like him? The man's touch got me going every which way. Yesterday, he'd wound me up and driven me higher and higher until I was as close to a lovesick puppy as I'd ever been. He had me feeling loyal and optimistic. Did I want more?

Everything felt different as Jack handed over a mug of freshly made cocoa. A long moment passed between us while I blew on the liquid before Jack cleared his throat.

"Look, I know that it can't happen again. I know you don't like me like that, and you know I don't date. I think we just got caught up in the moment."

My breath hitched in my throat at those words. *I might like you*, I wanted to tell him, but he turned his back on me, writing the conversation off as done. He cleaned his mug and stacked it onto the dish strainer.

"Yeah," I said numbly as he moved around me and stopped to put his Crocs on, which squeaked as each foot hit the floor. My eyes widened at the sound.

"Shut your cute mouth, Nat. These Crocs are necessary on the boat."

"You don't need to justify your nerdy side to me, Jack."

He shook his head. "You do need to justify your snark, Natalie."

I folded my arms across my chest and gave him a cutting glare. "I'll do no such thing. You love it anyway. Admit it."

"You're making me late," he huffed, turning from me.

"And you're avoiding the true issue at hand," I called after him with a smirk.

"You wish." With that, he shut the door.

I could picture the smile on his face as I got into the shower. I still had time before my first activity started today, and I was going to give myself a thorough pampering.

All week long, I'd been making my favorite jasmine and honey bodywash last, but it was ready to give up the ghost as only a tiny droplet squeezed out. I reached without thought for Jack's oak and bergamot orange bodywash and squirted a large dollop onto my loofah.

His curved smile, nerdy bird hat, and binoculars popped into my mind. Man, I loved that smile. Ugh. What was wrong with me? Maybe I just *liked* his smile. Just like I liked the close-shaved beard he always wore and how it rubbed against my face when we kissed. I liked how his touch was confident and how the tone he took with me when he was all dominant and dirty talking made my legs weak. I liked that he was competitive and passionate—that he now cleaned our cabin every night before bed.

I liked him.

Only, as I lathered myself up, there was no point in denying that I really loved the smell of oak and bergamot.

TWENTY-FOUR
Jack

I'D LEARNED A FEW THINGS ABOUT MYSELF FROM LIVING with Natalie Breckenridge.

One. *I loved that she was a formidable opponent.* As exhibited by our current standings in Camp Wars and in every argument we'd ever had. It both made me want to put up resistance and bow down to her will at the same time. It was confusing. And a little hot.

Two. *It was getting harder and harder to stay away from her.* That meant I wanted to stick around the cabin when she was home. And I wanted to check in with her throughout the day. I even went so far as to suggest we combine our two activities one day, because painting on a motorboat made perfect sense. I'd played that off as a joke, but was I joking? Kind of.

Three. *I didn't like to see her upset.* This included her being angry, sad, or unfulfilled. And that was the vibe she gave off lately, as if something were missing for her. And just as was my role in this camp as Mr. Fix-it, I wanted to figure out exactly how to rectify that.

It had been a week since our craft cabin hookup, and things were good. Nat and I maneuvered around the cabin easily—especially after I'd stopped storing all my work shit in the living room and took extra time to keep my space clean.

Another unexpected benefit was how the tidy environment did wonders for my mental health. I'd made a project list of things I could do to improve my own space, not just the ones I'd been working on for the camp. I realized just how long I'd been putting off improving my own living situation and chastised myself for doing so. I didn't need to work myself to the bone on the camp every day. I could do that and work myself to the bone on my own place sometimes.

I still needed to finish Nat's cabin first before I even thought about retiling my bathroom or changing out the shitty sink in my kitchen.

Thankfully, the cabin was coming along. She'd helped me with parts that didn't require a contractor and occasionally hung out with me while I worked, asking questions and handing me tools I couldn't reach. It was nice.

I'd told myself she was spending time with me only because she wanted her space back sooner, so I didn't make anything of it.

But as much as I tried to tell myself there was nothing there, the one thing I couldn't write off was my frequent need to keep up with her social media account. She'd been making basic posts, but there hadn't been much heart behind them, and considering I knew where she was, I could tell they had been planned so she could post them when she wasn't traveling as much. I started to question if she'd been uninspired lately, and the residual guilt from the way I'd treated her made me realize it was probably partially my fault. But things had been good between us since I'd apologized, and her posts remained the same, so maybe I had nothing to do with it.

Either way, I was resolved to get to the bottom of it.

"We're going out tomorrow, Breckenridge. Pack an overnight bag." I flopped onto my shitty couch.

She stopped scrolling on her phone and turned to me, her face deadpan. "I can't say I didn't know this was coming. This is when you kill me, right?"

"Why would I want you to pack if I wanted to kill you?"

She gave me a look that said, *come on*. "To make it look like it was an accident."

I tapped my chin, looking to the ceiling as if I were pondering this. "I guess you're going to have to trust me." I didn't give her a chance to retort as I left the room. "Noon tomorrow, Nat. Be ready."

All was quiet around us as we climbed single file up the rustic ladder to the fire lookout tower where I'd secured our lodging. Our positioning meant that I knew Nat was staring at my ass, making me grin as I climbed each rung. I tried not to let that minor distraction trip me up, reminding myself to stay balanced to avoid falling back under the weight of my heavy hiking backpack.

We'd hiked a mile in on a trail that didn't allow cars. Good thing Nat was outdoorsy. She'd perked up when I'd told her to bring her hiking shoes today instead of her pink tennis shoes. I could tell she was curious, but she didn't pester me to ruin the surprise, which I'd appreciated.

I was excited to show Nat this place. She'd been all over the place, but after scouring her socials, I was fairly confident she'd never been to a fire watch.

The location was remote and a little primitive. The brush was overgrown with weeds and fallen tree branches. Nat and I cleared the path as we went. We stood at the base of the fire watch. It was a medium height at close to forty feet up in the air, with a single ladder. This particular watch was being transitioned into a rental, but that also meant it hadn't been serviced or maintained recently.

So I went first and made sure everything was safe and not already occupied by wildlife.

We opened the door and put down our packs and Nat's gasp of excitement set my heart racing. She took my hand and dragged me to the windows overlooking the valley that stretched out below us for miles, her face practically glued to the view. Her reaction pulled a smile from my lips. The confirmation that I knew her made me want to puff out my chest. I had imagined her enjoying the panoramic view that only a place like this could offer, but it was a massive relief to see the happiness written on her face. She went to the view and pointed out Mount Hood and Mount Jefferson off in the distance.

"How did you find this place?" she asked, tucking a rogue chunk of her silky hair behind her ears.

I cleared my throat outside the door. "One of my bird-watching friends used to work for the Forest Service when this was active. There are twenty or so fire watches that can be rented out year-round, and soon this will be one of them." I leaned in conspiratorially. "What I'm saying is, it pays to know bird nerds."

Nat scoffed and patted my shoulder condescendingly, but it was in good fun. "Well, this certainly looks familiar." She gestured between the two small beds on separate walls from each other.

I'd been so focused on her reaction, I hadn't taken in the space fully. I hadn't considered the bed situation before and knew some fire watches only had one bed. It was perfect that ours had two, so she knew that wasn't my intention for setting this excursion up.

She pulled her lip into her mouth as she met my eyes. Was there a question in that look?

I dropped my backpack on the bed closest to me. "This one's mine."

She took a seat on the bed across the way without argument and tapped the heel of her boot against the rustic wood grain.

The room was slightly smaller than the room we shared at home. The living quarters weren't much, but it wasn't about the accommodations. This was about the view and the experience. Nat tilted her head against the window, looking out over the vast Pacific Northwest.

I pulled out a pair of binoculars and handed them to Nat, then grabbed my own—sans eyeblack this time. I tilted my head toward the door and we moved outside, leaning against the railing to take in the windowless view. Nat's elbow bumped into mine and I held my breath as she left it pressed against me. Everything felt like a watercolor painting, treetops tickling the sky, a mirrored lake reflecting the sun. Flocks of birds navigated through puffy clouds and mountains stood at attention, turning the serene sweeping hillside into jagged terrain.

"I can't believe you planned all this," she said in an awe-tinged tone.

"Just wait until later." I waggled my eyebrows at her, trying to cut some of the tension, excited to see her reaction tonight.

Nat's eye roll was as predictable as it was adorable. By the time we made our way through the woods to the truck, I wondered just how many more of those looks I was going to get.

Nat and I pulled up to the viewpoint at dusk to find more than a dozen vehicles ready to take in the rare passing of a comet. These kinds of celestial events were perfect for outdoorsy people, and I knew she'd love it. We could have stayed at the fire watch, but Nat's content always placed a spotlight on people's stories, so I'd hoped it would be like this.

As if reading my mind, Nat said, "This is one of the things I love about events like this. It brings people together."

A group of children ran between us, giggling as they made chase. She smiled at the couples setting up chairs and blankets in truck beds, a large portable speaker playing for everyone to hear.

We found a free spot, and I laid out the blanket before emptying my bag. Her gaze seemed to track every new item I placed on the ground. She lit up at the various Tupperware with Camp Starlight written in black marker, giving away that I'd gotten Azalea's help. And I was so glad I had. Nat looked ready to tackle me as I pulled out our salads, sandwiches, and cut up fruits and vegetables each with their own camp twist. I couldn't wait to get my mouth around some bacon-wrapped dates, and Nat had the same idea as she eyed the honey-glazed carrots.

Once we were settled, she took a bite of one of Azalea's brie and apple baguettes and sighed. A piece of arugula fell from her lips, and I held back my smile behind a sip of my water bottle.

"What?"

Apparently, I wasn't as covert as I thought I was. I reached over to pick the greenery off her shirt, careful not to graze my hand over her cleavage. I'd touched her there, sure, but this was different.

She laughed as I shoved it in my mouth, taking the last bite of my sandwich to chase it down. She reached over to wipe something off my lip and sucked the residue off her thumb until she pushed me away, giggling. I started listing Oregon mountain ranges in my head to take my mind off the image.

A butterfly landed on our blanket, and Nat reached for her phone before pulling her hand away, rethinking the motion.

I frowned. "Why aren't you taking the picture?"

"I figured pulling my phone out at something like this would take away from the moment. Or would annoy you, I guess."

I raised my eyebrows. "Did I ever say anything to give you that impression?"

"No, I've just been on dates where I saw something pretty and was reprimanded for not appreciating my surroundings or caring about living life in the present." Her eyes widened. "Not that this is a date."

I nearly laughed at her nervousness over what we'd call this outing, instead focusing on the problematic part. "You can photograph something and still be in the moment. I love how you look at the world and how you document things. I'm sorry I misjudged you in the beginning."

Her eyes softened. "You really don't mind?"

I shrugged. "That's why we're here, princess. I noticed you haven't done any excursions lately and figured you could use some inspiration."

I had one more surprise up my sleeve.

She watched me as I went into the bag and pulled out a glass container of Fritos that I had melted chocolate over.

Nat touched her chest, taken aback. "You thought of everything."

After cleaning up the trash from our meal, Nat pulled her camera out, practically bouncing at the chance to immerse herself in the event.

This was Nat in her element. I watched her talk with people and film a couple talking about their favorite Oregon viewpoints. I took a photo of her as someone offered a telescope for her to see Saturn's rings before the event started. When I showed her the image, her eyes went glassy.

That had me taking a dozen or so photos of her doing various things: standing in front of the mountain view, our food strategically arranged on a Starlight-themed paper plate. Our sticker-covered water bottles. Her looking out with her binoculars, the happiest smile on her side profile. She was absolutely stunning.

She thanked me profusely each time, and it had me wondering how often people helped her with her job. I pictured her with selfie sticks and tripods trying to get a shot of her for her brand, as she'd put it. There were so many artistic and vivid portrayals of places off the beaten path and people she'd met in various towns, but as she'd told Jordan during their hangout, photos of her had higher engagement, so she interspersed them.

I'd seen firsthand the amount of time Nat put into her work. It was impressive, the way she'd taken on Starlight as well. She did both without breaking a sweat. She'd told me that she had a system she stuck to because of her ADHD, and it obviously worked for her. She put so much work into getting things right, even if this was technically a *break* from her normal routine.

Nat looked invigorated as she lowered herself onto our blanket. We were probably minutes from the beginning of the event. She swiped through photos of people and the surrounding area on her phone. She lit up as she told me stories of her new friends. "This is Cameron and Sarah. They've been married for more than forty years and live three hours away, but this was the spot they met during a solar eclipse in the 1980s. I'm going to post about their story this week. Aren't they the cutest?"

She waited for my answer, which I realized I hadn't given her. I gave her a quick smile in response, hoping that was enough after realizing I hadn't even seen the photo. I'd been looking at her.

The stars sprinkled out of the night sky, fading out to make room for other miracles, but I was focused on this one, right here.

The gathered crowd appreciated the sky in a nearly reverent silence. Nat leaned backward, placing her hands behind her, and touched one of mine. Instead of pulling away quickly or apologizing for it, she wrapped her fingers around my palm and squeezed, turning to smile at me. I felt small in this universe and in this moment, but no matter how small I might be in this world, I had the power to make Natalie Breckenridge smile, and that was all I needed.

I wanted to be the reason she brought out that smile even more.

Nat shook beside me, and I saw the goose bumps on her arms. I reached into my backpack and pulled out a sweatshirt, which she gratefully accepted. I also pulled an extra blanket out and placed it over our legs.

"Thank you, Jack. This is perfect."

The word didn't do it justice. In the silence, as dozens of us gazed upon the passing comet, I found myself questioning what everything meant. Because the last thing I learned about myself when it came to Nat was that I couldn't get her out of my head. Not her laugh, not her ability to bring me to my knees, and definitely not the way she looked when she was filled with unadulterated joy.

That was the thing about Nat. She was unforgettable.

TWENTY-FIVE
Jack

STILL FEELING LIGHT AND EXCITED, I TOOK A STEP INTO our living quarters, forcing my thoughts back to my mental checklist. Heat: it shouldn't get too cold tonight, but there were blankets, chopped wood, and kindling for the woodstove. Pillows: check. Gallon of water: check.

Suddenly, Nat's hands were on my hips, tugging me backward.

Soft, sweet lips smashed against mine as she pulled me closer. I caged her against the door, instinctively gripping her waist. She kissed me once on the lips, then planted a luxurious kiss on my jaw before pulling away. Her gaze took me in, grazed down my body, then moved back up to mine.

I knew that look. She had a clever idea, and whatever it was, I was ready and willing to play it out.

"What are you up to, princess?"

Her hands were still on me, her lips a breath away. "I'm sure you'll figure it out."

Nat slid down the door to her knees. My throat went dry, and every nerve bunched together at the action. What a magnificent sight.

"Nat, you don't need to—"

"Oh, but I do." She brazenly winked at me as her hands found the button to my jeans. She paused as if waiting for me to push her away or urge her forward. She continued her path at my nod. There was nothing I wanted more than for her to keep going.

My boxers and jeans hit the floor a moment later. She looked back up at me and opened her mouth slightly as her hand wrapped around where I needed her most. I was grateful for the door. The sturdy wood kept me upright as I leaned my forearm against it, because when Nat licked the underside of my cock, I swayed. Fucking swayed. As if my dick had never been touched before. My knees felt like jelly, and then, as if she knew exactly what she was doing to me, Nat did it again. There was a slight hum as she licked up the evidence of my arousal, swirling her tongue around the head. And the way those big brown eyes latched on to mine had me. Mercifully, she took me into her mouth then, giving me a couple of strokes as she sucked.

I gently tucked her silky hair back before stroking her cheek as she set our pace. "Nat, shit, that feels so good."

This feisty, gorgeous woman was on her knees for me. Holy fuck. Maybe the keychain in my pocket really was lucky, because there was no way I deserved this.

Her enthusiasm sent shivers up my spine. With uneven breaths, I forced myself to remain still and go at her pace. I took in the way her purple nails made a pretty fist around the base as she bobbed up and down the length of me, her tongue making my blood pump wildly.

Without thinking, I dipped my hips forward, causing her to gag slightly. My brain wasn't capable of conscious thought, or I would have remembered the fact that her head was trapped against the door. I almost apologized, but she kept sucking, even as her eyes watered. She grabbed my ass and pulled me closer. The action was primal communication. She was okay. She wanted more.

Slowly, I thrust into her mouth, easy and rhythmic. I kept my hands off her, giving her plenty of space to take back the control if she preferred, but she took me in deeper and acclimated to my size. She whimpered around my cock, and I was in over my head. I ran my hand along her hair and cupped her cheek, and she didn't just suck my cock and take my gentle thrusts. No, Nat recalibrated every nerve ending in my body. She let me reset our rhythm, slow and steady, to stave off this burning, needy current rushing through me.

I balanced on a fine line between calm and chaos with Nat's lips around me. This was madness, torture, intoxicatingly perfect as she took me in again and again. All the way out, taking a reedy breath and kissing my tip, before sucking me down to the back of her throat. She let out the prettiest-sounding noises, and I realized I had a new addiction.

"Princess," I rasped. "Look at you, taking my cock so perfectly."

She hummed, and the vibrations she made sent the need to release into her through my every vein. Just like that, something snapped in me, and I needed to be inside her. Oh, hell, there were those eyes again. I was coming undone.

"Fuck, I'm about to lose it." I pulled back. She gave me a hazy sort of look before catching her breath and wiping her mouth. "Tonight's not the night I come in your mouth, princess. It's my turn to make you lose control."

I pulled her up and licked her pink, swollen lips and tasted myself as our tongues collided. She let out another needy sound, and her fingers went through my tangled hair, lingering gently across my scalp as little sparks lit me up. She was still fully clothed, and I became hell-bent on righting that wrong.

My hands found the hem of her shorts, and I unbuttoned them, keeping our gazes locked as she shimmied out of them. Her hands found the bottom of my shirt, and she tugged it up before doing the same to her tank top.

I was in awe as I took in every perfect inch of her.

Her underwear was heavenly. There was no other word for the

silky, tiny things that let her round ass peek out. But even more hypnotizing, there was an undeniable wet spot that had me nearly growling for more.

I palmed her breast over her bra. "Can I fill you up, Natalie? Do you want that?"

She nodded frantically and parted for me, like she needed this acute, sharp hunger between us sated. I ground my stiff cock against her fabric-covered core, kissing her neck and shoulder, then her lips. Her hands were all over me, gripping my shoulders and running down my back as I backed her up against one of the beds.

I hooked my fingers into the silk waistband, about to slide them off, when she laughed breathlessly. She moaned and clutched my forearms, pulling me closer to her. Maybe she needed this as much as I did. Doubtful. Because I needed to feel her taking her pleasure from me, sliding into her.

"Dammit." I pulled back from her a couple of inches. My thoughts were finally catching up.

Nat let me have the space. "What do you mean, dammit?" She took a deep breath and looked deeply into my eyes, as if they held the answers to everything.

"I didn't bring a condom. I wasn't planning on this. It wasn't why I—"

She pressed a finger to my lips and lightly pushed me away from the door with a grin on her face that promised she was going to save the day. I watched her dig into her overnight bag, where she produced a condom.

"For the record, I didn't plan on this either, but your girl is nothing if not prepared." She tossed the foil packet to me, and it hit me square in the chest. I dumbly caught it before it fell to the floor.

Your girl.

The image of Nat's lips wrapped around me just moments ago was eclipsed after those words left her mouth. She said *your girl* so casually, as if they didn't hold weight, but it sparked something in me, filling me with a primal need to call her mine. I knew I had no claim to her, and as she'd confirmed, this wasn't something either of us had planned. But that fact didn't stop the possessive feelings pressing against my rib cage.

Of course, Nat didn't help with said thoughts as she moved to the window, still wearing her elegant, albeit useless, underwear. She looked over her shoulder and arched her back out, shifting her ass tantalizingly toward me. Her gaze met mine from over her shoulder.

"Come check out this view," she told me, and I was behind her in a second. I pushed her hair off the back of her neck, making the little hairs on the tender spot rise. She made a soft sound of assent, and I pressed myself up against her, letting her feel me.

"It's an incredible view," I agreed, not bothering to take in the view outside. There were many more interesting things to look at in here. Such as running my fingers through Nat's long hair as I'd imagined doing a hundred times.

She tilted her neck, giving herself over to me in soft surrender. I gave her a playful tug and released her, then ran a reverent palm from the top of her shoulder down her underwear-clad ass. Nat pushed herself away from the cool glass until she was flush against me. I slid the tiny material off her hips with ease, and she stepped out of them without a sound. I playfully pulled her bra strap between my teeth and let it snap back.

She let out an impatient huff at my leisurely pace. "Take it off," she demanded.

I nipped at her ear in admonishment, and goose bumps climbed up her arms. After I'd teased her to my liking, I helped slip her bra off, encouraging it to join her underwear on the floor.

I cupped her perky breasts, squeezing them gently. "You're so beautiful."

Nat smiled at this, and I slid my hands lower, gripping her waist. I guided her forward until her perfect tits were pressed against the glass windows. The high-pitched gasp she made going from my warm, rough palms to the cool, smooth glass was something I'd be imagining for years to come. I made it up to her with kisses along her ear and neck that had her squeak before melting into a moan again.

"How wet are you for me, baby?" I whispered in her ear.

Her answering breath came out more pleading than snarky. "Why don't you find out?"

I hummed against her lips, kissing her once before I slid my finger along the wetness gathered at her center. She was already soaked and trembling as I stroked her pussy again.

Her hungry movements told me she didn't want games or soft lovemaking. Her impatient noises told me she wanted ferocity, her gripping fingernails told me she wanted a little roughness, and most of all, her every breath and each delectable moan all said that she wanted me. I tore open the packet and hastily sheathed myself while her hands touched me everywhere.

"Yeah, there you go. Show me how much you need it."

"I need it." She panted, squirmed, and pushed back against me.

And I needed to see her face. Roughly, I turned her around so she faced me. Nat bit her lip and wrapped her legs around my waist. I lined myself up and entered her in a long, sensual movement. She moaned beautifully as I filled her up just like I'd promised. I gave her a moment to adjust before I pulled almost all the way out and pushed right back where I belonged.

"Jesus, Nat, you feel so good. Your pussy is perfect."

She moaned in agreement. I sank deep into her, then as we adjusted, I picked up the pace, and just like I'd expected, Nat didn't back down. She met my intensity, just as starved for this as I was. Her nails gripped me, and she planted kisses all over while I whispered nonsense against her skin. I supported her with one hand and snuck my other between us to stroke her clit. Her whole body tensed and her hands slid down my chest as she let out a high-pitched whimper, unable to hold back.

I was obsessed. I loved being enveloped in her sweet, floral smell. I loved making her feel so intensely.

She tipped her head, letting it rest against my shoulder. "Jack, oh—"

I gripped her tightly, playing with her clit again, and Nat broke apart. Her moans were hypnotic, and the way my name rolled off her tongue had me trying to navigate the space between sane and whatever this was. Her body was pliant against mine. I almost lost myself then, but I wasn't ready for this to end. I wanted more.

She rode through her orgasm, clinging to me. She tilted her head to the side, and I kissed the corner of her lips. Her hair was a mess, and her smile was alight as she gazed into my eyes. I gazed right back. Those pretty, playful eyes I never got enough of.

But I needed to set her down. Gently, I cupped her ass and lowered her until her feet hit the ground. I steadied her a moment, and who was I kidding? I steadied myself, too. We took that moment and kissed, long and hard.

When we broke away, both smiling and breathing heavily, she glanced over my shoulder.

"We should put them together," she said breathlessly, tilting her head toward the beds.

She was right. I didn't think I'd fit on one of these beds on its own, anyway. She nipped at my earlobe, and I nodded and reluctantly pulled away from her.

"This isn't over," I promised.

"Good." Nat shot me a mischievous look, and I loved her fire. I wanted to dance in it. To celebrate it.

I quickly heaved the mattresses onto the ground so they were side by side. She watched me with a grin. She had her back to the window, still using it for support, and I loved that maybe a little too much. I strode over, feeling a fresh wave of energy, and lifted her boneless body up and carried her the short distance bridal style to the haphazardly tossed beds before tossing her onto her hands and knees.

Nat made an *umph* noise as she hit the bed, then giggled as I prowled over. She turned her head so I could kiss her deeply, and she seemed more than happy to follow my lead in this position.

She looked at me from over her shoulder and I curled around her.

I pressed kisses along her shoulders and up the side of her neck. Nat moaned, and soon we were moving as if there'd been no interruption. The heat and dedication she gave me had my head spinning. I kept my arms tight around her hips, locking her to me, sealing us with every deep thrust. She squirmed and moaned as she moved with me. The rhythm was made of bliss and anticipation, and we chased it together. Sweat and heat and need, all braided together. I lifted us up to kneeling, changing the angle. Her moans were guttural, and her long hair tickled my arm with each thrust.

I'd never fit this well with another person. Whether we were arguing, kissing, or fucking, everything with her just felt serendipitous. She matched each moan of mine with a gasp or a whimper of her own, and it felt as if she were made for me.

"Right there, Jack. I'm so close," she panted, breaking me out of my possessive thoughts.

Her words gave me a rush of adrenaline. I pinched her clit for good measure, holding her back tightly against my chest, and kissed her again as I moved. My balls tightened up as they smacked against her. Everything was overwhelming and so, so good. She stiffened and arched against me.

"Gonna let me feel you come again, princess? Let me feel you lose control?" I reveled in the way Nat mewled, as if she were incapable of full sentences. "Gonna say my name when I make you come?"

She was riding the edge. Every sound and movement she made was euphoric. I massaged her clit in slow circles until she was incoherent with lust.

And then, on a long gasp, she cried out, "Jack!"

Her pussy spasmed and clenched hard. My body reacted

intensely to feeling her pleasure. My orgasm hit me like a truck, and I filled the condom up. I pressed my forehead to the side of her head.

"Natalie," I said mindlessly.

We collapsed together onto the bed, and I was completely powerless to do anything but hold and kiss her while we both came down from our climaxes.

Eventually, I slowly pulled out of a blissed-out Nat, dealt with the condom, and collapsed back onto the small bed, pulling her into my arms.

She ran her fingers over the short beard along my jaw. "Good boy."

I chuckled and pulled her close. "You're such a brat."

She giggled sweetly, and soon my eyes were too heavy. Nat's gentle touch was relaxing, and within moments, sleep coaxed me under.

TWENTY-SIX
Nat

THE MATTRESS IN THIS FIRE WATCH WAS SO MUCH better than I thought it would be. I languorously stretched out. I was warm and so comfortable and—

Wait a second.

My eyes blinked open. Jack was under me, and not in just the sweet *my head is on his chest by mistake* sort of way. But in the *apparently I've become a koala bear, and this mountain man is now my tree* sort of way.

And then I noticed Jack's soft snore. Jack, who never slept, was dead to the world.

I didn't move.

After what I could only guess was an hour later, Jack shifted under me, and his hand clutched the back of my head as he pulled me tighter against him and placed a chaste kiss on top of my head. "Natalie?"

His voice was rough with sleep as his fingers glided through my hair.

"Yeah?" I asked, not moving an inch.

"You're sort of crushing my junk."

I took stock of where my legs were and realized my knee was pressing directly into his abdomen. I tried not to laugh, removing it carefully and garnering a relieved sigh from him. "Sorry about that."

"All good." We lay there like that for a minute before he broke the silence. "Want some hot cocoa?"

I grinned and went through the Herculean effort of pulling myself off him.

A little while later, I sipped hot cocoa out of a chipped mug, a baby-blue wool blanket wrapped around my shoulders.

"We can't ever do that again, can we?" I asked, looking out at the vast view.

Jack stepped up behind me and placed his chin on top of my head. "Probably not."

I nodded, which was a feat with his heavy head on top of mine. He lifted off me and curved his neck so that we were looking into each other's eyes.

"Do you regret it?" I asked, my voice just above a whisper. It was the last thing I wanted to hear, but I had to know.

He shook his head. "Not at all."

"Good. Neither do I." And I didn't. I'd had an amazing time with him last night. The date that wasn't a date and everything that followed would leave an indelible imprint on my mind, and it was all because of him. But this moment was just that: a moment. Something fleeting that could never be replicated for fear of it messing everything up. "We're friends now, and I'm happy to be okay with you."

"I'll take friendship over what we had before, hands down. I thought you'd never be able to forgive me."

Had I forgiven him too easily? I took a sip of my cocoa as I pondered this. One of the mini marshmallows dissolved on my tongue as he smiled sadly.

I never wanted to see that sad smile again. "Stop beating yourself up about it, okay? You've more than made up for it."

"If you're sure. I keep feeling like I'm messing up with you. Even last night feels like a turning point. Did we go too far?"

"I'll never think about it that way. I can move on if you can." I swallowed, hoping that if I said the words, I could mean them. "If all else fails, we'll just blame it on the stars."

This conversation was worth being late for, but as much as we'd tried to postpone the inevitable, it was time to go back to Camp Starlight. The next cohort of campers would be arriving shortly after we returned.

We freshened up, cleaned up after ourselves, and headed back home.

Home. Starlight had felt more and more like that special place I could rely on. I imagined all the counselors felt that same sense of safety. There was this acceptance and love that I'd only felt when I was there. Of all the places I'd traveled, nothing had clicked for me as it did there.

As we took off, the truck made a growling noise, eager to take us back home. I noticed Bernice hanging out with us, swinging back and forth on Jack's key ring as we traversed the bumpy road leading back to the highway.

"Did you bring that just to taunt me? You're such an asshole," I groused, but there was no anger or hatred, and I realized I didn't miss that push-pull between us. It felt like a natural evolution.

I like being his friend.

Jack grinned at me, and I tried not to swoon at the way he looked in a backward baseball hat. "If you're going to call me an asshole, Nat, you may as well add the word *champion* to the endearment. Don't forget what really matters here. I won this shabby thing fair and square."

I scoffed at his blatant disrespect. "Don't knock Bernice. She's a worthy prize, and you just got lucky."

Jack's fingers grazed the toy talisman. "How'd you get her anyway?"

"It was on my first solo hike. I'd always wanted to see Crater

Lake and decided to hike the perimeter. I got completely lost in the moment, but there was a flash of lime green that caught my attention. I walked a couple of feet off the path toward it. Out of nowhere, a branch crashed onto the ground in the exact place I would have been walking." A tremor went through me when I thought of the secluded miles I'd hiked, and pictured myself injured or worse. But I kept that part to myself. Jack's face was already twisted in concern, and I wanted to make him smile again. "It taught me that straying from the path can be a good thing."

"That's beautiful, Nat."

I shrugged, ready to lighten the mood. "She's been my good luck charm ever since. In most things."

"Most things? You mean, except when it comes to beating me?"

I chuckled. The nerve. "You'll be eating your words soon enough."

Jack shook his head. "Then what did you mean?"

"Well, Jack, if you knew any of my exes, you'd understand."

"You act like you're the only one with bad exes." He grinned at me.

My eyebrows flew to my hairline. "Excuse you. I've cornered the market. Did *you* date someone who sold your socks online?"

Jack's face scrunched up, and I smirked. In a game of comparing bad relationships, that anecdote usually won out.

"No, but that's gross. I did have an ex who had her mom break up with me."

I gasped. "She did not."

"She was supposed to meet me at a coffee shop, and then in walks Rhonda."

I burst into laughter. "I'm sorry," I wheezed. "I can't stop."

"It's okay. Rhonda was hot. Kind of wish I'd hooked up with her instead."

I kept laughing until my sides hurt. When I'd regained my

composure, I had another flop locked and loaded. "I once had a guy ask me to join his cult."

Jack literally turned away from the road and stared me dead in my eyes.

"They worshipped goats, and he was their leader. After the goats, that is." The dude and I only went on one date. You'd think someone trying to indoctrinate you would play a little bit of the long game. I laughed at the memory. I'd never actually laughed about my fucked-up dating history before. It was oddly cathartic.

Jack looked both entertained and dumbfounded. "Do you have any normal breakup stories?"

"Do you?"

Jack and I had gotten to know each other over our time living together, but I frequently found myself wanting to know him more, any crumb he would give me.

"Can't say that I have, but I did have an ex who liked my best friend more than me, which made things a bit awkward when they hooked up."

"Oof. That had to hurt."

"It hurt enough for me to move to California for a couple of years."

I looked down at my fingers, twisting them at the idea of anyone hurting him. He'd been cheated on twice?

"It worked out. I needed a change. Plus, that's where my dad lives, so I spent some time with him. Although that didn't go great either."

I'd gathered that Jack and his dad had a tumultuous relationship that he probably didn't want to rehash, so I decided to bring some levity to the situation. "Okay, that definitely sucks. But did your doorbell camera catch your best friend and ex kissing during your Halloween party?"

Jack grimaced. "Tell me that didn't happen to you."

"Oh, it did. And I have it on good authority that Captain America and Regina George should not be making out."

Jack ran a hand over his brow, shaking his head in disbelief. "That's so not fetch."

"I also found out someone I thought I was dating was only hanging out with me for publicity."

"Wait, what?"

I cringed. "Yeah. She thought dating would help our numbers go up by twenty-five thousand. She was aiming low, though. Dating me would get her at least fifty." I leaned forward and rubbed the keychain between my fingers. I didn't want any disparaging remarks toward my favorite charm. "Maybe Bernice has a bit to learn about love, but that doesn't make her unlucky."

"Your exes really are the worst."

I shrugged. "Yeah, well. There are two sides to every breakup. If I had a dollar for every time I heard I'm too much, I'd be able to pay for a therapy session."

There was some reason people didn't love me the way I wanted to be loved, and it had to be me. It was hard to hear something was wrong with you and not take it to heart. So I adjusted, because that was what you did, but sometimes those facets of my personality came out, and inevitably, my relationships went south.

Jack's jaw tightened at my admission, his face pinched into a scowl, and his energy shifted as if he had the distinct desire to punch something. Hard. I knew that feeling. It was the same one I used to get when I wondered if anything I'd had with any of my exes was really true, or if everyone just existed with ulterior motives I tended not to see until they were right in front of me.

We stopped at a light, and Jack met my eyes, which held a fire I'd seen before. Only this time, it was for me, not against me. I looked away, but his deep voice pulled me back.

"Let me be clear with you, Nat. You may pick the wrong people, but there's nothing wrong with you."

TWENTY-SEVEN
Nat

IT HAD BEEN A WEEK SINCE OUR DATE UNDER THE STARS, and the magic still lingered between us. Not enough to impede our competitive spirits, but enough that it was starting to feel... fun.

Jack and I made our way up the trail with childlike squeals as we raced to the archery range. Jack barely beat me there. Stupid longer legs. Not that it meant anything when we were both doubled over trying to catch our breath as we listened to the end of Sawyer's explanation on how points worked in the counselor-only archery event before they caught us barging in.

"You're both late." They looked between us, along with all the rest of the staff, and I felt my face go even hotter. I was never late. Damn this man, upending my sense of time.

"And out of breath," Emerson unhelpfully pointed out.

"We're just getting warmed up. We take the Camp Wars very seriously," Jack wheezed, and I held back my laughter. I tied a bandana on and noticed Jack did the same, securing his to his bicep just as he had in flag football. All that was missing was the eyeblack.

"Oh. We know." Hazel's tone was teasing.

I glanced around at all the cocked eyebrows that told me we

had not been good at hiding our rivalry. It was weird being the center of counselors' attention like this. Why were they so invested? I guessed there had been undeniable tension between Jack and me.

In a way, the fact that they cared felt good. When I was growing up, my family had barely paid attention to me, and I'd tried hard not to care too much about their lack of attention or the fact that I'd never earn their approval.

Apparently, we didn't give the group what they wanted. Everyone dispersed and headed to their targets. I was one of the first to go, having a stare-down with the bull's-eye fifty feet away from me. I nocked the arrow and aimed with precision. It had been years since I'd partaken in this activity, but boarding school meant I'd been exposed to rowing, show jumping, fencing, polo, and, as luck would have it, my favorite, archery.

With a steady breath and determination, I pulled back and let loose. Bull's-eye. Well, that would shut him up. Only, when I turned to Jack, he didn't have any cutting remarks. Instead, he was laughing and clapping like he was rooting for me. I couldn't let that thought distract me as I drew back the bow for my second and third targets, getting close to perfect with each of them. My third shot was so close, Autumn went up to confirm if it was in the bull's-eye. It wasn't, but for not having shot since last summer, not too shabby.

With my turn done, I glanced back at Jack. He gave me a lopsided smile that stunned the butterflies in my stomach. I grinned back and stood in line to watch the others take their shots.

"How many bull's-eyes can one person get?" Chase practically groaned, but his face said he was proud of me.

"You looked like Katniss out there. Sans braid," Hazel added.

Felicia mimicked my stance. "Damn, Nat, who knew you were an archery prodigy?"

I rolled my eyes. All of this praise made me blush.

Lamar, Chase, and Emerson took their turns, but no one came

close to my score. Then the real challenge stepped up. Well, maybe he was just a challenge for me. Jack held everyone's attention as he aimed. He looked like he was concentrating too hard, and the shot was nice but not a bull's-eye. Two more hits came close but not close enough, proving me to be the victor.

Autumn's teasing voice came up from behind us. "Didn't I teach you better than that, Hawthorne?"

Jack threw up his hands in happy defeat. "You can't expect me to beat perfection."

Autumn turned away from him, rolling her eyes as if he'd been sarcastic toward me, but I knew Jack's sarcastic tone, and that wasn't it.

"Looks like Nat's the winner," Autumn proclaimed, and suddenly, Jack's arms went around me. He picked me up in front of everyone, as if he couldn't wait to celebrate with me. As if he hadn't been there competing for himself.

This was all so new, and I'd be lying if I said I didn't enjoy it. I hugged him and then slapped his shoulder. "Put me down, Mr. Lumberjack."

He complied immediately, still grinning. I had the sudden urge to kiss him, but I remembered our surroundings—and the witnesses. Not to mention, we'd already talked about how *that* wouldn't be happening again. So, instead, I raised my hand for a high five.

If he noticed my awkwardness, he didn't show it. "Nice job, princess."

His tone was caring and sweet, and the nickname felt fond and not at all mocking like it had the first time Jack had used it. Even in this case, where my spoiled rich girl really was showing, but Jack looked at me with pride for it this time.

And it felt good. I'd done it. Not for my family or the boarding schools where I'd never truly belonged. But for myself. Everything was different at camp. Here, I fit in, and nothing could take that away from me.

"Thanks," I gushed.

Autumn pulled out a spiral notebook and added a tally to my name. "All right, people. This isn't over," she announced. "Standings are neck and neck. After this event, Nat is in the lead. But Sawyer, Chase, Jack, and Lamar are all still in it. Which means this could lead to a tiebreaker, so make the talent show count. We'll have campers vote on who they think the winners are for the talent show on Wednesday."

Jack had been secretive about what his talent would be for the next show, though so had I. I was excited to be performing a song. While I wasn't as good a singer as Hazel and Leo by any means, I could carry a tune, and I knew how to pick a crowd-pleaser. So suck it, Jack. This competition, at least the one between the two of us, was in the bag.

I smiled to myself, feeling confident.

Autumn came by my side, breaking my delusional fantasy of winning the competition, shitty little trophy in hand. "Can we talk?"

I stiffened. What could this possibly be about?

"Look, I heard about the whole Gia thing. I'm sorry about the misunderstanding." Autumn's face turned serious. She'd never hated me, I knew that, but she'd probably thought the worst of me. Just like Jack. "Jamie saw what happened that night and had to tell Jack."

I nodded. The truth was that I liked how Jack had people looking out for him. "Don't worry, Jamie and I can still be friends."

She hugged me, something we hadn't done once since camp ended last summer. I couldn't fault Jamie for protecting Jack's heart from a person who didn't appreciate him. How could anyone be mad at that? And better yet, how could anyone not appreciate him? Sure, Jack was a cocky, imposing man, with a love of monster trucks and terrible taste in music, but despite the man's many, many flaws, he was also becoming important to me. Maybe being with him was a bad idea, but regardless of what Jack may or may not ever feel, I'd protect his heart, too.

I WAS METICULOUSLY FOLDING CLOTHING WHILE listening to Noah Kahan, which balanced my thoughts that had been oscillating between the high of winning our archery competition and the gentle space of clearing the air with Autumn, when Mandy called.

"Mandy, what's up?" We didn't usually speak before her workday was complete.

Her words tumbled out of her. "Just on a break, but I have news. It couldn't wait."

"News?" Well, that was vague and disconcerting. Only she sounded happy. I grinned at my phone and put aside the stack of T-shirts. "What sort of news? Spill right now."

"I'm getting married," she screamed into the line.

I jumped for joy, not caring if anyone saw me. "Sho proposed? Or did you propose? Back it up right now. *Details.*"

My sister's voice trilled upward as she poured out the story in a quick staccato. "It happened this afternoon. Sho was bummed. I mean, rightfully so. I'm working on our anniversary. I'd promised to take her out for dinner, but she said she couldn't wait that long, so we went for lunch instead. I wasn't sure what she was up to, but then there was this gorgeous emerald on my appetizer plate and an eager-looking Shoshanna on one knee. Oh my god, Nat, you should have seen it. I completely forgot how to speak."

"Congratulations." I laughed with her, and when she texted me photos of the ring and the two of them together at the restaurant, looking elated, I couldn't help but be excited. "I'm so happy for you both."

"I know it's last minute, but, Natty—"

"Just say when and I'll be there."

"Can you come out on Saturday? Please? I need you there," she squeaked, realizing this was a big ask.

That filled me with shock. "Wait, are you eloping?"

She barked out a laugh. "God, no. Can you imagine? Mom would kill me. But we wanted to do the engagement party this weekend. Cherry Hill had an opening." Ah, that made more sense. Cherry Hill Country Club was the Breckenridge family's preferred venue. I'd practically grown up there. "Mom's already setting everything up. You know how she can be."

Didn't I know it. "Saturday is fast, but I'll try. We'll talk soon, okay?"

"I know you'll find a way," she said happily.

I SET MY SUITCASE DOWN AND PACKED UP MY TOILETRIES from Jack's shower. I looked longingly at the turquoise decorative tiles and flicked the light off just as quickly. I was excited to finally have my own space again. Jack had been putting in extra hours, and it had been an excruciatingly long week of not jumping him every chance I got.

He and I had been good lately. We'd agreed we didn't belong together, and that was okay. Even if seeing his messy, tousled hair had me panting. Even if seeing him put on his daily SPF did something to me. What was wrong with my libido? Sunscreen wasn't sexy. So why did I have to control myself when Jack did it?

I rolled my eyes and finished gathering my things. I had my own cabin, which meant privacy, which was good. But as I looked around at Jack's place one last time, I was filled with a sense of yearning. Was I actually going to miss this?

I grabbed my luggage and toiletry bag and headed over to Andromeda, not looking back. From the outside, everything seemed perfect. The cabin looked as though nothing had happened. It felt like another cute place. It would make a lovely home, with all its new charm, but it didn't feel like mine.

That was, until I opened the door and saw Jack standing there, taking up most of the space. He was sweaty and focused, but his face smoothed out its hard lines when he saw me.

"Hey, you're back. Welcome home." Jack gestured around my cabin like Vanna White on *Wheel of Fortune*, and I melted. He looked good here, smiling at his own cheesiness. Too good.

And just like that, my eyes filled with moisture. This was a big change and something I wasn't ready for. I didn't want to leave our space. But most of all, I didn't want to leave him.

Jack jumped into action, taking a step toward me, and before I could convince myself that this wasn't one of the several dreams I'd had since our time at the fire watch, his hand was caressing my cheek, making me feel safe and whole, as though he'd solve all my problems if he could.

"Natalie."

There was a pleading note to my name. I'd never heard it uttered like that before.

"I'm fine. It just looks so pretty," I lied, gesturing at the room. I told myself the newly clean bedding and curtains in my favorite colors weren't put there just for me. That he hadn't gone above and beyond because he was doing it for me. "Jack, I—"

He cut me off with a kiss, his lips moving in slow, languorous swipes against mine. A surprised sound escaped me before my body caught up. I tugged at his shirt and reactively arched against him, suddenly needing so much more.

His controlled movements contrasted with this crazed thing I'd somehow become, but Jack put his hand on my face, cradled my cheek, and met my eyes. "I'm going to take my time with you, Nat." The promise in his words had me instantly slowing down to enjoy this.

My hands ran up his arms and looped around his neck. He

lifted me, and my legs instinctively wrapped around his waist. His eyes never left mine as he walked us to my bed and gently laid me down.

Then Jack kissed me again. A deep, passionate kiss that told me this was the start of more between us.

I didn't know what this meant exactly, but it was already too late. I needed this. Needed to be closer to him. Needed to feel him inside me.

Everything about this was suddenly very intimate. I wanted him, even if it was a bad idea.

Jack's lips caressed mine intensely. We took breaths between every kiss, as if this was a normal form of communication. A beautiful conversation we spoke as our bodies melded together.

I wrapped my leg around his thigh and brought him even closer.

He groaned into my mouth. "That's it, sweetheart."

The way Jack spoke the endearment made my stomach swoop. His gaze felt charged as his fingers toyed with the waistband of my pants and underwear. I nodded softly, urging him on, and he took them both off in one pull.

By the time my shirt and bra hit the floor, a self-consciousness had washed over me. It had been so dark at the fire watch, and we'd moved so quickly that I was sure he hadn't seen much of my body, but being completely naked now felt intimate in a whole new way. He gave me a slow, appreciative look, taking in every freckle and curve.

He's seen you naked before, I reasoned. But this was naked naked. All the emotions I was terrible at ignoring made everything feel more intense.

"You're beautiful, Nat." He said it with such adoration, I nearly faded away into the new mattress. He ran his hand up my stomach, his blue eyes checking in on me as he cupped my breast, running his thumb over my nipple. He lightly pinched one, making me moan softly. His strong hands splayed out over my inner thighs, gently pushing them apart.

Jack applied pressure, opening me and holding me in such an exposing and beautiful way. I met his eyes, which were lit up with intensity, as if he was excited to taste me. Jack worked me into a frenzy with his tongue as if he wanted me stripped down and completely undone. As if he wanted me turned into a needy, whimpering mess. And he got exactly that.

He became a forge master as he melted me down to nothing, leaving only my obsession with him. Until his name was the only word I knew.

Jack licked and sucked my clit like he knew exactly what I needed to get there.

I'd go anywhere with him.

Soon, I was grinding against him, and Jack's large hand cupped my ass and pulled me closer against his face, his mouth driving me closer. My hands threaded through his hair, and he emitted a low growl as I gave it a gentle tug.

That sound pushed me deeper into my pleasure. I was overtaken. My legs tightened and shook as I came undone for him. I let out a whisper of his name that turned into a moan. Jack carried me through every sensation, encouraging me to take more from him.

He took a deep breath and grinned at me, messy-looking, hot as sin. And yet, that thought felt too simple and didn't match the tenderness of the moment. Jack wanted to take his time, and I was in no position to argue. He pressed gentle kisses to my inner thighs as I slowly came back to earth.

"Perfect, princess."

I cupped his cheek, and Jack crawled up my body like he was on a mission. His lips were on mine, and he pinned me with his weight. I kissed him deeply. The erotic taste of me on his tongue had my head spinning. Jack looked at me and then at my end table. I grinned, turning toward it and pulling out a condom. The foil pack easily opened, and I held the thin latex in my hand. Jack took short, thin breaths and made the most lovely sigh as I gave his cock a few appreciative strokes as I rolled the condom down him.

"Nat."

I looked up at Jack, the movements between us, the breaths we shared, everything was emotional. There was no better word for it. I smiled softly and kissed him. "Jack."

He hooked an arm under me and hitched my leg up over his shoulder. Jack entered me in one long, tight thrust, and my back arched up off the bed to meet him. We locked gazes and moved together. It was a hot position, but the way we were taking creative liberties, it was more slow and passionate. Intense sensations crested through me as I let out hard, breathy pants.

In no time at all, Jack was thrusting deeply, hitting that place within me that had me feeling watery and uncontainable.

"Jack," I whimpered.

He pressed a kiss to my leg and stroked my clit while he gave me maddeningly slow, deep thrusts. His eyes weren't leaving mine. "I've got you, princess."

And as if I'd done it a hundred times, I rode the wave and came again for him.

Jack gave me a moment to catch up, but soon he pulled my leg down and wrapped it around his waist. We changed positions so that he was sitting up and I was straddling his lap. We were hugging, as close as two people could be. A cosmically sensual feeling washed over me. I didn't want to let go.

Jack kissed my neck as he gently thrust into me. Pleasure built as we moved together, kissing as if it were our new language. My whole body tightened around him and spasmed until I erupted, a sparking sensation spreading to my fingers and toes.

Our foreheads pressed together while we shared the same air back and forth. Jack looked at me like I was everything to him as he grunted my name, clutched me tighter, and finally let go, coming inside of me.

His face tucked into my neck, and his breath danced on my

collar as we panted. Neither of us moved for a long moment. There was a deep sensation of peace as our hearts beat in sync and we held each other.

"You're so comfortable." I swooned, my limbs feeling like jelly, as Jack tucked me closer into him.

"That's because you fit right here." He was half-awake, and I loved this contentment between us. Secure in his arms, I was in no hurry to leave this moment. I'd linger in it as long as possible and dream of it even longer.

Last time was fast, intense, and fun. But this, the hugging, the eye contact, everything felt as though it had been ripped out of my heart and served on a platter. Raw and romantic in ways I hadn't expected. This chemistry between us couldn't mean nothing.

I listened to his steady heart, fiercely holding on to this moment, hoping he felt the same way.

TWENTY-EIGHT
Jack

I COULDN'T REMEMBER THE LAST TIME I'D SLEPT through the night and woken up so refreshed and ready to start the day.

But the beautiful brunette lying on my shoulder had me rethinking that last part.

I breathed in the scent of my former enemy's hair and smiled as a wave of that jasmine and honey scent washed over me. She always smelled wonderful. The time I used her shampoo because I ran out had not been a hindrance. And maybe I'd done it multiple times instead of just solving the problem sooner.

Something I hadn't realized the first time I woke up with her in my arms? The way her eyelids softly moved when she dreamed. And how she loved to nuzzle, which she was doing right now. I didn't hate it. Instead, I squeezed her closer, which was a mistake because it woke her up.

She took a whiff of my skin as she blinked awake, and it gave me the smallest amount of gratification that she'd done the same thing as me. Though I'd been awake when I'd done it. Not relevant.

A smile tugged at her lips. "Hi."

That scratchy quality I rarely heard from her was music to my ears.

"Morning." I clutched the back of her head as locks of hair cascaded over my fingers. Was there a better feeling? Why was everything so good with her?

She reached up and pushed a piece of my hair behind my ear. "How is it that you look like a perfect Norse god right after you wake up?"

A puff of air left my lips. She was so cute when she was drowsy. "Maybe I am a god. Ever thought about that?"

"Careful. We just fixed this cabin. Can't have your ego busting down the walls."

Fuck, she was adorable. "I think we'll be fine. I built them sturdy."

The eye roll that followed had to have hurt her head. The knock on her door sure did hurt mine.

"What was that?" Nat rolled over to find her phone and scowled. It was a quarter past six.

Two more knocks sounded, and she groaned as she awkwardly rolled over my body to get to the ground. She yanked open her dresser and pulled out a silky robe. Instantly, my mind went to all the ways that tie should be used, but we didn't have the time.

I chuckled under my breath as Hazel's voice came through the door. "Nat, I know it's early, but it's freezing out here. Can you please open the door?"

Nat's eyes widened, and she shoved my pants into my chest. The chuckling turned into laughter.

"Shh."

She was right. Someone could hear me outside of this studio-sized cabin of hers.

"Coming. I'm coming," she said in annoyance.

"Remember saying that last night?" I whispered.

She threw my shoe at me. The first one missed. The second one got me in the stomach.

"Oof."

"Oh no, did I bruise your eight-pack?" she whispered harshly.

The cocky grin I gave her must not have been the result she was looking for, because she threw my shirt at my head.

Nat pulled on a pair of yoga pants. "Hide."

It was as if we realized the problem at the same time: her studio didn't have many hiding places.

"Please, Nat," Hazel whined. "I really have to pee."

Shit.

I scanned the area as I pulled up my pants. There was her couch, but it was in the wide open, and Hazel would walk past it. Her kitchen faced the door. Her bed was also in wide view. Why was this cabin so open? My eyes darted around anyway as if another option would materialize. Nope.

Nat must have been watching me, because she stood next to a window, waiting for my attention, like she already knew the answer.

"No."

Her smile was downright gleeful. "Yes."

She opened it and pointed. I lifted my chin and stared at the ceiling. Apparently, I'd be going through the window.

I was not graceful about it. I landed in a bush, my shirt falling behind the house. I frowned as my foot landed on a branch, pausing to see if Hazel heard me. I heard her mumble a thank-you and the front door slam.

"Oh my god, it looks so nice in here," Hazel praised, her voice moving away from the window. "Would you mind making some coffee? I'm dying."

I could hear Nat's sigh of relief. "Not at all."

A sock pelted me in the head. At least I wouldn't be walking away from this place half-naked. I could hear the sound of the toilet flushing, then the sink being used as Nat stumbled around the kitchen.

"So I wanted to talk to you about something," Hazel said.

I zipped up my jeans.

"Sure."

"That counselor you replaced last year, Lucas? He just reached out to see if we had any roles available, so I figured I'd talk to you."

Wait, what?

"Talk to me..." The hesitancy in Nat's voice was nothing compared to the worry running through mine.

"You didn't know if you wanted to stay the whole summer, right?"

I'd been expecting this a month ago. Nat had a career already, but I'd thought she was having a good time here.

"Sure. I did say that." Was she hesitant? Or had she been waiting for this?

I tied my shoe and fell over.

"What was that?" Hazel asked.

Nat looked outside, holding back a laugh as she saw me in my state of undress. She closed the window. "A deer."

The word was barely distinguishable through the glass, which meant that I wasn't going to be able to hear the rest of their conversation. That fact was confirmed when placing my ear against the siding produced no results.

Was Nat leaving?

My head was fuzzy. It usually took me a solid twenty minutes to wake up, and gazing at Nat had maybe taken up ten.

She'd been so beautiful this morning. And last night. The way she'd looked me in the eyes as we came together. It filled my chest with something I couldn't name. There was a reason this attraction kept winning out, and I didn't necessarily want that to stop. The sex was so good. It had gotten to the point that being near her meant I needed to touch her, and that had me wondering why. Was it just our chemistry?

Hypothetically, if I were thinking of extremes, would we be able to make a relationship work?

Why was I even questioning that? We weren't meant to be

together. For one thing, I didn't even want a relationship. Or at least I'd thought I didn't want one.

For another, she was here just for the summer. Though it wasn't like we couldn't find a way to make that work. I had more downtime throughout the year, and she traveled a lot, but she'd still come home. After all, she seemed to want a place to land. Maybe that place could be here?

Maybe I could put that light in her eyes. It was there last night. Maybe that was a one-and-done, but maybe...

Did that mean something? Of course not.

But the way she'd felt in my arms. And when I was between her legs. We just fit.

This was a problem. Did I have feelings for my former enemy?

TWENTY-NINE

Jack

I STOOD SIDE STAGE AND WITNESSED THE ENERGY AND laughter emanating from the crowd as Hazel did her magic show. Our weekly talent show tradition had always been a hit. It was a final chance for campers to goof off and spend time with each other and their counselors. Tomorrow, this cohort would be heading back to their regular lives, and we'd have our time off before the cycle started again, and we'd be welcoming the next group of campers.

Over my six years of working at Camp Starlight, I'd tried many different talent show acts to impress our wide-eyed, fun-loving guests, but nothing felt right or perfect just yet, so I kept trying new hobbies. Experimenting with different pastimes had always been fun. For our first year, I'd tried out ventriloquism, which went about as well as you'd expect. When I gave it up, Sawyer took it on, and even though they weren't nearly as hopeless as I was, they went back to interpretative dance, which they were phenomenal at. At one point, Lamar told us he could do better and gave the puppeteer lifestyle a try until he realized his heart was and would always be with his dad jokes.

I'd taken up yo-yo tricks last year. I was pretty good at it, but I liked to change up my talent to keep things from going stale.

This summer was no different. I needed to get a leg up on my competitors, so I wasn't about to phone it in. Which meant my current juggling act wasn't going to be enough. I decided to go back to an old hobby that was muscle memory for me: skateboarding. I'd been grateful for the escape into the boathouse, where my deck and grinding rail I'd made were stashed. It was a bitch to move, but Sawyer, Lamar, and I managed.

The crowd screamed for Hazel. Leo was entertaining as hell, parading around in that damn pink wig as Hazel's trusty assistant. Campers always adored their camp mom and dad yuking it up. After tonight's hilarious performance, they relinquished the stage to a group of campers who did a *Top Gun* reenactment before Leo was back on to perform his one-man-band routine. Watching him use the foot tambourine Autumn and I had found last summer at Wildwood's thrift shop, the Treasure Trove, had been truly priceless. Hazel watched him in awe, even though she'd seen the act a million times.

This morning's conversation between Hazel and Nat still plagued me. Hazel had reminded Nat that she wasn't planning on staying the whole summer, and Nat had just agreed.

Why hadn't she told me?

Even if Nat wanted to go, I somehow expected Hazel to tell her that we needed her to finish out the summer for... morale. Something. Instead, there was already a possible replacement. That fact sat like bile in my uneasy stomach. I didn't know what I'd been expecting.

I shook my head, chiding myself. Nat was always going to leave. The world was a big place, and she loved exploring it. I guessed, subconsciously, I'd always thought we'd have more time together before that happened. But this was for the best anyway. At least now I didn't have to analyze the feelings I was having. I didn't have to interpret the half-assed lie I'd told myself about not wanting to spend every waking moment doing stupid shit together. Even sitting in silence with her was preferable to her not being here at all.

I sighed. She was leaving. It should feel like a problem solved. So why did that idea hurt so much?

I put those thoughts aside as I performed my skateboarding set, which resulted in resounding cheers from the crowd. I pulled off every trick I attempted, surprising even myself, and the crowd loved it.

A smiling Leo caught me as I wiped sweat from my brow. "Hey, good job up there."

I turned to him, smiling. "The knees might argue later, but it did feel good."

"It's gonna be close between you two."

I nodded. "I mean, Emerson's slam poetry act was incredible, and there are a couple more to go."

The rest of the counselors hadn't had as much applause as we had, so I was ruling them out. Only a couple of acts were left: another camper, Chase, and then Nat.

"I really love talent show night." Leo gave me a boyish grin, and it looked the same way it had years ago, during our first camp talent show. Leo had gone in front of the campfire with his guitar, and I'd been up next with mine. Later, I'd jokingly complained that I was supposed to be the camp guitar guy. He'd conceded and said he'd be the one-man-band guy instead. At the time, I'd thought he was joking. I never expected him to best me with an instrument, but as I'd watched him up on stage in his full ensemble, he officially had. His act was always a hit, and if I were being honest, it was always my favorite to watch.

Leo gave me a knowing look before cleaning his glasses on his T-shirt. "Zel and I aren't competing, and Emerson, while amazing, didn't perform well enough to beat you. There's no way any of the counselors are taking the whole competition. Looks like it's between you and Nat. It always was."

"So, who has your vote?"

"I may be biased, but I've seen Nat's act, and it will be tough to beat." He elbowed me with a cocky grin. "She's singing, and yours truly is playing guitar." Leo beamed at me until his phone rang, interrupting before he could explain himself. "Just a sec."

He turned away, walking a couple of paces. Then he ran his hands through his hair, one of his frustrated tells. I turned away to give him some privacy, but a moment later, Leo was beside me, his voice was strained.

"I need your help, Jack." The worried look that overtook his usually happy-go-lucky face was all wrong.

"What is it?"

My mind rushed to Nat leaving unexpectedly, but that was insane. She was performing last according to our set schedule, and she'd at least say goodbye.

Leo's voice was tight as he answered. "Hazel has a family thing."

I put my hand on his shoulder. "Shit, sorry to hear that. What can I do?"

A determined look crossed his face as he entered his *fix something for Hazel* mode. I'd seen it before when Hazel needed a spider "evicted" from her cabin. Hazel had gone right to Leo, who dropped what he was doing to take care of it for her.

"It'll be all right," he said, more to himself than to me, and then his guitar was thrust into my chest. "I'm going to go be with her. Can you play for Nat? The song is 'Unwritten' by Natasha Bedingfield."

Uh, what? "Yeah, you go. I'll help her."

On the stage, Chase was apologizing to a camper, despite the loud applause and laughter. Apparently, he'd lassoed the guy a little too hard, and they'd fallen over. There were several other hoots and offerings to be lassoed next. Were they mostly women? His expression of regret and graceful stage exit only made him more enduring. The crowd really loved him.

I quickly looked away from the commotion and jumped into problem-solver mode. I didn't know the song Leo had mentioned. "Unwritten"? Nope, never heard of it. I was surprisingly good at picking up songs, so I yanked my phone out to look it up, but it was already too late. She was setting up her microphone and looking around for Leo.

I stepped up onto the stage and smiled at her. "Leo had something come up," I whispered.

Her shoulders dropped. "Well, I guess you've won this event," Nat said solemnly as if she had accepted her fate.

I didn't like that one bit. "If I'm going to beat you, princess, it's going to be at your full strength," I teased. I'd give up the competitive edge if it meant Nat having fun and enjoying herself up on this stage.

She looked shocked, then relieved as I pulled the guitar strap around my shoulder.

"We're playing a different song," I told her. Her eyes widened in surprise. I lowered the strap around my neck and began to play.

She perked up, and her lips curved into a smile as I whistled while strumming the bars to "Home" by Edward Sharpe and the Magnetic Zeros. She'd been playing it nonstop in our cabin for the past two weeks, whether she was doing her evening skincare routine, editing videos, or cleaning. I had the damn thing memorized through sheer proximity.

Still, I surprised even myself when I knew every line of the duet as we faced each other, singing with our whole hearts for all of camp. Even with my help, it was clear who the star was. I lost myself in Nat's voice. There was a raw, honey-smooth quality to it that had me transfixed as we pulled off the unpracticed tune. In the quick moment I pulled myself away from her and looked at the crowd, I found them enthralled.

The song ended, but Nat and I stared at each other, locked in the moment. We must have pulled off sounding completely in sync, because a whistle blew, and resounding cheers broke me out of my haze. We collected ourselves, bowing once for the audience before exiting the stage. Autumn's cheery microphone voice took over from there.

The crowd was still cheering, but I wasn't paying attention. Our hands were clasped tight as I led us away from the crowd. We walked at a brisk pace filled with adrenaline and surrounded by joy in the air.

Nat stopped between some expansive trees, away from the bonfire. The excitement from our performance buzzed between us, but I couldn't take my eyes off hers, noting the catches of pretty moonlight in them. It was enough of a distraction that I was caught off guard as she went up on her toes and pressed her lips to mine.

With our foreheads pressed together, she let out a soft sigh against my lips, sending goose bumps down my arms. "I can't believe you did that," she said quickly. "I love you."

My heart faltered. Blood whooshed through my ears as I looked at her. Her eyes were wide as saucers. I must not have heard her right.

My brain tried to explain it away. She hadn't meant it. It was a colloquialism. A meaningless phrase that had spurted from her lips in the heat of the moment.

But she went from looking like she'd had a slipup to looking determined, and I knew it was too late.

"You... love me?"

THIRTY
Nat

An indistinguishable look crossed over Jack's face as he held my heart in his hands.

A nonspiraling version of myself would give the man a minute, but the anxious version wanted to fill the silence. She won out.

"You don't have to say it back," I said calmly, like someone trying to stop a bear from approaching. "I just think there's something here. We've spent all this time together. We had that night under the stars. Look what you just did for me. I know we've spent this summer at each other's throats, but the past few weeks have been different. And it's not like I didn't feel anything during all that anyway, even if...well, you know what they say about love and hate."

Radio silence.

I cleared my stinging throat. "You're leaving me hanging here, Jack. Say something."

The pained look on his face deepened, his voice sounding like sandpaper. "You don't mean that."

I didn't expect him to say what I wanted him to say, but did he have to choose the dumbest thing in the playbook?

I stood stock still. "Don't try to tell me how I feel."

Jack's brow furrowed as he took on a different tactic. "I told you I don't do relationships. I've seen them fail, and I've been through enough. I was clear, Nat."

I shook my head, stepped forward, and touched his hand. This poor guy had been through the wringer, and I just wanted to make him feel better. But what better words were there to make you feel better than *I love you*? "I know you've had your heart broken. I've been there, and I know how hard it is to come back from that. But you can't believe you're going to be alone forever. We have something worth fighting for. So why not me?"

Why not me?

The crinkles around his eyes came out, but only for an instant, before his face went back to immovable. He was stone, and I was what I always was: malleable clay, ready to be squeezed into whatever someone wanted me to be. Something that wasn't me. It was why I'd run from my family, from my previous life. I'd chosen to fit my own mold.

But not right now.

Right now, I would do anything to make him happy, to make his impending *no* become a *yes*.

"We've been having some really good sex. It's easy to get confused—"

"I'm not confused—"

"And the winner is Nat Breckenridge!" Autumn's voice carried over the applause and whistles coming from the stage. "Has anyone seen Nat?"

Cheers of "Nat! Nat! Nat!" filled the air.

"This was a mistake." Jack flinched as he said it, giving me a modicum of hope that this was going to turn for the better, despite the painful words. "We won't fuck up again."

And there it was. Like a blow to the stomach. I could barely catch my breath. The space between us grew wider, an uncrossable crevasse filled with all my hope. *A mistake*? I bit my lip and stared at my shoes as tears blurred my vision.

"Nat—" From his mouth, the word was heartbreaking. This was killing him, too.

The flicker of warmth that went across his face made me pause, but only for a moment. He was scared. Too scared to do something here, even with my heart on a platter.

Then fight or flight kicked in, thank god, and I turned from him. "I'm sorry you think we were a mistake."

He said nothing as I ran from our hidden place behind the trees.

The jubilant crowd cheered on the person who'd won the camper talent portion, and he was bowing and blowing kisses back at them. I took a deep breath, shaking off my feelings. I somehow put back on the Breckenridge mask I'd thrown away so long ago. I had never felt like myself with my family and their friends, so I'd leaned into this more palatable version of myself. I hated that I'd done this before, and it was even more unsettling to do so now.

But still, I made myself smaller and ignored what I felt. Only, right now on stage, I was thankful for it. I smiled at the crowd and bowed, accepting my place as winner of the Camp Wars competition, glad it wasn't going to be dragged out the whole summer. I shook the bedazzled kids' soccer trophy above my head, faking enthusiasm. The Kevin Blevins Award was practically falling apart. Just like my heart.

I'd won, but it felt like I'd lost everything.

The crowd cheered for me. Jack didn't cheer. He was nowhere to be found.

The realization hit me full force. These campers didn't know me. My friends barely knew me. But Jack did. And he'd made it clear exactly what I was to him.

It'll be okay. It was a lie I'd told myself a thousand times. It had to work now, too.

I stepped off the stage as fast as I could. Putting on my brave face was the most I could manage, but I'd done it. I made my way back to my newly constructed cabin in a fog.

I looked at the situation from a reasonable person's perspective and knew he was right.

I was great at making mistakes.

How many wrong moves could a person make in a lifetime?

Because I was pretty sure I'd hit the cap, and I was only thirty-three.

I threw clothes into my bag, rushing around my newly fixed room like the Tasmanian Devil.

I couldn't believe I'd told him I loved him. I wasn't known for holding in my emotions these days, but I'd thought I could when it came to my romantic feelings for Jack. My other feelings, those of animosity and frustration, had been loud and clear.

He'd shown up for me. Stopped caring about the competition we'd been fighting our way through because I was left hanging. And he'd done so much more than that. He'd fixed my cabin and took me on an excursion perfectly tailored to me. He'd carried me in the pouring rain, for fuck's sake.

Maybe that was just who he was. Maybe, to him, it didn't matter that it'd been me.

That fucking hurt.

And the worst part? He'd told me in advance that he wasn't into the idea, and I hadn't listened. I let good old too-much-Natalie blurt the most vulnerable thing she could to a man she knew wasn't interested.

She was too emotional. Too quick to give her heart away. Too good at scaring people off.

I thought I'd outgrown her, but I guessed I was still that girl.

I thought Jack knew me. I thought he understood me. I thought he was different from everyone else.

Maybe Jack's relationship avoidance had only been a front for the woman he saw becoming obsessed with him. Maybe he just wasn't interested.

Once my bags were packed, I made my way to Hazel's place. Campers usually hung out at the campfire for a while after the talent show or by their cabins, so I was lucky to avoid people on my way out of my pod.

I could see Hazel and Leo's duplex in the distance, right as I heard some voices coming up the trail. I jumped off the path and dipped behind some trees. I wasn't proud of it, but I was committed.

"Did you see the way she looked at him?"

"I wasn't looking at her. I would cut off my right tit just to get a man to look at me like that."

Some giggles followed as a very loud hiccup came from one of the campers.

"Wow. You're cut off."

My mouth went dry. Was I that obvious to other people? To the staff? Would I be able to show my face at camp? God, I'd have to come back to camp. This was a nightmare.

When they passed, I booked it to Hazel's. I knocked quietly and whispered her name as I waited for a response. Nothing. Then I knocked harder. Still nothing. Tears filled my eyes as I turned from her place, dropping my phone in the process. It lit up on the ground, and I lifted it to find a message from my sister with four simple words.

"So, are you coming?"

THERE WAS NOWHERE QUITE AS DEPRESSING AS AN airport hours before a red-eye flight after you've had your heart stomped on. I used to find them fun and exciting, but right now, it just felt depressing.

A man lying on his duffel bag by our gate let out a snore as a couple shared a wilted airport salad beside me. I checked my phone again when another couple approached hand in hand. They hugged each other as if they might not see each other again. They must have been going to different gates. I hated that I wanted to know. What was their love story? Maybe in the past, I would have talked with them and found out.

I tore my gaze away from their affectionate display. A flash of the last couple I'd interviewed popped into my brain. Married for forty years, still watching the stars together. My chest ached, and I willed myself not to cry here.

Three. More. Hours.

And no message from Jack.

Which was good. The last thing I needed was some pity response or a request to talk. I'd gotten out of there like a bat out of hell, and I wanted to burn my phone rather than hear from him. Mostly.

I'd texted Hazel that I'd decided to see my sister sooner than expected, and she'd given me the okay. I felt bad leaving my campers without saying goodbye, but I would have been a mess if I'd stayed.

Would I be a mess if I came back after this trip?

After my and Jack's last hookup—and that was what I had to see it as now, a hookup—Hazel had interrupted our cuddle to tell me that a former camp counselor had reached out about working the remainder of the summer. That it meant I could leave my position. She'd reminded me it had been temporary anyway but I was welcome to stay. I'd tried to get a read on her that day, on what she preferred, but I hadn't been able to.

Somewhere in between the storm and all the competitions, I'd decided to stick around, even if it severely impacted my traveling. I'd come to the conclusion that I needed Camp Starlight, but maybe I needed it more than it needed me.

I could easily lift right out, and that realization hurt. Hazel had been so busy this summer that we'd rarely hung out. The person I'd spent the most time with was Jack.

He didn't need me around either.

THIRTY-ONE
Jack

I WOKE UP WITH A HEADACHE. I HADN'T TOUCHED A SIP of liquor the night before. So why did it feel like I was hungover?

Oh my god, I love you.

She loved me?

I had to admit that these feelings I had weren't exactly those of friendship, but love? Wasn't that too far?

Yes. It had to be. The last person I thought I'd loved had taken my heart and stomped on it. And the way I felt about Nat was completely different. Did that mean something?

Two knocks sounded at my door, and I swear, it was like someone punched their fist through my brain. Maybe it was her. Why did I hope it was her?

"I'm coming!" I shouted, throwing on some sweatpants before yanking open the door.

There, at the bottom of my steps, wide-eyed and nervous-looking, stood my ex-girlfriend.

"Hey, there."

"How you doing, buddy?" Gia visibly cringed. Like me, she was probably thinking how weird the word buddy felt. I used to be baby, but that had never felt right either. "Yikes, I mean... hi?" she corrected.

"Hi," I returned, my brain not fully caught up to why my ex would be here. Sure, she'd been calling, but this was out of the blue, even for her.

"I know you hate me."

I pondered this. I certainly wasn't losing any sleep over the woman anymore, but I didn't hate her. I didn't hate anyone, except maybe myself right now. "No, I don't."

"It's okay. I've been trying to get through to you. But you already know that."

I opened my arm to the living room, and she took a spot on my shitty couch. She'd always hated that thing. Honestly, anyone who sat on it hated it. I couldn't believe I'd slept on that piece of garbage.

There wasn't much room on the loveseat, but I sat as far from her as possible. "Why would we need to talk, Gia? You got my package, right? That was months ago." I hated the hesitation in my voice. A part of me wanted to sound firm and unwavering. This was the woman who'd ruined my life for months.

"Yeah, it was the best breakup box I've ever gotten. Everything thrown in with no thought." She lifted her head to find my eyebrows raised. "Okay, maybe it's what I deserved. But I'm here for a reason. Firstly, I wanted to apologize."

"It's been ten months."

Gia's face fell as she chose her words. "I know, and I should have done it sooner. But the thing is, Mike and Lisa are retiring and want me to take over their vet practice. Obviously, I'm doing it. I just wanted to do you the courtesy of telling you that we may run into each other occasionally."

May was an understatement. The vet practice was right next to Wildwood's general store. I went there probably twice a week.

"Congratulations." I meant it. In our early days of being together, she'd planned on moving here if there was a place for her to work. She had gotten along with Mike and Lisa well, and she loved working with animals. Over time, I'd started to think it was a little too small-time for her, but maybe that wasn't the case anymore. "I bet you'll love it."

Everyone had gotten along with Gia. At one point, I'd pictured her perfectly as a Wildwood resident. Now it was happening, even though she wasn't with me, the way I'd originally thought.

The tightness in her body loosened, and her stiff posture took on more of a wary look. "Either way, an apology is long overdue."

"You already said you were sorry."

After Jamie had told me what he'd seen the night before, I'd gone back to my cabin. Gia had been there, drinking tea, full of nervous energy. It had hit me all at once that things had been ending between us. She'd apologized profusely as she told me the truth, right before I'd kicked her out of my cabin. In my defense, she had just cheated on me.

At one point, I'd been grateful. At least it'd happened during the last session of camp. I hadn't handled being cheated on again well. A lot of hammering took place afterward. The new pod came together much faster than it was supposed to because I'd wrapped myself up in work. That anger had festered for months.

But I didn't feel that way with her sitting beside me. That was surprising.

"I did in the heat of the moment, but it wasn't enough. You deserve an explanation. I thought about sending you an email or something, and I just couldn't. I was embarrassed because of how bad I fucked up." She paused and took a breath, as if she were waiting for a response from me, but I didn't know what to say. "I got drunk, Jack. That week was sort of a test in my eyes. To see how we were doing. Whether you want to admit it or not, we were having problems. So, when I'd had too many, I made a big mistake.

It's not an excuse. There is no excuse. But it's the truth. I don't even remember her name."

"Nat. Her name is Nat." It annoyed me that she didn't even remember when I'd given Nat such a hard time. Man, just saying her name put a tightness in my chest I still didn't know what to do with.

Gia's eyes widened, almost as if she were embarrassed, but it further cemented what she was saying. She gave me a pondering gaze, and I wondered if I'd given myself away. "Right. Nat. I know someone told you what happened, but I promise I was going to tell you myself. I just didn't get a chance to."

I wondered how that would have turned out, had Jamie not witnessed it. Probably the same. It would have hurt the same.

"I accept your apology." The words left my mouth without a thought. I wasn't holding on to that pain anymore. "And I guess you did me a favor, anyway. Because we were always going to go south. Relationships just don't work. At least not for me, anyway."

Gia's face softened as if she felt pity for me. "That's not right. Please tell me I didn't ruin relationships for you."

I shrugged. "I think I have more than enough proof that I'm right."

Gia narrowed her eyes. "I'm going to be frank here. I think you get emotionally invested in relationships that are wrong from the start. We're a perfect example. It was for the best that we broke up. We weren't meant to be."

I tilted my head. She seemed so sure. We'd been having problems for months. We'd hardly communicated about our issues, though. It'd been easier to ignore them. Our original plan had been for her to move here, but she'd changed her mind at some point and had asked me to leave Starlight. I'd hated the idea, but I'd considered it. Deep down, we'd both known that was never going to happen. I loved it here too much. I'd helped build this place. Literally.

But our problems hadn't stopped there. Gia was kind of

immature, even if she was two years older. We'd get in these passive-aggressive fights where we didn't talk for days, and she wouldn't answer the phone. She knew I worried about her during these moments, but she kept doing it.

And I was pretty sure she hated the outdoors, which was basically my life.

But Gia's words had me starting to analyze my past breakups. The woman before Gia had been a commitment-phobe, and I may have convinced her to be in a relationship, one that had epically failed after six months. Then there was the woman who had acted like it was an inconvenience every time I wanted to hang out with her. Preceded by my first love, the one who had liked hanging out with my best friend more than me. There was a smattering of months-long relationships, but none of them had been right.

My brain was starting to hurt.

Gia let out her hands, which she'd been wringing in the silence. "Look, we had a lot of barriers, but I think the biggest thing was that there was no passion. No spark." The apology in her eyes prevented me from getting defensive. Instead, despite my protesting brain, she made me actually think about whether or not that was true. "We were more like friends than anything. You know? And I didn't challenge you. You need that."

I sighed. Maybe she was right. I wondered if my feelings over the breakup were less about it ending and more about how it was ending. This feeling I had over my treatment of Nat hurt so much more than my and Gia's breakup, which, in hindsight, was unsettling. Were my feelings for Nat deeper than those I'd had for Gia?

Shit.

No one could argue that there wasn't a spark between us. If I were looking at our relationship through Gia's lens, we checked all the boxes. We had passion, she challenged me, and the spark could have lit this entire forest on fire.

I remembered waking up with Nat in my arms and the feeling of the world falling away. With her, I was happy. With her, I felt complete. I'd seen glimpses of possibility when I was with Nat. Like maybe I could be in a relationship. Maybe it just took the right person to prove not all relationships were doomed. I may have been an idiot.

No, scratch that. I was definitely an idiot.

Nat had put herself out there. For me. For the hundredth time, I wished I'd talked to her that night. The way she wore her heart on her sleeve around me proved she trusted me. Maybe that meant she wanted to do this, and the prospect filled me with such an immense joy that I could hardly breathe.

Maybe I still had a chance with her. Maybe it wasn't too late.

The first barrier to finding Nat came from one of my campers, who didn't realize they were allergic to bees, and a sting caused their hand to swell up. I'd had to run to the office to get an EpiPen and calm them down before Sawyer took them to the hospital.

By the time I got away from my pod, I was sweating.

Then I got a radio call from Azalea asking for help when our commercial ice machine wouldn't stop spitting out ice cubes.

Followed by another call asking where the hell I was because Hazel needed help with checkout. Normally, there was coverage, but for some reason, they needed me. I figured I'd find Nat in the chaos of today and pull her aside at the very least, but I hadn't seen her. Which meant I was heading in the direction of her cabin now, in a rush, high on adrenaline.

I could do this. I could fix this.

I was almost to her place when I heard the two words I was tired of hearing today. "Hey, Jack?"

Leo stopped me when I was thirty feet from Nat's pod. I wanted to get rid of him.

"What's up, Leo?" The annoyance in my tone must have caught him off guard, because one of his eyebrows quirked.

"Did you happen to submit your monthly expense report? I'm too inundated to strong-arm it from you the day of, like Hazel does."

No. The priority was begging Nat for forgiveness. And then kissing her. And living happily ever after?

I must have lost my mind.

"No, I didn't."

He zeroed in on my tapping foot. "Are you in a hurry or something?"

I stopped instantly. "I'm trying to find Nat."

"She's not here. Why do you think Sawyer is handling her end-of-session list? She left. Don't know why, but I didn't have time to get it out of Hazel."

My world toppled over as the breath whooshed out of my lungs. And was that a high-pitched ringing in my ears? I hadn't seen her after she confessed her love, but I'd sort of been avoiding her. I thought again about what I'd heard when I climbed out of her window. Hazel had come to talk to her about a possible replacement counselor. Had Nat taken the option? I felt sick.

"I did this." The words felt bitter on my tongue, but it was nothing compared to the churning in my stomach.

Leo's eyebrows lifted in surprise before narrowing. "Please tell me you didn't fuck up with her. Again." Leo was back to his chastising face. I'd never seen it before this summer, but I was finding it more and more frequently.

I put my head in my hands and watched his feet come closer through my fingers. He placed his hand on my shoulder, and I lifted my head to find a look of understanding. "I'd been telling myself I didn't want a relationship, and like an idiot, I pushed her away. She told me she loved me, and I pushed her away."

"Then you know what you have to do, Jack." His determination had me feeling like maybe I could fix this, but that didn't mean I didn't have doubts.

"What if I'm too late?"

Leo shook his head. "You won't know until you try. Putting yourself out there is hard. And maybe you offer her your heart, and she crushes it, but that doesn't mean it wasn't worth the risk. Love is always worth the risk."

THIRTY-TWO

Nat

The hotel lobby had been a shit-show. I'd dragged myself out of my rideshare to find total chaos in the form of loud kids of all ages here for the statewide spelling bee, just my luck. I'd tried to put on a smiling facade for the receptionist, but could barely muster up a wave.

By the time I'd made it to my room, I had five missed calls from Hazel. She'd left me a couple of messages while I was in flight, and I couldn't put her off for much longer. So after a shower and some self-care, I picked up the phone.

"So, how's it going?"

I twirled the sash to my hotel robe and stared at my newly painted toes as Hazel asked the question of the day over video chat.

"Oh, you know." My stomach was upset, and I questioned why I went from one mortifying situation to another. Tomorrow's party was going to suck. "Mandy and I are about to go to dinner, just the two of us. It'll be nice."

More like it'd be difficult to mask my emotions about what I was diving into and what I'd just been through with Jack.

Jack.

The name I couldn't even think of without tearing up. But I

couldn't tell Hazel that. Not now. Not if I was going to make it through this day.

"Are you okay, Nat? I mean, I know you're about to go into this terrible situation, but it just feels like there's something else."

My throat stung as I swallowed down the words I wanted to say. Instead, I blurted out a completely different thought, as though I hadn't been vulnerable enough in the past twenty-four hours. "I think I'm hard to love."

The silence that followed was deafening.

"Forget I said that," I choked out. "I just heard a knock at the door. It's probably room service."

"No, Nat. Don't you dare."

"Listen, Haze, it was a stupid thought. I think I'm just down on myself," I tried. "It's because of the whole parents thing, and you trying to fill my role and—"

"Whoa, whoa, whoa. What do you mean by me trying to fill your role?"

"I mean, you found a replacement, and that's cool," I lied.

Shock covered Hazel's face. "I had someone reach out to me, but I'll kick them to the curb right now, babe. I want you to stay."

"You want me to—"

"It's not even a question. Do *you* want to stay?"

Did I? That question wouldn't have even crossed my mind forty-eight hours ago, but now, with everything happening with Jack, I didn't know.

Hazel's kind eyes hit me right in the gut. "You don't have to answer that just yet. Let's start with you telling me what's actually wrong."

"He doesn't want me."

"Who? Jack? Bullshit."

The woman with her jaw hanging open on the small screen on our call didn't look like me. "You..."

"You really think after weeks of bickering and sexual tension that we wouldn't notice you two finally getting along? I know

Daddy Leo putting the hammer down wasn't the only reason you two could suddenly stand each other. I never should have bet Leo about you two in the beginning. Now I owe him fifty bucks. Dammit."

I didn't know how to wrap my head around this revelation. They knew. And who were *they* exactly?

"I don't know what I was thinking. He doesn't want a relationship. He doesn't want to open himself to anything. I don't know why I thought I would be the thing that changed his mind."

Hazel's strong gaze had me feeling like she was in the room with me. "Look, Jack needs time to digest. He has ever since I've known him. He hasn't had the best luck with love, and he closes himself off when he's scared. And what's scarier than giving your heart to someone else?" Her gaze drifted from the screen, as if she were lost in thought about something, before glancing back to me. "I have a feeling he'll come around."

The idea sparked hope in me, but I didn't want to believe it, just in case she was wrong. Was it smart for me to wait around? Was it smart to take him back after he rejected me?

"Can you answer a question for me? Why didn't you think you could talk to me about this?"

I swallowed. "Because he's your friend."

"I think that's a cop-out." Hazel had always been direct. It was jarring and often caught me off guard when she was being real with me, but I had to respond honestly. She deserved that much.

"I didn't want to be a burden. I'm always afraid I'm one step from pushing you away."

The sorrow that spread across her face was telling, and yet I still felt that tug to keep myself from her. What if I lost her? Who would I have left?

"I wish I were there to hug you." That was a surprise. Hazel definitely wasn't a hugger. The moment you received one of her hugs, you knew it meant something. And how I wished I could feel her arms around me. Maybe cry on her shoulder. "You're one of my best friends. You could never be a burden to me. Why do you always think you're too much for people?"

"Because I am. You think I haven't heard it enough? I'm too annoying. I'm too emotional. I'm too complicated." And yet, I wasn't enough at the same time. Not enough for Jack to love.

"When was the last time you spoke to your therapist?" There was a slight smile on her face, and I laughed, the tears in my eyes loosening. I hoped the video quality was poor enough for her to miss that. Hazel leaned forward, as if the proximity would drive her point home. "Because I think they would tell you the same thing. You are not too much. You're amazing. There's nobody like you, and that makes you special."

I was ugly crying now. "You think so?"

"I know so." Her face was no longer recognizable through my tears. "And whether it works out with Jack or not, you need to remember one thing. You are completely lovable. I know this because I fell in love with you the day we became roommates. The day we became friends."

"Your eyes are puffy." My sister stepped forward and touched the apple of my cheek, concern written all over her face.

I wrapped her in a hug. "Gee, thanks. I missed you, too."

We took our seats in the cozy booths at our favorite art-deco-inspired restaurant. It had been a long time since I'd been here. It'd been a long time since I'd been home, if I could even call Maryland that anymore. But some things never changed, and this place, with its wood-paneled bar, brass accents, geometric art prints, and to-kill-for horchata panna cotta, inspired warm feelings in me.

"Grandma Carol would tell you to put cold spoons on them."

I chuckled. "Can you imagine what that would look like?"

"Better than forks," Mandy joked. "She says hi, by the way. She wanted to come, but she's on that cruise in Ensenada."

She'd been looking forward to it for months. The last time I saw her was in February for our Galentine's tradition. She'd told me she'd been plotting how to hit all the buffets on the luxury liner. She had a map and everything. How she and my mom had the same genes, I'd never know.

"It means so much that you came out here. I know I didn't get to say it during our last phone call, but I'm sorry about our fight." Mandy's eyes were downcast. Guilt was written all over her face.

The server came to take our order, and I was relieved for the opportunity to work up the nerve to say what I needed to say. "I'm sorry, too. But I need you to know, there is precedent for me saying the things I say about our parents." Maybe I'd learned something else from Hazel. Being direct was the only way to be about this.

She sighed loudly, and it filled me with frustration.

"No, Mandy. Listen to me. They kicked me out of this family. All because I didn't let them control me any longer."

After years of running from conflict with my sister, I realized I didn't need to do it anymore. It was time to face things head-on, and the first thing I needed to do was stop sugarcoating the past and tell her the truth, whether or not she liked it.

Mandy narrowed her eyes in disbelief, and I knew I'd have to prove myself. "They told me you turned your back on them. On us."

I clenched my jaw painfully before releasing it. "Mom's exact words were, 'If you think you're going to shame this family by going off and being an Instagram model, don't bother coming home.'" I couldn't let her off the hook. For once, I was going to hold her accountable. I wasn't going to be passive and let my sister believe her lies. "I've tried to tell you this before, but you keep fighting me every time I do."

Mandy's eyes narrowed. Was she surprised? Ashamed? Disbelieving? "I don't know, Nat."

That was disappointing, but I wasn't about to beg for her understanding. "Well, now you know my side of it. Take it as you will."

We silently took sips of our blackberry mojitos until our server came by and dropped off our food. After that, we were back to superficial conversation about wedding stuff, which was a welcome reprieve, given the emotional conversations I'd had back to back. But it left me wondering if this was yet another relationship I needed to push aside for my own mental health. When someone didn't believe you, how real could things actually be?

THIRTY-THREE
Nat

IT WAS THE KIND OF PARTY MY FAMILY LOVED TO throw. Cocktail hour, followed by a big dinner, coming in at a little over a hundred people. I'd been to a million of these things, and I'd never felt more out of place.

Was it all in my head, or were most of them looking at me?

A loud clatter came from across the elegant ballroom, and as I found the location of the commotion, my eyes bugged out of my head. All heads were turned Jack's way, as if everyone here could tell that he wasn't supposed to be here.

My breath caught in my throat, and the ringing in my ears didn't let up as I took him in. Jack in a sports coat and slacks. Jack. *Here*. Was I hallucinating? He and the server he'd obviously run into had bent over to pick up the spilled food from a tray the server had been carrying. I left my conversation with my sister's sorority without explanation and rushed over to the mess. My stepfather would definitely chastise me if he knew this was because of me.

Jack let out a string of apologies to the man holding crushed canapés on a silver platter. When he left, Jack stood up and swiped at his knees to brush off the dirt from the floor. Then he straightened, his eyes trailing up my legs to my face.

"What are you doing here?" I whispered in exasperation.

A charming grin spread across Jack's face, and it nearly had me buckling. He placed his arm on my bicep and moved me away from the swinging kitchen door. "I needed to talk to you."

How had he even found me? I swallowed the question, mostly due to shock.

Jack answered as if I'd asked it anyway. "Hazel told me you were at a country club, and I called around looking for the Breckenridge party. Do you know how many there are in this city? Fourteen. That's just excessive, don't you think?"

Someone tinked a glass and alerted us that it was time to take our seats.

I swallowed, choosing to focus on the pink dahlias and eucalyptus crowding crystal vases that were centered on each of the round tables. The head table's bouquets were giant poofs of peach and white. It was all very classy and reminded me of a world I used to belong to. I turned to the table I was meant to be at. It was just twenty feet away. I could make it without falling apart. "I can't do this right now."

Any hope that he would leave quickly went away as I pulled out my seat. A sharp scraping sound came from behind me. The sound of a chair being pulled across parquet wood flooring. This place was dated as hell.

"Do you mind?" he asked as he pushed the chair between me and my cousin, Paige.

She did, in fact, mind. She glared at him as he moved between us, unsuccessfully, since he could only fit a leg in the space, his other leg crammed up against my chair. "You look beautiful," he whispered in my ear. The hairs on my neck stood on end as his breath caressed the skin there.

I turned my head, ready to unleash hell on the man with the utter gall to say such a thing, when more glass tinking filled the space.

My mother and stepfather stood behind my sister and her

fiancée's chairs. My mother took the mic. "Thank you all for coming to celebrate Amanda's engagement."

I rolled my eyes. No mention of Shoshanna, but sure.

"Many of you know how much pride I have for my two daughters, Amanda and Natalie, who have both achieved great things."

Wait... What? My mother had only expressed pride for me on a few occasions: after I'd done well at political events, at my graduations, and when I'd accepted a job at her company. Maybe this was the turning of a new leaf? Maybe the estrangement was finally over. "We are so excited to welcome yet another daughter into the fold. To Amanda and Shoshanna." She raised her glass. "May your impending marriage be fruitful and full of possibility."

Everyone repeated, "To Amanda and Shoshanna," before taking sips of their drinks. I did the same, but my smile made it difficult to consume anything. Had she actually admitted she was proud? What was happening?

I turned to find Mandy, who looked every bit the happy bride-to-be, beaming at her intended. I was happy she didn't make eye contact with me. After all the foot-dragging I'd been doing, I'd clearly been wrong about our parents wanting me here, but I was much happier being wrong than being right.

Mom and Dean sat down on the other side of our twelve-person table, and I was resolved to break the ice despite the barnacle attached to my side. "How are you, Mom?"

She glanced up from her champagne glass. "I'm fine, Natalie. Happy for your sister."

She gave me the perfect in to start a conversation. "Has Mandy talked about a date yet? I know she wants a destination wedding, so I'm not sure how that affects timelines."

"We don't have a date, but we'll be doing it at the club," my mother said, tight-lipped.

"Oh. I thought she wanted to get married in Italy."

"Things change." The pointed glare she sent my way would have had fourteen-year-old Nat shivering in her astronomically expensive pumps. I'd never been a heels girl, but that didn't matter to my mother.

"Oh. Well, I'm sure it'll be nice here, too." Though I'd be sure to talk to Mandy about her actual feelings regarding her wedding venue.

My mother nodded and turned to Dean.

Seeing an opportunity, Jack jumped at his chance to talk to me. "Can we take a minute to—"

"You know, Natalie, I'm surprised you even came," Dean interjected, just above a whisper. The rest of the table seemed tied up in their own conversations, but I heard him loud and clear.

I turned away from a dumbfounded Jack and faced my stepfather's barely restrained rage. His fists were clenched at his sides, his rigid posture and previously guarded stare had become dangerous. He zeroed in on me as though I were the cockroach who dared to cross his path.

My heart shriveled, and I hated the way just a comment like that could make me feel like I was ten years old and coming home with a report card that wasn't all A's. I treaded lightly because staying neutral around them had always been best. "It was last minute, but I made it work."

That little vein on the side of his forehead twitched, and I knew I was in for it. "That's not what I meant. You haven't been a part of this family for a long time. Why are you here?"

I returned his shitty question with a glare. "Because she's my sister. The next thing you're going to say is I'm not allowed at the wedding."

My mother took over. "We'll see if you get an invitation."

My mouth dropped open. "Wait a minute." I barely got the words out. "You just said you were proud of me."

"We're not going to tell our closest friends what a stain you have been to this family's reputation. They think you're tied up in the London offices."

Now I wished my social accounts had my full name on them.

I'd always thought keeping my real identity separate from Naturegirlnat was because of safety and the fact that I wanted to have something based on my own merits, but I was starting to wonder if I'd been hiding behind it. For them.

"You're an embarrassment. What did you think we were going to do? Say our daughter is being groomed to take over the company while our other daughter is frolicking through the woods?" Dean added as if my life were a punchline to a joke.

I looked down at the julienned carrots on my salad and swallowed back the lump in my throat. I didn't think I'd be able to hold back the tide of tears on the verge of cresting, much less get words out.

"What is wrong with you?"

I turned to find an enraged Jack in the stare-down of his life before pivoting back to my mother, who, for the first time, had some fear written on her face as she glanced at our tablemates, whose ears were starting to perk up.

"Who the hell are you?" Dean asked, doing a cold, judgmental once-over and deciding that Jack was unworthy of his time. That was something we had in common.

Jack ignored the question. "Nat has nothing to be embarrassed about." He took my hand and squeezed. "She's the hardest working person I know. She's built her brand all on her own and has more than a million people interested in what she puts out into the world. She's brilliant and kind. She'll drop anything to come to the aid of people who need her. You should be proud of her, not disparaging your own daughter. I can't believe you call yourself parents."

I'd thought the warm feeling spreading throughout my chest was the sign of a heart event, but it turned out that having someone jump to my defense in a way no one had filled me with satisfaction. It was invigorating.

"You'll forgive me for ignoring the opinion of a man I don't even know," Dean countered.

Jack bulldozed right over him. "Really? Because it seems like appearances are all you care about."

"It's time for you to go, Natalie, and take whoever this is with you." Dean shot daggers at Jack, and I wished my dad were here and not some sorry excuse for a stepfather.

"What's going on?" Mandy came up from behind our parents. I was so mortified about being told to leave that I hadn't noticed her standing behind them. "Why are you telling Nattie to go?"

My mom jumped in. "She's making a scene, honey. The last thing we need is to bring her failures to the forefront of your party."

Mandy was taken aback. "Failures? What are you talking about?"

"That girl has been falling short since she was a child," my mother said. "That's why we're so proud of you."

Their praise didn't impress my sister, who turned to me, her eyebrows downcast. "I didn't realize it was this bad." She wrapped her arms around herself in the same way she had when she'd been nervous as a child, before looking up at Jack quizzically. Then she turned to Mom and Dean. "You really are awful to her. I can't believe I didn't see it."

Mandy wasn't known for confrontation. Our parents' word was law in our household, and deviating from what was expected could lead to disastrous results. I was a perfect representation of that. That was why my mother and stepfather's open-mouthed stares weren't surprising. If it had been me, my mother would have told me I looked like a trout, but she was too focused on her stepdaughter's spiraling.

Instead of waiting for their response, I decided it was my chance to say something. "I thought you might want to see me after all this time, but clearly, I was wrong. All I want is parents, but you can't even meet the bare minimum. Parents are supposed to love their children no matter what. Parents are supposed to be proud of their children's accomplishments. If you can't love me for me, then I'm going to surround myself with people who will. If you want to call and apologize, you have my number."

Back when I worked for my mom's company, I'd constantly tried to make her proud at the cost of my self-worth, but that had been wrong. I'd thought I'd gotten away from allowing people to dictate how I lead my life when I'd left my family behind, but I had a pattern of doing this in relationships as well. I tried to hold on to people even when they weren't right for me. Now I realized I had been masking, trying to be someone else to please them, just like I'd done as a child, all in the hopes that they would love me.

I had to accept who I was. I liked myself, and I was lovable. I just needed to stop internalizing other people's criticisms. It was time to stop making myself smaller for people to love me.

I waved to Shoshanna, who'd witnessed the whole thing, as Mandy came around the table and kissed me on the cheek, whispering in my ear, "You don't need them. You'll always have me."

The smile I gave her had to be watery, but it was more than that. It was full of pride for her and acceptance that our parents were the disappointments, not me. I didn't need them to love me, but I could allow myself to be sad that everything I'd once had was over. I'd allow myself that much.

Once that moment was over, I reached for Jack, who looked like he was ready to go to battle, and pulled him from the room. I didn't need to be here anymore.

THIRTY-FOUR
Jack

Nat couldn't get out of there fast enough. We ignored the stares of nosy guests who needed to mind their own business as I pulled her to the side of the building. I wanted it to be just us. Unfortunately, it was us and the tension that felt like a physical presence.

I hated the way Nat was guarding herself. Her posture was rigid, and she had a deer-in-the-headlights look that quickly transitioned to her I've-had-enough glare that I knew all too well.

I'd witnessed so many aspects of her personality. The soft, vulnerable parts. Her worries about being too much. The joyful parts when we were happy together, joking around, or holding one another in the early hours of the morning. The way she needed competition and the fierceness with which she dedicated her whole self to it.

She challenged me like no one ever had, and the spark Gia had mentioned we'd lacked in our past relationship was never in question with Nat. There was this unequivocal need to be in her orbit. Sometimes, that looked like pushing her buttons. Other times, it made me want to pull out the smile she shared with only me.

Without her, an ever-present hole expanded in my chest, and it was all my fault because I'd pushed her away. I was the reason she was gone.

That was nothing compared to the way her spark had dimmed just from being around her family for a night. It was dimmer than I'd ever seen it. It made me want to hold her tighter.

I couldn't believe my ears when Nat's mother had called her a stain on their family's reputation. Her stepfather had actually used the word embarrassment, and I'd nearly lost it.

Nat had proven she was so much more. Her family clearly had no respect for the life she'd built.

They didn't see the hard work, all the thoughtful ways she crafted stories and shared them with the world. Her artistic eye and the care and respect she showed everyone she met. The heart she led with at Camp Starlight and beyond. None of it mattered to them. And yet she'd come back here, to be treated like that? My blood boiled. My hands clenched. I would have done anything to take her pain away.

Even with my messed-up family situation—the messy divorce, the way my mom and dad pitted us against each other—at least no one questioned what I chose to do with my life. Unlike with Nat's family, where they seemed to want her only if she fell perfectly into step. I didn't understand it. I never would.

But I did understand her better, especially when it came to the weight of the expectations put on her and how difficult it must have been when she'd finally gone against her family. Her light was undeniably brighter when she was at camp, and if I were lucky, I'd get to see that light again.

"Are you okay?" I pressed my hand to her cheek, noticing how hot and sticky it felt after some rogue tears had escaped.

Nat tilted her chin down as if she didn't want to meet my eyes, and I hoped I hadn't ruined this already. "That was mortifying."

"I'm so sorry, but I had to say something." She could fight her own battles, but I also couldn't sit by and watch someone tear her down like that.

Nat's eyes widened. "Not you. Them."

I could see now how little support Nat must have had since choosing herself. My heart broke for her. She needed so much more love and acceptance than she'd received. Yet she'd somehow still carried herself with grace despite the scraps she'd been given. I wanted to spoil her with it and show her she deserved so much better than she got. Based on what I'd been told, her sister seemed to love her, and she clearly wanted her there, but her parents were missing out on knowing their amazing daughter.

Nat's wet eyes pinned me in place. She let me hold her hand, but her voice was small. "You were right, I do pick the wrong people. And I did it again." She looked down at her feet and said it as if she were the one to blame.

"No, that's not it. Natalie, listen to me. I was an idiot." I tipped her chin up, and she looked at me with desperation in her eyes. "I never should have treated you the way I did. I'm sorry for the animosity I built between us, and I'm sorry that I called you a cheater. Also, for saying a meteor should have destroyed your cake. And for replacing pipe cleaners in the craft cabin with rubber snakes."

Nat gaped at me, glaring daggers. "I knew that was you."

This confession might not be going exactly as I imagined, but I had to stay on point. I turned the little keychain over and over in my other hand, my fidgeting going unnoticed. When I tore my hand out of my pocket to run my fingers through my hair, the keychain clattered onto the pavement.

Nat let out a teary snort as she bent down to pick up the little frog. Her face lit up as she dangled the charm in front of my face. "I didn't realize you had a stowaway."

"Bernice wanted to come. And I knew I'd need all the luck I could get for this."

Nat's body softened, and she met my eyes. A wave of emotions slammed into me, but I took a breath. I had to get it all out.

"Listen, I'm so sorry I pushed you away. The truth is, I was scared. Scared to risk everything again. I thought love and I were not compatible, and each of my failed relationships only proved that. After Gia, I convinced myself that it was better to avoid it altogether. I just thought there was no way I was going to put myself on the line for love again, but you made me realize that you're worth risking it all for. You're the one I want to be good enough for. No, not just good enough. I want to be worthy of you. I want to put my all into each day to prove to you over and over again that I can be the man you deserve."

I grabbed Nat's hand and brought it to my lips, kissing it gently. Her nails were newly polished in a subdued pink color, instead of a bright one, like she usually wore. It wasn't her. None of this was.

"I was wrong. You picked the right person. And I'm so sorry, princess. I'm sorry I froze that night. I'm sorry I didn't hold you and kiss you and say it back. Because I do love you, Natalie. I'm so in love with you it hurts. And I want you to move in with me for real, if you want. Maybe that's too fast?" I pushed on before she could answer me. I hadn't meant to blurt that one out, even if it was true. "What I'm trying to say is, I'm all in. I want to be your person, because you're already mine. I want to be your landing place. And I'm not going to fight this anymore."

Now it was Nat's turn to make me wait an agonizingly long time, during which I nearly turned tail and ran, until suddenly she was in my arms.

"You love me?" Her voice wavered as she stared into my eyes. She knew how to break me apart and put me back together with one look. "Are you sure?"

I nodded. It pained me that she'd question it and that it had taken me so long to come to this conclusion when it was so obvious. But I never shied away from hard work, and if Nat needed more, I'd prove it to her every single day.

"Yeah, Nat, I'm sure. I know what I need now. And it's you."

She smiled, and it filled me with hope. "Even when I ruin a

good song by playing it to death?" She threw my words back at me, but there was no heat in them.

"Silence is overrated."

"What about when I can't go to sleep until our space is cleaned?"

"Well, you know I have insomnia, so I won't be going to bed until then, anyway. We can do it together."

"That's the hottest thing you've ever—"

Our lips found each other, our bodies melding as if we were two magnets finally coming together. I ran my fingers up the side of her face and clung to her as she tightened her hold around my neck. I never wanted to let her go. She gave me one more kiss and held onto me, as I looked deep into her eyes.

"I'm not moving in with you. Pretty sure it's too soon for us to live together."

I loved that her attitude was back. That teasing tone I wanted to hear forever.

I pulled back and looked at her face. All her tears had dried up. She was so beautiful. My thumb glided across the apple of her cheek. *Nat loves me.* She wanted this, too. The thought filled the aching chasm in my chest, making me feel secure. Everything clicked into place. I never wanted to let her go.

She'd been right all along. This was worth fighting for, and I'd spend my days proving that to her.

"As long as you're coming back to Starlight, I'll be happy." I tucked her hair behind her ear and smiled. "You'll always have family there, and you'll always have me." I kissed her softly before taking her hand. "Come on, princess, let's go home."

Epilogue

JACK

One week later

I'd woken Nat up with hot chocolate every morning this week.

We still had a little over two months of the camp season left, and it'd been a little strange at first, with the competition being over, but we hadn't fully let go of our tenacious natures. We'd do dumb shit like race to see who could get the mail from Hazel first. Or we'd casually practice archery together, and even though she always kicked my ass, I still believed I'd get her one of these days. And there was the ongoing swimming rematch we'd never let go. Autumn was getting fed up with us taking her lake and growing tired of judging our dumb swimming competitions. Our races were always closer than I'd like to admit.

Every day with Nat was simply fun. She lit up my world with her presence. She sang in the shower and danced when we made dinner together. Some days she'd even wake up to go bird-watching with me.

She knew that it would take work to help her through her baggage. She'd had a virtual therapy appointment yesterday and planned to keep up with it because, as she put it, she'd been slacking. After seeing Nat taking steps to get back into therapy, I decided to start going as well. So just last night, I'd researched local Wildwood doctors since I preferred to meet face to face.

Every night this week, I'd held her at the campfire. Sometimes Autumn and Jamie would hang out with us, but Hazel and Leo were the ones who put up with our antics the most.

Today, however, I was owning up to my defeat.

"Are you ready for this?" Nat asked sweetly as she squeezed my palm. I handed her my folded boxers and T-shirt, staring off the platform as if I were being led to my doom. But a glance at her had me rethinking my negativity. Seeing her look at me like this, I knew I'd be fine.

"Yeah, but you're feeding me after this." I hadn't been able to eat beforehand. Maybe I was more nervous than I wanted to let on.

The small crowd of counselors gathering on our day off had been hooting and hollering since Nat and I had climbed up the ladder. I'd hoped we could avoid the audience, but of course, they knew what today was. Nat squeezed my hand encouragingly, and I did what I promised I would do.

I had to admit, the breeze felt refreshing as I stood next to my girlfriend, whose pink cheeks over my nudity made all of this worthwhile.

She made life worthwhile.

"I like the suit," Emerson shouted from below, cackling as I struck a confident pose, grateful for the platform we were on. They could probably only see me from the waist up. Nat shoved a harness at me, shaking her head.

"What? I look good naked in the daylight."

"Yeah, but you look better spread out on my bed at night." She winked.

Our friends laughed and cheered me on as I stepped into the safety harness on the zipline platform.

Nat made sure I was secured to the cable, her eyes sparkling. "You're all set, loser."

"I wouldn't say I lost."

She gave me a disbelieving laugh. "Oh, you definitely lost."

"I got you, didn't I?"

With that, her face softened, and I kissed her cheek. She slapped my ass before I dove off the platform and into the great unknown, or more aptly, into the life I was more than happy to call mine. My job, my friends, my girl… I didn't take any of it for granted. Every day, I remembered how lucky I was.

As I floated in the breeze, arms outstretched and naked as the day I was born, someone from down below me said, "I'd hate to be the guy that has to wash that harness."

Six Months Later

Best friends weren't supposed to have this many opinions about couches.

"What about this one?" I sat on a perfectly fine leather couch, just like the last few we'd sat on, but Autumn had a checklist.

At first, it was kind of funny, but we'd been shopping here for hours, and I had my own checklist to finish. Although I had to admit, she was right that it was a big decision. She'd declared my job was to picture Nat on the couch with me. That had me thinking dirty thoughts, which distracted me from the task at hand. It also garnered a look from Autumn that said *Really?* each and every time.

"Why not this one?" I asked.

"It doesn't meet the criteria. Leather is a pain in the heat. Imagine getting your ass stuck to that thing in cutoffs. Nat will thank you."

"That's a good point. I don't want her wearing clothes on this thing very much anyway."

She mock-gagged before transitioning into snarky Autumn again. "Look, I know the couch you're buying has to last the next fifty years, so it needs to pass the checklist."

She had a point. I did tend to use things until there was no use left in them.

I moved to the next couch, which wasn't leather, and it was one of the approved colors on my color palette, so it had that going for it. "This one's good," I said, trying to make it seem like I'd put just as much energy into deciding on it as my best friend had required, but truly, any of these couches would be a significant upgrade to what I've been subjecting Nat to since last summer. We'd usually watch movies at her place, on her normal couch.

I smiled, remembering the one time we hung out at my place for movie night when, in the middle of *Crazy, Stupid, Love,* she'd gotten up and moved to sit on the floor, telling me without preamble that we weren't having sex that night.

I took a breath and reminded myself I had eight days to complete the final changes before Nat got back from her solo trip to the Philippines. She'd been most excited to visit Palawan Island to take in the limestone and lagoons.

"Does it have USB ports?" Autumn asked, hunting for said feature. I nodded. She was acting as if I didn't have these questions memorized by now.

"It does." I'd been the one to add the USB option to Autumn's list. I hoped Nat would probably work on the new couch, and her phone was always dying. She made do on the kitchen table, but it couldn't have been comfortable for more than an hour or so.

Autumn hummed around me. "How about a built-in recliner?"

"Check."

"And it's comfortable enough to sleep on—"

"We don't have to test that." I scoffed, exasperated. "This is the one."

Autumn laughed and sprawled out on the couch, pretending to sleep anyway. She kept her shoes off it at least.

"Fine choice," she said to me with a smile. Then she turned to the couch, bouncing on its luxurious cushions before patting it. "You passed the test. Come on, let's get you to your new home."

I grinned at her silliness.

We were both covered in a sheen of sweat as we pulled out of the furniture store. My new couch tested my truck's shocks as we headed from the city back to camp.

Leo and Hazel met us in the parking lot, and the four of us hauled the partially assembled gray sectional couch the rest of the way into my cabin. There was a minor snag when I had to detach the door to get it to fit, but eventually, we got it settled inside. Autumn had been right, the couch did set the tone for the space.

I took in the living room, with its fresh coat of paint I'd finished last night and now with the new couch. It was warm in a way it had never been before Nat's influence. Now, the room was inviting.

My friends all collapsed onto the new couch. Leo, of course, sat on top of Hazel, which turned into wrestling together until I cuffed him on the ear, and Autumn popped the first of a few beer tabs, which got them to settle down.

When we were finished, I walked them through my cabin. It was so different from when the four of us had slept in the same space because we were paranoid that it was haunted, thanks to the scratching in the walls. It'd turned out to be squirrels making a nest, but it'd been freaky for those of us who didn't read horror books at night.

Leo looked at the new office, approval written on his face. Only a couple of months ago, it had been full of accumulated junk and tools, half-finished projects, and half-used paint cans. The mess had taken long nights and some strategic organization of a storage shed to get under control. I'd kept the door closed, and Nat hadn't asked me about it. She knew I was organizing it, but now it was a real room. There was new hardwood flooring and light fixtures, as well as a large desk underneath the window. I still had some corner bookshelves to put together, so she'd have a place to store all her books. She'd recently joined a book club Dr. Alyse hosted in Wildwood.

I wanted Nat to see herself in this room and know that she had a place to call home.

Hazel held up a can of paint. "Ooh, you picked my favorite color. It looks just like your eyes, Leo."

I caught Autumn looking at me from the corner of my eye, but I didn't want it to be obvious that we'd caught Hazel's slipup. I did notice Leo tilt his head in her direction as if he were intrigued. We tried not to bother the two of them about their chemistry anymore. The same couldn't be said for the people of Wildwood, but what else were small towns for?

"That's why I picked it," I joked.

Leo patted me on the shoulder. "It's okay that you're obsessed with me, Jack. I won't tell your girlfriend."

I shook my head. "She'll understand. We're all a little obsessed with you, Leo."

Autumn turned to me with soft eyes. "Nat's going to love what you did. You turned out to be boyfriend material after all," she affirmed, pulling a laugh out of me as the four of us moved over to the primary room.

My three closest friends had all seemed a little nostalgic and even baffled when I asked them to help move out the bunk beds tonight, but they'd been eager to help when they learned I needed assistance so that I could finish on time. A couple of pizzas from Raphael's made for perfect bribery. We'd all done it before, in those beginning days of camp. Part of me wondered if a piece of Nat would be strangely disappointed to see the bunk beds go, but it had to be done. We needed the space to feel like a room built for a couple. Not a space for reluctant roommates who couldn't stand each other.

The memories of me ever thinking I could hate Nat were laughable now. Once she got under my skin, she had quickly become my whole universe.

"It's going to look like a grown-up lives here," Hazel commented after we got the bunks out. Her dry tone made it sound like more of an insult than a compliment.

"Thanks?"

Maybe we were grown-ups now. I liked that idea. Mostly, I liked the idea that Nat could settle here long enough to become comfortable and feel like this was her permanent home. Nat's place was cozy, but beyond Trudy, a finicky house plant I took care of while she was away, she didn't make it her own. There weren't bookshelves stacked with books or knickknacks she collected from Wildwood, and she hadn't hung photos from her travels on her walls. I hoped that, if this worked, we'd be doing exactly that in a cabin we called ours.

After we finished dismantling and cleaning up, we toasted to new beginnings. I was more than ready to move on to the next phase of my life with the woman I loved.

Traffic to the airport was easier than I'd expected, and I made sure to arrive early.

Two hours early.

Okay, so maybe I was anxious to see Nat. Eight days had gone by fast with how busy the projects kept me, but the nights had dragged. I missed random moments where we'd argue over what movies to watch or listen to her random playlists while doing soothing face masks. I missed how she'd tuck into my side and kiss me each morning. But today was the day, and I was eager to have my girl back in my arms.

Nat had texted me photos throughout her trip. My favorite one was of her on a gorgeous hike in front of a waterfall. Sometimes knowing she hiked alone gave me anxiety, but she was always careful. Plus, she had Bernice with her since we shared custody now.

On the fifth night of her stay, she had sent me the first draft of her review of the place she had stayed, which was off the beaten path and in need of tourism. Any time Nat wrote about a previously undiscovered place, there was usually a significant bump in their business in the coming months.

Then there were photos she'd send me at night. Full of beautiful smiles and local food she discovered. And the best part? She looked happy. We'd talk a few minutes here and there, but I didn't place any expectations on her when it came to calls and texts, apart from proof of life. She always surprised me, though, finding the time to spend at least an hour a day talking.

Sometimes I went with her, like the trip to Puerto Rico for a week in October, and to Ireland last month. Traveling with Nat had been the experience of a lifetime, but I also enjoyed standing on the sidelines when she had an impromptu trip. All I wanted was for her to keep doing what she was passionate about.

Summers would be a little different going forward, since Nat wasn't a counselor anymore, but I knew every trip she had planned. There was a lot of time for just us. Nat had been busy. She was primarily running Starlight's and Sunlight's social media accounts with the help of a new assistant, MacKenzie, who was based at Camp Sunlight.

Nat was able to set her schedule, which worked perfectly, so she could balance between both camps and her travel blog. Her role could be done anywhere, so she could travel as much or as little as she wanted. And I was more than happy to celebrate with her when she returned. Knowing she would always come back to me was the sweetest reward I could ever ask for.

After zoning out for a while, I looked up to find Nat's purple rolling suitcase at my feet. She had a backpack slung over her shoulder, and her cheeks were sun-kissed, pink and full of joy. I kissed her, and we hugged before we said a word.

When we did talk, I'd always start with my initial question. "What trouble did Bernice get you out of on this trip?"

She laughed. "That's just between me and her." She kissed the tip of my nose. "I'm glad to be back. I'm all yours for the next four weeks."

"You'll be all mine longer than four weeks if I have my way."

She kissed my lips. I'd take all the time I could get with her.

We got back to camp, and when we made it to the front steps of my cabin, I pulled a blindfold out of my pocket.

"Jeez, Jack, let a girl unpack before you get all frisky."

I laughed and shoved that thought down for later. "Will you put this on? I have a surprise."

She nodded with a grin, and I tied the material over her eyes. She didn't even question me. Was she just going along with this? I thought for sure we'd argue outside of the cabin for at least five minutes before I'd get my way.

Was I disappointed about that? I shook my head as she lifted her chin, granting me easy access to place the blindfold on her.

"We're not getting frisky." I held her hands to my face, then kissed them.

She laughed and smirked. "Not with that attitude." Then her face went soft. "Leo may have already spilled the beans." She winced under the blindfold, as if she didn't know if she should tattle on our friend or not.

I heaved out a long sigh. Trusting Leo with secrets was my own damn fault. "Well, can you just pretend you don't know?"

Nat nodded and smiled under her blindfold again, and my heart melted. I carefully led her inside our cabin, fingers crossed. I walked us to the middle of the room and put her luggage down.

"Hold on one sec." I didn't care that she already knew. I still wanted this moment for us.

I hit play, and the music to our song, "Home," filled the air. Nat stood patiently, smiling so beautifully.

"Okay, you can take it off now."

Nat slid the blindfold down, and she took in the new couch, then slumped onto it before proceeding to bounce her butt up and down on it. To be fair, it was a perfect couch for bouncing.

I joined her on the other side of it. "What do you think?"

"I love it. And maybe now I'll stay over for a movie night once in a while."

I grinned. "I hope so. There are USB outlets."

She grinned like I was talking dirty to her.

"Now for the rest. I won't make you wear the blindfold, though," I said, pulling her up from the cushions.

"The rest?"

Nat held my hand and followed me, and even though I knew she was playing into the whole act-like-you-don't-know-anything thing, her sweet question made my heart flutter. Our song followed us down the hall, albeit softer, as I opened the door to the once junk room, now turned into what I was hoping was a Natalie-approved office.

Nat's eyes went comically big. So maybe Leo hadn't revealed everything.

"Jack," she breathed out and stepped into the room. We still held hands, so I was right behind her as she took in the restrained hardwood floor and the freshly painted walls.

Nat sat in the desk chair, ran her free hand over the curtains, and took in the outlets and shelving. I turned on the newly installed twinkle lights and the neon Naturegirlnat sign I'd commissioned, and she looked around, speechless.

"I know Leo told you. But I hope you like—"

She shook her head as she took in every minute detail. "Autumn asked for my home mood boards, which was a little strange, and Leo told me about the couch. But this… I didn't expect this."

I was beyond thrilled. "If you want more plants, they can go up here." I indicated the custom shelves. "But we can always put in a skylight if you need more light later."

"Later?" Nat was teary-eyed and happy, and I knew she knew where this was going, but I wasn't ready yet.

I squeezed her hand. "Yeah, later." I gently led her out of her new office and toward the bedroom. "Now what was it you were saying about getting frisky?" I teased, wanting to lighten the moment as I scooped her up and carried her over the threshold of our bedroom. "I'm sorry about your bunk."

When I set her down, Nat reverently touched the new dresser. Well, it was a new used dresser I'd refinished last month and tucked away in storage for this week.

"Where will I sleep?" she asked, as if she'd slept a wink on that bunk bed since we became a couple. She was in her bed in Andromeda, or where she belonged, in mine. But it was cute.

I cleared my throat, suddenly nervous. "I'm hoping you'll sleep here. Every night. With me."

Nat opened a large wooden drawer to find it empty. She didn't say anything for a moment, and regret flooded me. I should have had her pick out the new furniture. What if she hated the dark stain I'd used? Or worse, what if she didn't want to live here again?

I moved to open the closet, cutting off those thoughts. I showed her the three-fourths vacant space while she processed the changes. "See? There's plenty of room for both of us," I said dumbly.

She turned back to me. Her face was unreadable, and it was killing me. "You want me here every night?"

I nodded back. "More than anything," I confessed.

She turned from the closet back to me. "Every morning?"

My hands found her face and drew her closer. "Every minute," I corrected. Nat kissed me and toppled us onto the perfectly made bed. I laughed and went down with her easily. "Move in with me, princess. I promise you won't regret it."

"You want me to move in here? Not to Hazel's friend's place, with the room to rent?"

She'd been worried about not having a place to live once the camp sessions started back up. I never wanted her to live anywhere else, but this wasn't my decision to make.

"I want you here, in our home, more than anything. No separate beds or tape down the middle. One shared space for both of us."

Nat nodded, peppering my face with kisses, telling me how happy she was. All the time I'd spent working for this moment had been worth it. She was excited. Giddy, even, as she hugged me. "Okay, Jack, let's do it. And maybe this time around I won't hate you."

I barked out a laugh and kissed her sweetly. "Maybe this time I'll tell you how much I love you, instead of how much I think I hate you."

Nat pretended to scoff at me, and I booped her nose. It was my turn to be giddy. All my bets were paying off. All my previous skepticism and avoidance of love were entirely gone now that I had her. The way she loved with her whole heart was more than I could have ever imagined. Everything felt meant to be with my girlfriend, happy in my arms, in a home that belonged to both of us.

Want more Nat and Jack?

Sign up for our newsletter for a bonus scene and to stay up to date with the Camp Starlight Universe:

elliebelmont.com/bonus

Acknowledgments

We've learned a lot since writing and releasing *Camp Love*, but the biggest takeaway is that we are two of the luckiest authors out there. To our readers: Thank you for giving us a chance. Thank you for your reviews and kind messages. For coming up to us and telling us what you liked about our book. We are so lucky to have so much excitement and encouragement around us.

To our friends and families: Words cannot express how special you have made us feel since the release of our first book. You've celebrated with us, recommended us, and playfully harassed passersby to read *Camp Love*! Your love and encouragement are like a warm hug. It reinvigorates us on the tough days. It helps us stay excited for what's to come. Without you, we wouldn't be able to do this.

To the indie bookstores and booksellers who took a chance on *Camp Love*: Thank you. We have had such wonderful conversations with you and have experienced such amazing support. It's so wonderful to find spaces where we can nerd out about things we're passionate about, and to see our work on your shelves? It's a feeling we'll never get over.

To the Portland Romance Writers: We are so fortunate to have found such an amazing community. We love talking to you, learning from you, and standing beside you at events. Thank you for the writing retreats and sprints. We've had some incredible times and can't wait for more!

To our wonderful editors: Thank you for helping make this book into what it is. We know it must be tough to do what you do, and we appreciate you so much for taking our work and making it shine even brighter. Making it more readable, but also something we're really proud of.

Camille, we are always grateful to hear your feedback. Thank you for your perspective and for keeping track of the number of campers and other logistics with the competitions. It helps so much.

To our beta readers: You've seen us at our rawest, before the book has been edited, and your feedback has been instrumental in workshopping and developing scenes to make our stories truly sparkle. All of you are geniuses in your own right. We understand it takes a ton of time to read through our work and share your feedback. We really appreciate your insight and attention to detail as well as the reactions and words of encouragement.

To our ARC readers: Thank you for taking the time to pick up our book with the intention of reading and reviewing. Your cute social media posts make our day, and we know your word of mouth gets our books into the hands of readers.

And a special shout-out to MacKenzie. Your unhinged comments had us laughing one moment, to cursing your name every time you found an error, to awwing with joy that you'd fallen in love with our characters again. We loved how excited you were to see Jamie and Autumn, how you looked out for Emerson, and especially how you connected with Nat. Everything you shared with us only made *Camp Enemies* better. Thank you from the bottom of our hearts.

About the authors

Writing duo Lacey Cole and Ellie Belmont met working at a video store, and have been best friends ever since their first friend date, where they danced around an empty theater while watching Step Up. They live with their partners in the Pacific Northwest and this is their debut novel.

linktr.ee/ellieandlacey

www.ingramcontent.com/pod-product-compliance
Lightning Source LLC
Chambersburg PA
CBHW030538130726
48054CB00020B/84

* 9 7 8 1 9 6 7 3 8 3 0 3 0 *